"You're too arrogant for your own good, Slayer,"
Veronique hissed, smiling.

Buffy leaped up into a roundhouse kick.

At that precise moment Veronique ducked past her. Buffy started to come down, thrown because her target was no longer in front of her. Veronique grabbed her around the neck and flipped her into a glass partition. It shattered, and Buffy crashed down on the broken shards of glass. She staggered to her feet, bleeding from a dozen tiny cuts.

"That's the point you're missing, Slayer," Veronique said. "You don't have anything to say about it at all. I've fought you enough, girl. You've killed me too many times. I've studied you; I've paid attention. I know your style now. Every time you make a move, I'll have already guessed what it's going to be."

Buffy's instinct was to thrust her legs out behind her, to sweep Veronique off her feet. But she couldn't do that.

It was what Veronique would have expected.

Buffy the Vampire Slayer™

Available from ARCHWAY Paperbacks and Pocket Pulse

Buffy the Vampire Slayer adult books

Available from POCKET BOOKS

BUFFY THE VAMPIRE SLAYER™

IMMORTAL

CHRISTOPHER GOLDEN and NANCY HOLDER
An original novel based on the hit TV series created by Joss Whedon

POCKET BOOKS
New York   London   Toronto   Sydney   Singapore

Historian's Note:
This book is set during the third season.

POCKET BOOKS, a division of Simon & Schuster Inc.
1230 Avenue of the Americas, New York, NY 10020

™ and copyright © 2000 by Twentieth Century Fox Film Corporation. All rights reserved.

Originally published in hardcover in 1999 by Pocket Books

ISBN: 0-671-04175-4

First Pocket Books paperback printing May 2000

10 9 8 7 6 5 4 3 2 1

POCKET and colophon are registered trademarks of Simon & Schuster Inc.

Printed in the U.S.A.

For my grandmother, Alena Pendolari,
And in memory of my grandfather, Romeo Pendolari
—CG

For Brenda Van De Ven,
who gave me immortality
—NH

Acknowledgments

The authors would like to thank all of Team Buffy, including Lisa Clancy, Liz Shiflett, and Micol Ostow at Pocket Books, Caroline Kallas at *Buffy* central, and Debbie Olshan at Fox. You guys are the best! Thanks, also, of course, to Joss Whedon and the cast and crew, all of whom continue to inspire us.

Christopher would also like to thank his wife, Connie, and his sons, Nicholas and Daniel, as well as his agent, Lori Perkins, and all the people at the Bronze, who are always so welcoming and supportive.

Nancy would also like to thank her husband, Wayne, and her daughter Belle Claire, as well as her agent, Howard Morhaim, and his assistant, Lindsay Sagnette. Thanks, also, to Ida Khabazian, April and Lara Koljonen, Bekah and Juli Simpson, Julie Cross; Kathy and Charlie Grant; and Leslie and Elise Jones.

Prologue

*T*he island of Kefi was a hollow place, where nothing stirred but the warm breeze off the ocean and the ghosts of the moldering dead. At sunrise, though, the spirits were laid to rest for another day, leaving only the wind. It was strong enough, at times, to ring the three bells that sat in their whitewashed arches, one straddling the others, on the stony cliff overlooking the Sea of Crete.

Sometimes, like this morning, the bells were enough to rouse the attention of the presence that haunted the tainted church, built into the cliffside. Once, the faithful of the tiny isle had worshiped there. But there were no more faithful on Kefi.

Within the white walls of the church, Veronique's mind whispered to life. She heard the bells, and the wind rattling the rotting, empty window frames, and the surf pounding the cliff far below. What there was of her—not much more than a spirit, really, but far greater than those memories that flitted about the island at night—drifted amid the pews and out toward the doors, shattered so long ago.

Veronique had no eyes with which to see the sun, and yet she was witness to its magnificent beauty. Bound here to the church, she had watched as the decades passed and the sunlight had bleached the church and its crosses and the little bell tower the color of bone. So perversely appropriate for something so brittle and dead.

When first she had been trapped here, one hundred and twenty-seven years earlier, the sun had been a precious gift, a novelty. With her own bones turned to dust, her lingering essence had not needed to fear the rays of the sun. But the novelty had worn off quickly. The sun was not an equal trade for her freedom, for the ability to traverse the world in service to her masters.

She had been foolish, coming here, allowing that girl to lead her to such a remote place. The Triumvirate had punished Veronique for her foolishness by leaving her bound to the island, unaided.

But this morning, this final morning, she relished the sparkle of the sun on the sea and the way the very air shimmered above the white roof of the church with its heat. For she knew her punishment was about to come to an end. The Triumvirate had need of her once more and so would forgive her vanity and find some way to free her.

They would find her a shell, a vessel into which she might pour her essence. Then she would serve them once more. With all the omens finally coming to pass, the stars told the tale: it was time for her masters to walk the Earth. And Veronique would be their harbinger, announcing the doom of the world, preparing the way, performing the ritual. She would baptize the world in the blood of her victims, in the name of the Triumvirate. She would feast until she could not bear another drop of blood.

Veronique would not miss the sun. Not when there was so much pleasure to be had by moonlight.

On the deck of the *Charybdis*, Cheryl Yeates raised a hand to shield her eyes from the sun and studied the crescent-shaped coastline of Kefi. The boat had been a fishing trawler, once upon a time, but its owner had converted it for sightseeing in the Greek islands. From the look and smell of it, the conversion hadn't been made all that long ago.

"What do you think, honey?"

Cheryl looked at the island a moment longer before turning to face her husband, Steve. He sat, legs astride the bow, with a beer in his hand. His skin was a painful red, already peeling in some places from their days traveling around Greece. Cheryl's own skin was a deep brown by now, but Steve never seemed to tan. He just burned and then burned on top of that.

All in all, he was a good sport.

"I don't know," she told him. "Dimitri was pretty insistent, or I wouldn't have agreed to come out here at all. I'm not getting paid by the day, y'know?"

Steve climbed to his feet, careful not to slip on the deck, and moved up beside her, holding his beer bottle by its neck. He squinted, even beneath his sunglasses, to get a clearer look at the island.

"You don't have to tell me," he told his wife. "We've already spent the first half of your advance, and I've used up all the vacation I'll get this year. But it's been worth it, hasn't it? I mean, doing this with you has probably been the greatest time of my life."

Cheryl smiled, shook her head, and looked at her husband. She reached for his hand just as the boat hit a swell, and she lost her balance. Just as she began to fall to starboard, Steve grabbed her and went down on his knees, pulling her down with him. Despite the fear that had momentarily surged up within her, Cheryl started to laugh.

"Y'know, what I was just saying?" Steve asked. "Drowning would ruin it."

"It has been something, hasn't it?" she said, nodding to herself. "What an adventure."

"Frank and Julie said we'd be killing each other by the third day," Steve reminded her. "Seven weeks, honey, and I don't want to go home. I wish we didn't have to."

Cheryl nodded regretfully. "Well, then," she said, "one more little adventure can't hurt. Hell, we're already here. Might as well see what we can see."

Steve turned to face the island, and Cheryl slipped over to sit in front of him, leaning against his chest. It felt so good, just to have him with her. And he was right: they had fought hardly at all. This trip had been such a wonderful reminder of what they could be to each other when the rest of the world didn't get in the way. He was a junior partner at a small but well-respected law firm in Philadelphia. Cheryl had only recently received her Ph.D. in anthropology, the same week, in fact, that she had signed the contract for her first book. It was going to be called *Myths and Legends of Greece: From Antiquity to the Modern World,* and she hoped it would be the first in a long series.

Just as she hoped this would be the first in a long series of adventures she shared with her husband.

"I see something," Steve said, pointing.

Indeed, there was some kind of structure atop a cliff almost directly ahead. As Cheryl tried to focus, she realized that it wasn't alone. There were a number of other smaller buildings—all the same glaring white as the first—that dotted the island.

"Must be the village," Cheryl said. "The bigger building could be the church, I guess." Even as she said it, she could make out something atop the white dome that could have been a cross.

"Looks like," Steve agreed. He paused a moment, then kissed the top of her head. "A creepy little story, if it's true."

Cheryl couldn't agree more. Local legend held that the island of Kefi had been attacked by a *bucolac*—a vampire—more than a century before. The islanders fled one sunrise, taking everything that would float, leaving the vampire trapped on the island.

"What's fascinating is the way in which this legend differs from other vampire lore. Not just here in Greece but all over the world. I mean, you leave a vampire alone on an island for ten or twelve decades, you've got to figure they starve to death, right? But if you believe Dimitri, nobody's been out here except for day-trippers in all that time. Okay, the island's remote, but it's not *that* remote."

Now that she thought about it, Cheryl was glad they'd come. It was a long way for just one story, but it was an oddity that would add something to the book. Before this trip—in fact, before Dimitri, the scholar they'd met in Athens, had told them about Kefi—she'd never even heard of the island.

"What I don't understand," Steve said, "is why the vampire didn't just swim for it."

Cheryl turned around far enough to see him trying not to smile. She laughed and punched him lightly in the shoulder.

"What?" he protested. "It's a legitimate question."

She shrugged. "All right, then, smart guy. Any theories?"

"Yes, in fact, I have a theory," Steve said archly. "Vampires are basically corpses, right? Okay, a short swim, no problem. But a while in the water, the fish start coming around, taking a nip here or there. Dead flesh in the water, he's basically shark bait. Nothing but chum."

"That's gross," Cheryl said, frowning.

"It's your book," Steve reminded her.

"Besides, this vampire's a she, not a he."

"I like this trip better already."

"Yeah, if only they were real, honey," she said. "I'm sure all those vampire chicks would love you."

Eyebrows raised, Steve leaned in to kiss her. "Want to suck my blood?" he asked.

"We'll see," she replied, and kissed him back.

A short time later, the couple watched in silence as the boat drew close to the island. The captain, a thin, muscular Greek named Konstantin, came out of the cabin briefly to inform them that they'd be mooring in a small cove to the east, where the cliffs turned to sloping hills.

They made their way up the coast a little way, until they were almost out of sight of the church. Just as the captain dropped anchor, Steve turned to Cheryl with an odd look on his face.

"What?" she asked.

"Are you sure we need to spend the night?"

She smiled. "It's not much of a story if we don't," she told him. "Why? Scared?"

"Nah. Just not very romantic with Konstantin along as chaperone."

Cheryl looked over at the captain, who was lowering the

dinghy over the side. "He's not coming along," she said. "He's staying with the boat. We're on our own up there."

"Great," Steve mumbled.

They didn't speak as they dropped their packs into the boat and then slipped over the side.

Cheryl had gotten some extraordinary pictures. The landscape was just beautiful, and the view of the ocean from the top of the cliffs by the church was breathtaking. But what remained of the village itself was chilling. Haunting. The island ought to have been a Club Med or something by now. Instead, it was a ghost town.

"I feel like the last man on Earth," Steve said quietly.

She turned to see her husband standing next to a small structure that housed a trio of bells. They were curiously free of rust, and when Steve had hauled on them, the clappers had gonged within, the bells pealing clearly, reaching across the water below.

Cheryl walked up behind him. "If that means I'm the last woman on Earth, I guess I got pretty lucky to end up with you."

He turned, and they embraced. Cheryl kissed him. But she felt as though Steve was holding something back. Something was lurking behind those baby blues, and she didn't know what it was.

"Hey," she said. "You all right?"

"I'm okay," he promised. "Just . . . it's so remote here. So far from anyone else. Look out at the horizon."

She did.

"What don't you see?"

"Land?"

"Besides that."

"Boats. I don't see any boats."

"Exactly." Steve nodded. "It isn't that nobody comes here. Nobody even comes *near* here. But here we are . . ." He spun around to face the church, arms raised. "I feel like we're desecrating a graveyard or something. Overturning tombstones."

Cheryl laughed. "We're taking pictures, Steve. Come on. Are you really that spooked?"

He glanced down, chewed his lip thoughtfully. Then he nodded. "Yeah," he said. "I am." Then he turned to look at Cheryl, gestured toward the camera. "You have everything you came for?"

She thought about it. They'd been in several of the homes, all through the church. She had plenty of pictures, and they were losing their light anyway. Cheryl had been sort of looking forward to snuggling up inside the church for the night, maybe getting some sunrise photos. But she could see how much the place was really getting to Steve.

"I never thought of you as the superstitious type, hon," she told him. "This stuff has never bothered you before."

He looked embarrassed. "We can stay," he said, as though it meant nothing.

But Cheryl could tell it did.

"That's okay," she said. "By the time we walk all the way back to the boat, it'll be dark anyway," she reasoned. "We can say we were here until nightfall. That's more than enough investigation for this particular myth. Besides, maybe we can wake up in Mykonos tomorrow. That'd be nice."

"Yeah," he agreed, smiling at last. "I can live with that."

Together, they gathered up their things and started the long trek down off the cliff to the cove where the *Charybdis* was moored.

The sky was an angry pink, bruised with blue, where the last bit of sun burned the ocean. Cheryl and Steve were both exhausted by the time they came in sight of the cove and the boat bobbing just offshore. There were no lights on the *Charybdis*. No lights anywhere, save for what remained in the sky and what little the stars would provide now that dusk had come.

The moon was barely a sliver up above.

Cheryl reached into her pack and grabbed her flashlight. Steve didn't bother. He seemed much more relaxed now. Had, in fact, since the moment they'd started down from the island's peak.

"I guess we should just try to signal Konstantin," she said.

"Some shouting might help, if the light doesn't work," Steve told her. "I can't imagine he'd be sleeping already. It's barely dinnertime."

Her flashlight on, Cheryl began to sweep the beam across the water, its light splashing across the boat again and again. For a moment, Cheryl had a horrible thought, that the *Charybdis* was as abandoned as the island itself.

Steve shouted the captain's name several times, but Konstantin did not appear.

"Keep it up with the light," he said after a bit. "I'm going to drag the dinghy down to the water. We might as well just head out there. He'll hear us as we get closer, and the water isn't very rough. I don't think there's much of a chance of our being carried away on the tides."

Cheryl didn't argue, but now it was her turn to grow anxious. Steve grabbed hold of the dinghy and dragged it over the sand as she swept the light back and forth across the water. She was about to stop, to help him with the little boat, when her arm dipped down, and the beam of the flashlight splashed across something that was moving.

In the water.

In fact, it was *two* somethings. Two men, to be exact, swimming to shore from the boat.

"Steve . . ."

He came up beside her, staring at where the flashlight beam illuminated the two men moving toward them in the surf.

"Konstantin?" Steve called out again.

The captain paused in his swimming and raised a hand to wave amiably at them.

"He must not have wanted to shout back before to save his breath," Steve reasoned, looking at Cheryl.

"Maybe," she said dubiously. "But who the hell's the other guy, and why are they coming ashore?"

She kept the beam focused on the second man, the one they'd never seen before. He was swarthy and bearded, but she could barely make out his face in the surf. He was a fast swimmer, too.

"Some kind of problem with the boat?" Steve suggested.

Cheryl's stomach did a little flip. "God, I hope not. We're in the middle of nowhere. But what about this guy? He didn't swim here from Crete."

"We were gone all day," Steve said. "Konstantin could have gone and picked him up somewhere."

But even as he said it, Cheryl could tell from his tone that Steve didn't believe it. Together, they watched the two men moving toward the sand. Even now, Konstantin stood up in the water, and it only came midway up his chest.

"He must have been belowdeck all that time," Cheryl said.

"If all they wanted was to rob us, there are easier ways," Steve contended.

He was right about that, but he didn't sound all that convinced. Cheryl didn't understand it, either, but there was something very off about this whole thing.

Steve reached down and grabbed one of the oars off the dinghy. He held it in one hand as the two men walked, sodden with seawater, up the sand toward them. Both were clad only in their pants.

"Konstantin, what's going on?" Cheryl asked in Greek, trying to mask her nervousness.

Steve nodded toward the other man. "Who's your friend?" he asked the captain of the *Charybdis*.

The man nodded toward the bearded newcomer and smiled. "Ephialtes," he said.

"That's your name?" Cheryl asked the man in Greek.

In response, Ephialtes moved closer to Cheryl, studying her face. He reached out to touch her. She slapped his hand away and stepped back. Ephialtes looked angry and moved after her. Steve stepped between them, holding the oar out in front of him in both hands.

"That's a mistake," Konstantin said.

In English.

Cheryl didn't know the man could even speak the language.

That was the moment when Ephialtes snarled. He reached out for the oar in Steve's hands, and when her husband wouldn't give it up, the dark, bearded man struck him with the back of his fist, knocking Steve to one side. The oar fell to the sand between them. Even as Steve scrambled to get back to his feet, Ephialtes grabbed the oar.

When she saw what was about to happen, Cheryl screamed. She leaped for Ephialtes, but Konstantin grabbed her from behind and held her. From behind, she watched Ephialtes bring the oar down on her husband's head. Again and again. It cracked on the third stroke. Shattered on the fourth. Ephialtes did not stop.

The thick, broken shaft of wood was covered with blood.

Cheryl sank to the sand, mind numb. Hot tears streamed down her face, and she made an effort to free herself, but Konstantin was a man of the sea. Though thin, his body was covered with muscles thick as heavy cables. She could not free herself.

Finally, Ephialtes let the oar drop to the sand. Cheryl stiffened, for she believed she knew what was to come next.

But then Ephialtes turned, and she realized she had no idea. His face was inhuman, his brow ridged and protruding. His eyes blazed yellow in the dark, and his lips were curled back in a snarl that revealed horrible fangs.

"*Bucolac*," she whispered, the truth shattering what remained of her rational mind.

Ephialtes sank down onto his knees on the sand before her. Konstantin released Cheryl, and Ephialtes drew her to him. For one brief instant, she screamed and tried to squirm away from him, but he was even stronger than Konstantin. There was logic to that, in her mind. Konstantin had captained the boat. Konstantin was human.

Holding her tight, Ephialtes sank his fangs into the soft flesh of her throat and began to drink.

The wind blew hard across the cliffs, and the bells rang loudly. In the darkness of the church, the spirit and memory,

the invisible, Hellish thing that was all that remained of the
vampire sorceress Veronique, shuddered with pleasure.

"At last," she said to herself.

"At last."

Veronique's eyes fluttered open. Her eyes now. And yet only
hours before, they had belonged to a woman named Cheryl
Yeates. From the traces that remained in Cheryl's mind,
Veronique quickly assimilated much of what she would need to
know to survive what the world had become. Not merely to
survive but to thrive.

For a moment, she only looked up at the stars, looked at the
lovely night and felt it caressing her flesh. It was a sensation she
had forgotten many years before, and now it filled her with a
lust for the shadows.

Finally, Veronique noticed the two creatures before her. A
vampire and a man. Both servants of the Triumvirate. She
could sense that from their mere presence.

"Your name?" she demanded of the vampire.

"Ephialtes," he replied.

Veronique smiled. "An excellent jest, young one," she said.
For he had named himself after another Greek, one who had
betrayed his people millennia before. Ephialtes had been at
Thermopylae, where a handful of Spartans held hordes of
Persians off for days before finally falling. The Persian king,
Xerxes, who fancied himself a god, called his elite guard the Im-
mortals. Ephialtes betrayed his own people to the Immortals,
and they were slaughtered.

"Yes," Veronique repeated. "An excellent jest."

"Thank you, mistress." He stared at her. "I am your descendant," he told her in an awed tone. "I was made by one you
made, long ago. I have been searching for you, waiting for you.
Waiting to be called."

She touched his face. "And do you know why I am here?"

He nodded slowly, his face radiant. "Yes, mistress."

"Excellent." She was very pleased.

For a moment, she studied the human, then she looked at the boat and the ocean beyond.

"How far to Crete in this vessel?" she asked.

"Two, perhaps three hours," Ephialtes told her.

With another glance at the sky, Veronique estimated at least eight hours until dawn. More than enough time to reach Crete and find shelter.

Which meant they didn't need the human.

Veronique smiled at him. "Come here," she instructed. "It is time for you to serve the Triumvirate."

He looked frightened and began to back away.

But he didn't get very far.

The feasting had begun.

Chapter One

Several months later . . .

At first glance, the town of Sunnydale was like so many other small towns that made up the endless suburban sprawl of Southern California: it promised much but delivered very little.

There were no real neighborhoods, only differing amounts of distance from the nearest freeway. Life went on at the other end of a commute: at the office, the magnet school, hangouts based not on proximity but on flash. Although the school board talked about the excellence of Sunnydale public education, everyone really believed the key to success was whom you knew and how charming you could be.

But there were other things wrong with Sunnydale, in the light of which the worship of style over substance seemed the tiniest of faults. Unlike the other, similar towns that dotted the coast of Southern California, Sunnydale was cursed. Below the ground, the mouth of Hell sat dormant, ready to erupt at the appropriate provocation and to disgorge the demons, monsters, and forces of darkness that raged for the death of the world. Evil was drawn to the Hellmouth as though it were a magnet, drawn to Sunnydale, and it flourished there.

Sunnydale was the epicenter of the dark forces that lurked in the shadows of the world, a constant threat to humanity. It was evil's very own ground zero.

In its way, Sunnydale was the heart of darkness.

And if you want to destroy a thing, you aim for the heart.

Which was what had brought the Slayer, Buffy Summers, the Chosen One, to Sunnydale three years before, though she hadn't known it at the time. Forced to leave her old life in Los Angeles after her war against the darkness led her to burn down the high school gym, she and her mother had come to Sunnydale because Joyce Summers thought it the perfect place to start over. The perfect place to run an art gallery the way she'd always wanted.

Buffy believed in that dream. She had been thrilled to have an opportunity to put the whole vampire thing behind her. She knew now that it was naïve to believe she could escape her destiny. But back then . . . for one brief, shining moment, she'd thought she could be a normal kid again.

The first day at Sunnydale High, Rupert Giles, her new Watcher, had made himself known—and any hope Buffy entertained of having a normal life had evaporated.

Now, on this cold and gray February night, torrential rain bulleted the metal siding of the Bronze. Wind rattled the windows as if they were the vertebrae of a frozen, abandoned graveyard memory. The Bronze stank with the odor of wet wool laced with coffee. People dashed into the club completely drenched, because, as a rule, Southern Californians didn't own umbrellas. Or if they did, they never remembered to use them.

Buffy slipped back into her chair at the Bronze, sipping at her newly purchased—and lusciously warm—mochaccino, and grinned broadly at her friend Xander Harris, who sat across the table from her.

"Isn't this great? Flash-flood warnings, and I'm chillin' with my friends. No vamps to stake. No demons to destroy. Just me, my pals, and an extremely mediocre band."

Xander nodded happily. "Yup. It must be great to be a Slayer in Southern California. When the weather's bad, even the forces of evil take the night off."

"Actually, business *has* been a little slow all week," Buffy said.

"I'm having trouble filling my empty nights. Almost." She raised her hands. "I gave myself a manicure last night."

Then she made a guilty face at her best friend, Willow Rosenberg, who slid, burdened with a pair of huge coffee cups, into an empty seat at the high, round table.

"Of course, the manicure was accompanied by the whole study thing. Since I would never want you to feel that all the time you've spent tutoring me is wasted."

"My time is freely given," Willow announced, sliding one of the cups to Xander, who had held the table for them. "And the band's not that bad." She paused. "Which is actually the definition of mediocre, so, okay." She sipped her latte and smiled in the direction of the coffee counter, where her boyfriend, Oz, was buying some pastries. As if he sensed her gaze, he looked up and smiled back, blue eyes shining.

Buffy was wistful. She could hardly remember what it was like to be in a relationship that wasn't tormented and awkward. Oz was a werewolf three nights a month, but that was the extent of the major weirdness between them. It wasn't like her and Angel's deal.

"Uh-oh, your smile is fading," Xander chided. "Remember, Wendy, if we don't think happy thoughts, the pixie dust won't work, and we won't be able to fly anymore."

"Hey, I'm weightless," Buffy protested. She took a sip of her mochaccino to prove it. She licked her lips and sighed with contentment. "Time off from slayage doesn't get any better than this."

"Or shorter," Xander said slowly as he gestured toward the entrance to the Bronze.

"No," Buffy moaned. "No, no, no."

Giles was closing his umbrella as he scanned the crowd. The sort-of-haphazardly-dashing forty-something Brit's expression was serious in the extreme, and that, combined with the fact that he usually avoided the Bronze like the plague, was a fairly good indication that he was here on business.

"You guys distract him while I hide under the table," Buffy grumped.

Giles spotted her and headed on over. Willow frowned in sympathy, and Xander wagged his finger in Giles's direction.

"This Slayer's out of service," he said by way of greeting. "In serious need of downtime."

"Hi, Giles," Buffy said wanly. "What's the haps, not that I really want to know?"

"I am sorry, Buffy." At least he was contrite. "I've just learned that the medical examiner conveniently failed to mention to the media that Jackson Kirby's neck was torn open and he was drained of blood."

Jackson Kirby had been something of a local celebrity. A homeless panhandler, he had been a fixture on the corner of Avenida Ladera and Escondido Boulevard for seven years. "WILL WORK FOR FOOD," the sign around his neck had read. Whether anyone ever actually called him on the offer seemed unclear.

He had been found dead in an alley early in the morning. With no family and—according to the local news—nothing suspicious about his death, he'd been quickly interred at city expense.

"He was buried at Restfield," Giles continued. "If he rises, we need to make sure he doesn't stay risen."

Sigh. Life as the Slayer, Buffy thought glumly. "Don't you think he'll wait until it stops raining?" she asked. She started pulling on her raincoat.

"I've got my car," he told her.

"And an umbrella," she noted. She picked up her coffee cup and examined it. "And, happily, I have finished my piping-hot beverage."

"So, the glass is half full," he ventured.

She gave him a look.

"One-third," he amended.

"Hey, that's my line," Xander said. "Buffy, you want some company?"

"Xand, that'd be above and beyond the call of duty." She flashed him a wan smile. "But you're sweet to offer."

"I've got nothing better," he insisted.

"It's just one dusting. It'll be over like that." She snapped her fingers.

"So, I'm thinking, company," Xander insisted.

Oz walked up with a buttery croissant on a plate, which he offered to Willow. "Is there a rumble?" he asked.

"We're rumble-free," Buffy assured him. "Or, rather, you are." Then she shrugged and said to Xander, "If you're all pumped to be wet and cold and bored, who am I to stop you?"

Xander smiled and hopped off his stool. To Oz and Willow, he said, "Duty calls."

Willow pulled off a piece of croissant and popped it into her mouth. As she chewed, she said, "Do you want us to come with? Cuz we're happy there."

Buffy smiled. "You guys have something better to do."

"Hey," Xander protested, miffed. Then he shrugged. "Okay, I was first to comment on my lack of social engagement, but let's not all rush to help out."

Giles cleared his throat. "Let's be off, shall we? I imagine this won't take long."

"Yeah, that's what they all say," Xander said. Then he flushed. "Forget I said that."

Buffy smiled slightly and picked up her Slayer's bag. *Poor Xander.*

She led the way out of the Bronze just as Cordelia Chase sauntered in, killer in a trench coat and heeled boots, completely dry. Xander tensed at her side, but Buffy didn't let on that she'd noticed.

A moonstruck kid about half as tall as Cordelia carefully lowered his umbrella from the heights of her hair. A single droplet of rainwater tapped the end of Cordelia's nose, and she glared at the guy. He withered.

"I'm sorry, Cordelia."

She gave him an impatient scowl. He stared at her. "Coffee?" she prodded. "Muffin?"

He snapped his fingers. "Double latte, nonfat milk. Peach, nonfat."

"And?" She raised an imperious brow.

He strained for the answer. Looked not so joyful. Here he had made it all the way to Final Jeopardy, and he was drawing a blank.

"Possibly, two packets of blue sugar substitute," Xander suggested.

Cordelia moved one shoulder. The boy stared at her as if he had never heard of blue sugar substitute. Then his lips parted. "Oh!"

He scampered away.

"He must have a really nice car," Xander said evenly.

"His father owns the Porsche dealership." Cordelia nodded at Buffy and Giles, removing her coat. "What exciting adventure are you running off to? Another tour of the lovely Sunnydale sewer system?"

Buffy shook her head. "Naw, we did that last night, saving the world from the Unbengi Serpent."

"Well, on behalf of the world, thanks. And excuse me. You're blocking everyone's view of my outfit."

Xander huffed and rolled his eyes at Buffy. Buffy was thinking up comebacks, but Giles tapped his watch and said, "We really must be going."

"Have fun." Cordelia gave them a wave. She had not spoken one single word to Xander, nor even acknowledged his presence.

"Porsches. How common," Xander grumbled.

Xander and Giles flanking her, Buffy made a point of giving Cordelia a wide berth as they exited the Bronze. The rain was really coming down, and even the short walk to the car was daunting. Giles unlocked the doors to his ancient gray Citroën. Xander climbed into the backseat while Buffy sat shotgun up front with Giles.

There was that inevitable exciting moment when she wondered if the Gilesmobile would start. Once again, Buffy was astonished when the engine sputtered to life. Then they were off.

*   *   *

Alone at home, paperwork spread before her on the kitchen table, Joyce Summers listened to the rain and wondered what time Buffy would be home. As she stared at the night-blacked windows, she felt another cough coming on and tried to stifle it. She had been coughing for days, and sniffling, and now was the worst time to get a cold. There was so much to be done at the gallery. She had been working for more than two months to mount the Malaysian shadow puppet exhibition and organize the artist's reception. Working too hard, that was a given. But it was going to be a wonderful exhibit.

She sipped her tea, which had grown lukewarm. She didn't feel well at all, and, truth be told, she wanted Buffy's company as much as she wanted to be reassured that her child was safe and warm.

It was hard to be a mother, harder still to be the mother of the Chosen One, the only girl in all her generation to be pitted against the forces of evil. At first, Joyce had not believed Buffy's story about being a vampire Slayer, to the extent of pretty much forcing her out of the house. Her reward for that lack of faith was an entire summer spent hoping and praying that her absent daughter was not dead and that she would come home.

But as the days and nights had dragged by in one long, agonizing vigil, momentary flashes of debilitating panic—*she's been killed, she's never coming back*—pierced her grim determination not to break down. It had never occurred to her until then that she might actually outlive her child, a nightmare reserved, she had assumed, for bad parents. Careless parents, neglectful parents. Despite her work with the runaway shelter, she couldn't shake the notion that if something . . . bad happened to Buffy, it would be her own fault entirely.

But feeling guilty had not been a priority. Finding Buffy had. Giles scoured the country in search of her, while Joyce took on what was to her the more difficult task of waiting by the phone. Jumping at every sound, imagining she had heard the door open.

As she was doing now.

How could any mother stand by, night after night, while her child was in danger? And yet that was precisely what was required of her.

She coughed again. She was tired, and her chest was very sore. Her throat was raw. All she wanted to do was sleep.

Cold, she thought glumly. *And no wonder, with all this rain.*

Her mind drifted back to happier times, when Buffy was little and she and Hank thought happily-ever-after applied to all marriages, especially theirs. Her ex-husband had sworn by chicken soup whenever she was sick, and he would bring her a piping-hot bowl on the wicker tray he had brought home from the Philippines. *Saltines,* she remembered.

Then the marriage died, rather quickly, and they were divorced. He had remained in Los Angeles. And though she knew Buffy blamed herself for her parents' breakup, the two of them had no one to blame but themselves. They were the adults. She was the child.

Restless, feeling bilious, Joyce got up and walked to the refrigerator, mostly for something to do. She wasn't particularly hungry. It occurred to her that she hadn't had much of an appetite lately.

Maybe I should just go to bed, she thought. But ever since she had learned that Buffy was the Slayer, she had made it a policy not to rest until her girl was home.

She coughed again, much harder. Grabbing a tissue from the box beside her calculator, she put it to her lips. The copper taste of blood seeped into her mouth, and she daubed the tissue against her tongue.

Her breath caught in her throat as she examined it.

I'm coughing up blood, she thought. *There really is something wrong with me.*

The thought terrified her, not only for her sake but for Buffy's. *I can* not *get sick. She needs me too much.*

But this wasn't mere paranoia on Joyce's part. The blood was real. She had never coughed blood before, and she knew that such things didn't happen unless there was something really *wrong.* And suddenly she felt small and cold and did not want to be alone on a stormy night in a house in Sunnydale, with blood in her mouth and her daughter patrolling the dark for monsters to kill.

She rose and stared at the window, willing Buffy to come home. Or, at the very least, to be safe.

Buffy muttered to Xander, "Sing it with me now. 'It never rains in Southern California.' "

"It's our state song," Xander said brightly.

They had been huddling with Giles under his extra-large black umbrella for almost half an hour. Buffy stood close to Xander, a stake clutched to her chest. They had run out of small talk—or at least the other two had—and Xander knew prattling could be annoying, though he had no clue why, and now they waited quietly, each with his own thoughts. Lightning flashed, and the rain poured down.

They stood there.

We look like an Edward Gorey print, Xander thought, and he was just about to share this observation—which would no doubt prompt Giles to ask what exactly Xander knew about Edward Gorey—when the mound of mud on top of Jackson Kirby's economy-style gravesite started to move.

"Finally," Buffy said.

She started to dart from beneath the umbrella. Giles said, "Oh, here, we'll move," and the threesome edged in concert closer to the mound. Rainwater sluiced down through the newly created rings of mud as the newborn vampire began to rise, like a baby chick breaking open its shell.

Or maybe not so much, Xander decided, as one pale hand burst through, followed by the other. Then the head emerged, fully vamped out—ridged forehead, wild, glowing eyes, and the feral, senseless grin of a mouth stuffed with fangs.

The demon that now inhabited Kirby's corpse saw them and growled savagely, renewing its efforts to leave the grave. As soon as its chest was clear, Buffy murmured, " 'Scuse," to Giles.

"Mmm? Oh, yes, certainly," he said, stepping out of her way.

She stooped down, just about to run the newborn through, when something came flying through the cemetery and launched itself at the three of them.

A vampire.

Three, actually.

They seemed to flow through the darkness and the rain, attacking quickly and viciously. Buffy, Xander, and Giles all moved to defend themselves. The Slayer sized up her opponents—one petite blond female and two males, one thin but tautly muscular, one large, swarthy, and bearded. And the newbie, who had cleared the grave, made four. With a mindless snarl, he rushed Buffy and the group from the opposite direction.

The hairy one lunged for Buffy; she dodged and shot out an elbow to the back of the head which sent him into the mud.

"I'll take the new kid," Xander shouted, and pulled out a stake from his jacket.

Giles was likewise armed. Dropping the umbrella to the ground, he pulled out a cross as well and fended off the thin vampire as it rushed him. Recoiling, it turned as if in search of easier prey and spotted Xander, who had rushed forward to take out the newbie. The vampire grabbed his shoulders from behind. It clamped one hand on his forehead and caught him under the jaw with its other, arching his head back. Snarling, it bared its fangs.

The female vampire moved on Buffy, circling her, expertly dodging each kick and body blow Buffy attempted. Buffy swung again, and the vampire laughed.

We're in trouble, Buffy thought, casting an anxious glance at Xander. Then she saw that the olive-skinned, bearded vamp was deliberately backing Giles up in the direction of the newborn, whose only impulse was feeding as soon as possible.

"Giles, behind you!" she cried. She feinted another side kick at the blonde, who took the bait, jumping out of range as Buffy took off in the opposite direction. Instead of aiding Giles, who was not in immediate danger—he had, like, two or three seconds before that happened—she charged the vampire who held Xander in a death grip, fully expecting the staking to be a simple matter.

But at just the right moment, the vampire released Xander and ran to the blond female's side. Together they came at Xander and Buffy.

And Giles's three seconds were up.

The newbie shrieked while the swarthy one pushed Giles toward him, bellowing, "Eat, brother!"

They were the first words any of the vampires had spoken since the battle began. "So, not deaf-mute vampires after all," Buffy said as she struck the thin male in the face.

"What shall we say? You are beneath notice," the blonde replied in an exotic accent, thrusting Buffy out of the way in order to save the thin vamp. Buffy's back slammed into a gravestone, and she grunted as the air was expelled from her lungs. Then she popped back up into fighting stance.

The female, obviously the leader, glanced quickly at the others. "Konstantin, Ephialtes, what is wrong with you? Kill them, and be done with it. We have no time for such things."

Buffy frowned. "Nice accent. Foreign talent. Did you check in when you came to town? Cuz, you see, the local vamps don't let just anybody chomp people in their territory."

"This is my territory now," the blonde retorted.

"No, sorry, it's really not." Buffy jumped into the air, executed a three-sixty, and finally landed a good solid kick to the side of the female's head.

She grunted and staggered back. Buffy took advantage by going on the offensive, pummeling her with brutal punches to her face and neck. The vampire seemed slightly off balance, but she was obviously ready for more.

Buffy glanced quickly around. Xander was once again under attack by the swarthy vampire, the one the blonde had called Ephialtes. And the newbie, Jackson Kirby, was doing its best to grab onto Giles, who ducked down just as it tried to throw its arms around him. It lost its balance, and Giles aimed his stake for its chest from his squatting position.

Good, Giles, she thought. But then Ephialtes lashed out and drove Giles to the ground. He grabbed the Watcher's arm and dragged him through the mud of the grave and across to the other side, where Jackson Kirby licked his chops.

Meanwhile, Xander was grappling with the thin vampire, Konstantin, his stake pointed toward the sky instead of directly at the vampire's chest, as it should be.

Worried about her friends, Buffy almost didn't realize how much danger she was in.

"How dare you ignore me!" the female roared, and struck out at Buffy.

The Slayer took the hit, went down on the wet ground, and rolled with the momentum. When she came up, she was only a couple of feet away from Giles.

This is harder than it should be, Buffy thought as she went to Giles's aid. Flashes of lightning in quick succession lent the scene a strobelike effect as Buffy took Ephialtes down. She raised her stake above her head, anticipating the dusting, but then the female was there, wrenching the stake from her grasp.

"I think not," she said.

Buffy pumped forward, her palms flattening on the male vampire's chest as she threw her weight on her hands and brought her legs up behind her, smashing her heels into the blonde's face.

When she dropped to her feet, she leaped over the vampires' fallen leader and went to Giles's aid again. Jackson Kirby was about to take a bite out of the Watcher. Giles tried to stake him, but the newborn vampire grabbed his wrists.

"I'll take that," Buffy said to Giles, yanking the stake out of his hand. She pushed him out of the way and ran the newbie through.

The thing that had once been Jackson Kirby exploded in a shower of ash that was immediately saturated by the rain and absorbed into the mud.

"Thank you," Giles said politely, and went to help Xander.

"Kinda what I do." She smiled briefly and gave the swarthy

vampire, who was trying to sit up, a good, stiff kick in the head. The force sent him rolling, sprawling facedown in the mud. That, more than the kick, seemed to piss him off.

"Who is this girl?" he said to the blonde, scrambling to his knees. "How does she dare get in our way?"

"Giles, note. We need a better publicist," Buffy sighed, and kicked the vampire in the head again. "And speaking of daring, how dare *you* guys spoil our evening? You keep this up, I'm going to miss *Felicity*."

She whipped her arm down to dust the dude—*easily done*—but the blonde intercepted her with a body block to the side. Buffy sprawled but managed to trip the blonde as she charged. Then they were all down there in the mud, the dark, bearded vampire and his blond mistress, and Buffy.

The female climbed onto Buffy, who tried to force her off but without any luck. She was latched on tight. Buffy staggered to her feet, fighting to break free. Suddenly, Ephialtes loomed up before her, and she wondered if it was all over.

Which was when Giles slapped a cross on the back of Ephialtes's neck. Without a stake, it was his only weapon, and he made good use of it. Ephialtes cried out and turned to crack Giles hard across the cheek. Then it was two on two, Xander and Giles against the two male vampires.

Buffy grunted angrily and thrust herself backward, slamming into Jackson Kirby's headstone. The female vampire grunted, and they both tumbled down into the disturbed earth that had been Kirby's grave.

The Slayer was on top.

"Ephialtes, Konstantin, go!" shouted the female.

Now, Buffy thought, and brought the stake down swiftly. Just before the point struck home, the vampire smiled sort of oddly and said, "Until next time, Slayer."

Then she burst into a sodden pile of dust.

"In your dreams, moron," Buffy spat.

She straightened, ready for more, only to realize that the other two vampires were trying to escape. Xander and Giles—

bless their souls—were giving chase. Buffy joined the hunt, leaping over broken gravestones and exposed tree roots. The rain was so heavy it obscured Buffy's vision; she narrowly missed an overhanging branch until it was illuminated by a flash of lightning.

Thunder rumbled, the bass accompaniment to Buffy's steady footfalls in the sticky, slippery mud. The vampires were faster than Xander and Giles, and they had had a head start. When she caught up with her guys, she stopped, muttered, "Damn," and scanned the area in case the two vampires had come with any friends who were slower.

"Two out of four's not bad," Xander ventured.

She gave him a look. "Don't let it get around."

"For good money, I won't. Or a massage." He flinched at her glare. "Or a quarter."

"Put it on my tab."

"Well, that was rather more arduous than I would have expected," Giles said as they trudged back toward the umbrella.

"Same here. They weren't exactly amateurs," Buffy said. She smiled at Xander as they ducked under the tree branch at the same time. "I'm glad you showed."

"I'm glad you're glad. Personally, I'm freezing. I'm going to—"

At that moment, Konstantin dropped from the upper branches of the same tree and took off. Buffy couldn't help a brief smile—*I've got him this time*—and hauled after him.

"Go, Buffy!" Xander shouted.

She pulled out all the stops, ticked at having lost him once, determined not to let it happen a second time. *Boots, meet mud,* she thought as her bounty from a recent mall excursion with her mother was soaked through, and she felt the cold, slimy mud seeping into her socks.

The vampire looked over its shoulder and kept going. All it had had to do to survive was stay hidden in the tree for about two more minutes. *But no. That flight-or-fright thing gets 'em every time. Or fright-or-fight. Or whatever.*

Feeling smug, Buffy matched its pace, then put on a burst of speed to get the job done. Lightning flashed, momentarily disorienting her, and she sailed along blindly for a moment before the ground seemed to open up in front of her. Buffy stumbled, fell, slammed against a wall of earth, and then landed butt-first in an open grave.

"Buffy!" It was Giles.

As she sputtered and fumed, he and Xander peered over the edge. Giles had pulled out a flashlight, which he was shining down at her.

"Oh, dear," he murmured.

"Hey, no big," she shot back. "I've fallen into freshly dug graves before. I just don't know why they didn't cover it."

"Merely a shot in the dark," Giles ventured, "but I don't believe the *they* you refer to dug this grave at all."

Confused, Buffy looked at him more closely. He gestured to the gravestone behind her. She turned to see that the date of death on the stone was six months old.

"Wait a minute. That means . . . someone dug him up?"

"So it would appear," Giles agreed. "Certainly, no vampire waits six months to return to life. The hunger, never mind the condition of the body, would not allow such a thing. Add in the obvious 'freshly dug' quality you mentioned, and, well, it seems we have a grave robber on our hands."

"Um, would it make me less manly if I said *eeew?*" Xander asked.

"Considerably," Giles informed him.

Xander nodded. "Right. Of course. Which is why I would never. So who'd want to dig up dead bodies?"

Buffy sighed. "In this town? If we rounded up the usual suspects, there wouldn't be any town left."

Xander brightened. "Now, there's a happy thought."

Chapter Two

In her dream, it was still raining. Buffy stood in the middle of Restfield Cemetery, alone this time, and glanced nervously around. She knew that she should be bored, and confident, and she was. But something lingered in the air, in the dream mind, the flow of her consciousness, and it told her that what was to come was to be feared. So despite her outward calm, the current that flowed beneath the dream was laden with anxiety.

Dream lightning flashed, illuminating the deep open grave only a few feet away. Her feet moved beneath her, and Buffy tried to look down at them, or even at her hands.

She couldn't see her hands. Her subconscious mind, monitoring the dream reality, was slightly relieved. That was good. *In normal dreams, you can't see your hands.*

Dream rain spattered her face. Lightning flashed again, and Buffy looked down into that hole in the ground, and she saw them there, piled one upon the other: Giles, Xander, and Oz. They were dead, eyes staring blankly, jaws slack and gaping, almost accusing her of some complicity in their deaths.

The illumination of the lightning seeped away, eaten again by the dark, and still Buffy stared in horror and revulsion, fear and guilt, at the dark pit beneath her and the bodies that lay there in the shadows. After a moment, something rustled in that empty grave, and three sets of pinprick eyes glowed red in the ebon shadows of that hole.

Buffy recoiled in horror and whispered something aloud, though she could not hear her own voice. Dreams could be like that.

Thunder boomed across the starless night sky, and in the wake of that noise, a sound more sinister and subtle reached her ears. The slippery, sucking sound of mud, the crumbling of sodden earth. Buffy spun, the grave forgotten in her dream, and saw a pair of hands thrust up through the soil of the nearest grave.

As Buffy watched in horror, Willow dragged herself from her grave, face slack and white, eyes red and bloodshot.

"God, Will, no," Buffy whispered.

At that, Willow smiled, her skin cracking at the edges of her mouth as she did, and as her lips drew back, fresh rainwater poured out the sides and down her chin.

Buffy wanted nothing more than to turn and run, or simply collapse there in the rain among the dead and sob. But beyond Willow, something else stirred in the ground. Beyond and beyond and beyond, things shoved their way up through the malleable, sucking soil.

All women. Girls. With familiar faces.

Cordelia was there, beyond Willow. And Amy Madison. Her old friend Jennifer from Hemery High in L.A. Chantarelle. But the worst was the one in the back, the one even now making her slippery way past the others to the front of the pack, her long, wavy blond mane slicked back with rain.

"Mom," Buffy whimpered, lip quivering.

She reached out for her mother, hoping to help somehow, and she realized with a jolt of horror that now she could see her hands. This wasn't just a dream anymore. This was something else.

In that moment of realization, Joyce smiled. They all smiled, even the ones so far back in the dark that Buffy could not see their faces through the shadows. Then the lightning crackled across the sky again, illuminating the cemetery in sharp detail.

And all their faces changed. Eyes blazed yellow, features contorted, mouths hissed wide, rainwater now sluicing over jutting fangs.

Buffy screamed, tried to back up, to get away, but her feet found no purchase in the mud. She slipped and fell backward. She fell for a very long time, and when she landed, flat on her back, she was surrounded by walls of crumbling dirt. She lay in that open grave, in several inches of accumulated rain, and water poured in around the sides. But she knew she wouldn't have time to drown.

Thunder rolled across the sky, and lightning picked out the faces bent over the open grave above her, peering down, leering with cruel intent. And then, above them, another face. Evil, yellow-eyed, vampire face. But changing, becoming human and beautiful. Becoming Angel.

"Buffy," he said grimly. "There's forever, and then forever."

Before she could reply, the night sky was suddenly torn asunder, and her eyes were blinded by a flash of the brightest white light she had ever seen, and all the vampires were incinerated, exploding to dust. For just half a moment, there was a malformed shadow silhouetted in the light, and three pairs of red eyes glaring down at her from within the shadow.

Then they, too, were burned away from the light.

Buffy's eyes fluttered open.

"Buffy, honey, wake up."

For a moment, Buffy couldn't breathe. She stared at her mother's concerned expression and felt disconnected from her own body, from the waking world.

Then, suddenly, her breath returned, and she sucked air in quickly, as though she'd been suffocating. Her heart was pounding in her chest, and Buffy sat up, staring around her room with eyes wide. She picked up Mr. Gordo from the bedside table and held him tightly in her hands.

"Whoa," she whispered.

"Honey, are you okay?" Joyce asked, reaching out to stroke Buffy's wild bed hair away from her face.

Buffy twitched as her mother's hand came near.

Joyce blinked and looked at her, coughing, a hurt expression coming over her face. Buffy shook her head in apology, let out another long breath, and reached out to pull her mother to her. They embraced briefly, and though she was the Slayer, though the darkest evils of the world cringed at the mention of her name, Buffy only started to feel safe in the protective harbor of her mother's arms.

It wasn't until after breakfast that Buffy began to dispel the anxiety that her dream had produced. During her shower, and while she dressed for school, she'd felt as though she were nearly sleepwalking. The horrible images of her nightmare did not fragment and dissipate as such things have a tendency to do. Instead, they lingered, and as hard as she tried to turn her mind to something else, her thoughts went back there, time and again, as though the hideous dream were a melody repeating itself over and over in her head.

Finally, though, when she came downstairs, ready for school, and noticed for the first time that the rains of the night before had given way to clear blue skies, Buffy began to relax again. Her mother had taken the time to make an egg scramble with ham and cheese and wheat toast for both of them.

"Rough night, huh?" Joyce asked as she handed Buffy the carton of orange juice. She had a tissue over her mouth, and she was still coughing a lot.

There was something in her mother's voice that made Buffy look up and frown. "I'm okay," she said. Her mom looked pale, and her eyes were rimmed with red.

"I know. I just thought, with that dream you had, your patrol must have been pretty dreadful."

"That's one way to put it. We ran into some out-of-towners who were a little more durable than your run-of-the-mill Sunnydale vamp. Kinda proves my theory about inbreeding around here. Anyway, their leader was mucho macha. Gave me bruises on my bruises, even with the whole no-Band-Aid-required bonus of Slayerism."

Joyce looked at her bravely, trying not to seem as concerned as she already was. Buffy wished there were something she could do or say so her mother wouldn't worry so much. But there wasn't. Except, perhaps, in this case . . .

"I dusted her."

Joyce smiled with relief. Coughed. "Well, that's nice," she said. "Want some more eggs?"

"No, thanks. And you've eaten so much yourself."

Joyce shrugged. "I guess I'm not in much of a breakfast mood." She wiped her nose and tossed the tissue in the trash.

Buffy sucked back the last of her juice and got up from the table, reaching for her bag. She kissed her mother's cheek and headed for the door. When she was about to pull it shut behind her, she remembered that they were supposed to shop for shoes that afternoon. Her mother was going to take off early from work for some girl time. Buffy felt guilty, but she went back inside and poked her head into the kitchen.

"Hey, Mom?"

Joyce looked up, pausing with a tiny piece of toast halfway to her mouth.

"I'm sorry, but I don't know what time I'll be home this afternoon. I really want to go, but can I just call from the library when I have a clue?"

Her mother looked at her oddly for a moment, and then her mouth opened in a little "Oh."

"You know what? I sort of forgot about that. I may be tied up this afternoon anyway."

Buffy was a little hurt. She may have screwed up their plans, but at least she'd remembered them. With a shrug, she started to turn away.

"I'm sorry, honey," Joyce said. "It's just . . . I'm trying to get in to see my doctor this afternoon. I've already placed one call to her answering service this morning."

"They'll just tell you it's a virus," Buffy said, smile askew.

"That's all they ever say. Then they collect the bucks from the HMO."

Joyce blinked and hesitated. Buffy didn't like that hesitation. Not one bit.

"I'm sure you're right. It's probably nothing," her mother said. "But I keep coughing." She took a breath and went on in a rush. "Last night, I coughed up a little bit of blood, and—"

"*Blood?*" Buffy cried. "Mom, excuse me, why are you even calling? Get in the car, and go to the doctor. We're not talking head cold." Buffy paused, realizing how dire her words were. "I mean, I'm sure it's nothing." She backpedaled. "But nothing's more sure than sure, you know? You can't fool around when it comes to your health. You told me that about a thousand times, right?"

"And that was just last week," Joyce said slyly, a small smile playing at the corners of her mouth. Then she coughed again. "I'm sure you're right, Buffy. It's just a bad cold or something, maybe even bronchitis—"

"Which, okay, no fun, but not the end of the world," Buffy interrupted, realizing as she did so exactly how desperate she sounded.

Joyce smiled. "You're going to be late for school."

Buffy nodded. Her mother was right. She turned to go, and just as she did, she saw her mother's smile disappear abruptly. Buffy didn't turn back around, didn't try to catch her mother with fear and worry engraved on her features.

She didn't want to see.

All day, she worried about her mother. She had come to school late and decided just to go in to see Giles when classes let out. Not that it did her any good to attend her classes. For that entire day, her mind was completely preoccupied. Between her mother's health, the events of the night before, and the awful dreams she'd had just before rising that morning, Buffy could barely remember she was even in school to begin with.

Several times, the teachers noticed. By calling on her for answers to questions she could not possibly have, given her lack of attention, they attempted to embarrass her. Buffy didn't rise to the bait, paid no attention to the looks she received from other students in her classes. Her mind was simply somewhere else.

Until lunchtime.

"Saturn to Buffy," Xander said. "Hello? Bonjour? Saturn to Buffy?"

As he slid into an ugly orange plastic chair with a plate full of baked manicotti on an ugly orange plastic tray, Oz raised an eyebrow and glanced over at Xander.

"Shouldn't it be 'Earth to Buffy'?" he asked.

Xander shot a glance at Buffy and pointed at her with his thumb. "You kidding?" he said. "Wherever she's gone, it's way past the point where she can receive the signal from Earth."

"Okay, not defending *herself,* so 'Hey!' " Willow said, frowning at Xander. "Buffy's just, y'know, replaying the events of last night's patrol and trying to decipher the mystery of the missing corpse. Not to mention getting an ID on these new vamps."

Buffy smiled weakly and put a hand on Willow's arm. "Thanks, Will, but Xander's right," she confessed. "I'm not even in the Milky Way. My brain molecules are drifting across the galaxies." When she'd called to check in, her mother had told her she hadn't been able to get in to see the doctor today. But she did have an appointment for tomorrow.

And now she was home, having left the gallery early because she felt too ill to work. *My mother?* Buffy thought. *The workaholic?*

"Case. Rested." Xander looked smug.

"Ooh, but now we're drawing you back," Willow told her, sounding excited. "So, *do* you have any ideas about last night?"

Buffy shook her head. She really was drawing a blank. "Ask Xander," she said. "He was there."

"And I have the back brace to show for it," Xander replied happily. "Or I should. They were tops in their infliction-of-pain-and-bodily-harm class at vampire college."

"What's up with the body-snatching thing? We got Dr. Frankenstein on our hands?" Oz asked out of the blue.

Of course, Buffy thought, *with Oz, most everything comes out of the blue.*

"Nah. We've been there," Xander told him. "Someone was trying to build Cordy out of other women's parts. Sort of. It wasn't pretty."

Buffy chewed her lip. "Gotta say, with all my heart, I have no clue as to what's going on," she said. "But the mysteries do seem to pile up quickly lately." Buffy glanced at Willow. "Ready to play Nancy Drew?"

"Nah. She gets caught too much," Willow replied.

"Cool!" Xander exclaimed. "Does that mean Oz and I get to be the Hardy Boys?"

"You'll have to be a Hardy *Boy,*" Oz told him. "I've never been much good at make-believe."

"Sad for you," Xander told him. "It's what I live on."

They all looked at him, and Xander looked away sheepishly. "Okay," he confessed. "Maybe sad for me. But I'm not bitter. Nope. My life is forfeit to my duties as weak, human distraction for cannibal creatures from Philadelphia. I don't have time for make-believe."

"Good to hear," Buffy told him. "I'm going to need you tonight. All of you."

"Very sound thinking, Buffy," Giles said proudly, pushing his glasses up on the bridge of his nose. "Just what I had planned myself, actually. We don't know if there's any connection between last night's two graveyard mysteries, and so we must assume none exists for the moment."

"Are you sure it isn't dangerous, y'know, splitting up?" Xander asked meekly, almost pleadingly.

"Well, of course it's dangerous," Willow explained to him gently. "But we're up to the challenge, aren't we?"

"We're very much of the challenged," Xander agreed. "Though I don't know that anyone's ever described me that way and meant it as a compliment."

He leaned back in his chair at the library's study table and glanced around, apparently hoping for someone to interject, maybe with the suggestion that Buffy's plan was a bad one. But Buffy knew that despite any inherent dangers, it was the most logical way to follow up on the events of the previous night.

"Guys, there's no reason to think this is connected to those vampires from last night. I don't think either of the ones who got away was hiding a corpse in a coffin under his coat. Just in case, we'll make sure you're armed to the teeth."

"Does that mean we get to play Commando Raid?" Xander asked.

"As retro-funky as that might be, I don't think that's where Buffy's going with this," Oz replied, with as much sympathy as he was likely capable of.

"Cordelia used to play Commando Raid with me," Xander said wistfully.

"Too much knowledge," Willow said in alarm. "Gonna have to cleanse soon."

"With you," Buffy told her. "But can we move along? Giles already talked to Cordelia before cheer practice. The four of you should hook up at the Bronze after dinner. Oz can transport whatever weapons you need this afternoon, keep them in the van. Just take your time, patrol all of the cemeteries."

"All twelve?" Xander asked.

"Consider yourselves fortunate," Giles broke in. "The mayor is considering charging visitors to our fair city for just that very tour."

"No rush. Just look for anybody with a shovel. Digging after dark is a dead giveaway in the body-snatcher biz."

"Where will you be, in case we need you?" Willow asked Giles.

"I will be here, attempting to see if I can find mention of either of these chaps, Konstantin or . . . Ephialtes, I believe you said, in the Watchers' Journals."

"And we'll probably cross paths," Buffy told Willow. "I'm going to patrol, see if I can track down these bad boys, find out what they're up to, why they were so concerned about a newborn."

"Perhaps you'd best go by Angel's first," Giles suggested. "With vampires with such strength and fighting prowess . . ."

"Backup's good," Buffy agreed. "Great minds think alike. And, coincidentally, so do we."

Buffy rarely found Angel asleep, even when she went to his house during the day. There had been times when she'd roused him from slumber, and in those times, he'd looked so nearly human that the wishes and hopes that went through her mind in those moments caused her heart to ache. But for the most part, she would arrive, enter through the back as she usually did, and find him wandering quietly somewhere in the house. Perhaps doing his martial arts *kata* or reading an old book that had been out of print since before Buffy's mother was born.

That was the real Angel, she knew. The sleeping Angel was just an illusion of normalcy. An illusion shattered if she looked too close. Then she might notice that while he slept, his chest did not rise and fall. She would see that he looked like a corpse, and she might be tempted to realize that in some ways . . . ah, but she wouldn't allow herself to think in those terms.

Even now, as she walked across the broad expanse of lawn in front of the house, the sun still gleaming just above the horizon, throwing long shadows that hinted at the things that might creep about after dark, Buffy did not expect to find Angel sleeping. In her heart, she knew that he didn't truly *live* in that house. More truthfully, the way he moved silently through its corridors and lingered in certain spots for long minutes at a time, it might be said that he haunted the place.

Certainly, such thoughts disturbed Buffy, when she allowed them to creep into her mind. But they were easily dispelled. All she had to do was look into Angel's eyes, to see how much he cared for her, and everything else, questions of life or death, just disappeared.

But not tonight. For this evening, she found herself thinking about her mother. Buffy had checked in after school, but her mother still hadn't spoken directly with the doctor. His office had promised to fit her in the next day, but they were going to get back to her with a time.

Whenever it was, it wouldn't be soon enough for Buffy.

A fire burned in the hearth inside Angel's house. It wasn't necessary for warmth, though there was a cool breeze blowing outside. Nor for light, as it was not quite dusk yet. But it comforted him, in a way. He enjoyed the sound of wood burning, crackling. And when he leaned against the masonry around the fireplace, he could feel the heat of the fire through the stone, and it gave him a great deal of pleasure. Without the sun, without a heart beating inside his chest, there was very little warmth in Angel's life.

The fire, and the stone, and holding Buffy in his arms.

Angel was a vampire. He didn't need anything but blood to survive. But there were other things he needed to *live*.

He leaned against the stone fireplace, reading a weathered collection of short stories by Algernon Blackwood he had stolen from a bookseller in 1938. The author didn't seem to have had any real understanding of the horrors that existed in the world, but somehow, Angel felt he managed to capture the essence of horror, of evil, and through them, the secret of humanity. Which was, of course, fear. Of pain and death and what lay beyond.

The fire crackled behind him, and the light from the sun began to diminish. When Buffy entered the room, he felt her presence even before she spoke.

"Hey," she said, voice low, as though they stood in a museum rather than his home. "Good book?"

Angel smiled and slipped a battered leather marker into the pages before closing the book. "Ghost stories," he told her.

Buffy looked at him oddly. "Can't get enough, huh? Maybe it's me, but if I lived in Norway, I'd go somewhere warm for vacation."

"They're just fantasy stories," Angel said.

"Not my fantasies."

He stood up as she approached, and then they embraced.

They held on to each other like that for a long minute, until the intimacy of it began to become too much for them, too dangerous for them. They could love but dared not share their love, for fear of the consequences. But when Angel released Buffy from his embrace, she did not withdraw. Instead, she held him closer, tighter, as if she clung to him for fear she might drift away if she let go.

"What is it, Buffy?"

Finally, she pulled back and looked up at him, expression troubled. She opened her mouth, began to speak, but then she faltered, searching for words. After a moment, she glanced away, brow still furrowed with secret concerns.

"Hey," Angel whispered, and lifted her chin.

Buffy offered a weak, unconvincing smile. "I love you," she said, and rose up on her toes to kiss him.

Angel bent to the kiss, cold heart momentarily warmed. But still, he was concerned for her. "Something's on your mind," he said. "I'd like to help, if I can."

"I know," Buffy told him. "But now might not be the time. Can we pick it up later, after I try to make some sense of it myself? Not to get so *All My Children* on you, but I just need to do a little Summers-brain spin control first."

His first instinct was to say no. To prod her so that he might learn what was bothering her. Part of that, the admirable part, was his need to help her. But he understood that the other part was merely his selfish need to have the answers now so that the questions would not stay with him, worrying him until she was willing to share.

Reluctantly, Angel nodded. "So, what else is going on?"

With the conversation turning to what passed for business in their lives, Buffy brightened noticeably. The turmoil in her heart was too much for her, but monsters and dead things she could handle.

"The usual chaos, but with a twist," she told him. "We've got a rise in vamp activity—in itself sort of a big yawn, I know—but we've also got some grave robbing going on."

Angel frowned. "You're sure they're thefts? Not just vampires rising?"

Buffy shook her head. "Nah. This grave was dug up, not dug out of. Anyway, the Mod Squad's gonna try to track down the grave-robbing angle—which I figure is safer, especially if they're just on stakeout—giving us the space to start culling the vampire herd. Actually, I'm starting to wonder if it's seasonal, y'know? Vampire breeding season coming around every few months. I should ask Giles to track the figures. Willow could make a computer model. That would elicit squeals of geeker joy."

Angel went into the hall and grabbed his coat off a rack, then slipped the long black duster on.

"For vampires, it's always breeding season," he said darkly.

"Yeah, well, whoever's riding shotgun on this undead posse must have an extra special itch, 'cause they were real concerned about reproducing last night, waiting for a newbie to rise."

As they left the mansion, Angel pondered that. Buffy was right. Vampires usually employed a kind of scorched-earth policy, killing without thinking, changing a kill over on a whim, and not looking back. Newborn vampires came into the world as alone as they were when the last of their blood was drained away. Sometimes vampires killed for companionship, but then the body would not be likely to receive a burial in the first place.

It wasn't much of a mystery. More of a curiosity. But at least it was something for Buffy and Angel to focus on while they both pretended not to be thinking about whatever had her so preoccupied.

Outside, only the last angry red rays of sun lingered on the western horizon.

Pepper Roback had taken a job waiting tables at the Fish Tank to make enough money to finish college. Six years later, she still didn't quite understand what had happened to that dream. Granted, she didn't make very much money at the Tank, even on the busiest of nights. The kind of guys who drank there weren't much into tipping, unless they were trying to get a girl into bed. And the ones even vaguely interesting enough to go home with had a habit of forgetting her name the next time they came in.

Still, they always tried. Though she felt worn down inside, Pepper knew she was still attractive. Her curly red hair got a lot of attention, and her freckles, and her size as well. She was a very small woman, barely five feet tall, and ninety-two pounds pretty much forever. But despite her size, most guys didn't give her a hard time. They might flirt, but if she wasn't interested, they wouldn't pursue it. The regulars respected her, and the others just didn't want to make trouble with a woman who seemed as hard as Pepper Roback.

But Pepper wasn't hard at all. Not inside. She had simply learned how to survive. It was vital that she know how to get by, to take care of herself. Nobody else was going to do it. Pepper had stopped briefly at the Fish Tank, and stayed too long. And the rest of the world had moved along without her.

With seven hundred dollars in the bank, Pepper knew she wasn't going back to college. Wasn't going much of anywhere, in fact. She'd wanted to be a teacher. Later, when she'd started to realize that the stale smell of beer and the raucous laughter and deep depression that permeated the Fish Tank were now a part of her life, she'd thought that maybe she might get a job doing day care.

No question, she loved kids. But over time, she'd come to wonder if she had anything to offer them. Pepper knew she wasn't much of a role model. There was a rawness to the Fish Tank, and to the people who spent time there. And there was an element of danger to the place as well. The men and women who went into the bar night after night didn't mind a fight or two, didn't worry about using a broken bottle or a blade to hurt someone if they felt it necessary. Those things didn't give them a moment's pause, because they didn't fear going to jail.

They didn't fear going to jail, because they had nothing to lose. Not really.

It wasn't much of a life. Not at all. But Pepper had finally done something about it, found something to enrich her life and make her smile, to give her something to look forward to, week after week. Every Monday, Wednesday, and Friday afternoon, she spent two hours reading to schoolchildren at the Sunnydale Public Library. Sometimes they were wild, those kids. But they were always glad to hear a story, and Pepper always left the library with a smile on her face. Her stories made the children happy, and that was all she had ever wanted.

But no matter how happy Pepper might be when she left the library, went out to the lot, and started up her car, the minute she began to drive, the smile slipped from her face. For she was always driving to her real job, driving to the Fish Tank. Which meant that she would need to don, once more, the cold, hard mask of the tough woman the place had made her. A smile as happy as hers would only make her vulnerable there.

Pepper couldn't afford vulnerability.

On Monday afternoon, she read "The Seven Chinese Brothers" to the kids. The boys always liked that one, because the story's characters all had strange powers, like superheroes. And they were family. They took care of each other, kept each other alive. It was a fantasy story to Pepper, just as it was to many of the children to whom she read.

When she left the library, a light breeze had sprung up, and Pepper shivered. Sitting in her car, she opened a brown bag she'd kept in the library fridge during the afternoon and ate the sandwich she'd prepared for dinner. Ham and swiss on wheat, with mustard. Then she had the apple she'd brought along and put the core back into the bag.

Then, ever so reluctantly, she started the car and headed for work. Her battered Chevy Corsica stuck out in most of Sunnydale, receiving disapproving stares from other drivers, and even from people just walking by. But by the time she reached the Fish Tank, she had started to blend. Sometimes her car stuck out in that part of town for the opposite reason: compared to the others parked on the street or passing by, it was in great shape.

The Tank was only a few blocks from the docks, where ocean-shipping warehouses and fisheries provided much of the clientele. The people there worked hard and came to the Fish Tank mainly because they didn't have the time or the energy or the inclination to go anywhere else.

She had to drive around a bit before she found an acceptable spot, in a side alley a block from the Tank. There were tow zone signs posted everywhere, but the owners of the building never had anyone towed. The car would be fine. The only thing in it worth stealing was the radio, and that was a piece of junk as well.

Pepper tasted the salty tang of the air as she stepped out of the car, and she thought of the ocean. Once, she had loved to swim, even to sail when she got the chance. But now the ocean only meant customers—the regular influx of men just off fishing boats or fresh from unloading freighters at the docks.

She shivered slightly with the cool breeze and wrapped her arms around herself. The alley was dark and empty, save for several other cars parked there. Out on the street, it was too early for many of the regulars to be about. Some of them didn't get started until after ten o'clock.

Wrinkling her nose at the odor of a Dumpster just a few feet up the alley—the wind had shifted, and now it brought the noxious smell of garbage—she began to walk to the corner, to make her way up to the front door of the Tank.

Pepper didn't even hear anyone come up behind her.

"Cold?" the stranger asked.

She turned to see a large bearded man looking at her expectantly.

"Do you want my jacket?" he asked, an exotic accent to his voice.

For a moment, she almost smiled, almost said yes. This was a different sort of man, after all, from the usual crowd at the Fish Tank. This was a man who would not be spending the rest of his life, or even another hour, in this dump. He was well dressed, very handsome, and so very foreign. She almost said yes.

But there was something about him that unsettled Pepper. Something in his eyes.

"You know what? I work right here. But thanks for the offer," she told him.

Anger flashed in his eyes, and then they changed. His nostrils flared, his features seemed to flow and contort. His eyes glowed.

He was a monster.

Pepper opened her mouth to scream, and then he struck her. She slumped forward, tumbling toward the ground, and he caught her. Groggy, unable to find the energy to cry out now, she felt unconsciousness cradling her, carrying her down into the dark. Somewhere, she heard a car start.

Then nothing.

When Ephialtes entered the crumbling stone structure with its boarded-up windows, he had the woman over his shoulder. Konstantin saw immediately that she was alive. He watched as Ephialtes brought the unconscious human to a darkened corner and set her down. To Konstantin's eyes, she was a fine creature, a bit weathered by her life, but humans were so fragile in general.

Except for the Slayer. He remembered her strength, and it both infuriated and aroused him.

This woman was a pale shadow of the Slayer. But she would not be for long. Not long at all. Soon she would be changed.

He watched Ephialtes from across the room. Behind him, in what had once been the office of the chief of police—before a new police station had been built years earlier—three newborn vampires, all sired by Veronique herself, set about building the nest.

The nest. Konstantin was not precisely certain what the nest would contain, but he knew it would be soon. And they would be horrible.

There was a short cry of pain and a grunt of pleasure, and when Konstantin glanced back at the corner of the entry hall, Ephialtes was drinking deeply of the woman's blood, long teeth sunk into her soft throat. Konstantin was jealous.

Ephialtes was the harbinger of the mistress, just as she was the harbinger of the Triumvirate. He was preparing her place in the world once more. Konstantin hoped one day to have that honor.

When Ephialtes laid the woman gently on the floor—for she would soon rise with the essence of Veronique within her—Konstantin stood behind him, watching carefully.

"Is there something you wish to ask?" Ephialtes demanded, his tone an admonition.

"Why bring her here to take her?" Konstantin asked.

"For the quiet. And out of respect. And because the place I found her might have been too far away from where the mistress's last host met its destruction."

"We are not like her, are we?"

"I forget how young you are," Ephialtes said dismissively. "We are not like her, and never shall be. Veronique is a true immortal. Where we have only these flimsy shells, and are tied to them once we have taken up residence within, she lives on forever. Do you not recall the prophecy she shared with you that first night, on the Sea of Crete?"

Konstantin did recall.

"From my scion, the three faces of Hell shall be born.

"Through my offspring, three shall become one.

"In their name, shall I live on from flesh to flesh.

"And when the three-who-are-one have had their fill,

"I will drink the blood of the last man on Earth."

Such had been the words of Veronique, some of the first words she had spoken to Konstantin when he awoke to his new life, slathered in their shared blood. The prophecy had chilled him and thrilled him to the marrow, giving his cold blood the illusion of warmth.

The blood of the last man on Earth.

Chapter Three

Constantinople, A.D. 543

It was close to midnight, and the horns of the crescent moon dripped with magick and death. The signs and portents were clear: the hour was at hand. She must make haste, or she would miss her chance.

The youth struggled and screamed as Veronique dragged him down the filthy street, his head caught firmly beneath her arm. His thin arms flailed; he dragged his sandaled feet and kicked his heels, but he was in no condition to cause her trouble. He obviously had not eaten in days. His face was sunken, and his eyes were ringed with exhaustion. He stank, but these days, everyone stank.

Constantinople, once the flower of the empire, had become more vile and disgusting than Hell itself. The plague of Justinian, now in its second year, killed more than it spared, and there was no one left willing to bury or burn the bloated, pustule-ridden corpses of the common folk. People were left where they fell, to die and to rot. The fouled air, an unbelievable stench of decomposition mingled with the oily smoke of noble funeral pyres, served as the only shroud for the majority of the deceased. Flies and maggots attacked the bodies in huge hordes, like locusts; and the rats, which had brought the plague, feasted on the blackened carrion, multiplied, and perpetuated the disease.

The scent of her captive's fear made Veronique weak with hunger. She was starving. The plague had tainted the blood of the human population, making it impossible to drink, and there were not enough uninfected people to feed even the handful of vampires in Constantinople. The animals had already been devoured long ago. The hunt for sustenance had become a terrible contest that was rapidly winnowing down the vampire population to a hardy few.

But the blood of this lovely boy was clean. And his terror would surely enhance its flavor.

She felt her face change, and the captive's screams reached fever pitch. Veronique slapped at him peevishly to silence him. Every impulse within her told her to drain him here, now, but she kept reminding herself that he would fill a higher need, if only she could hold off long enough.

A pretty one, Veronique thought, *despite his condition.* Blond, blue-eyed. Perhaps a foreigner, as she was. Some poor young adventurer who had dreamed of making his fortune, never imagining the fate that now awaited him.

"Please," he tried again. "She's a monster!"

The only other living person on the street barely bothered to glance at Veronique and her quarry. Its sex was indeterminate, since starvation robbed men and women both of their essence. Nothing registered on the haggard face. The day-to-day business of survival took concentration and great force of will. No one ever knew which heartbeat was the last. The plague of Justinian came on without warning. First came shivering and vomiting, headaches and giddiness. Then an intolerance to light and a high fever. Within a day, coughing started, until it became spitting up blood. Then the stomach bloated, and blood boils bubbled under the arms, the sides of the neck, and the sexual organs, which turned black and, often, exploded.

For those who were fortunate, death came next.

But many lingered for a time, in unbelievable agony. A few miraculously survived the ordeal. But that was of no interest to Veronique and her kind. Once the blood had been infected by this insidious disease, vampires could not drink it, even if the host returned to perfect health . . . or what stood for health, in these desperate times of little food and no sanitation. She had never heard of such an illness, and yet here it was.

Still in vampire face, Veronique made a sharp left and dragged the young man through an alley. She stepped with distaste around corpses and piles of garbage, making an attempt to steer him past them as well. He must be as pleasing as possible for the ones she served.

After a very long walk, during which the youth finally gave up the struggle and hung limply in her arms, she came to the gates of her sanctuary. It was a small but exquisite villa. Its crowning glory, a sizable dome, had crashed through the roof three years before, collapsing large portions of the building in upon itself. She had been present, for it was a brothel, and she had been one of its star attractions—foreign, exotic, and skilled.

Long ago, even before she had become a vampire, Veronique had begun her life as a prostitute. Later, she had discovered it to be the perfect way to find victims. She might nip one of the men who came to her, take only a little, or follow him as he left to come upon him again in the shadows, this time to fulfill her own needs rather than his.

When the brothel's dome fell, almost all the other *hetaerae* and patrons had been killed. A number of the courtesans were horribly disfigured, and they ended their lives rather than endure the shame. In a few cases, Veronique could have restored their beauty with magick, but she opted to do nothing. She could afford no scrutiny, not even from the clever, witty women who had warmly befriended a stranger such as she.

Then, a fortnight after the accident, the empress Theodora came to the ruin in secret, to pay homage to the spirits of the dead prostitutes. Theodora herself had been a courtesan, who through her incredible sensuality had captured the heart of the emperor, Justinian.

As the empress poured wine on the floor over the mosaic of

Leda and the swan, where so many had died, Veronique dared to approach her from the shadows, one sister courtesan to another. Theodora had taken an instant liking to the beautiful, accomplished, and very bold woman, never dreaming that she was a vampire.

They began to meet, as friends, then confidantes. The beautiful empress shared Veronique's interest in the occult arts, though to the world she attempted to present a different picture altogether—pious in the extreme, a reformed sinner and champion of the state religion.

"I conjure endlessly for eternal beauty," she told Veronique as they lounged in the women's baths at the palace. "To be young and to savor pleasure forever is all I require of an afterlife."

She leaned toward Veronique in the warm, perfumed water. "And I believe I am on the path. Shall you join me?"

At last, Veronique exulted. Her sire, Pere Augustine, had been a powerful sorcerer, in life and as a vampire. He had taught her much . . . and expected much in return. When she had tired of him, she had staked him—only to regret it later when she ransacked his laboratory and discovered vague notes about incantations and rituals that could prolong life indefinitely. She couldn't piece much together, only that he believed that these rituals might allow a vampire to continue to exist even if its human shell had been destroyed. Pere Augustine had believed that the answers lay here, in Constantinople. That was why she had come here, three years ago. She had never imagined that Theodora would be the one to reveal the mysteries to her.

So the Byzantine empress and the vampire began the work. On auspicious nights, dressed in ebon shadow, they distilled elixirs that took them to other states of being, allowing them to journey to other dimensions. For their searches, they gathered talismans and amulets to ward against evil and possession . . . and to invite it. Steeling themselves against the pain, they carved arcane and powerful symbols into their flesh and branded themselves as daughters of the unholy.

They sacrificed together—first lambs and goats, then slaves.

Next came the occasional freeborn virgin, plucked from the countryside by discreet and greedy members of the royal household guard.

They grew in knowledge and power, and the bond between them was formidable.

Then rumors began to get back to the city. The empress was suspected of witchcraft, and her enemies fanned the talk against her. Many of the lofty and powerful hated Theodora because of her distasteful beginnings and her licentiousness. Her life was in danger. Assassins followed her everywhere, and servants were paid enormous bribes to report her every move.

"I can no longer meet with you," she bitterly told Veronique, embracing the vampire in the shadows of the ruined brothel. "I must abandon the work."

In truth, Veronique was relieved. She had learned all she could from Theodora. But she feigned tears and sighs as they parted for the last time.

Now I can get on with it, she thought gleefully, *without that silly cow slowing me down.*

After countless journeys through time and space, her senses made contact with something ageless, eternal, and so evil that she withdrew. But she recognized that within that evil lay immense power . . . and that if she served that power as its handmaiden, her desire would be granted: she, among all the vampires, would be truly eternal.

So she returned to that special place in the abyss where the evil dwelled. She found it there, the Three-Who-Are-One, and it was called the Triumvirate. As she forced herself to surrender, it slowly began pouring its evil into her, transforming her into its creature.

Bring us forth into the world, it bargained, *and we will share eternity with you.*

From that time, she devoted herself to fufilling its desire. The mosaic floors of the ruined brothel, which she kept in a state of disrepair in order to deflect attention from her activities, were soon stained with blood from countless attempts to provide it with a suitable vessel to be born into the world.

And it is this lovely boy, she thought excitedly. *This time, I shall succeed.*

The hem of her white robe dragged through the dirt and cobwebs, and her jeweled headdress gleamed in the torchlight her minions brought to greet her arrival. Preceded by her small but loyal retinue, she swept into the grand salon and stood proudly with her captive as her followers bowed before her. The stars were in alignment; the portents were right. She had gathered the required thirteen vampires, all of her bloodline. This young man would not be among those performing the ritual but, rather, the vessel. The portal.

In a way, it was a pity, for he would suffer horribly. But in another way, his death would exalt him. For he would bring forth upon this Earth the Triumvirate.

"Greetings, Harbinger," one of her minions murmured. Bowing and scraping, he carried an elaborately carved ebony tray. On it, a human heart had been cut into four large pieces. Runestones had been tossed between the four bloody clumps, and she read the signs with delight.

"So, I was right," she said to her follower. His name was Belasarius, and he was one of Justinian's finest generals. She had turned him only recently, and no one in the royal court knew his secret. "Tonight is most auspicious for our purposes."

"It is the most auspicious night in the next one hundred and sixty-nine years," Belasarius agreed, and they smiled at each other. Thirteen years times thirteen years was one of the most powerful spans of time in existence.

"Then we shall proceed. Prepare the vessel."

He held out his arms, and she handed over the burden of the unconscious man. Frowning, he looked down at the human. "I think he's dead."

Her rage was terrible.

Her terror was worse.

*   *   *

Buffy and Angel crouched among the headstones at the Shady Hill Cemetery. After a while, she said, "We should have brought a deck of playing cards."

"For Faro," Angel said.

"Don't know it." She moved her shoulders and cricked her neck. They had been there for almost half an hour, and Buffy was a little chilly and very restless. "Hearts, now that's a game."

He glanced at her, shrugged. "I don't know it."

"Hearts? Where've you been?" she demanded.

"Underground," he shot back.

"Geez. What a stiff."

They smiled at each other, Angel far more faintly than Buffy, who was putting on a big show that she found this kind of talk in the least bit amusing.

See, the problem with loving a guy you're not supposed to love is that you tell yourself there's an upside, she told herself. *Such as, you get to be such great friends with him. Which, frankly, sucks in a lot of ways because friend is a major demotion from girlfriend. And let's not even go to the higher planes of relationshiphood— such as what comes after girlfriend. Because that ain't gonna happen, and it would make a lot more sense to jump off the train before it leaves the station. Because it's going nowhere near the place you want to be.*

Problem is, the alternative—being nothing to him—sucks worse.

Angel looked at her. He didn't say anything, just looked. Her cheeks got warm, and she muttered something about being in a bad mood.

"You've been in a lot of bad moods lately," Angel ventured.

"Hormonal. Strictly." She frowned and waved her hand. "Nobody's digging up anybody around here. Shall we move along?"

"Is it me?" He squinted at her as she flushed. "I'll take that as a yes."

"What?" she asked defensively. "Why would it be you?"

He stared at her.

She sighed. "Pleased now? Thrilled that I want to kiss you and . . . and be with you, and I can't? Does that give you some kind of whacked-out happy? Flatter you?"

"Of course not." He kept staring. "Buffy, you know that I . . ." He sighed.

She sighed, too. "You can't even say it, you can't even tell me you love me, because next thing you know, your soul will be gone, and you'll try to destroy the world. And I'll be sending you back to hell all over again," she muttered.

"You *know* I do," Angel whispered.

Then she looked up, trying not to reveal her pain. "You're the only one I . . . you're someone I can talk to, but hey, I can talk to Xander. I can't do what I . . ." She looked away, because the pain was obvious, in her voice if not her face. "You'd think that after all these months and years of Angel-based awkwardness, I would be better at it."

"Awkwardness is a moving target." He shrugged. "My aim is off, too, if it makes you feel any better."

"Why would it make me feel better?" she echoed back at him.

At an impasse, they sat gazing at each other. Then Angel stood. He turned his back to her and said, "Buffy, when we were together, part of me . . . I gave it to you forever. It will be yours, forever."

She took that in. Her voice dropped below a whisper. "No. It won't. Because I won't be around forever."

He cocked his head. "Did you say something?"

"No." She swallowed hard. "Let's just sit here and wait for the grave robbers, okay? We can pretend we're at the movies, like the more normal dysfunctional couples of today."

"Next time, playing cards *and* popcorn," Angel said.

Buffy shifted her weight. She was getting a cramp in her thigh. Or maybe it was her heart. "What's it like, to know you'll be here at least another century?"

He paused. "I don't know that."

"Barring stakings, I mean. Stay on your toes, you're pretty much a shoo-in."

He bent down and wrapped his hand around hers. He pulled her to her feet and put his arms around her. His skin was cold, but the contact warmed her nonetheless. "It's not all that different, Buffy. I can still die."

"It *is* all that different," she insisted. "Because I *will* die."

For a moment, he was still. His eyes glittered in the moonlight. Then he raised a hand and pushed her hair back, looping it behind her ear.

"Every evening, when I get up, I wonder where you are. How you are. I never wonder if you're still alive."

"Gee, thanks," she huffed.

"Because I can't imagine that you won't be."

Something moved among the gravestones. Buffy tensed. Beside her, Angel said, "I think it's the wind. I don't smell anything."

"Of all the superheroes, your power is the weirdest," she drawled.

Suddenly, Angel was kissing her. His arms were tight around her body, and his mouth was pressed against hers. She caught her breath; her hand rose in weak protest above his shoulder, and then she was clinging to him. Every part of her was hungry for him, starving. *Just once more*, she thought. *Once, because if I had known it would be the only time, that I could never have him again . . .*

She tried to catch her breath as Angel sank to the earth with her in his arms.

If she had known that the night they had made love would be the only time, nothing would have been different. Because it had been Angel, and first love, and lust, and so much that she had not known about, could not have prepared for. She had been overwhelmed with passion, and joy, and astonishment, believing that night to be a miracle, a wonderful gift to compensate her for her life as the Slayer.

But now, as her desire mounted, so, too, did her pain and dread. *Never, never again.* As good as it had felt. As happy as she had been.

Never again.

"Angel, stop, we can't," she said, gasping.

Then he broke away. She gave a little cry and began to reach for him. He turned his back on her.

"Don't touch me, Buffy," he said. "This is all the strength I have left."

She ran from the graveyard.

He did not follow.

"Nighthawk?" squeaked the walkie-talkie.

"Roger that," Xander whispered. "Nighthawk here."

"Hi, Xander." It was Willow. "Restfield's a bust. And, um, I have a big calculus test tomorrow."

Xander nodded gently into the speaker. "Okay. Call it a night. Nothing's happening here, either."

"Maybe that one was a fluke. You know, like a Norman Bates thing. Maybe somebody got dug up for sentimental reasons."

"I love the way you think, Will," Xander drawled. "Or are you just trying to impress Oz?"

"I have other ways to impress Oz," Willow retorted. Then she giggled. Xander grimaced, imagining all the smoochies Oz and Willow had shared in the graveyard while he, king of Cretonia, had shared nothing with anyone except the stray cat that tried to snag half his Taco Bell Gordita.

"If this were a horror movie, you guys would be toast," Xander grumbled.

Willow giggled again. "But it's not."

Xander harrumphed. "That's debatable."

"So, Xander," Oz said, "okay if we book?"

"Sure. I guess I'll pack it in, too. Jennifer Love Hewitt is going to be on Leno."

"Signing off, then," Oz said. The walkie-talkie fuzzed out, then went to dead air.

Xander turned his off, too, picked up his empty Taco Bell bag, and sauntered out of the cemetery and onto the sidewalk.

He had started toward home, when who to his wondering eyes should appear, but Cordelia and a guy.

A guy who was pawing at her and making weird noises, while she was huffing and writhing in his grasp.

"Hey," Xander said.

The guy ignored him. It looked for all the world as if Cordelia was trying to pry the guy's hands off her shoulders, but she was getting nowhere fast.

Xander sprinted toward them, tackled the guy, and threw him to the ground. He straddled him and pulled back his fist, ready to deliver the first blow, when Cordelia smacked him on the back of the head.

"What the hell are you doing?" she shouted.

Xander looked up and over his shoulder at her. The guy on the ground punched him in the jaw, and Xander fell backward onto his elbows.

Staring down at him, Cordelia narrowed her eyes. "This is so pathetic. What, are you stalking me and my dates now?"

"Your . . . date? I thought he was your mauler," Xander said, rubbing his jaw. "Aren't you on patrol?"

"Patrol? What's he talking about?" the ground guy demanded. Xander took a good look at him. *Oh, fabulous. It's Troy Harper. Rich, football team, scholarship to USC.*

"Oh, he saw this stupid video," Cordelia said meaningfully. She wound her arms around Troy's. "Xander doesn't understand about passion." She gave the X-man a withering look. "Just jealousy."

Xander exhaled slowly and raised his hands. "Sorry. Misread the situation. I thought you were in trouble because of the thing you were supposed to be doing tonight."

"And if I had been, you would have saved me." Her voice was loaded with contempt.

"Yes," Xander said evenly. "I would have."

Without another word, he brushed past them both.

"Well, I *did* patrol," Cordelia shot back at him. "But Giles said I could stop."

As Xander stomped away, he heard Troy say, "What video?"

Man, what a one-watt, Xander thought savagely. *If she had any brains at all, she'd be bored with him in two minutes.*

"Who's Giles?" Troy went on.

Pepper Roback had a roommate named Tanisa Johnson. Sacrificing her privacy had been one of Pepper's cost-cutting measures, an artifact of saving for college that she'd never done anything about, even when it became obvious college was no longer in her long-term plans.

Tanisa worked two days a week as a manicurist at Jada's Nails and three days a week at Barron's Bazaar, where she sold Oriental rugs. To her surprise, she had discovered she was good at selling things. And when Mr. Barron offered her full-time work at his larger store in Los Angeles, she jumped at the chance.

When she got off work, she hurried home to give Pepper her thirty days' notice. Not that it was required in an informal roommate situation, but it was the nice thing to do, after all.

Thing was, Pepper did not show. Not after work, and not before it was time for her to go to the library to read to the kids.

So Tanisa filed a missing person's report as soon as the cops would listen to her. She wrote a note for Pepper with the address of a friend of hers who lived in Brea. Then she packed all her stuff and took a cab to the bus station.

When she never heard from Pepper again, Tanisa simply figured Pepper was angry with her for splitting and forgot all about her.

Without anyone to prod them, the Sunnydale police forgot about Pepper, too.

In the middle of a violent coughing fit, Joyce heard Buffy come in. The kitchen door slammed, and Joyce pushed her wad of tissues against her mouth, struggling against the violent urge to hack up all her internal organs. She was alarmed by how much worse she felt this evening compared to the morning. *I should have tried harder to see Dr. Martinez,* she chastised herself. *If not for my own sake, then for Buffy.*

She looked up from the John Updike novel she was reading. Only, not reading. She had been on the same page for the last hour.

I've been worried about Buffy, she thought. And while that was true—she was usually worried about her daughter—she found herself thinking about her doctor's appointment in the morning.

Buffy paused at her bedroom door and called softly, "Mom? I'm home. Everything's okay."

"Thanks, honey," she called back, with difficulty. "Are you hungry?"

"Naw. Just going to bed."

"All right. Sleep well."

"You too, Mom."

"I will."

There was a pause, and then Buffy said, "What time's your appointment?"

"Ten-thirty."

"Oh." Buffy sounded disappointed.

"Sleep well," Joyce said again.

"Well, good night." Buffy was clearly distracted.

Joyce stared back down at her Updike book.

Now, where was I?

In the morning, Joyce overslept—a rarity for her—and Buffy had already left for school. Joyce was disappointed. Some part of her had needed to hear Buffy wish her good luck, maybe even favor her with a rare hug. Instead, she got dressed and drove herself to the medical building, assessing her various aches and pains to see if they were worth mentioning. Her ex-husband used to tease her about having "TV Hospital Disease" every time she saw a doctor about anything: on TV, it was usually the one strange little symptom the patients forgot to mention that resulted in their nearly dying. If only they'd remembered first thing that they had a little bump on the end of their ear lobe, or that their shoulders ached, but now it was too late . . . or very nearly so.

Except for missing the chance to talk to Buffy, the morning was just as Joyce imagined it: sitting forever in the waiting room, reading old fashion magazines. They contained an endless number of questionnaires, which she eventually filled out because she had already read all the articles. She discovered she had a spicy personality and that her dominant personality trait was "nurturant-aggressive."

That's what comes of being a single parent, she thought wryly.

And then the nurse was at the door to the waiting room, calling her name with brisk efficiency. Joyce got to her feet, the magazine sliding off her lap, and she smiled nervously as she caught it.

As they walked back to the scale beside the bathroom, the nurse asked her in a loud voice about her symptoms. How much blood? How often? Was she feeling especially tired? Did she smoke? Did she consider herself an alcoholic?

Joyce blanched at the woman's obvious lack of sensitivity and made a mental note to discuss it with the doctor. Then she decided she'd wait until another time. The nurse was not the topic of discussion here. Joyce was.

They went into an examining room. Joyce sat down in a hard plastic chair, and the nurse took her blood pressure. "Very good," she said, as if praising a little child. Then she picked up her papers and added, in as impersonal a tone as seemed humanly possible, "Doctor will be in in a moment."

Joyce looked around for something else to read.

At school, Buffy stared at the clock. Willow watched her. She smiled when Buffy glanced at her, and Buffy made a little face. Willow's smile faded. When the bell rang, she immediately went over to Buffy.

"Hey. What's wrong?"

Buffy walked slowly down the hall. "My mom. Something's

wrong with her." She moved her shoulders. "At least, I think something is. She coughed up blood."

Her face felt hot, as if she were telling Willow something that she shouldn't. She didn't understand her reaction, but it was strong.

"Oh." Willow looked worried. Then she looked as if she knew she looked worried. She tilted her head slightly, contemplative-ly. "It could be her tonsils. Does she still have them?"

Buffy raised her brows. "No clue. Do you know if your mother does?"

"Oh, yes," Willow assured her. "She thought having them taken out was just one more example of the overly aggressive medical establishment finding a quick way to make a buck. She also didn't want to immunize me against anything."

Buffy's brows rose higher. "But then you couldn't go to school."

"Oh, yes. In California, you can. If you say it's for religious reasons." Willow smiled. "But my dad insisted. So I've had all my shots."

"Wow." Buffy was impressed. "My parents didn't even think about it. They just did it."

"Well, you know my mom." Willow rolled her eyes. "Every-thing's a study."

"She's big on the research," Buffy agreed. "She and Giles would make a good cou- . . . not going there."

"Nowhere near there," Willow agreed. Then she frowned suddenly and started away from Buffy. "Hold on a second, okay?"

"Uh, sure," Buffy said.

Willow strode down the hall toward a dark, tall girl dressed in an outrageous orange mohair sweater and matching fuzzy skirt. She stood in front of an open locker, head bent, crying silently. Mainly because of the tears, it took Buffy a moment to realize the girl was Damara Johnson, whom Willow had tutored briefly during their sophomore year. As Buffy watched, Willow and the girl spoke quietly to each other.

Buffy almost didn't notice as Cordelia came up to stand beside her.

"What is Willow doing talking to that fashion catastrophe?" Cordelia asked snippily. "Oh, wait, forgot. You people just don't have the standards I do."

Cordelia's attitude was no surprise to Buffy. She'd learned to expect that sort of thing, not to mention that Cordelia and Damara weren't exactly compatible. Damara shopped almost exclusively at Buffalo Nickel, the vintage clothing store frequented by the arty types who weren't into black berets and coffee houses. Cordelia wouldn't have been caught dead inside that store.

Buffy ignored her. A moment later, Willow gestured for her to approach, and Buffy did. Cordelia tagged along.

"I swear, it was her roommate, but she looked all weird," Damara was saying as they walked up. "I mean, really, really hideous." Damara wiped her eyes. "And I kept thinking, what if Tanisa didn't get on that bus to Brea? What if Pepper did something to her, and she's making us all think Tanisa is okay?"

"Are you on drugs?" Cordelia asked bluntly. "Because if you are, we really don't have time to take care of your hallucinations."

"Who's Pepper?" Buffy asked.

"My sister's roommate," Damara explained. "Well, she was, but then she disappeared. And Tanisa moved, and now . . . I'm so confused."

"You think something's happened to Tanisa?" Buffy asked.

"I don't know." Damara wiped her eyes. "But Pepper came by last night and stared in the window. And she looked . . ." She moved her hands. "She looked like she should be in a horror movie. Like a gremlin or something."

"Oh, yeah, gremlins. Can we *go* now?" Cordelia sneered.

Buffy peered at Cordelia, who stared blankly back. Then Cordy said, "*Oo-ohh.*"

"Damara, would you mind coming with us?" Buffy asked. "I think Mr. Giles might like to hear your story."

"The school librarian?" Damara asked, clearly confused.

"He really cares about all the kids," Willow added, taking Damara's elbow. "He'll want to help you with this . . . story."

Buffy and Cordelia walked behind the other two girls, herding them gently toward the library.

Buffy came home a little later than she'd planned. Giles had been most keen to ruminate on Damara's story, and then he got really hepped up when Willow located the missing person's report on Pepper Roback. He wanted to go over it and speculate and discuss it for, oh, at least another hour or so, but Buffy slipped out during a lull—*or was that when Xander nodded off and started snoring?*—and got home as fast as she could.

"Mom?" she called.

Joyce was in the kitchen, putting the finishing touches on a platter of pork chops. She smiled at Buffy and said, "How was your day?"

"What did the doctor say?"

Her mom scrunched up her nose. "Doctors. Do they ever say anything? He ordered a chest X ray. I'll go in for that tomorrow."

"Why? What's it for?" Buffy demanded.

"They want to see what's going on in there," Joyce said, as nonchalantly as possible. "It may be nothing, but . . ." She trailed off. "They just need to see."

Buffy was frustrated. She had waited and worried all day. *This . . . this is bogus*, she thought.

"But didn't he give you any kind of indication about what might be going on?"

"He said we should wait for the X ray." Joyce wiped her hands on a dish towel. "I have a meeting at the gallery in fifteen minutes, so I have to scoot. Save me some applesauce?"

"Mom, you shouldn't go out. You haven't been feeling good."

"I feel much better," Joyce said. "It's about installing the exhibit, and I have to be there." She smiled at Buffy and picked up her coat and purse. "Are you going out later?"

"I guess." She looked down at the pork chops and then at her mother's retreating back. "Mom?"

Her mother either didn't hear her or chose not to answer. In either case, she walked past the window to the car, got in, and drove away.

As soon as she was out of sight, Buffy was on the phone to Willow, who was more than happy to do a quick Net search for information on X-ray technology, the reasons for its usage, and how that might connect with someone who was coughing up blood. After about five minutes on the Net, Willow reported back.

"They may be looking for, um, a mass," Willow said.

"Mass?" Buffy frowned. "English, please?"

Willow took a minute to reply. "Oh, like a cyst."

"Oh." Buffy's stomach flip-flopped. Willow wasn't coming clean. *She's so terrible at lying. Or not telling the truth.* Which were, Buffy reflected, sometimes two different things.

"Buffy, don't worry, okay?" Willow said. "Just don't worry."

"All right." Buffy frowned.

They both pretended not to know she was lying.

Chapter Four

At dusk that day, the darkness seemed to spread very quickly, traveling across the sky, slipping through the streets and avenues of Sunnydale with a kind of gleeful anticipation, as if it knew, somehow, what was to come. Evening flowed across the town as though it conspired with those creatures that could not come out by light of day. And why should it not? Vampires, demons, goblins, and ghouls, they were the champions of the darkness, after all.

After dark, many of Sunnydale's residents made it a habit to stay indoors. They were just homebodies, they told themselves and others. Fogies. They watched television or played cards or read books. If they did go out, it was likely to be a trip to the mall or the movies in the car. Californians loved their cars, but none so much as the people of Sunnydale.

There were, however, a great many people who braved the night, not allowing even their subconscious minds to recognize that there was a real, tangible foundation for the little tingle of anxiety or fear they felt. But even those hardy souls, the young and the stubborn, for the most part, stayed to the well-lighted areas, or where they might find groups of people. Nightclubs and bars and restaurants. The busy downtown strip with its trendy shops and the Sun Cinema. Sporting events. The point, where young couples parked almost nightly.

Conversely, there were certain areas of the town that were almost completely deserted after dark. The warehouses near the docks. The parks. And the two-block stretch some people still called Old Town. Once upon a time, it had been a bustling, trendy little strip, similar to that which now existed only a quarter of a mile away. But that had been a very long time ago, before earthquakes had undermined the foundations of half a dozen buildings, weakening their foundations enough that eventually the town was forced to condemn them. Abandon them. Every year, there was talk of a major renovation of the area, of destroying the buildings and constructing something new and wondrous in their place.

But for the moment, they stood empty, crumbling, unsafe. The perfect refuge for runaways and drug dealers, and several of the buildings did have illegal squatters living within. Until recently, the former police headquarters had been a popular place to crash for those who existed on the fringes of society. Not anymore.

Nothing lived inside that shadowy, condemned structure. But it was, nevertheless, quite inhabited. And those unfortunate enough to have been inside the building when its current inhabitants arrived now lay in the basement, stacked against a wall like so much cordwood.

Rotting.

For when the hatchlings were born into this world, they would not desire fresh meat.

In the silence of dusk, only Veronique and Ephialtes dared wander the halls. The others were new and, as such, victim to the images of their kind made familiar by modern entertainment. It would take them time to realize that an errant ray of diffuse sunlight, as it slipped beyond the horizon, would not kill them instantly. To understand that they could look out upon the arrival of dusk, the last lingering efforts of the perpetually dying sun, and taste the coming of night and all the things that darkness would bring.

For the moment, Veronique was pleased that her new brood remained in the dark recesses of internal offices, sleeping under desks and in closets. The quiet was bliss to her. Particularly in that it was a good-bye of sorts.

"The last time night will ever fall for me," Ephialtes whispered beside her.

Veronique turned to look at him, becoming accustomed, now, to the new body she wore, the flesh of Pepper Roback, with her flaming red hair and tiny shape. She could see in Ephialtes's expression that he admired this new body.

She leaned in and kissed him gently on his darkly stubbled cheek. "Yes, my dear one. But your memory will burn forever in the fires of the new Hell that your life will bring."

He had nothing to say to that. Ephialtes returned her kiss and then merely stood with her, there in the huge open foyer of the old police station. The desks had been moved, stacked against a far wall. The room was large enough for their purposes, and they could sleep upstairs. And off to one side, of course, within a large office, there was the nest.

"You are the eldest of my descendants," Veronique reminded him, for Ephialtes had been sired by Belasarius, her spawn, who in his turn had been staked by a Slayer in A.D. 1011. She had no doubt that others of her blood roamed the world, but the Triumvirate had chosen Ephialtes to aid her.

"The Triumvirate smiles upon you tonight," she whispered to him.

"I will be with you, within you, when your sharpened fangs stab the throat of the last man, my love, dark Harbinger, when the blood spurts into your mouth, dripping thickly down your throat. I will be with you there, won't I?" Ephialtes asked.

Veronique smiled. A rare sight. "You will live in my blood."

"Let us wake the others, then," he replied grimly, determination etched on his features.

Veronique glanced out through the gap between two large boards. She could see another dilapidated building across the street and the road below. Cars drove by from time to time, their lights splashing over the face of the building. But the later the hour, the fewer vehicles went by.

"No need to wake us."

Ephialtes and his mistress both turned to see that the others had begun to gather in the gloom behind them. Konstantin was the one who had spoken, and now he stepped forward and knelt before Veronique.

"We abase ourselves before you, Harbinger," he said, but he did not lower his eyes. Instead, he stared at her.

"Is there something on your mind, Konstantin?" she asked angrily.

Finally, he dropped his gaze. "No, mistress," he said. "I was only . . . looking at your eyes."

"Why?" she demanded.

Konstantin looked up. Once again, it seemed as though he wished to look away but was unable. "You are not the same, Veronique, and yet you are. Still the Harbinger inside this new body. I am the demon within, yet I am still Konstantin, in many ways. But you . . . change completely, and yet your eyes do not change."

"My nature has been explained to you, Konstantin."

Ephialtes turned toward Veronique then and smiled. "It is one thing to be told something, Harbinger, and something else entirely to understand it. Seeing you struck down only to rise again in this new form reminds the rest of us that though we are so much more than human, we yet suffer from some of their frailties. You do not. You are truly immortal."

Veronique glared at him. "Would that it were true," she whispered thoughtfully. "But nothing is truly immortal save evil itself."

At that, they all fell silent in momentary contemplation. Beyond Konstantin, the four she had thus far gathered looked at her in awe and adoration, amazed by the truth of her eternal nature, her demon soul residing within Pepper Roback's corpse. *Newborns*, Veronique thought dismissively. They were such fools. But the ritual could not be conducted without them.

"What are you all waiting for? You know how vital this evening is to the fulfillment of our goal, to the future of our kind.

"Prepare the way," she snapped.

The vampires scattered. Save for Ephialtes. As the others went about their business, setting candles at intervals throughout the room, drawing the appropriate symbols within and around the wide circle she had chalked onto the floor the night before, Veronique watched them, checking each one. It must all be perfect for the spell to work.

It had taken several hours to prepare, but all was now in readiness. Veronique looked upon Ephialtes, her descendant, who even now stood proudly, unwaveringly. He was at the edge of the circle, the others hovering around him, tending to him as best they could. In their eyes, Veronique could see the conflicting emotions within each of them. Jealousy, that Ephialtes should receive such an honor. Respect, that he should face it with such fortitude. Relief, that they would live to hunt another night and feel the spray of warm blood in their mouths. They were new to it, these babes, but the demons in them were ancient things, and the lust for murder and the hunger for the flow of life were strong within them from the moment they rose.

No, none among them would have willingly chosen to take Ephialtes's place in the ritual. In the sacrifice. But they knew what an honor he was about to receive, just the same.

After all, what they were about to do, the unnatural horror that was about to befall Ephialtes, was something that this world had never seen. In a world rife with decadence, prurience, and cruelty, both human and inhuman, Veronique was sublimely pleased to be introducing to the world an entirely new perversion.

Perhaps several.

For a moment longer, she admired the way Ephialtes looked, simply standing there. The others had painted his body with symbols to match those on the floor. Painted his flesh with their own blood. He stood naked, adorned with those bloody runes and scrawls, his olive skin rippling with the power of the body, the engine beneath.

He is a fitting tribute, Veronique decided. *So nearly perfect. A worthy vessel.*

"Enough!" she said, and moved forward, herding the sycophants away. "You will all stand at the edge of the circle, but you will turn your backs toward the center. You will not look, you will not see. Ephialtes will come to glory, but you must not turn. Should one of you dare even to glance over his shoulder, I will tear your eyes out with a single talon and pop them between my teeth. Do you all understand?"

They all nodded, moved to the edges of the circle, and turned their backs to Ephialtes. Veronique watched Konstantin for a moment. There was a curiosity to him but a strength as well. She thought that with Ephialtes gone, she would make Konstantin her lieutenant, or something more. Veronique was a creature of desires, always had been. It was her habit to take a lover from among her followers, and she wondered whom she might bestow that honor upon when Ephialtes was gone. Perhaps Konstantin. Perhaps not.

But for the moment, she knew she must push all such thoughts aside. Veronique had every expectation that the ritual would be successful. It was a simple thing, really, once the appropriate preparations had been made—and she had been meticulous about doing so.

Yes, shortly . . . shortly . . .

Veronique shuddered as a wave of depraved pleasure, of filthy ecstasy, swept over and through her. The sudden thought, the realization of all that she had been taking for granted, nearly overwhelmed her. After so long, all the centuries she had survived, dying again and again, the time had finally come. The Triumvirate would soon emerge into the human world, and all the things they had promised Veronique for so long would finally be hers.

Another shudder passed through her, and Veronique realized that she had transformed without intending to do so. Her face was feral now, the face of a vampire. Her eyes were yellow, and her mouth was open, fangs glistening. With a smile of vicious pleasure, she crossed to where Ephialtes stood, alone and naked and ready to die.

With a thin smile, Veronique kissed him. To his credit, Ephialtes returned her lustful attentions but said nothing. Then, after a moment, she nipped his lip with a fang, grinned, and moved with him toward the center of the circle. She nodded, gesturing for him to lie on the cold floor, surrounded by arcane images and flickering candles. She ran her hands over his body, gently at first. Then her lengthening fingernails dug into his skin, and Veronique sliced bloody furrows into his flesh.

Ephialtes grunted, tensing slightly, and his face transformed as well. But he did not cry out. Did not even blink. He went to his glorious destiny without hesitation.

She wanted him then, but she did not act upon it. The time for such indulgences had passed.

"Open yourself, Ephialtes," she whispered in Greek. "Empty your mind. Prepare yourself as receptacle for all the power of Hell, and be blessed."

Veronique stepped back beyond the edges of the circle. Within, Ephialtes spread his arms and legs wide, so that his body was an X upon the floor.

Then the Harbinger closed her eyes and began to sing. The language was ancient, belonging, as it had, to those twisted souls who had first torn away the veil between the world of man and the realm of demons and peered beyond to come away only with visions of madness. But it had been a beginning. Man had evolved a great deal since then, but he still feared the dark.

The five vampires she had sired stood around the circle, their backs to Ephialtes, and not one of them dared so much as a glance. Veronique swayed as she sang. The candles flared impossibly high, raging infernos of wax and wick and infernal flame. The fire roared. Ephialtes bucked, shrieking, his voice high and ragged and then suddenly silent. His mouth remained open, screaming in pain and terror, but no sound came from it.

"Yes," Veronique whispered. She had attempted this so many times, and each time she had been thwarted. At first, her own ignorance had prevented her from succeeding. And later, after she had determined what she had been doing incorrectly, she had been interfered with. The last time, long ago in Venice, it had been that damned Slayer.

Veronique hated Slayers.

On the floor, the symbols etched there seemed to glow with a hideous light.

In an instant, it ceased. Ephialtes settled back with a heavy, sweaty slap onto the floor. The candle fire was snuffed, each leaving little more than a black mark in its place, casting the room into darkness, save for the light from the streetlamps outside.

As she stared at Ephialtes, Veronique was momentarily frozen with the fluttering of hope within her cold, dead heart. For another moment, she hesitated, then she moved into the circle and knelt quickly at his side. The wounds that she had made were sealed, the blood that had been spilled gone as if it had never been. Ephialtes's mouth was gone, his lips sealed together so tightly they seemed little more than a scar running across an otherwise unmarked face.

So, too, his eyes.

So, too, his nostrils.

His body had been completely sealed in order to protect that which even now incubated at extraordinary speed within. He had reached the last stage of the metamorphosis of his long life. From man to vampire and, now, to egg.

A beatific smile spread across Veronique's features as she truly realized, for the first time, what she had done. Not brought her master to Earth, not quite yet. But the seeds had been planted, that much was certain.

She rejoiced.

Then she got down to business.

"Konstantin. Get him into the nest," she ordered. "Immediately."

The vampire responded instantly. With little more than a glance at the others, he indicated that they should help him. They went to Ephialtes's still form and lifted him quickly. One of the vampires grunted as they lifted him. As they carried Ephialtes across the room to the open door of the office where the nest had been built, Konstantin glanced over at his mistress.

"He is quite heavy, Harbinger," the vampire said, his voice hushed. "What will happen now?"

Veronique's smile faded. Her nostrils flared. Without an ounce of amusement, but only wonder and the slow gnawing of her bloodlust, she whispered a reply.

"Something wonderful."

One of her vampire servants, a tall, tawny-skinned female named Catherine, who had been an exchange student from Taiwan before Veronique claimed her, gasped and nearly let Ephialtes fall from her grip.

"Fool!" Veronique snapped.

"I'm . . . I'm sorry," the girl stammered, as though she were still nothing more than human. "It's just . . . something moved."

"Harbinger, look at his belly," Konstantin said in a ragged whisper.

She did. His stomach was distended. Beneath the skin, something moved. Or, rather, *things* moved, pressing against the skin from beneath. Veronique stared a moment in amazement, in spite of herself.

"Hurry."

They did. Quickly, Konstantin, Catherine, and the others settled Ephialtes's body into the nest that had been constructed within the office. The materials had been cobbled together, for the most part, from the building itself. Wood from shattered furniture, stone and brick from crumbling walls, cloth lining that had been the clothing of the human prey whose corpses even now decayed in the basement.

As one, they stepped back to allow Veronique through the door. She stood and looked upon Ephialtes's naked form. His skin had taken on the sheen and texture of wax in just the moments that had passed since the end of the ritual.

But she spared only a brief glance for the rest of him. Her eyes were otherwise riveted on his bulging gut. They were all silent now. None of them even made the pretense of breath that was common among newborns. And in that absolute silence, they heard the ripping. Tearing. Chewing.

Ephialtes's stomach stretched upward, and then the skin tore and split, three sets of talons ripping at their surroundings. Three pairs of eyes glowed a deep, mesmerizing red in the darkness.

"The Three-Who-Are-One," Veronique whispered. "The Triumvirate."

The hatchlings were covered in golden scales, awash with blood and gore. Their talons were razor sharp, their mouths filled with gleaming, gnashing teeth. Their heads and snouts were lined with jagged ridges, topped with needle-thin spines, almost reptilian, but some nightmarish vision of a reptile.

Still, they ate, moving in a stew of Ephialtes's organs and intestines, feasting, their eyes roving around, studying the vampires who even now looked upon their hideous savagery.

"They're like horrible little dragons," Catherine whispered in wonder.

"They're magnificent," Veronique said. "And this is only the beginning. They're nothing but hatchlings now. But in the time between this night and the night of the Reunification, when the portents are right and the stars aligned, the hatchlings will grow. Oh, they'll grow."

Somehow, she was certain of that. They'd whispered as much to her in her dreams. And something else besides.

"But in order for them to grow," she added, turning to Konstantin, "they'll need to eat. Go, now, and bring one of the dead up from the basement. Begin with the oldest, most rancid meat. I expect they'll turn their noses up at a fresh kill."

Konstantin blinked. "But Ephialtes—"

"—had been dead a very long time," Veronique cut in. "Now go." Then she turned to the others. "Catherine. I charge you with a vital responsibility. I must continue the Gathering of Thirteen. I leave it to you to continue your cemetery visits. We must not run out of sustenance for the hatchlings.

"Even if you have to rob every grave in Sunnydale."

"Maybe Dr. Frankenstein *has* all the corpses he needs?" Xander suggested.

"Let's hope not," Cordelia replied. "I mean, if he's dug his last grave, we'll never catch the guy, and then we'll never know what he's doing, and if he's trying to build the perfect body, you know he's going to need part of me."

Oz and Willow both turned to stare dubiously at her.

"What?" Cordelia protested. "That always happens."

Oz shrugged. "She has a point."

"A very small point," Xander admitted.

"Wait, so now we're actually *hoping* our grave robber hasn't completed whatever perfidious thing he's got going with the missing corpses?" Willow asked, looking down sadly. "Somehow, I have the feeling our priorities got majorly out of order somewhere."

Xander frowned. "Perfidious."

"Oz gave me one of those word-of-the-day calendars," Willow explained. "Today equals perfidious."

"Perfidious," Xander repeated.

Cordelia sighed. "God, Xander, it means—"

"I know what it means," he said defensively. "Just don't necessarily recall ever hearing it used in a sentence. Except maybe at a spelling bee. Anyway, are we really thinking our guy's given up the ghost? So to speak."

There was a moment's pause as they all contemplated that question. Willow's research had revealed that no fewer than seventeen graves had been ransacked in the previous ten days from the dozen cemeteries within the town limits. And those were only the ones Willow could find by hacking police and town hall records.

But last night, nothing.

They'd patrolled for hours, split into two teams. Oz and Willow, and Xander and Xander. It was supposed to be Xander and Cordelia, but she'd had other priorities. Tonight, though, she'd apparently realized that the threat was serious . . . or, and to Xander's mind more likely, Giles had simply guilt-tripped her into behaving herself. Once again, they'd split off, but after hitting five cemeteries apiece and coming up empty, they'd decided to do the last two, Restfield and Shady Hill, together.

Now they stood in the middle of Shady Hill Cemetery, completely baffled.

"I don't know, Xander," Willow said at length. "I mean, just because we don't have a record of a grave robbing last night doesn't mean there wasn't one."

"Even if there wasn't," Oz added, "doesn't mean the groovy ghoulie has given up. Maybe he had a date last night."

"Maybe he's been digging up his dates," Xander suggested.

"Eeew," Willow and Cordelia said in harmony. Even Oz wrinkled his nose.

"Sometimes I just can't help myself," Xander said, head hung in mock shame.

"Do you think we could move on to our last stop so I can get home? Believe it or not, I do need some beauty rest from time to time. Unlike the rest of you, I have people who expect me to look my best. It's not a responsibility I take lightly," Cordelia said snappishly.

"Cordelia," Willow said, chiding her like a patient schoolteacher. "We are trying to figure out the pattern of a series of pretty gruesome crimes that make no sense at all. You offered to help."

"Actually," Oz noted quietly, "I'm sort of trying to figure out how a place with no trees and not much of a hill could be called Shady Hill. But that's me."

Cordelia ignored him, giving Willow a scandalized how-dare-you stare. "Help? Um, hello? What do you think I've *been* doing?"

"Mostly carping about how knowing all of us has ruined your life. Which, by the way, gives me an immense happy," Xander told her.

Cordelia just glared.

"Tell you what," Oz said. "We spread out, do a quick run through this place, buzz over to Restfield, and do the same. Then home. Tomorrow . . . you look even better than you did today."

Now Cordelia beamed. She reached out and grabbed a flashlight from Xander, glared at him, and started off in the opposite direction. "The sooner we get this done, the better," she muttered.

Xander was staring at Oz.

Oz raised an eyebrow.

"That was more than I think I've ever heard you say at one time," Xander said in astonishment. "And you . . . complimented Cordelia."

Oz just grinned, then started up the gentle rise toward a huge old family crypt with the name "HART" engraved above the door. Xander watched him go, then turned to see Willow shaking her head and sighing, staring after Oz lovingly.

"What?" Xander asked. "You're not jealous? He just said Cordelia was beautiful."

"No," Willow replied. "He didn't. That was only a compliment if you're as vain as Cordelia."

Then, vastly entertained by the cleverness of her taciturn boyfriend, Willow turned and started off on a path perpendicular to the line between Oz and Cordelia. Shaking his head with confusion, Xander sighed and moved off the other way.

Shady Hill Cemetery wasn't much to look at. Angel's house wasn't that far away, and like most everything in that part of Sunnydale, this particular cemetery had been really something in the forties and early fifties. The people who'd been buried here back then were wealthy enough to be remembered with enough pomp and circumstance that Xander thought it bordered on the silly. There were enormous angels with swords drawn and fat little cherubs with open, loving arms. There were vast crypts with intricate carving, some of which, according to the plaques outside, had only two or three people laid to rest within.

But as the years had passed, and many of the wealthiest families moved to newer areas, or even more ridiculously ostentatious dwellings, the neighborhood around Shady Hill had sort of faded and cracked, like an old photograph. The cemetery was the same. There were broken headstones that looked as though they might have lain that way for years. Weeds had spread wildly in some places. It was all just . . . old.

"Old," Xander whispered.

He frowned, mind working, moving in unusual patterns. Without missing a step, he turned and started after Willow. After a moment, he jogged lightly. He hadn't gone that far when he saw her and let out a little whistle, a terrible imitation of a bird that they'd used to call out to each other when they were kids.

Willow stopped in mid-stride and looked back at him. Xander beckoned to her, and she started back, walking fast. He saw movement in his peripheral vision and turned to see Cordelia coming toward him as well. He took a quick glance up the hill, but all he could see was the enormous Hart crypt. Oz was nowhere in sight.

"What is it?" Willow asked, frowning with concern as she reached him.

"Just a thought," he said. "You were sort of rattling off the names and stuff on the missing bodies, and . . . they're all recent, aren't they?"

Then Cordelia was there with them. "Nothing that way," she said. "Home, please."

They ignored her.

"Well, they were all in the last year or so," Willow said, "but I don't know if it counts as recent."

"A lot more recent than anybody buried in this place," he reasoned. "They're not exactly lining up around the block to get in. And if our guy knows that, would he even come in here to begin with?"

"Hello?" Cordelia said, more loudly.

"But there must be *some* recent graves here," Willow said, frowning. "And he can't just keep hitting the same spots, or the police . . . would just do nothing. Still, though, it makes sense that he'd try to vary his activities."

"I don't know," Xander said. "I think we should just get on to Restfield. Ah, what do I know? Maybe I'm just—"

"A lot," Cordelia snapped. "You know plenty. You want to go, and I'm on board with that. Let's just get Oz, and maybe I can still be human in the morning."

"Still?" Xander asked.

Willow had think-face. Which, to Xander, was good. He'd had one logical stream of thought tonight, and he didn't want to risk hurting himself by trying for two.

"You do have a point, though, Xander," Willow said pleasantly. "Maybe we *should* just go."

"Y'know, if we just start with my plan in the future, these nights will go by that much faster," Cordelia observed. "Now, why don't we . . ."

Her face went slack.

"Cordelia?" Willow asked with concern.

Xander waved a hand in front of her face. "What's wrong?"

With a nervous glance at the ground, Cordelia took a step backward. "Um, nothing. Let's just go. I need to get home and . . . oh, all right. I can't stand these high-pressure tactics. You're like the old salesladies at Neiman Marcus."

Willow and Xander exchanged a glance.

"My mother's best friend's mother died last summer. They sort of grew up together, so my mother had to go. She dragged me. The old lady was buried here," Cordelia said disgustedly. "Right up over the hill."

Willow nodded slowly. "So there's at least one recent burial."

Suddenly, she blinked and glanced up the hill. "Oz is taking a long time."

Xander looked at her, saw that she was alarmed, and felt a little concerned himself. "Let's find out why," he said.

The three of them started up the rise. They made a direct course for the Hart crypt, and when they were within a dozen feet of the thing, Xander slowed, then reached out a hand to indicate that the girls should stop. He pointed at what had stopped him.

The door to the crypt, a heavy thing of thick iron, stood open five or six inches.

"You don't think Oz . . ." Xander began, then let his words trail off.

They were going to have to check inside. Or at least they would have, had Oz not appeared then, quite suddenly, from the deep shadows alongside the crypt. He poked his head around the corner and waved them on. Silently, he patted the outer wall of the crypt to show that they should stay close to it, just as he was doing.

Willow followed right behind him, then Xander, and finally Cordelia. When they reached the back of the crypt, Oz leaned forward slightly and peered around the edge. He pulled his head back and motioned for Willow to do the same. When *she* pulled her head back, Xander didn't like the look on her face. Not at all.

But he looked anyway.

Just down from the crest of the hill upon which the crypt sat, three figures moved through the shadows around a marble headstone with a roaring lion on top. Two of the three had shovels and were quickly unearthing whatever poor soul lay at the bottom of that grave.

Xander pulled his head back, leaned against the cold stone of the crypt, and sighed.

"I don't need to look," Cordelia whispered.

"See, this is what makes Sunnydale different from other towns," Xander said in a harsh, frustrated whisper. "You might get your random grave robbery in Denver or Tucson or Bismarck-freaking-North Dakota. But around here, it's a spectator sport."

"Quiet," Willow said, barely speaking at all, eyebrows raised for emphasis.

"Fine, fine," Xander sighed. "So what now?"

"We go to the van, find a phone, and leave an anonymous tip for the police," Cordelia said slowly, as though they might have trouble following her train of thought. "And I never leave my cell phone in my purse again."

"But, well, what if they're gone?" Willow asked. "They'll get away."

"And your plan would be what?" Cordelia snapped, a little too loud perhaps. "A little witchery? Maybe a little axe murder? These are criminals. That's what the police are for."

"Maybe in other towns," Oz said grimly.

They all looked at him, but Oz was still looking around the corner at the grave robbers. Finally, he looked back. His eyes passed over Cordelia but lingered on Xander, then finally went to Willow.

"I vote citizen's arrest," Oz told them.

"That could be fun," Xander reasoned. "It's four against three. They have two guys and a girl, we have two guys, a girl, and a bulldog."

"If I do the math on that one, Harris, you're in trouble," Cordelia snarled.

"Then I'd say I'm pretty much safe, wouldn't you?"

She glared at him but said nothing more.

"This is just wrong," Willow whispered, looking around the edge of the crypt. "We have to do something."

"Fine," Xander said. "Let's do it."

As one, Oz, Willow, and Xander moved out from behind the crypt and started down the slope. After a moment, Cordelia sighed and followed. At first, the grave robbers didn't even notice them.

"Hey!" Xander shouted. "You never heard of resting in peace?"

He was feeling pretty pumped up at that moment. Between him and Oz, they'd done more than their share of vamp fighting, not to mention demons. And these were just grave robbers. At the very least, they had to be evenly matched. And it counted that they were the good guys, at least in his mind.

But then the Asian girl standing behind the headstone looked over at him, and her face changed, became feral, eyes blazing yellow. She bared her fangs.

"Okay!" Xander said, holding up his hands. "Have a great time, kids. We'll just be moseying."

He started to back up, and the others with him. Then the female vamp slapped one of the males in the back of the head.

"Kill them," she said, sneering.

The two vampires pulled themselves from the grave, dropped their shovels, and started to sprint after them.

"I wanted to go home," Cordelia reminded everyone.

"Wishing you had," Xander replied. "And that's the last time we go with the werewolf's plan."

Then they were just running. They passed the crypt, and they could hear the vampires calling out, hooting, behind them. *Having a grand old time*, Xander thought. *Meanwhile, we're screwed.* They didn't really have any vampire-slaying weapons. That wasn't what the whole grave-robbing investigation was about.

Or so they'd believed.

They'd never be able to get back to the van before the vamps caught up with them.

Six feet past the crypt, Xander stopped, reached out, and grabbed Willow and Cordelia.

"Turn around!" he snapped.

"Failing to see that as a better plan," Oz told him, remarkably calm as always.

But Willow had already figured out what he wanted to do. She ran toward the open door to the crypt and shoved it with her shoulder. Xander was next to her a second later, and the iron scraped against the granite of the crypt itself. It took Oz's additional weight, but they got it open enough to slip inside. Willow went first, then Cordelia, then Xander, and finally Oz.

"Now, that's a good idea!" Xander heard one of the vampires cry in delight as he and Oz put their full weight into closing the door. "This way, they don't have to move you after we've had dinner."

The iron door squealed on the stone beneath, and it caught in the same position it had been in, six inches from closing. Xander stood back and gave it a hard kick, and it scraped a bit further, now open only four inches.

A vampire's hand thrust into the opening and grabbed Oz by the hair. He let out a shout of pain and batted at the hand. Xander was too busy trying to shoulder the door shut to help.

Suddenly, Cordelia slapped a silver crucifix down on the soil-encrusted hand. The vampire outside shrieked and pulled his hand back, his flesh steaming.

"Obliged," Oz told her, then gritted his teeth and redoubled his efforts at Xander's side as they tried to close the door.

"Don't leave home without it," Cordelia said.

"How 'bout some help, ladies?" Xander asked.

Willow moved up next to them. Cordelia hesitated, but only for a moment. With the four of them working together, straining, they forced the door closed, iron grinding on granite. The latch caught, and they leaned against the door to catch their breath.

The vampires slammed against the door from the outside. They tried the handle, but it wouldn't open. It was locked.

"Forget it, Niles," one of them said. "They're not going anywhere. It's more important that we bring the body back to the Harbinger."

"Girl burned me," the one called Niles complained in a whiny English accent.

"You'll get her another night," the other replied. "But if you displease the Harbinger, she might feed you to those hatchlings."

"Oh, all right, then."

Inside the crypt, Xander, Willow, Cordelia, and Oz stared at one another in the almost complete darkness. There was a crack in the ceiling, perhaps earthquake damage from some years earlier, and moonlight leaked in from there and from a gap above the iron door. Xander realized that was why it was so hard to close. It must have settled, somehow, and no longer hung right in the frame.

"Do you think they're gone?" Willow asked.

"What did they mean about us not going anywhere?" Cordelia added nervously.

"Might have something to do with the fact that the door's locked, and there's no handle on the inside," Oz said simply.

Xander's eyes widened.

"Well, sure," Willow said, trying to be helpful. "Why would you need a handle on the inside? Unless, y'know, you expect the dead to rise and try to leave, which is just . . ."

She looked at Oz. "We're trapped, aren't we?"

Oz nodded.

"Oh, wait," Willow said suddenly. "Maybe at least we can see what we're dealing with."

She reached into her pocket and withdrew a packet of matches. "For spells and stuff," she explained sheepishly. Then she struck a match, and it flared to life.

It didn't last very long. But it was more than long enough for them all to see that, unlike some of the other crypts at Shady Hill, this one was very much full. There were a number of coffins and stone tombs, and some of them had been broken into or cracked open sometime in the past.

From one rotted coffin, a skeleton lolled, its skull lying on one side as though its empty sockets were staring at them.

They were trapped among the dead.

Chapter Five

Buffy and Angel were patrolling in the bad part of town, within earshot of the Bronze. Matte shadows coated the maze-like warren of narrow alleys like a coat of cheap primer on a stripped-down chassis. A foul odor of age, neglect, and filth rose from the old warehouses and boarded-up businesses—a failed Vietnamese restaurant, a cobbler's, and a padlocked, burned-out gas station. In the darkness, rats scurried busily in the garbage and debris, making for a few tense moments when one is looking for jumpoutables.

Beside a stack of retreads piled against a chain-link fence, Angel stopped and made a strange face.

"What?" Buffy asked, on alert.

"Nothing." He started walking again, turning right to glide through a cramped, smelly, garbage-strewn alley.

Moving with him, she frowned. "That was *not* a nothing face."

He shrugged as he poked behind a trash can. Sometimes vampires left fresh kills there. It was also an excellent place to find winos, if that was ever important. So far, it had not been.

"Just wondering how the Bronze books bands," he said.

Buffy flashed him an ironic smile. The band tonight would get a D-minus for effort even if they graded on a curve. "You thinking of putting a group together?"

He smiled faintly at her. "Have you ever heard me sing?"

"Talent is not a requirement, obviously," she said, tilting her head in the direction of the very bad music echoing off the graffiti-laden brick. "I think the secret lies in being willing to drive all the way to Sunnydale. We're not exactly a dot on anybody's world tour."

"And yet." He shrugged.

"Some are really good," she filled in. "Well, we can ask Oz how all that complicated stuff works." She yawned. "Maybe we should just pack it in. We have seen neither fang nor talon of any vamps tonight."

"Yeah." He sounded eager to go, and Buffy was stung. To her, it was still an event every time they were together, despite that she hid that fact fairly well. When he phoned, his voice made her catch her breath. When he showed, she noticed what he was wearing. *Call it neurotic, call it dumb, call it what it is: seeing him gives me a happy, and not seeing him . . . is so very beyond what I can handle.*

"Sorry to waste your evening," she said through gritted teeth.

"And I had so much planned," he said wistfully.

"Oh." She aimed for casual, was pretty sure she stuck it like Kerri Strug after a vault.

"A couple of cereal boxes to read, a few reruns to watch." His smile told her he had her number. "Maybe we could grab some coffee?"

Like a date. She tried very hard not to make it a thing. "It's not like I'll catch up on homework if I get home at a decent hour."

As they headed for the Bronze, Buffy cheered up: no more patrol, and a chance to have a little normal fun. Such moments were precious and few.

"Hey, got a cig?"

A short, small woman with curly red hair stepped from the shadows and smiled at Buffy and Angel. *Major freckles,* Buffy thought, but something didn't feel right.

Then she remembered Willow's latest hack into the police files. *This is Pepper Roback.*

The Slayer smiled. "*Pepper*. How've you been?"

Pepper frowned. Tilted her head sideways. "You didn't know her," the redhead said with certainty.

"Oops, caught me," Buffy said, shrugging.

Then she backhanded Pepper across the face, hard. Even as she spun away, Pepper morphed into vamp face. Buffy went after her, Angel right behind her. She lunged at the vamp girl, but Pepper brought up her right arm in an expert block, and Buffy had to wonder if she'd taken self-defense classes when she was alive.

"How did you know?" Pepper demanded.

"Talking about yourself in the third person?" Buffy ventured. "Dead giveaway. Also the fact that you're a genuine missing person. Or were."

Pepper dodged a blow from Angel and snuck a lightning punch in at Buffy's face. The vampire's fist clipped Buffy's chin. She brought her leg up into Pepper's chest and kicked her back, but the vampire didn't go down. She was a good hand-to-hand fighter.

Almost too good. Buffy hadn't done the research on Pepper, but it seemed amazing to her that this woman, even with the demon now in the corporeal driver's seat, knew anything substantial about physical combat.

On the other hand, she'd have to wonder later. Now was clearly not the time.

Angel went after the vampire, but Pepper eluded him, then struck him a fast blow to the face. In the moment of his reaction, she grabbed Angel and slammed him against the alley wall. Buffy snapped another hard kick up into Pepper's chest, toppling her backward toward a recovering Angel, who grabbed her from behind.

Pepper hissed and said something in a foreign language— there were so many—and Angel reacted slightly.

"It's French," he announced.

"There goes graduation," Buffy shot back, since she was taking French and hadn't understood a word.

"Medieval French," he added.

The vampire turned her head and tried to bite Angel in the

face. He held her away from himself, his own face morphing, and growled deep in his throat.

"Slayer," the vampire said to Buffy. "I despise your kind. You had your little victory the other night, and I told you there would be a next time. You'd do well to keep out of my way."

Buffy took that in, but she didn't let it deflect her attention. "Sorry," she said. "I can't place you. It's just that we dust so many. After a while, you guys all look alike. Look, Pepper, let's just get this over with, and you can stop hanging out, peeping in windows, scaring the highlights out of your old roomie's little sis, 'kay?"

"Daylights," Angel corrected.

"Have you seen Damara's hair?" Buffy asked, not taking her eyes off the vampire. "Come on, Pepper, I don't have all night."

"Slayers! Always so sure of yourselves. Well, I will see you rot, just as I have seen others of your line molder in their graves."

Pepper snarled and leaped at her. Confused—after all, this woman was human until a couple of nights earlier—Buffy tried to defend herself, but the vampire feinted a blow toward her face, then ducked in for a swift uppercut to her gut. Buffy staggered back, surprised at the skill this little female vamp showed.

"Not bad, Pepper," she grunted, trying to catch her breath.

"Stop calling me that," the vampire snarled. "I am Veronique! You should know the name of she who will take your life."

Buffy bent down and picked up a broken piece of wood off the ground. The vampire saw what she was doing and laughed.

"Save your energy, Slayer. I've already prepared a new host," she said.

"Yeah, well," Buffy said, trying to figure out what was going on before she killed the vampire. She kept the stake at the ready, and she and Angel began to move around, trapping between them what she now thought of as the schizo vampire.

A shriek pierced the air. "Oh, my God!" shouted a man. Then a thirtyish couple was running up the alley toward them.

"Help!" cried the woman.

In that moment of chaos, when Angel turned toward them, Pepper lunged for him, drove him off his feet, and then raced down the alley in the opposite direction and was lost to the shadows in an instant.

"What the hell's going on around here?" the man said, his voice revealing his panic.

Buffy hesitated, but only for a second. "That woman just attacked us."

"There's a dead girl back up that way," the guy told them as the woman clung to him, whispering pleas to God and to her boyfriend that they just get out of there.

"We'll . . . we'll go call the police," she said. "Can you stay until they arrive?"

Buffy looked at Angel, who had morphed back to his human face the moment he'd seen the couple approaching.

"We'll stay," he said.

When the couple had gone, Buffy and Angel hurried down the alley in search of a corpse. The dim fuchsia buzz of a neon sign advertised the "Sunnydale Pawn Shop CASH OR CREDIT MONEY ORDERS WATER BILLS." In the glare, a woman with extremely bleached blond hair lay sprawled on her back, eyes staring glassily at the sky.

Her skin was whiter than her hair. There was a deep wound directly over her carotid artery.

"Pepper's been busy," Angel said gravely.

Buffy nodded. She picked up another piece of wood, just in case. It was quite possible this dead woman would come back as a vampire. Unfortunately, *when* was a good question nobody but Angel and Buffy knew to ask.

"Buffy," Angel said quietly.

The body was twitching, just a little. Buffy sighed, stepped forward, and rammed the piece of wood through her chest.

The newborn vampire exploded in a rain of dust.

Grimly, they walked back down the alley together.

"Y'know what's weird?" Buffy said. "That whole riff about Slayers. She was pretty much raw talent. What do you think that was all about?"

Lost in thought, Angel didn't respond. Buffy didn't really expect him to. After a moment, though, he glanced at her. "She called me *brother*," he said. "In medieval French."

"How does someone like Pepper Roback know medieval French?"

Angel shrugged.

Buffy sighed. "Weird."

They were down among the dead men, and Cordelia was really beginning to lose it. She, Xander, Willow, and Oz were seated in a close circle on the floor of the vault, but the smell of the dead was closing in on her. Every time she heard a sound, she imagined the skeleton they had seen, its empty eye sockets staring at them, its mouth opening slowly, as it crept toward them. In the pitch dark, she saw hazy white shapes and tried to remind herself that if you stare at nothing long enough, you're bound to see something. *Sort of like falling in lust with a loser like Xander.*

"Wait, here," Xander said quickly. "I found my flashlight."

He clicked the light on, and Cordelia breathed a small sigh of relief. Its beam was dim, almost as though the light were being sucked up by the gray of the Hart family crypt and the shadows around them. But it was something. It was light.

Even though it was getting colder by the minute inside the tomb, she could barely breathe. She was certain they were using up all the air and that they would suffocate. One by one, they would lose consciousness, and the next time the family who owned this vault opened it to lay a loved one to rest, the Mystery of the Missing Teens would be solved. Four dead seniors, so close to graduation . . . now just more Sunnydale statistics.

"In the olden days," Xander said, "they used to string up little bells on pull cords inside tombs and coffins. In case you were buried alive. You could sound the alarm, and they'd come and let you out."

"Have we looked for one of those?" Cordelia asked anxiously. "No?"

The beam from Xander's flashlight darted around the crypt. "No bell. So, any thoughts on getting out of here?"

"I'm trying to remember the words to a spell," Willow said helpfully.

"Are we sure leaving is the safest idea?" Xander asked. "Or are we thinking those were imaginary vampires?"

"They left!" Cordelia protested. "They had something they had to go do."

"Which might be done by now. And they might come back." Xander actually sounded kind.

"So much for my beauty rest," she snapped.

Silence fell over the group. There was some shifting as muscles cramped; with each movement, Cordelia stared at the indistinct shapes moving in the shadows beyond the reach of the flashlight—*just my imagination*—and thought about the bones in the coffins.

For a time, when she'd been little, she had become convinced that there was a dead woman inside her mattress. She was afraid to go to sleep, because if she did, the dead woman would stab her through the back with a huge, sharp knife. Now she didn't remember how she'd gotten over the fear, because as she thought about it, the hair on the back of her neck rose, and she shivered, just like a little girl. In fact, part of her couldn't seem to *stop* thinking about it, even though it was wigging her out.

"If we were about six years younger, we'd be telling each other ghost stories," Xander said. "I used to think there was this—"

"Don't," Cordelia said. "It's bad enough without you babbling on about some dumb nightmare of yours."

"It wasn't dumb." Xander sounded defensive. "It made perfect logic. My Uncle Roary's AA sponsor told me so."

"Scary stories. Maybe not such a good idea at the moment," Oz remarked.

He doesn't sound scared at all, Cordelia thought enviously. *Maybe werewolf and all, he doesn't get scared much anymore.*

"Guys, please, I'm trying to think," Willow said.

"Yeah, Xander. Zip it," Cordelia snapped. "Willow, what do you think? I mean, even if you can get us out of here, do you think the vampires are gone?"

"Let's worry about getting the door open first," Oz suggested.

"Everybody join hands," Willow asked.

Cordelia sneered at Xander, who was sitting next to her.

"Please," Willow urged.

Reluctantly, Cordelia took Xander's hand in her left and Oz's in her right. When they'd all joined hands, Willow closed her eyes and started chanting something. It was English, but she was whispering so low that Cordelia could barely hear her. Then, suddenly, Willow sucked in her breath, and her eyes went wide.

"Will?" Oz asked, concerned. "What is it?"

Willow's eyes darted around the crypt. "We're not alone," she said.

Then her eyes rolled back in her head. Oz called her name, but Willow didn't seem to hear him.

Angel was concerned by how sluggish Buffy was. At his insistence, they skipped the Bronze, and he walked her home.

I never wonder if you're still alive. Did I actually say that to her?

Does she actually believe it?

While it was true that Buffy was the Slayer, she was still human at the core. In the netherworld where he dwelled, another word for *human* was *mortal*. The life spans of humans were terribly short, but for Slayers shorter still. She had been so right. He could die. But she *would* die.

He wouldn't be able to see that. Maybe it was cowardice, or an excess of love, but even the thought of Buffy lying dead somewhere was more than he could bear. As soon as he pictured it, his mind shut the door, and a voice inside his head said, *Never.*

"Buffy," he said, turning to her on the street. For one insane moment, he thought of turning her, not even asking her if she wanted him to, because that would grant her some measure of immortality. Then he came to his senses; Buffy would be gone, and a demon would inhabit her body.

There was no easy way, then. In all the fairy tales, loving someone was enough to tame the beast, awaken the princess, live happily ever after. But in the real world, loving someone was often the shortest route to misery.

She didn't answer. Perhaps she didn't hear him. He doubted that; they were often so close that one knew—or suspected—what the other was thinking. So he kept his silence and was relieved when the house on Revello Drive came into view. Soon she would be in bed, and safe, and she'd live to fight another day.

They climbed the porch steps, and she unlocked her door. Whispering, she said, "My mom might be asleep. She tries to stay up for me, but she dozes off a lot."

He nodded. They tiptoed in and, without speaking, headed for the kitchen. Another night, years ago, she had innocently shouted, "Come in!" when they'd been chased by the Three, warrior vampires sent by the Master to kill her. She had had no idea at the time that her handsome Danger Guy was a vampire, too. Nor had she known, as she dressed the wound he had sustained in battle, what the tattoo on his back had signified: Angel had once been Angelus, the Scourge of Europe, one of the most savage vampires ever to have lived.

They went into the kitchen. It was then that she saw the note propped in front of a bouquet her mother had bought at the grocery store.

> Dear Buffy,
> I called Dr. Martinez from the gallery, and he told me to go to the emergency room at the hospital. I don't think it's anything, and neither did he, but I was just a little dizzy and my chest hurt. I guess you were right; I did overdo it. Please call before you come to the hospital. I'm sure I'll only be here a little while, and we might miss each other coming and going.
> Love,
> Mom

"Angel." Her eyes welled. "My mom's in the hospital."

He took the note. "At the hospital," he corrected gently.

Wearily, she slid off the stool. "I'm going there," she insisted. "No arguing."

Without a word, Angel put his arm around her and led her toward the door.

Willow could still sense her friends around her. She knew that they were safe, for the moment. She also felt no threat from the presence—the many sentient spirits—that swirled around her. She had begun the spell she thought would free her friends, and it had failed. Unable to recall the incantation completely, she had been about to give up when she felt them gathering, prodding her mind, trying to touch her.

Who are you? she thought.

The dead are reaching out to you, spellcaster, a voice echoed through her mind, and possibly even through the crypt, for all she could tell. *They are those whose bones lie here, in this sepulchre. Your magick spoke to them, touched them. They had long since surrendered any hope of ever having contact with the mortal world again, and you have given them a great gift merely through your presence.*

But why are they here, and not . . . Willow didn't even finish the thought, but she didn't need to. She sensed that the being she was communicating with understood her question regardless.

This crypt was desecrated by dark forces not long after it was first built, the voice told her. *Three generations of the Hart family have lingered here after death, lost, unable to find their way on the ghost roads to the afterlife that awaits them. Only if the crypt is reconsecrated will they be able to depart.*

"You keep saying 'they.' If you're not part of their, um, family, then who are you?" Willow asked aloud.

Xander, Oz, and Cordelia stared at her.

"Will? Is it flashback time?" Xander asked.

"Not funny," Oz told him. "Willow. Are you all right?"

But Willow didn't respond. She was talking, all right. But not to them.

I am a wanderer, the voice explained. *I have traveled the ghost roads for a very long time, but I have done so by choice. I have done my best to guide the lost souls of the dead to their final reward, giving them the direction that the circumstances of their death might have robbed them of.*

Willow understood. During a previous crisis, she and Buffy and the others had discovered a great deal about the ghost roads, the paths the spirits of the dead follow after they leave the human plane to move onto the next. Some people, victims of murder or other violent death, particularly, had a hard time finding their way. If what this spirit told her was true, she must have been an extraordinary individual in life to choose such a selfless existence after death.

But who are you? she asked again. *What's your name?*

In life, I was called Lucy Hanover.

Even within the landscape of her mind. Willow was startled into silence. Lucy Hanover's ghost sensed her astonishment and hesitation.

You know of me? the ghost asked.

You were a Slayer, Willow replied. *The current Slayer is my closest friend. We've . . . read about you. But what are you doing here, in Sunnydale?*

Ah, I knew you were no ordinary girl, battling vampires and casting your spells. As to my presence here, it is the Hellmouth, is it not? There are always a great many lost souls here. I return from time to time, hoping to aid them if I can. The spirits of the Hart family were crying out to you, but you could not hear them, so I came to speak in their stead.

Willow's heart beat faster. *Can you help us?*

After that, there was silence for a time. Willow sensed that Lucy had gone away, but not far. The spirits swirled all around her. Oz was beside her, stroking her hair and her face, but even he felt like no more than ghost to her now.

Then Lucy returned. *They will help,* she said. *We all will. But we must do so through you, spellcaster. And the spirits desire your help in return.*

Let me guess, Willow thought. *They want us to get the crypt re-consecrated?*

That is part of it, yes, Lucy agreed. *But there is more. They would like you to come back, when you may, and let them be with you, within you, for a time, so that they may see the world when the sun is high and the birds sing, see the world that their children and grandchildren live in. Then they can move on. Will you help?*

Of course, Willow replied. *It would be an honor.*

Very good, spellcaster.

Willow. Call me Willow.

Willow. It's a fitting name for a soul so grand. Prepare yourself, then, Willow, for we enter you now.

"Thank you, Lucy," Willow said, eyes still rolled back to white.

"Willow?" Oz asked in a soft, amazingly calm voice.

An incredible chill washes over Willow's skin, giving her goose-bumps, making her scalp prickle. She shivers violently. The shiver becomes a tremor. Earthquake, she thinks.

She is lying in a box, staring up through the lid, seeing people veiled in black as they weep and bend over her. Their faces swim above her, as if they are growing farther away. Rose petals float down over her face; she smells them. Then dirt clods drop down on her, clog her nose and throat, cutting off her air.

A deep, soul-wrenching grief settles on her chest like a night-mare goblin; she tries to take a breath, but her chest is constricted. Her throat aches with unshed tears. She is dizzy and disoriented, floating in free-form despair.

We die alone. The thought is unbidden, unwelcome. We deny it all our lives. We fall in love. We have children.

But the fact is, we die alone.

She hears distant voices, but they are drowned out by a chorus of moaning and sobs. She is aching with the sound. It is a funeral dirge; it is a lamentation.

Grief is a thing, she realizes. It's heavy, and cold, and its edges are hard and jagged. It can kill you.

In her mind's eye, she reaches out a hand. Icy fingers grip hers. Tears like brittle, frigid diamonds pelt her cheeks.

She stands, reaches out her fingers . . . but they are not her fingers any longer, they are tendrils of smoke and spirit and death. She reaches for the door . . .

"Oh, God, Oz, what's happening to her?" Cordelia cried.

Oz didn't know how to answer. He'd been keeping it together, assuming it was all part of the enchantment, or whatever. Something of the Wiccan persuasion. But this was too much.

Without warning, Willow stood and started toward the door. Her pupils moved now, but her eyes were wide, searching, as though seeing everything for the first time. She reached out her hands, and a swirl of glittering mist stretched from each finger.

Xander's mouth dropped open. "Whoa."

There was a shriek of metal, and the door opened, scraping against the granite floor of the crypt.

"How did she do that?" Cordelia asked, astonished.

"That'd be magick," Oz replied. But even he wasn't quite sure.

Willow seemed to deflate. She swayed a little on her feet, and Oz went to hold her up. She wrapped her arms around him, leaning on him heavily.

"Lucy," she whispered. "Thank you."

"Who's Lucy?" Oz asked.

Willow looked at him, focusing at last. Finally, it was really her, back among the conscious.

"Oz," she said. Then she hugged him tightly.

He didn't ask anything else, just happy to have her back. Willow, for her part, didn't offer much of an explanation. At least, not at first. But as they walked out of the crypt, and Xander and Cordelia started to badger her, Willow finally relented.

"Sorry, guys," she said. "I'm just trying to take it all in."

"Well, I, for one, say way to go, Will," Xander piped up.

Willow smiled. "Actually, it isn't me you need to thank," she confessed. "And . . . it isn't exactly over." Then she told them about Lucy Hanover and the ghosts of the Hart family and what they had done.

"So, what you're saying is we're in debt to a bunch of ghosts," Xander said, clearly not thrilled at the prospect.

"Up to our eyeballs," Willow confirmed.

"It could be worse," Oz reminded them. "We could still be in there."

They all looked back up at the crypt. Oz's arm was around Willow's shoulders, and he felt her stiffen.

"Lucy," she said.

They all looked. There, moving smoothly among the gravestones toward them, was the shimmering form of a dark-haired girl, perhaps in her early twenties. Below her waist there was nothing but a kind of green mist, and her body itself was translucent, seemingly ephemeral.

Before Oz or any of the others could react, Willow pushed past him and walked toward the ghost of Lucy Hanover. The ghost smiled, and Oz thought that, though her features seemed sad and cold, that smile revealed the beauty of the girl she had been, once upon a time.

"I . . . I mean, we can see you," Willow said happily.

It is possible for me to manifest my spirit, if I focus my will, Lucy explained. *I wanted to meet you all properly. The Harts will finally be able to move on once you have fulfilled your end of the agreement.*

"We will," Willow agreed. "As soon as we can."

I have no doubt, Willow. Thank you. The Slayer is fortunate to have such friends as you. Please tell her I wish her well. Now that we have met, perhaps I will visit in the future.

"That'd be great," Willow replied, grinning. "Um, just, not around my parents, okay?"

The ghost actually chuckled a bit at that. *Of course. Goodbye, spellcaster.*

" 'Bye, Lucy," Willow said.

As they watched, the ghost shimmered brightly and then simply disappeared.

"Wow," Cordelia whispered.

"Yeah," Xander agreed. "There's something you don't see every day."

"Not even in Sunnydale," Oz added. Then he took Willow's hand and led her toward the gates of the cemetery.

As far as he was concerned, they'd spent enough time among the dead.

With Angel at her side, Buffy approached a half-moon desk in the center of the lobby of the Sunnydale Hospital. An elderly lady with silver-blue hair and wearing a pink-and-white-striped jacket smiled up pleasantly from a *Chicken Soup* book and said kindly, "Yes, dear? May I help you?"

"My mother. Joyce Summers," Buffy blurted. "She came into the emergency room."

"Well, it's down the hall and to the left," the woman said.

"Is there any way to check if she's still there?" Angel cut in. "Her name's Joyce Summers."

"Let me see." The lady picked up a bookmark decorated with cat paws and carefully inserted it into her book. Then she shut the book and placed it flush with the desk blotter upon which many things were scribbled. Very slowly, she placed her hands over a computer keyboard and started typing. "That would be Summers as in the season?" she asked Angel. He nodded. "And the first name was Patrice?"

"Oh, *God*," Buffy groaned. Angel touched her arm.

"Joyce," Angel said.

The elderly lady squinted at the screen. "Oh, my." She stared at Buffy. Buffy almost fainted. Then the lady blinked and said, "Wrong screen. Which is a good thing, because that other patient, well, let me just see. Yes." She brightened. "Mrs. Summers was just admitted. She's in Room 401."

"Admitted?" Buffy echoed faintly. "*What?*"

"Yes, let me see." She started typing again.

Angel steered Buffy toward twin elevators. The receptionist shouted after them that it was past visiting hours, but they didn't slow for a second. As soon as the elevator doors opened, they were inside and on their way to the fourth floor.

The nurses' station on the floor was a strange mixture of efficiency and idle chitchat. Some nurses were punching things into computers, while others were discussing their vacation plans. One of them looked up at Buffy, who went through the rigamarole again. Angel stood by her side.

"Room 401," a nurse named Leyla said, pointing down the hall. "She's in luck; she's the only one in there right now. But it's really past visiting hours, you know."

Buffy was about to scream, but Angel laid a hand on her arm and looked at the nurse.

"It's her mother," he said. "We just found out she was here. Please, just a few minutes."

The nurse hesitated only a moment before nodding.

Buffy looked at Angel, and together they tiptoed down the hall.

She pushed open the door. Her mother lay in bed in a hospital gown. A trio of lights surrounded the upper part of her head, like some brain surgery contraption in a science-fiction movie. She was asleep.

"Where's her chart?" Buffy whispered.

Joyce opened her eyes and smiled groggily.

"Buffy."

"Mom." Buffy did a half turn. Angel had left the room. She saw his shadow from the overhead lights in the hall. "Mom, what's wrong?"

"I just felt so sick. Dr. Martinez was . . ." She waved a hand. "There's a specialist. Dr. Cole . . . Cole . . ." Her eyes fluttered. "I can't remember."

"It's fine, Mom." Buffy took her hand and leaned over her. She brushed Joyce's hair from her forehead. "Is there anything you want? Are you in any pain?"

"Not now."

When were you in pain? Buffy wanted to demand, alarmed, but now was not the time.

"Sleep, Mom. I'll come see you in the morning." Buffy smiled at her and kissed her forehead.

" 'Kay, sweetie." She was fading. Her words were slurring together. "Did you get the bad guys?"

"I had a perfectly dull evening," Buffy assured her.

"Leftover pork chops," Joyce went on. "New half-gallon of ice—"

"Mom, I'm fine. I'm not hungry."

"Too thin." Her mother's hand flopped toward Buffy's face. "Love you."

The hand slowly lowered to the bed. Buffy put her hand over it, then hurried from her bedside into the hall.

"Where's the doctor?" she demanded in a loud voice. "I want to know why—"

"Buffy," Angel said, looking a little odd. "This is Dr. Leah Coleman."

Dr. Leah Coleman was ancient. There was no other word for it. Her face was very pale and extremely wrinkled, and there were dozens of lines bleeding into her lips. Her hair was stark white and cut short, and pierced pearl earrings dangled from withered ear lobes which had obviously been fuller in their day.

"I'm a specialist visiting from New York," she said by way of greeting. "My colleague, Dr. Martinez, asked me to consult on your mother's case."

"Her . . . case? She has a case?" Stricken, Buffy looked to Angel for comfort.

But Angel, though beside her in body, was definitely elsewhere in spirit.

Manhattan, 1944

He sat in an alley that was plastered with posters urging people to buy war bonds and to comply with blackout procedures. Perhaps not realizing the irony, he was crouched beneath a poster that read, "IS THIS TRIP REALLY NECESSARY?"

He was filthy, and he stank, and even though there were far more rats in New York City than there were Huns fighting for Hitler, he was practically starving. He could barely bring himself to drink of them, because he wanted to die.

Angel, once Angelus, the One with the Angelic Face, still grappled with the paralyzing guilt that had overcome him when the vengeful Kalderash Gypsy clan had restored his soul. It was his punishment for killing a young girl of their clan. Now he must live with the guilt from all the evil things he had done while a demon had inhabited his body and his soul had rested in the ether.

He couldn't live with them. He could not bear another second of agonizing regret. He was more than half crazed with remorse, and he knew of no way to find relief.

A door to the alley opened, and Angel skittered away, like the rats whose lifeblood he disdained. Yet he couldn't help but turn and look, in case the person who stepped into the alley was the Girl.

And it was. She had lovely dark chestnut hair, usually braided around her head like a coronet, but tonight it was loose and flowed over her shoulders. She wore a starched white apron over a rather severe gray dress, but on her, the costume was feminine and appealing.

Her face was drawn, her features delicate, and her eyes were rimmed with tears.

"Leah?" a voice said behind her.

It was an older woman, who came out into the alley. She lit a cigarette and offered one to the Girl—*to Leah,* Angel thought, delighted by the knowledge of her name.

"Honey, you need to go home," the woman said.

Leah shook her head. "There's too much to do." She laughed bitterly. "I remember the Depression. I was just a girl, but I worked like a slave in my mother's soup kitchen. They keep saying the war's been good for the economy. So why are so many Americans starving?"

The older woman lit a cigarette, inhaled, and blew out the smoke. "There'll always be the ones who fall through the cracks."

Leah's features hardened. "When there are this many, they aren't falling through cracks. Society is failing them."

"Oh, Leah. You're so young." The woman touched her cheek. "I hope you never lose this . . ." She smiled softly. "What shall I call it? Purity?"

"I'm only doing what everybody should be doing." She stuffed her hands into her apron pockets. Angel saw her exhaustion in the hunch of her shoulders. She stared at the alley with a dejected frown and said, "I can't believe I'm supposed to clean this up."

"Fire hazard." The other woman shrugged.

"But we didn't even put this garbage out here." She surveyed the heaps of trash. "I'll make a sign-up sheet, ask the men to help us."

"They're here for the soup and the beds, Leah. Not to be nice."

"I can't believe that, Opal. They'll help."

"Miss Coleman?" someone called. "There's something wrong with the stove."

Leah Coleman sighed. "I'll be right there."

She glanced at the other woman and wordlessly walked back through the doorway. The woman threw down her cigarette, stepped on it, and followed her. She shut the door, casting Angel into darkness once again.

He stared at the smoldering cigarette. At the piles of debris in the alley—empty crates, broken milk bottles, newspapers.

Moving slowly, as if he hadn't moved any part of his body in more than a century, he bent down and picked up the cigarette. Squeezing it out between his fingers, he rifled through the mess until he located a wooden crate in fairly good condition. He tossed in the cigarette. And a few handfuls of newspapers. He picked the broken glass up carelessly and cut himself more than once. But he didn't mind the pain. At least it was feeling *something*.

Angel cleared as much of the garbage as he could. When he got tired, he caught a rat and drained it, so that he could keep going.

Chapter Six

Paris, October 11, 1307

From somewhere in the distance came the sound of a violin, expertly played, sweetly keening. The sound was odd and incongruous, punctuated as it was by the tolling of the bells of Ste. Genevieve. It was just past eleven in the evening, the witching hour near at hand, when a distraught Philip the Fair rode beneath the shadow of that grand church and continued on toward the home of his mistress.

His knights rode beside him, one on either side, the rhythm of their horses' hooves on the road a brutal counterpoint to the painful beating of his heart. He dared not bring more than these two, trusted men-at-arms, despite the danger should anyone see him for what he truly was.

Philip shivered beneath his cloak and held the reins of his mount all the tighter. It was a chill evening, more so even than might be expected after a gray October day. But he was not a fool. Philip suspected that the cold that seemed to spread throughout his body had little to do with the climate, and far more to do with the dawning horror of what he even now contemplated.

In the past several years, he had done a great many things he would never have imagined. Devious things. Despite the air of propriety that had surrounded them, they had been savage things. But he had a sacred charge as a servant of the Lord, as well as a duty to France itself. And he would do whatever was necessary to fulfill those responsibilities.

No matter the cost.

Or so he had thought. But this . . . this was inconceivable. He'd agreed to it weeks before, but now he could not even close his eyes to sleep for fear of the night terrors that would beset him.

Despite the ghostly violin that played somewhere ahead, there were few people out in the street, save for beggars and other poor, stricken ones who wandered about like soulless things, searching for a safe place to sleep. Philip wondered if they would not be better off in the arms of the Lord than wheedling for alms.

The bells of Ste. Genevieve fell silent as he and his men drew up before the residence of his mistress. They dismounted, his knights looking all about to see that they were not spied upon. Frederick nodded to him, and Philip handed over the reins of his mount and went to knock softly at the door as his knights led the horses into the darkened alley alongside the house.

After a moment, the door opened, and Philip looked in upon the face of his mistress's manservant.

"Are you going to let me in, Antoine, or just gawk at me?" Philip demanded.

Antoine seemed dumbstruck. He pulled the door wide as quickly as he was able and then fell to his knees in obeisance, eyes downcast.

"Oh, get up, you fool," Philip snapped. "Tell your employer I am here. I must not be gone very long this evening."

The pale, silent manservant rose and turned toward the grand staircase that curved upward behind him. But he needn't have bothered. Philip looked up to see that she was there already, smiling down at him, dressed only in a sinfully ravishing peignoir.

"Indeed," she said, "it would not do to arouse suspicion."

Philip could only watch the way her lips moved when she spoke. Then he whispered her name: "Veronique."

She descended to the bottom of the stairs and dropped her head, bowing deeply. "Your majesty," she said, a small smile flitting across her face. "Perhaps we may discover what brings you so late and so desperate this evening?"

King Philip shot a suspicious glance at Antoine.

Veronique smiled. "In my chambers," she said.

Then she turned and led the way back up the stairs. Philip followed, marveling for perhaps the thousandth time at the audacity of this extraordinary woman. He had ordered execution for less offensive behavior. But such a thing would not even occur to him where Veronique was concerned. He loved her. How could he not? She exuded a vibrant sensuality that seemed to overwhelm any effort at rational thought on his part. He was hardly a young man, but her mere presence was enough to rouse within him the most outrageous thoughts.

And she fulfilled each one.

More than that, however, Veronique was a brilliant woman. She understood the mandate that the Lord had set out for Philip and had several times suggested a course of action that aided in its advancement. Veronique understood the matters of state and church which consumed him, and, ridiculous as it would have seemed to him had anyone suggested such an idea years before, she had become not merely his lover and confidante but his most trusted adviser.

Philip followed Veronique into her chambers, watching the way the peignoir slid over her silken flesh. When he entered her bedchamber and almost unconsciously closed the door behind him, it was the first time he had not been completely consumed by his guilt in days.

"Oh, my darling . . ." he whispered as he went to her and buried his face in the honey silk cascade of her hair. Just the aroma of her was enough to transport him to some exotic elsewhere, the barest glimpse of heaven itself.

That was the truth he had come to understand over time. Veronique was a gift to him from God Himself, to aid him and offer succor in these most trying of times.

"Yes, majesty, I am here," she whispered in return. "But you did not ride out this chill eve merely for the pleasures of my company. Tell me, Philip, what disturbs you so?"

The king released her and turned to face the door, eyes downcast.

"I don't know if I can do it, my love," Philip said earnestly. "Jacques de Molay is godfather to my son. Come morning, he will act as pallbearer at the funeral of my sister-in-law. He gave me sanctuary in the Temple last summer when the people of Paris sought my head, understanding, as do you, that what I do I only do for them, and for God."

Beyond that, Philip could not speak. Veronique knew his heart better than anyone. He merely stood there, watching the flickering shadows thrown onto the wall by the candlelight. Then he felt her gentle touch on his shoulder, and she reached around him and unfastened his cloak. She draped it across her bed covers, then turned Philip to face her.

Veronique looked angry. Philip at first lifted his chin in defiance of that anger, prepared to deride her for her arrogance. But then he blinked and glanced away once more, for he knew it was well deserved.

"You are the king of France," she reminded him. Once more, he stood tall. "You are the chosen of the Lord. One day, you will be *Bellator Rex*, you will be nothing less than God's tool on Earth, emperor of an entire world suffused with the peace of the Lord."

"Yes," he replied, nodding. It was his destiny. He had known it since his coronation more than twenty years before.

"But your kingdom is failing. It is poor. The people have perpetuated an economy that cannot hold together," Veronique reminded him. "Everything you do, you do for them, to heal the wounds that they have made. Perhaps some have suffered—"

"Many have suffered," the king interrupted.

"And so they deserve to suffer. A less patient, less noble, less faithful king might have put such unfaithful subjects under a much more punitive rule. But you are not such a leader, my love. You are Philip the Fair."

Nothing that Veronique said came as a surprise to Philip. Yet there was simply something in the way she said it that gave him comfort. There were times—and he had admitted this only to her, not even to his confessor—that he began to lose faith in his destiny, and in his subjects. Veronique restored that faith, time and again.

The treasury of France was stronger than it had been in many years, but still it suffered. He had begun to rebuild it years earlier, of his own accord. Though it enraged many, Philip had imposed tithes on the church and banned the export of gold from the country. Keeping the gold and silver of France *in* France, that was a start. Then, from his wealthier subjects, he had appropriated serving plates and vessels made of fine metals, paying a mere fraction of their true value, in order to melt them down and make more coins for the realm. For the coffers.

Time and again, over the years, he had purposely devalued the currency of France. The subjects of his kingdom despised him for it, but France remained a powerful force in Europe, and his dream of Christian empire remained alive. If not for Philip, France might have collapsed into anarchy and ruin long ago.

In July 1306, thanks mainly to Veronique's wisdom, Philip had executed his greatest plan thus far. He ordered all of the Jews in France arrested and expelled from the kingdom. Their money and holdings were seized by the royal exchequer. It had been a triumph for the church in France, but more so, it had been an enormous boon to the treasury.

And now Veronique had fashioned an even greater and more audacious plan. One that would put a great deal of gold into the hands of the king, far more even than the expulsion of the Jews. Philip and Veronique had conspired to crush the Order of the Knights Templar.

Those warrior monks were extraordinarily powerful. They answered only to the pope himself. But now that the Holy Land had fallen to the Saracens and the Templars had failed, their power was diminished slightly. Their power, yes, but not their wealth and influence. In France, they numbered perhaps two thousand very rich men.

Indeed, they had been Philip's allies many times in the past. But he had always suspected something was rotten at the core of the order. And Veronique had confirmed it. She had a cousin, she had told him, who had been inducted into the order, only to seek refuge in a Franciscan monastery when he discovered the true nature of the Templars.

Difficult as it was for Philip to believe it, the entire order, including his friend Jacques de Molay, were worshipers of Satan. The rituals Veronique described to him were hideous. Long had whispers gone throughout Europe about the Templars and their ceremonies, which were held behind closed doors and covered windows. Now Philip understood their secrecy.

But still . . .

"I cannot help but feel as though I betray Jacques, who has been like a brother to me," Philip said helplessly.

Veronique caressed his face. "Who is the betrayer, your majesty?" she asked bluntly. "He has given himself over to the darkness, under the guise of a servant of the church. It is not merely your right to destroy him and all the Templars, but your duty."

"Pope Clement will be most agitated that I did not consult him," Philip said thoughtfully.

"The pope might warn the Templars by bringing the question into the open. Better to take them by surprise than give them the opportunity to bury their sins deeply. His Holiness does not know how close to his heart sleeps the serpent of the Garden."

Philip turned to look deeply into Veronique's eyes. She understood so well, and she did not have the weakness of affection in this instance. He realized that he was not being objective, and it hardened him to recognize this frailty.

"You are right," he said at last. "I knew it. I only needed to see my certain course reflected back upon me. The Templars shall be taken, and they will confess to their insidious evils, no matter what means must be employed to elicit such confessions. Then His Holiness will have no choice but to accept the charges against the order."

Veronique smiled and kissed him softly on the lips. She pulled Philip to her, and he felt her softness pressing against the bulk of his clothing. He thought he might crush her, though he knew such a thing would be impossible with a woman so formidable.

"And, of course, the Knights Templar are very wealthy," she said happily. "With their riches in your hands, you will be that much closer to the peaceful empire that is your fate."

"Yes," Philip whispered into the soft curve of her neck. But he was no longer responding to her words. "Yes."

The peignoir slipped from her shoulders and floated to the floor. Veronique led him toward her bed.

The fate of the Templars had been sealed.

After she'd crawled out of bed and into the shower, then stumbled out and dried herself off, Buffy had stared forlornly into the mirror above the sink, and fretted over the black bags under her eyes. She didn't remember ever looking so tired and haggard.

Try as she might, she couldn't remember ever wanting to climb back into bed quite so badly. Her worry for her mother crowded nearly everything else out of her head. And yet, after last night's run-in with vampy little Pepper Roback, she knew she had to go to school, if only to see Giles. Plus, somewhere in the back of her mind, she seemed to remember something about a math test.

She couldn't even get up the energy to worry about it.

After she'd dressed, Buffy called her mother at the hospital. Joyce told her she had to stay at least another day for observation. She sounded a little less dazed this morning than she had the night before, and Buffy was somewhat reassured. She promised to visit after school, no matter what other fun and funky reindeer games Giles had planned.

"Oh, honey, I know you have responsibilities. I'm fine, really," Joyce insisted. "I'll call you as soon as I know anything."

"You can tell me when I see you," Buffy said flatly. "I'll be there right after school."

There was a pause on the other end. "Well," Joyce said at length, "I know better than to argue with my daughter when she's determined. I'll see you later."

Buffy smiled. She thought she heard relief in her mother's voice. Joyce needed her but didn't want to say it. Which was fine. Buffy had a lot of people in her life with that particular reticent quality.

"I love you, Mom," she said.

"Love you, too, honey," Joyce replied.

After Buffy hung up, she felt a little better. She was still afraid of what the day would bring, what news they might get about her mother's condition. But they were in it together. Whatever happened, she was going to be at her mother's side. And she felt better just having a plan for the day. School, brain dump with Giles, then off to the hospital.

For as much as Buffy operated on her own, under her own terms, she honestly didn't know what she would do without her mother in her life. In fact, she wasn't even going to allow herself to think about it. She wasn't a fool. She knew that death came for everyone eventually. But now wasn't the time for her mother. Joyce was much too young.

Buffy needed her too much.

It wasn't until she was going out the front door for school, bag over her shoulder, that all the positive-thinking fantasies she'd been running through her mind simply collapsed in upon themselves. Her brief talk with Dr. Coleman the night before had been fruitless. She was a specialist, but even she didn't have any idea what was wrong with Buffy's mother. Dr. Coleman had said it was just too early to tell.

All the strength went out of her, and for fully two minutes, Buffy simply stood there in the doorway, leaning against the frame for support.

"Please, no," she whispered to herself. "Give me something I can fight. Something I can protect her against."

When she pushed through the swinging doors into the library, Buffy was a bit surprised to find everyone still there, even Cordelia. The bell had rung for first period to begin, but everyone was just sort of sitting around, chatting or lost in their own little world.

"Hey," she said softly.

"Well, look who rolled out of bed just in time to grace us with her presence," Cordelia said, raising an eyebrow. "And I do mean rolled out of bed. Did you sleep in that outfit?"

Before she could stop herself, Buffy actually looked down to see what she was wearing. Her brain wasn't functioning completely, so she'd actually forgotten. Still, the outfit looked fine to her.

"Buffy, are you all right?" Willow asked.

That's my witchy woman, always the perceptive one, Buffy thought.

She was about to respond when Giles emerged from his office, looking at her expectantly.

"Ah, good, you're here," he said. "A great deal is happening at one time, and I thought it best if we were all here to discuss it. There are mysteries upon mysteries here, and we've had no luck at all in unraveling them."

Buffy just sort of looked at him.

Giles paused to glance back in concern. "Buffy?"

"Sorry," she said, shaking it off. "Long night."

"Yes, well, it seems we all had rather long nights. I only hope yours aren't quite as colorful as the others' was."

Finally, Buffy felt as though she was coming out of the brain fog her fear for her mother had formed around her. She looked at her friends, sitting around the table when they ought to be in class. Waiting for her. Save for Cordelia, they looked at her with concerned expressions. Oz tapped his knee with a pencil. Xander held a book—one of Giles's dusty leather volumes—open on his lap, but he was looking up at her rather than at its pages. Willow was the most concerned of all.

"Sorry, guys," she said. "I'm a little out of it. We can deal with that later, though. Are all of you okay?"

"Other than scarred for life—" Cordelia began.

"We're fine." Willow cut her off.

"If you don't count the whole trapped-for-hours-with-a-bunch-of-corpses thing," Xander added amiably. "And, hey, what's a little abject terror among friends, right?"

"Always been my motto," Oz put in. "Right after 'Fools rush in.' "

"But you're not alone in foolishness," Willow assured him, and the two of them looked at each other with such adoration that it should have been nauseating but was actually rather sweet.

"Sorry, but huh? Let's all pretend my brain was hit by a semi, and it's limping, dragging several bloody limbs, from the accident scene," Buffy suggested.

Giles stared at her oddly. "Are you sure you're all right?" he asked gravely.

"Never said I was all right. Can we move on?"

"Please, I'm for that," Cordelia said snappishly. "Here's the sitch. We cruised the deadfill for grave robbers, and we found some. They were vampires."

"Whoa," Buffy said.

"With you on the 'whoa,' " Xander said, nodding.

"We hid in a crypt and got trapped in there," Cordelia continued. "Willow engaged in some illicit communication with dead people and then magicked us out. Can I go to class now?"

Buffy frowned and looked at Willow.

"Okay, Cordelia Translation Program?" she asked.

"Pretty much accurate," Willow replied, looking uncomfortable. "Well, except, y'know, the illicit part. I owe them a favor, though. The dead people. And we got some help from the ghost of Lucy Hanover."

"The Slayer?" Buffy asked, incredulously.

Willow explained the circumstances of their meeting with the ghost, and Buffy listened in amazement.

"Cool," she said when Willow had finished. "Nice to know there's somebody else on our side out there. Even if she's already dead. But why do I get the feeling there's more?"

"Good that you retain some optimism," Oz complimented her.

"Gee, thanks."

"Yes, well, there is more," Giles said reluctantly. "A great deal more, I should think. Further investigation into the phenomenon of Lucy Hanover's presence will have to wait until this crisis has passed. We still don't know why the vampires would want to take these corpses. Certainly, it isn't to fulfill their hunger."

"Possible they have other needs," Xander suggested.

Even Oz shot him a revolted look.

"I should know better by this time," Giles sighed, and looked at Xander. "But would it be at all possible for you to contain your outbursts for five minutes?"

Xander looked thoughtful. "It'd be an experiment."

Giles shook his head. "In any case, we need to discover what becomes of these bodies after they've been stolen. I'm certain the vampires are up to something. And it isn't merely this that concerns me. It also appears that they are marshaling their forces."

Buffy blinked. "They're what?" she asked. "Preparing for war?"

"Not necessarily," Giles replied. "But certainly preparing for something. I remained here in the library quite late last night and did a bit of research using the computer."

Now it was Giles's turn to be the center of attention.

"And he's really come through it well," Willow said. "No bruises or lacerations or any signs of hemorrhage."

Giles shot her a withering look, and Willow shrugged sheepishly.

"Willow took a look at my findings this morning and then infiltrated the newspaper and police computer systems."

"You can just say hacked," Xander told him.

"Do you ever use the computer for anything legal?" Cordelia asked, her tone as condescending as always.

"Not everyone can make their millions from setting up their own trampy Web site like you have, Cordy. It's a gift," Xander told her.

Cordelia scowled.

"I'm never going to finish with this," Giles huffed. "Perhaps you ought to all come back later, when the town has been decimated by the forces of evil."

They all fidgeted guiltily. Buffy went to the table and sat down.

"Enough, guys, come on. Giles, what's going on? Or what do you think is going on?" she said.

"Not only are the vampires stealing corpses, but there have been a number of live disappearances that we were unaware of, thanks to the spin control exerted by the powers that be here in lovely Sunnydale. Pepper Roback is one of many to disappear and not leave a drained corpse behind. Which would indicate that these people are not being simply murdered for food but purposefully turned. Someone is making new vampires.

"A great many new vampires."

Buffy nodded, leaned back in her chair. "Yep," she said. "Pepper Roback."

Giles blinked. "Sorry?"

"Pepper's your girl. Angel and I met up with her last night."

"But she only disappeared a few days ago," Willow argued. "There's no way she could be behind all this."

"Maybe she's not behind it, but she's in it deep," Buffy said. "Gotta say, this one's got my head spinning. It was definitely Pepper. She matched the description we got perfectly. But she spoke to Angel in medieval French, and she fought as well as anyone I've gone up against, with the exception of maybe Angel. You don't learn to fight like that watching repeats of *Walker, Texas Ranger.*"

Giles looked troubled. "Did she say anything else? Give you any idea what she and the others are up to?"

"Not really. But it's pretty obvious she's got a serious crush-kill-destroy thing going with Slayers in general, and she made some comment about seeing Slayers die before."

"That's impossible," Giles sniffed.

"She also said her name isn't Pepper," Buffy offered, then shrugged.

Giles paused and looked at her thoughtfully. "Did she happen to mention what it is?"

Buffy thought about it. Then she brightened. "I'm thinking Betty, but I know that's not right."

"Not real fearsome, either, as vampire names go," Oz noted.

"Betty," Buffy repeated. "Betty and Veronica! It was Veronica," she said, then looked puzzled. "Or something."

"Veronique?" Giles suggested.

"Give the man a gold star and a blueberry scone!" Buffy said.

But Giles barely responded. He looked deeply troubled, which, in turn, had Buffy deeply troubled. Giles turned and went back into his office. They heard him rummaging around inside, and when he emerged once more, he held a slim book open in his hand.

"Giles?" Buffy asked. "Can we assume bell, ringing?"

"Hmm?" he said, then glanced up at her. "Oh, yes." His eyes went back to the book, and he flipped a couple more pages. Then his finger jabbed the page. "Here it is! 'Veronique is unique among all vampires. Destroy her time and again, and yet her malevolence remains. God preserve us and all Christian men, for she is the ultimate immortal.'"

"But that's not possible," Willow said. "Once a vampire is dusted, the demon soul inside it is destroyed. Right?"

They all looked to Giles.

"Well," he said, blinking and nodding his head slightly. "That is the generally accepted principle, yes. But to every rule there is an exception, yes? Apparently, even this one."

Giles squinted and looked more closely at the page. "There

seem to be a number of cross-references here to various times in history when this creature's existence has been documented. I remembered reading about her in my studies, but I always thought the scholars must be in error. If she does exist, she must truly be unique."

"Oh, she exists," Buffy said. "In fact, the way she was talking, I got the feeling I'd fought her before. I'm having a really hard time buying all this, but if you're right, and this thing exists, I'm betting she was the vamp I dusted at the cemetery the other night. You remember? Jackson Kirby's undead welcome wagon."

"Yes. Quite possible," Giles agreed. "Give me a moment, would you?" He began to read again.

Buffy barely noticed. Her mind was elsewhere. All she could think about was the conversation she'd had with Angel about dying, about mortality and immortality. Buffy was only human, a fragile, mortal creature. But despite their supposed immortality, vampires were in some ways even more fragile. She could destroy them as easily as, even more easily than, they could destroy her—if she ever let them get that close.

Veronique was something else entirely.

"I have a question," Cordelia said.

"I know we have to figure out what she's up to," Buffy said, ignoring her. "But even if we do, how do we stop Veronique if her malevolence remains, whatever that really means in real English?"

"That was my question." Cordelia sniffed grumpily.

"You all should get on to class," Giles said absently. "It appears I have my research cut out for me today. Shall we all reconvene here when the last bell has rung?"

Everyone agreed, but Buffy was silent. Giles looked at her.

"I can't make it," she said.

"Buffy, this is rather—"

"My mother's in the hospital," she told them, feeling her throat constrict, fighting the emotions welling up within her.

"I'm sorry," Giles said. "I'd no idea."

"Is she going to be all right?" Willow asked.

Buffy wanted to say something positive and confident. Instead, she looked away.

"I don't know."

Paris, October 13, 1307

In the small hours of the morning, not long before dawn, Veronique slept pleasantly upon the wide bed in her private chamber. Enfolded in her arms, draped in the gentle fabrics of her bedclothes, was the still, cold form of Collette, the beggar girl whom Antoine had brought her the night before. The girl had been quite filthy at first, but Veronique had doted upon her. Once she had been stripped of the rags she wore and bathed and perfumed, her hair lavishly brushed, she had proven quite a beauty.

Veronique had taken care with her, not a drop of blood had she allowed to drip onto the bedclothes. Now Collette lay perfectly still, perfectly hollow, waiting to be filled with life once more. And soon enough, she would be, and Veronique would cultivate the girl as though she were a flower.

Rather than a vampire.

From below, there came a raucous crash and the sounds of men shouting. There followed a cry of profound agony, and Veronique's eyes snapped open. She sat up, slipping her arm from beneath the dead girl's head, and drew a robe about herself.

Veronique heard the pounding of boot heels upon her stairs and felt more curiosity than fear. There was very little that could frighten her, save perhaps the displeasure of her masters, the Triumvirate. So she stood with her arms crossed in front of her, angry at this intrusion but also looking forward to the violence she felt sure would follow.

She was not to be disappointed.

The door to her chamber was thrust open, to slam against the wall. There on the threshold stood a man whose face had become very familiar to her in the foregoing years: Jacques de

Molay, grand master of the Order of the Knights Templar. De Molay's forehead was cut above the right eye, and the wound bled down into the orbit, making for a grotesque countenance. His clothes were torn and dirty, and as she examined him, Veronique thought she saw a bloody wound in his abdomen through a tear in his clothing.

He'd been run through with a sword.

Veronique smiled pleasantly at the panting, bleeding man.

"Monsieur de Molay," she said. "To what do I owe the honor of this visit? If I had known you would be gracing me with your august presence today, I would have asked Antoine to prepare a meal for us to share."

De Molay sneered at her. "Antoine? Your man, then? I don't think he'll be able to serve you any longer."

"Yes, well, there are always more willing to serve, are there not?" Veronique said, and now she allowed her disdain, her hate, and her glee at his condition to show through. "You look as though you've had a bit of trouble. Might I be of any help?"

To his credit, de Molay was through talking. He reached down to his scabbard, wincing at the pain from the wound in his gut, and drew his sword. His eyes moved from Veronique to the pale, naked form of Collette, which lay so still upon the sheets.

"Monster," the Templar hissed, and he lunged for Veronique with his blade flashing.

She leaped to one side, but the point caught her side nevertheless. Blood seeped out from the small wound like tears, staining the robe instantly.

"Do you think I don't know what you are?" de Molay demanded, and he brought his blade to bear again.

Veronique knocked the sword aside with her arm, felt it carve the flesh to the bone, but ignored the pain. She grabbed de Molay around the throat with both hands, and her face changed, became gloriously hideous, yellow eyes glowing in the semidark of the heavily draped room, lips drawn back to reveal gleaming fangs.

As she choked the man, she whispered to him.

"I don't think you have any idea what I am." She sneered. "For eleven years, I have tried to use this city as my home, tried to create an environment suitable for the arrival of those I serve. I have spread the seed of my blood throughout the city, hoping that when the stars were properly aligned, I would be prepared. Time and again, you have thwarted me. You have crushed my offspring, you and your self-righteous knights, those foolish warrior monks who continue to believe in their own place in the hierarchy of religious power, when any idiot can see it has long since disappeared.

"But you have thwarted me for the last time, dear Jacques. For now the Templars are no more. Philip is my puppet. You are alone, and soon you will serve the very horror, the very darkness you have feared and battled against for so long."

"Never!" de Molay croaked, eyes beginning to roll back in his skull.

"Oh, no," Veronique whispered. "I won't let you die yet."

She threw him at the wall. His head slammed hard against it, and de Molay flopped to the ground, disoriented. His sword clattered down beside him. She was about to go to him, to drain him, to turn him. It would have been the ultimate humiliation for him, and thus the ultimate victory for Veronique. But then she heard the shouts from downstairs, and the saber rattling of knights who had come in pursuit of the very man she had just thrashed.

Veronique cursed softly and thought quickly. More swiftly than any mortal could have moved, she went to the bed and drew the bedclothes from Collette. She lifted the dead girl and ran toward de Molay, dropping the girl to the floor by his feet, even as the Templar began to rise again, reaching for his sword.

De Molay looked up at her with hatred burning in his eyes, this righteous, pious soldier of the Lord. And Veronique screamed.

Seconds later, three soldiers tramped through the door. Veronique swooned, leaning against the posts of her bed, her robe hanging open to reveal her nakedness, to draw their eyes not merely to her unclothed form but to the bleeding wound in her side.

Instantly, the three turned their swords on de Molay. One of them stood atop his blade so that he could not lift it.

"Madame—" one of them began.

"He is a devil!" she cried, staring fearfully at de Molay, ignoring the soldiers. "He burst in, killed my man downstairs, and then began to babble in some tongue I did not recognize. Not a minute ago, my cousin, sweet Collette, was standing by my side, cowering in fear as did I. He merely pointed to her, and she fell to the floor just as you see her! What manner of demon is this? What horrible magick? Is she dead?"

"Demon!" de Molay shrieked. "You fools, it is this creature, not me, who is allied with the darkness! She's the queen *vampire*. Look about this room. Do you not see the heavy drapery? See how the sun will burn her, and then we shall discuss these accusations about the Templars!"

Veronique looked pained and clutched her wound. As the soldiers looked at her with suspicion, she pretended only now to notice her near-nakedness and pulled her robe around her, glancing away in shame. Her eyes went to the dead girl on the floor, and she whispered her name.

"Collette."

The soldiers looked at de Molay with pure hatred and malice.

"Get up, monsieur," said the knight who stood upon de Molay's sword. "The word has come down from the king himself that you and your brothers are to pay for your idolatry. I have a family. If it were not for his orders, I would cut off your head for the horror you Templars have committed, the blasphemy! Demons cannot speak the truth, save under the pain of death.

"Rise, now, and come with us, or die there on the floor like the animal that you are," he said gruffly. "This lady has suffered your evil enough."

De Molay rose slowly. The soldier turned to another and gestured toward Collette's corpse. "See to the girl."

The other nodded and knelt beside the dead girl to examine her. Even as he did so, de Molay lunged forward. In that moment, the soldiers made a single error. A terrible mistake. They assumed that de Molay was going to attack them, to try to make good his escape, so they stepped back and held up their swords, prepared to defend themselves.

De Molay dove between them, then leaped up, powered by rage and perhaps even madness now. His wounds seemed to bother him not at all. With the swords of the soldiers close behind him, he lunged at Veronique.

She hesitated. It would not do for these soldiers to see her true face.

And in that moment of hesitation, he had her. The Templar's weight and momentum caught her off guard, threw her off balance, and then he was carrying her backward, completely out of control.

"No!" she shrieked.

"Oh, yes," de Molay grunted.

Then they were crashing through the windows, curtains tearing away, glass shattering. Dawn had come, and the sun shone warmly down upon Paris. Together, the master of the Templars and the creature who had engineered their destruction fell from the window to land hard on the road below.

Veronique roared in pain and fury as she burst into flames.

De Molay lay, broken and bleeding, on the road. But his eyes were clear and sharp, and he smiled at the sight of her agony.

"You may have destroyed the order," de Molay choked, blood bubbling from the corners of his mouth. "But we are yet victorious. Your evil is . . . expunged . . ."

His eyes went wide, his chest heaving, and more blood spilled down his chin.

Her skin blackening, hair engulfed in flames, burning down to her scalp, Veronique found the strength to stumble toward him.

"Your death is meaningless, mortal," she rasped. "Oblivion has come to claim you. All that you worked for is through. But I will be back. I shall return again and again, until I have fulfilled my masters' purpose. Until I have drunk the blood of the last man on Earth. Nothing can truly destroy me."

Then she began to laugh, as the roaring blaze withered her flesh and her eyes burst in their sockets.

At last, Veronique exploded in a cloud of fiery ash.

When the soldiers came to drag the broken and bleeding Jacques de Molay off to prison, he was weeping.

Within the condemned police station, Veronique stood just inside the nesting room and watched as the demon hatchlings ate. The sight suffused her with pleasure. But there was another feeling that lingered beneath the surface of her mind.

Frustration. Even despair.

In spite of her impending triumph, Veronique could not forgive herself the centuries that had passed while she attempted to fulfill her masters' plan. Certainly, she knew that it was not solely her fault. Many hundreds of years had passed before it even occurred to her to wonder if, perhaps, there was a way to achieve their desired ends other than the one known to the Triumvirate. As many times as she had tried the ritual as they outlined it and failed, she had begun to realize that it was not she who was at fault, really, but the ritual itself.

The Three-Who-Are-One could not be brought into the mortal world in their pure form.

Once she had realized this, it was merely a matter of trying to find another way to go about it. Finally, after several more centuries, she had happened upon a ritual that might be altered to fit her needs, to split the Triumvirate and have them hatched anew upon the Earth, where they might later be reunited to bring horror to the world, to the mutual benefit of the Triumvirate itself and the race of vampires.

Veronique's masters had been very pleased with her when she discovered that truth.

Which was, perhaps, part of the reason they had been so very enraged after her first attempt at performing the hatchling birth ritual had failed in Venice. And all thanks to that damned Slayer, Angela Martignetti, and Veronique's own overconfidence.

Slayer, she thought, the word like a brand upon her cold, dead heart. Now here was another of the accursed trollops, preparing to interfere once again.

Not this time, Veronique thought. For the Slayer was but a girl, a child. And now Veronique was prepared. The centuries had made her clever. *The shadow of the demon beast, the Triumvirate, will darken the streets of this place before the Slayer even realizes that it has come. And as the shadow falls, so are the souls of the humans in this little town damned for eternity.*

Even now, it was almost too late for the girl to prevent what was to come. Veronique was not satisfied with *almost*, however. They would stay well clear of the girl, and when the time came, they would kill her. For the moment, she had far more important matters to attend to.

"Catherine!" she snapped.

Even as she did so, the vampire was there. Veronique looked at her and smiled. This one had seemed almost soft at first, but she felt that Catherine would grow to become very powerful. Veronique was proud.

"They are growing, Harbinger," Catherine said, staring into the nesting room at the three demon hatchlings that writhed in the bloodstained remains of their most recent feeding.

When they moved, almost slithering as they'd yet to be able to walk, the bones of their many meals rattled beneath them.

"Yes," Veronique replied. "Aren't they beautiful? They must be fed again in four hours. I leave it to you to remember."

"As you wish, mistress," Catherine said, eyes downcast.

"Good girl," Veronique replied, and smiled thinly. *Oh, yes*, she thought. *I like this one very much.* "Now, gather the others and bring them here."

Several of her offspring were still sleeping, but Veronique

knew that Catherine would rouse them. Very shortly, they gathered in the foyer of the building, waiting for her to address them. Veronique stared longingly into the nesting room, still filled with awe at what she saw there: the Triumvirate incarnate. They might be merely hatchlings now, almost mindless because they could not properly function until they were reunited, but still they were sublime.

"Harbinger," Konstantin said quietly. "You wanted us?"

Veronique turned and frowned at him. "I favor you, Konstantin," she said curtly. "But that favor buys you no quarter from me. Impatience is not a quality I would cultivate, were I you."

The vampire dropped his gaze. "Yes, mistress. My apologies."

She glared at him a moment longer. Veronique had chosen Konstantin to be at her right hand, but she was beginning to wonder if that had been an error. Time, she supposed, would tell. Finally, she let her gaze drift over the others gathered before her. There were six, all told. One a newborn just this evening. But that was not nearly enough, and time was wasting.

"There must be thirteen of you when the stars align, thirteen of my blood children," she told them. "Thanks to this Slayer, your numbers have not been growing quickly enough. It is dusk now. This very night, we will remedy this situation.

"Each of you must feed this night. Feed, and, more importantly, you must turn a mortal. As I have sired you, so you will sire them, and they will also be my offspring, as the ritual requires. If you should see the Slayer, avoid her at all costs. Do not let her take you or your chosen. If you must fight her, then you must kill her."

Veronique turned to look back into the nesting room, heard the slither of scales and the clacking of bones.

"By dawn, I will have my thirteen. Then, all we need do is wait for the stars and portents to fall into place.

"And the gutters of this horrid little town will run with blood."

Chapter Seven

Just before the end of last period, Buffy received a note asking her to come to the vice principal's office. She was dizzy with apprehension as she wove down the corridor, hall pass in hand, not able to put into cogent thought the fear that was eating her up inside: *Mom is . . . Mom . . .*

She's fine, she insisted to herself as she waited for the vice principal in a chair beside the attendance desk. *They got me out of class to tell me that she's just ducky.*

Vice Principal Anderson was a well-meaning person. Rather nice, actually. Too nice to survive the regime of Principal Snyder. Buffy and Xander had a bet that she wouldn't last more than two semesters in Sunnydale. *She'll be begging to get transferred to a prison school.* "You, one more tardy, and it's the Big House for you—"

"Your mother called. She wanted us to know what's going on, in case you have some kind of emergency."

When Buffy said nothing, the woman pressed on. "You know we're here to support you if you need anything. The district provides a number of services—"

"We're fine," Buffy snapped. She couldn't help her angry tone. She had read somewhere that firefighters have problems with stress because they never know when the alarm will go off in the fire station. Maybe, say, they're watching a movie, or fast asleep, or talking to their kids on the phone, and the siren blares so loudly they all take to wearing ear plugs. It wears on them after a while. It makes them jumpy.

Huh. All they have to do is put on their little yellow outfits and slide down a pole with their buds, Buffy thought. *Then they go put out a fire.*

Me, I never know when something's going to jump out at me. Or at Willow, or any of them. Sometimes I walk around like I'm on a mine field. And I'm still supposed to study, and I'm still supposed to handle it like a champ when something's wrong with my family.

It wasn't self-pity; it was more a realization. So she didn't smile and thank the vice principal for her concern.

Instead, she walked straight out of the woman's office—cutting the rest of class—and ran to the hospital as fast as she could. As she was the Slayer, she could run very, very fast.

Sweat beaded on her forehead and chest by the time she burst through the door to Room 401. The curtain was drawn across the room.

"Mom?" she called, shouting, not meaning to. She lowered her voice. "Mom?"

There was a lot of coughing, followed by, "Hi, honey. Come on in."

Buffy was flooded with relief. *Okay, she's fine,* she told herself, tensing nevertheless as she drew the curtain back.

Her mother was sitting up in bed. An overhanging table had been pulled across her lap. On it sat a mauve plastic cup and a straw. There was more gray in her hair than Buffy could recall ever seeing, and she was pale and drawn. Her nose looked raw.

"Hey," Buffy said.

With a forced smile on her face, her mother picked up the plastic cup and took a sip. "Hi, honey," she answered. "How was school?"

"Schoolful. Filled with things of school." Buffy felt cold. She crossed her arms over her chest and realized that she was also a bit dizzy. Her throat constricted painfully.

Oh, no, she thought. *I'm getting sick, too. I can't get sick. I'm the Slayer. And I'm her daughter.*

I have to take care of her.

Her mother didn't seem to hear her. She coughed and sniffled, cleared her throat, and patted the bed.

"Sit down, Buffy."

Slowly, Buffy sat by her mother's feet. Her body was tingling. Her face was hot.

"I had an X ray this morning. It showed a mass on my lung," Joyce said carefully.

Buffy tried to be strong, tried not to react. Willow had prepared her to expect exactly this, but the reality of it was something she could never have prepared herself for. *A mass. What the hell is that?* There was a word forming in the back of her mind, but she didn't want to find it there, didn't want to speak it, or even think it.

The word was *tumor.*

Taking a breath, Buffy nodded. "So now what?"

"Tonight I'm going to have a CAT scan. They'll be able to tell a lot more after that."

"A lot more about what?"

Joyce's smile was filled with concern. "Why I'm sick."

Buffy tried to say something. She couldn't. She wasn't certain she was breathing.

"Dr. Coleman's an oncology specialist," Joyce continued. "That means she's a—"

"I know what oncology is," Buffy cut in. Her voice was shrill and petulant, sounding like the only child she was, someone used to stamping her foot and throwing tantrums to get what she wanted.

In this case, her mom.

Joyce reached along the hospital bed railing and took Buffy's hand. "I know you're frightened, honey. I am, too." She laughed shortly. "I guess that's fairly obvious."

"Mom," Buffy said uncomfortably. "I . . . this is about you. I'm okay."

Joyce cocked her head. "I spoke to Mr. Giles today." She briefly closed her eyes, then opened them. "He didn't go into details, but I know you're up against something big. I don't want to be a burden on you. I know you're fighting a bigger fight."

Buffy's eyes welled. "It's a different fight. Not a bigger one." *There can be no bigger one.* "Why do they think you have . . . ?"

"Cancer?" Joyce said bluntly. Buffy bit her lower lip and stared down at her mother's hand. "If you can name the monster, you can fight him."

Buffy was ashamed. *My mom is so much braver than I have ever been.*

"Oh, Buffy," Joyce said. "Don't be frightened. It's going to be all right."

Buffy's shame grew as the tears slid down her face. She buried her face in her mother's shoulder to hide that she was crying. She opened her mouth to murmur words of comfort, to tell her mother that she was fine, but she couldn't get a single word out. Her throat was so tight she had trouble taking a breath. She silently nodded.

They remained that way, mother and daughter, for a very long time.

In the condemned police station, the hatchlings were devouring the dead much more quickly than Veronique had anticipated. She was both alarmed and exhilarated. They were growing at an astonishing rate, and according to her understanding of their condition, the more mature they became, the harder it would become to unite them. There was a possibility that each aspect of the Three-Who-Are-One, having tasted life as an individual, would balk at submerging itself into the Triumvirate.

On the other hand, she must continue to provide them with carrion, or they would die. It was a delicate balancing act. Failure was not an option; these were her Masters, on Earth at last. Their lives were in her hands.

And so is my true immortality, she thought, clenching her hands as she waited for nightfall. *For this time, all is fragile. My hopes. Their survival.*

Her children were dozing, except for Konstantin, who, she realized, was watching her. *He's jealous. He wants what I have.* She didn't know if he truly understood that her immortality was a gift bestowed upon her, not something that was inherently hers by right. If he thought about it enough, it might occur to him to barter with the Triumvirate for the same gifts.

Or usurp my place. Get rid of me.

If necessary, she would destroy him first. He was valuable, but he was expendable. They all were. They had to believe, to know fully, that there was more to be gained in allying themselves with her than in turning against her, if Konstantin tried to betray her.

Maybe I should make him fall in love with me, she thought. *But oftentimes, lovers are the most ruthless betrayers of all.* She smiled, thinking of all the powerful men she had used and then destroyed. Down through the ages, she had exploited the power of the feminine life principle—power beyond measure—to bring herself to this momentous day.

She would not allow one male vampire to get the better of her now.

Ignoring Konstantin, she walked out of the room and into the corridor, the better to check the status of the sun. Oranges and fiery reds washed the wall at the end of the passageway. Sunset. How many more, until there were no human eyes to look upon them?

Someone came up behind her. *Konstantin.* She grinned to herself and said in Greek, "Put your arms around me, my dear one."

He touched her upper arm. She tensed slightly.

If he has a stake, I will have to use it on him. The thought saddened her greatly.

But all he brought his mistress was a kiss.

They were still locked in an embrace when twilight smothered the brilliance on the wall. Throughout the station, the vampires were stirring. As she had ordered, they would go out and sire new flesh of her flesh.

And they would gather old flesh, rotting and decayed flesh, as the hatchlings continued to cleanse the Earth of foulness.

In Weatherly Park, Catherine watched scattered children at play. It was dark, and indulgent parents, standing together on a square of concrete with some open bags of tortilla chips and jars of salsa, glanced over at the little ones now and then and made noises about going home for dinner.

A chubby little boy sat on a swing and frowned in concentration as he flung his legs straight out, then yanked them back in. Out, in. She was charmed. He was learning how to pump.

I'll take him, she thought, feeling her face change. *Veronique and I will raise him.*

Then she realized the foolishness of her impulse. They needed fighters, not offspring. Followers, not dependents. True children were a luxury for later, after their ends had been achieved.

Her face changed back to human form. She walked toward the boy, who smiled at her and cried, "I can swing!"

For a moment, she lingered, watching him. "So you can," she told him. "Good for you."

Reluctantly, she moved on. *I'll be back for you,* she silently promised.

Melting into the darkness, she glided more deeply into the park. She found a young man wearing a Crestwood College sweatshirt and a pair of earphones. He was carrying a couple of books.

He's lovely, she thought as she attacked him. He never heard her coming, never knew what was happening. But he fought. How he fought.

Delicious. She drained him completely. But not before she'd given him some of her own blood.

Some people are brilliant. Some can barely fend for themselves. Others need constant care, because demons rage inside them.

In that respect, the forces of Hell are very like the humans they seek to destroy.

The vampire lurched along, its demon brain half-formed. It had not fully understood what the leader wanted of it. Dazed and disoriented, it waited with the others for the brightness to go away, and then it had stumbled out of the building and wandered off alone. It went, partly out of instinct but mostly out of chance, to a nearby graveyard, stumbling in confusion over headstones and tree roots.

It was hungry.

That was all it knew.

The nurses brought an extra tray for Buffy at dinnertime. Buffy pushed bits of roast turkey around on her plate. She couldn't swallow anything, not even water. But she didn't want her mother to know that.

But years of motherhood clued Joyce in. When Buffy smiled briefly and said, "This was really good, for hospital food," Joyce rolled her eyes.

"I'll ask them to make you a sandwich for patrol," she offered.

Buffy sighed. "I'll just trade it for cookies."

Joyce sipped broth. "Well, then, I hope you stop somewhere."

"My first break, I'm Denny's-bound," Buffy promised.

A young woman in a pink scrub top and white drawstring pants took the tray away. Then she took Joyce's blood pressure and temperature. In a loud voice, she said, "Joyce, do you want something for the pain?"

Joyce looked caught as she murmured, "Yes." She shrugged and looked at Buffy. "My chest. It's a little sore."

She lifted her plastic cup. "May I have some more ice water?" she asked the woman. Buffy wanted to tell her not to lift anything, not even to move, but she knew how much her mother hated things like that. They both did. Summers women were strong women, and they didn't like to be patronized. Coddled on occasion, perhaps. Babied now and then, of course. But they didn't like to be reminded that they were not invincible.

My mom is the bravest woman on Earth, Buffy thought with a sudden rush of feeling. Pulling up roots when L.A and being a married woman were all she knew, getting the gallery gig, dealing with a kid who turns out to be kind of a freak. Bumps along the way, most certainly, but Joyce Summers had passed all the initiation tests. She was a full-fledged amazing person.

Joyce turned to her and said, "What? You're looking at me so oddly."

Buffy couldn't think of any words. Instead, she made a face and offered a small shrug.

"Honey, if you don't mind, I'd like to take a nap before the CAT scan. Why don't you go home?"

"But—" Buffy protested. She had planned on staying through the CAT scan.

"I'm so tired, sweetheart."

Buffy nodded, capitulating. "All right." She got up and kissed her mother's cheek. "Call me as soon as you can?"

"I will." Joyce smiled.

Buffy walked into the hall. She paused for a moment.

That was when her mother started sobbing. Buffy stopped herself from going to her. Listening to the fear, and maybe the pain, she knew, somehow, that this was not the time for comfort.

This was the time for naming the monster.

A strange voice drew me to the graveyard . . .

In seventh grade, Xander had gone through an intense teenage death song phase, and Willow, as his best friend, had suffered right along with him. Now, along with calculus equations, spells, incantations, the phone numbers of all her friends, and probably a hundred and fifty interesting factoids about wolves, she knew all the words to "Strange Things Happen in This World."

"Remind me again why this is a good idea tonight, when last night it turned out pretty darn bad," Xander said.

"Well, for one, we're better armed tonight," Willow said optimistically.

"Ready for vampire shenanigans," Oz agreed.

"Oh, sure, that's it," Xander said. "Those vampires and their shenanigans. I'm still rooting for a frothy cappuccino, myself. But if you guys want to hunt vampires—"

"Want to?" Cordelia asked, glaring at him. She threw up her hands, a cross in one and a stake in the other. "I don't even know why I'm here."

"Comic relief?" Xander suggested.

Cordelia glowered at him.

Everybody was armed—with holy water, stakes, and crucifixes. Xander had pleaded with Willow to ask Buffy to accompany them, but Willow had refused. Her best friend needed to be with her mother right now. They could pick up the slack when necessary. They'd done it before.

They walked on, around the crumbling headstones and weeping angels, crosses and stakes at the ready. The moon gleamed on the Hart family crypt, where the vamps had sort of imprisoned Willow and the others—*okay, technically, we imprisoned ourselves.* She reminded herself that she would have to come back soon, during the day, and fulfill her promise to them, to let them use her as a kind of window on the mortal world. The thought made her shiver.

As they passed the crypt, Willow heard something moving inside.

With a finger to her lips, she got the attention of the others and pointed at the crypt. Oz nodded. He'd heard something, too. Willow took a few deep breaths and murmured her favorite warding spell, just to be on the safe side.

"By the light and the heart of the Earth,
I forbid all evil spirits my bedstead and couch;
I forbid you my house and my home;
I forbid you my flesh and blood and body and soul.
I irrevocably forbid you entrance to my mind and my
*   thoughts;*
My fears and my strengths;

Until you have traveled over every single hill and vale;
Forged every stream and river;
Counted all the grains of sand on all the shores;
And every star in the sky.
I forbid you."

The door was still open, as they had left it the night before. Willow brought up her flashlight and clicked it on, its beam piercing the darkness of the crypt.

And the mindless newborn vampire, which had been shambling around inside the tomb, starving and desperate, lunged at them.

Buffy reached Angel's mansion and stood outside for a few moments, struggling to compose herself. Half the way there, she had started shaking so badly she couldn't walk. She simply slid to the ground and gasped for air, her throat aching with each labored breath.

She had no idea how long she lay there. The stars seemed to move crazily across the sky, but maybe that was just her. At any rate, she finally got up and got going. If she could just make it to Angel, she would find strength from being in his arms. For a few moments, she wouldn't be the Slayer, just Buffy, and she would bury her face against her boyfriend's chest, and maybe she would cry. Maybe he'd tell her everything was going to be all right.

Maybe she would believe him.

She walked to the door and pushed in. The Art Deco living room was bathed in diffuse light from the sconces on the walls. How many times had she come here? She had lost count. But tonight everything looked different to her. She felt almost as if she had never been here before.

"Angel?" she called softly. They were all supposed to meet at Shady Hill Cemetery later on, though her friends had decided to start patrol at dusk without her. But she had told Angel she'd try to come by first.

She called his name again. When there was no answer, she tiptoed deeper into the house. *Maybe he's still asleep.*

She walked into the hall. "Angel?"

On his bed, she found a note, in the handwriting she had once come to hate. After they had made love on her seventeenth birthday, he had lost his soul again. Fully taken over by the demon inside him, he had once more become Angelus, the One with the Angelic Face, one of the most hated and feared vampires of all time.

He had left sketches of Buffy on her pillow to taunt her. Of her mother. And of Jenny Calendar, the Gypsy spy sent to watch him and Buffy, who had fallen in love with Giles. Whom Giles had loved in return, despite her betrayal of the Slayer.

Angelus had murdered Jenny and left her in Giles's bed, luring him upstairs with a note Giles thought Jenny had written.

And now there was an envelope on Angel's pillow.

She shivered as she opened it.

> *Buffy,*
> *I figure you're spending some time with your mother, so I went out for a bit. I'll meet you at eight-thirty at Shady Hill with the others, as agreed.*
> *Love,*
> *Angel*

Her heart skipped a beat at the word *love.* She was embarrassed that it meant so much, at the way she stared at it like some dumb kid. But she did stare. And it meant the world to her.

Carefully, she folded the note and slipped it into the pocket of her sweatshirt. She sat down on the bed and placed her hands on the sheets. They were cool to the touch. It was chilly in the room.

He won't get old, she thought. *He won't get . . .*

She burst into tears, echoing her mother's heavy, heartbroken sobs. She gathered up his pillow and pushed her face into it, smelling him. *He won't get cancer.*

Alone in Angel's house, she wept as if her mother were gone. The pain was unbearable. It was too much for her to handle alone.

But she was glad he wasn't there. He was already hundreds of years old. All around him, people aged and died, and he remained untouched. He must have left this kind of grief behind a long time ago. *Rolling with the punches, while we plain old human beings go down for the count.*

Willow screamed as the drooling vampire reached for her. The others had their crosses up in an instant, and the vampire roared like the Frankenstein monster confronted with fire and backed away.

"You messed with the wrong girl, Chumley!" Willow cried, staking the slobbering creature. It exploded, and that was that.

Oz looked at her. She looked at Oz. "Okay, so my tough chick banter needs work."

"Hey."

They all turned.

Buffy stood beside the tomb. She looked awful. Her eyes were huge and puffy and lost, like a Precious Moments figurine that had just lost its best Precious Moments friend.

"Oh, God, Buffy," Willow whispered, running to her.

"I'm okay," Buffy rasped.

But Willow held on tight.

The silver-haired woman waited for the driver to get out of the cab and hold the door open for her.

Those days are long gone, Angel thought, then smiled faintly when the cabbie, clearly irritated, stomped around to the passenger door beside the curb and yanked it open.

Like a queen, Leah Coleman climbed out, moving precisely, if not exactly slowly. Most elderly people took care. It was hard to heal broken bones this late in the game.

Except it's not a game. If it was, we'd all be having a lot more fun.

He thought back to the alley, and the young woman she had

been. So lovely. Despite her energy and drive, however, a much less confident woman than the one who now walked with caution—not fear—toward the front doors of the Sunnydale Suites Inn. That she was residing here indicated that her stay was too long for a regular hotel but not long enough to rent an apartment.

From what Angel had learned of her, that made sense. Since those days in the alley, she had gone on to medical school at Harvard and pursued postdoctoral oncology studies at several prestigious institutions, including the Mayo Clinic. She spent most of her time consulting with doctors and hospitals all over the world. Apparently, she had come to Sunnydale to discuss some new findings about gene therapy with the cancer staff.

Somebody at Sunnydale Hospital must have a lot of clout, to get her to come out here. Joyce Summers probably doesn't realize how lucky she is. She's got the best looking after her, and it's all just co-incidence.

Leah had never married. Her fiancé, Roger Giradot, had been killed in the Pacific during the war. But she had done a lot with her life. She had made a difference. Especially to Angel, though she probably didn't even know it.

Does that make the prospect of death any easier?

He had no idea. As he searched inside himself, he found that he had no concrete opinions about his own death. Had he lived so long it was simply an abstraction? How far apart from other people did that set him?

I am not a person, he reminded himself. *I'm a vampire.*

He had faced death many times. Time and again, he would have willingly sacrificed himself for Buffy. *Or Willow. Or any of them. Or is that just talk, because I truly can't imagine death anymore?*

If you die and come back, were you ever really dead?

Does it matter?

He watched silently as Leah pulled open the door to the Sunnydale Suites Inn and carefully crossed the transom.

Yes, he thought. *It matters a lot.*

Chapter Eight

"This sucks."

They stood on the minuscule rise that made up the "hill" part of Shady Hill Cemetery, and for a moment no one spoke. The Slayer and those closest to her. The ones who backed her play, time and time again. Who were always there for her, even if it wasn't for her, exactly. Like Cordelia, for instance. Buffy often marveled at Cordelia's willingness to fight the good fight. Whatever else they might say about her—most of it unkind but true—there was no denying that she just wasn't made the same way as other beautiful, shallow, popular, bitchy girls. There was a bit of steel in her, the courage to face what lurked in the shadows instead of turning away. Despite the massive inconvenience to her quest for social supremacy.

Then there was Oz. True, he was a werewolf and all. But he'd been willing to help out even before he was in love with Willow, even before he knew the score in Sunnydale was Evil, several million; Slayer, one.

Willow and Xander were another story. They just loved her. Buffy knew that, and it meant more to her than she could ever explain to them in her fractured version of English. They were always there to watch her back, to play cavalry when the evil was too much even for a Slayer to handle. This time, though, there just wasn't much they could do. There was nothing for them to help Buffy fight. It was a battle she had to wage on her own.

No. That's not even true. It's a battle Mom has to wage on her own. And I have to just stand by and watch and hate myself for not being able to do anything to help.

Buffy looked around at her friends and realized that maybe they were all in the same position after all.

"Man, this totally sucks," she said, even more gravely.

"Which part?" Oz asked.

"My thought, too," Xander said. "The vampires-and-grave-robbings-have-us-mightily-confused-and-we-have-to-find-this-immortal-vampire part, or the Mom's-not-healthy part, or the it's-ten-past-eight-and-Angel's-late-again part?"

"I've never been Optimist Girl, but you're depressing even me," Cordelia said.

Buffy smiled thinly, unsuccessfully. Her eyes met Willow's, and she realized her best friend had said nothing. They looked at each other a moment longer, and when Buffy spoke, it was Willow she was speaking to.

"She has a spot on her X ray," the Slayer whispered. "Some kind of mass. They don't know if it's . . . cancerous, so they're going to do a CAT scan."

Willow held Buffy's hand tightly, sharing her strength.

"Hey, Buffy," Xander said gently. "I know you're scared, but don't freak. People have tumors and turn out fine. My Uncle Roary's had two tumors removed from his lungs, and both have turned out to be harmless if disgusting growths. And the doctors aren't even sure if what he's got a little lower can even be *called* a liver anymore, but he's fit as a drunken fiddle."

Buffy rolled her eyes. "Thanks, Xand. That's a comfort. Truly."

Xander puffed up proudly. "Score," he said in a hush.

Shaking her head, Buffy looked at Cordelia, who would not meet her gaze. Buffy was stupefied. For once, Cordelia Chase had absolutely nothing to say. Or, more accurately, Buffy figured she had no idea what she *should* say.

"I'd like to suggest, dwelling, bad," Oz observed.

"Right," Buffy said, nodding. "Been doing way too much bad dwelling. Unhealthy stuff. As of now, we're moving on to that place where I internalize my anger and fear and sadness and express my feelings by kicking the crap out of anything that gets in my way."

Willow smiled. "That's my girl," she said gently.

"For starters," Buffy went on, "we're not waiting for Angel. If he doesn't find us here, he'll head for the library. Let's rendezvous with Giles and see if we can't figure out what our next move should be."

Nobody argued. They didn't dare.

Buffy pushed through the library doors a little past eight-thirty, with her friends in tow. Giles poked his head out of his office a moment later. She expected his let's-get-on-with-it face, but instead, he looked upset about something. For a moment, she was thinking demons. Then she recognized the sad look in his eyes and the way it was directed at her, and she knew.

"Ah, Buffy," he said, rather absently but in that way that proved he wasn't absent at all. "I'm glad you're all here. I presume your mother told you I spoke to her earlier . . ."

"She mentioned it," Buffy said. "But don't worry. I'm not gonna drop the ball."

"Yes, well, I just want you to know that whatever you need to do, whatever time you'd like to spend with her, the rest of us will persevere. Time with your mother should be your priority," he said.

Buffy frowned, staring at him a moment.

"What is it?" Giles asked.

"She's going to be fine, Giles," Buffy insisted. "I appreciate the thought, and I'll need to be with her some, but I'm on this stuff with Veronique and her annoying resurrection habits. My mom's going to be fine."

"Well, very good, then," Giles agreed, nodding. Then he looked directly at Buffy, eyes narrowed. "Be that as it may, you'll do as you must, as always. Whatever we can do to make that easier, you can rest assured it will be done."

Buffy looked away, a bit ashamed by her initial response. Giles was only trying to be kind, to reach a comforting hand out to her.

"Thank you," she said quietly. "I really do appreciate it. Now, though, I think we have more immediate things to worry about. Did you find anything useful?"

Giles had nodded and was lifting a book up from the study table when the doors swung open again and Angel stepped in. They all looked at him, and Buffy wondered if they were all thinking the same thing. It wasn't their mother who might have cancer, but they had to be super aware of Angel just the same. He was a vampire. Cancer would never claim him. He was immortal.

But even that was only to a point.

Veronique was a different story. If what they believed was correct, she was immortal in a much truer sense. It made her one of the most formidable enemies Buffy had ever faced. Buffy still had a very difficult time accepting it as reality. She was so used to just dusting vamps and being done with them that the idea of a vampire that was essentially invincible, unkillable . . . it simultaneously astonished her and disturbed her profoundly.

"Sorry I'm late," Angel said, speaking to them all but looking only at Buffy.

"It adds to your mystique," Willow told him.

"See," Xander said. "That's what I need. How do I get some mystique?"

"It's like credit," Cordelia sniped. "Can't get it if you don't have it."

"Back to square one, then," Xander said in surrender.

"You never left square one, so you can't go back to it," Cordelia reminded him.

"I know it's a great deal to ask of this group, but do you think we might have the smallest bit of decorum?" Giles asked.

"Night has long since fallen, and this particular pack of vampires seem to be quite a bit more industrious than their more dimwittedly hedonistic cousins."

He glanced at Angel. "No offense, of course."

"None taken."

Giles opened the book that he'd picked up from the table and bent his head slightly to glance over a few pages as he skimmed.

"Now, then," he mumbled, and continued to skim.

"This is riveting," Xander said. "Thank God for decorum."

Giles shot him a withering glance, then looked back down at the book and tapped his finger on the page.

"Here we are. 'As for the recovered pages from the journal of Peter Toscano, they seem to indicate that this Veronique received her own immortality—a kind of perpetual resurrection wherein she revives inside the next vampire born within a certain distance of the site of her previous destruction—from a demon referred to alternately as the Triumvirate or the Three-Who-Are-One. Veronique appears to prefer the female form but has also been known to inhabit male host bodies when necessary . . .' "

Buffy listened carefully. When Giles finished, she looked at him expectantly. When she realized there was nothing more, she sighed.

"I kinda hoped it would tell us how to shut her off," she said.

"After our patrol, I'll continue my research," Giles assured her.

"Who's Peter Toscano?" Willow asked.

"He was a Watcher, mid-nineteenth century," Angel explained. When Giles looked at him in surprise, he shrugged. "That was my prime. You think I didn't keep tabs on Slayer/Watcher doings? The Slayer at the time was the Martignetti girl, right? As I recall, though, Toscano disappeared."

Giles looked at him a moment longer. Then he nodded. "That's one way of saying it. Actually, he was burned to death in his home, along with most of his journals and, apparently, the rest of his library.

"In any case, I'll continue trying to find more information about Veronique and this Triumvirate. I've found no information as yet pertaining to precisely what sort of a demon it is, what kind of threat it represents, or what its agenda might be.

"For the moment, then, we must concentrate on Veronique. I presume her presence here serves it or them or what-have-you in some way. It seeeems possible we could stop her by trapping her somewhere far from any vampire activity," Giles suggested.

"Not forever enough for me," Buffy said. "But it's something to think about. Problem is, how do you catch her and keep her long enough to get her somewhere remote enough that there wouldn't be any vampire activity. I mean *ever.*"

"You could try someplace smelly and dirty, like Newark or Detroit," Cordelia suggested. "I doubt even vampires would hang out there."

"Okay, so what's the real plan?" Xander asked.

Giles cleared his throat slightly. "Though it would be helpful to know what Veronique and her followers are doing with the corpses they are retrieving, it would seem our first order of business is to try to prevent any more vampires from being born into her service."

"So, saving lives," Willow translated helpfully.

They all looked at Buffy.

"Weapon up," the Slayer said. "Then we split into teams, and we go hunting. If they're really going at this new membership drive as hard as they seem, we should be able to dust a few of them tonight."

"You make them sound like Jehovah's Witnesses," Oz observed.

"These guys are even heavier into recruitment," Buffy told him.

Then she paused. She looked around the room at her friends. At Giles. At Angel.

Angel. She'd needed him so desperately earlier, and he hadn't been there. Now, she wanted badly to talk to him, to tell him what was happening with her mother. To have him hold her and tell her it was going to be all right.

Even now, he looked at her with those soulful eyes, such love there, and Buffy wanted him to explain. To make the hurt and the fear go away.

But nobody could do that. And in some ways, Angel was probably the least qualified of all. He couldn't give her what she did need. And what he could give—a reminder that people were mortal and that her mother would die someday, even if not this time around; supportive, whispered, loving words that would ring all the more hollow because they came from lips already dead, from a soul that survived only inside a shell of evil—those things were not what Buffy needed now.

For a long moment, she looked at Angel, heart troubled with a conflict that was new to her. She loved him. But in that moment, part of her hated him as well. For being alive. For having gone on living while so many died around him.

She took a deep breath, then turned to Willow. "I'd like you to come with me."

Willow blinked, glanced at Oz, and then moved toward Buffy. "I'm your girl," she said. "Not in the girl sense, but in the on-the-team sense, that . . . maybe I could have a weapon and I'll be quiet now."

Buffy didn't smile. She really couldn't. Not then. Instead, she glanced over at the others.

"Guess I'll stick with Giles," Oz said reasonably.

Cordelia glared at Xander. "I am not wandering around dark places with Mr. Chicken."

"Fine," Buffy said gruffly. "You go with Giles and Oz."

Xander nodded happily. "Good, I don't want to be anywhere near our little scream queen. So that leaves me with . . ." Realization dawned on him, and he sighed and looked over at Angel. "Guess it's just you and me, Dead Boy."

Angel looked at Buffy. "This happens too often for my liking."

"Yeah. It's a conspiracy," Cordelia said happily. "You spend enough time with Xander, we're sort of hoping you'll be aggravated enough to kill him."

"Ha-freakin'-ha," Xander said blithely.

Angel turned to look at him, face deadpan. "I don't know. It could work."

They gathered in the darkness in front of Sunnydale High, each armed with the accoutrements of vampire hunting: cross, holy water, stakes, and the courage to stand against the undead. Giles had a crossbow, as did Xander. Willow whispered a little charm and spread her hands wide to include all of them.

"Maybe it's late to bring this up," Xander said, "but has anyone noticed all the people with transportation are in one group?"

Oz quickly went to Willow and handed her the keys to his van. Giles glanced at Cordelia, and the two stared at each other for a long moment. Cordelia was the first to look away.

"I hate riding in that corroded death trap you call a car," she said firmly.

"You'd rather have Oz and me as passengers in that cramped little sports thing you drive?" Giles asked, surprised.

"No," she sneered, and pointed at Xander and Angel. "But I'd rather that than have one of those two bozos drive *my* car."

Giles chuckled and tossed Angel the keys.

"This just keeps getting better," the vampire muttered. Then he turned to walk toward the parking lot. "Come on, Boy Wonder. Let's see if we can track down the Joker before he strikes again."

"That's not fair," Xander grumbled. "I was planning to make the Batmobile joke."

"Just losing your touch, Xand," Willow said sympathetically.

Then they were all heading to the three vehicles parked in the school lot. Oz climbed into the backseat of Cordelia's candy-apple-red sports coupe, and Giles dropped into the passenger seat with a look of terror on his face. Willow climbed into the van and started it up. Xander hopped into the passenger side of

Giles's car. Buffy and Angel stood together in the lot between the van and the Citroën.

"How's your mother?"

Buffy looked away. "She's got something on her lung."

Angel reached out to run a hand lightly along her arm. Buffy marveled at his silence. Somehow, he must have known. He must have understood what she was feeling.

But then, he always had.

"Thanks," she whispered, and stood on her toes to kiss him. "Be careful."

Angel smiled. "In *this* car?"

Giles, Oz, and Cordelia sat in her car in front of the Bronze, looking for anything out of the ordinary. Though he tried to maintain his focus, Giles found Cordelia's incessant nattering about shopping and fashion and her responsibility to less socially cogent teens to be quite a distraction. At length, he had to get out of the car, if only to clear his head. Oz followed quickly after.

Giles left his crossbow in the trunk. If they were going to be hanging around outside the Bronze, or venturing inside, he couldn't exactly carry it with him.

"Make sure you have your keys to hand, Cordelia," he said. "I don't want to have to search through your purse if we're under attack."

"Seems quiet," Oz noted.

They all looked at the Bronze. There was a bouncer at the door, and the low thrum of music could be heard from inside, but it was definitely not a standing-room-only night at the Bronze.

"You really think anyone's going to get grabbed right out front?" Cordelia asked.

"No," Giles said patiently. "Though I do expect some moronic teenager to wander off with the object of his or her affection and receive a very nasty surprise for their troubles."

"Pretty much par for the course, then," Oz muttered.

Neither Giles nor Cordelia responded to that, but the Watcher certainly understood it as a sad truth of youthful romance. Or romance in general, in some respects. Very rarely did people turn out to be precisely what you expected, or perhaps hoped, they would be. When it happened, though . . . sometimes that could lead to the nastiest surprises of all.

Giles knew that better than anyone.

The three of them stood in the shadows or leaned against Cordelia's car in front of the warehouse across from the Bronze for better than an hour. More than once, Giles found his eyes drooping, his head bowing, only to snap awake again. He had spent too many nights up till all hours doing research, and it was catching up with him now. Again. He could not help but think his time would be better spent getting the information they needed, perhaps precluding them from needing to make another all-out effort tomorrow night.

"Can we go home now?" Cordelia said a while later. "Standing around like this is bad for my posture."

They both looked at her quizzically.

"I slouch when I'm bored," she explained.

"All right," Giles said tiredly. "Another fifteen minutes, and we'll make a pass in the car through the dock area and around the Fish Tank, where Pepper Roback disappeared."

"I'll need to wear a hat and cover my license plate with mud," Cordelia said with resolve.

Giles didn't even want to ask.

"Hey," Oz said.

Over the past year, Giles had come to understand that just as the Eskimos had dozens of ways to say *snow*, a simple "Hey" from Oz could carry a greatly varied array of meanings. This one, very plainly, meant "Here comes what we've been waiting for, guys, have a look."

Giles narrowed his eyes and gazed at the two couples emerging from the front door of the Bronze. Immediately, he recognized the male in front. He was tall and wiry but muscular: one of the vampires who had been with Veronique that first night in the cemetery.

"Follow them," Giles said, his voice low.

Quietly, Cordelia, Oz, and Giles slipped around the car. As the vampires whispered sweet words into the ears of their intended victims and led them along the street in the general direction of the cemetery several blocks away, Giles flashed back to the first time he'd been to the Bronze. That night, Buffy had saved Willow and Xander from a fate almost identical to the one these girls were surely headed for.

"Not tonight," he whispered.

The vampires, however, had no intention of going as far as the cemetery. As they passed a dark, open alley, one all too familiar to the Watcher and the others from past conflicts, the two male vampires attempted to herd the girls into the darkness. One of them seemed to be going along willingly enough, but the other balked. Instantly, the vampires gave up their charade. Their faces changed, fangs protruding, and they clapped their hands simultaneously over the girls' mouths and began to drag them, kicking, into the alley.

"Move," Giles spat.

They ran as one. Cordelia's great show of reluctance was gone completely, and she kept pace with Giles and Oz as the three of them burst into the alley. The vampires had pressed their intended victims against opposite walls of the alley. As Giles pounded into the alley, one of them, a stout bulldog of a creature, saw him and snarled.

"What the hell—"

But that was all he managed before Giles shouldered the girl aside and slammed the vampire against the wall with all his weight behind him. The girl screamed and ran from the alley, nearly knocking Cordelia down. By then, the bulldog had recovered and gave Giles a mighty shove that sent him sprawling in the garbage-strewn alley.

"Nobody likes a hero," snarled the stout vampire, and lunged for Giles.

"Not exactly true," Cordelia told him, and splashed holy water into his face.

He brought his hands up, shrieking in pain. Giles leaped to his feet, took out his cross, and drove it against the vampire's forehead. He slammed the creature against the wall and held it there with all his strength.

"Now, Cordelia!" he shouted.

She slammed the stake home, and the vampire erupted in a cloud of ash. Giles breathed a sigh of relief. But it didn't last long. They turned to aid Oz against the other, the one Giles had recognized.

Oz was bleeding.

The girl had run off, but Oz had twin scrapes on his throat from where the vampire must have tried to bite him before being shoved away, raking his fangs over the flesh. Oz was struggling to bring his stake into play, but the vampire was very strong and held his arm away, moving in once more with his fangs.

Giles brought his cross up and shoved it between Oz and the vampire. The creature hissed, turned, and hit Giles with a vicious backhand across the face. He staggered backward, but his interference had been enough to allow Oz time to recover. Now, he and Cordelia stood facing the vampire, moving on him with stakes.

"You just think you're something else, don't you?" Cordelia said dismissively to the vampire.

Who looked disconcerted for the moment. Then he grumbled something angrily under his breath, turned, and ran off.

"I'm intimidating," Cordelia announced.

"Always thought so," Oz agreed.

Giles stood up, leaning against the wall for a dizzy moment. Then he frowned and looked at them. "What was that he said?"

"Something about how he had to stay alive. 'For the Harbinger,'" Oz explained.

Giles frowned but put off wondering too much about the vampire's words until he had taken a closer look at Oz's neck. It wasn't going to require stitches. But they'd have to find a rather large bandage.

* * *

Xander and Angel had been through Hammersmith Park and had come up with nothing. When Angel pulled the Citroën to the curb in front of Weatherly, it backfired loudly, and Xander jumped in his seat, heart trip-hammering wildly.

"God, this car's even more crotchety with you behind the wheel than it is when Giles drives it," he huffed as he got out and slammed the door.

"The car's ancient. It's falling apart," Angel argued.

"The *car's* ancient? What about the driver? You're used to horse and buggy, right? These newfangled contraptions are a little confusing for you, I guess," Xander said.

"I've spent more time driving than you've spent breathing," Angel said, his jaw set angrily. "Could you just shut up and get on with it? The only reason I agreed to this is to give Buffy some space."

Xander turned to look at him. "Give her another few thousand miles, why don't you? I mean, her mom's sick, maybe with cancer, maybe gonna die, and you hanging around is only a reminder that one of these days it'll be *her* in a hospital for 'tests.' And you'll be just as perfectly dead-alive as you are now.

"Space. Yeah, you're a champ."

Angel glared at him but said nothing. Instead, he turned and started across the street. Xander swallowed uncomfortably. He regretted his words, his anger, but that didn't make them any less true. He'd never really liked Angel, but the vampire had saved his bacon enough times that he knew he should ease off, especially now.

With a sigh and a shake of his head, Xander followed Angel across the street and through the gates of the park. According to the sign, they had half an hour before the gates would be locked for the night. As they walked in, a couple with their arms slung around each other exited the park.

"Looks pretty deserted," Xander said as he came abreast of Angel.

"Only an idiot or a tourist would hang around in here after dark," Angel replied darkly.

"Guess we're from out of town?" Xander asked hopefully.

A small smile played over Angel's features. "I am."

Before Xander could balk, he spotted two women sitting together on a park bench. They leaned against each other, talking quietly and laughing in that girlish way that . . . girls have. *Friends on their way home from a party, maybe,* Xander thought. *Stopped for a rest. A little too much spiked punch.*

As he and Angel drew closer, one of them, a sweet-looking honey who didn't look much older than Xander himself, glanced up at him and smiled.

"Oh, my," Xander whispered.

Angel looked at him dubiously, but Xander ignored him and quickened his pace, strutting over to the girls on the bench. He set his foot on the edge of the bench and gave them his most debonair grin.

"Evening, ladies," he said. "I'm sorry to interrupt, but I couldn't help noticing you two sitting over here, and I knew I'd be betraying my civic duty if I didn't warn you that it gets awfully dangerous in here after dark. Maybe you should let us walk you somewhere safer. Say, home?"

The girl who'd smiled at him did so again, but her grin was even broader now.

"That's so sweet," she said. "And I'd heard chivalry was dead."

"What are we supposed to be afraid of, anyway?" the other asked.

Xander fumbled with that one. "Um, well, there's muggers and . . . wild dogs . . . and gangs. On drugs. Don't you read the papers?"

The Asian girl laughed. "Oh, is that all?" She rolled her eyes. "We thought you were talking about the vampires."

"Vampires?" Xander said, alarmed. "What vampires? Oh, you guys are a riot. Vampires!"

He looked at Angel for some help in recovering from the spot he was in, for some kind of verbal backup at least. Angel only shook his head, raised his eyebrows, and shot Xander an impatient look.

"Xander, look around," Angel said. "The park is deserted. They're going to be locking the gates. Nobody's around."

"Missing your point, big guy," Xander replied.

Angel sighed. "They *are* the vampires."

Xander's eyes went wide, but even as he turned to face the girls, he saw that their features had changed. They were horrible to look at now, hideous, with their fangs bared and their yellow eyes blazing. Even as he whipped out a stake, he heard someone hissing and turned to see Angel, also in vamp face.

He froze. *Note to self. Make it a point* never *to be the only human at the party.*

"No, sister," said the one Xander'd had his eye on. She laid a restraining hand on the other girl's arm. "This one must be the Angelus. He is with the Slayer. Our mistress had given us instruction."

"Yeah, well, so has ours!" Xander shouted before he realized what he'd said.

Then he went after the one closer to him, stake in hand. But the vampire women weren't attacking. They turned and ran along the path, toward the street. Xander looked at Angel, dumbfounded.

"What's *that* about?" he demanded.

But Angel was already in pursuit. Xander ran after him, after them. Angel was much faster than he was, but the girls had a head start. Just as Xander started across the street in front of Weatherly Park, he saw Angel staking one of the vampires up against Giles's car. The girl was dusted.

The other one, however, the cute one, had disappeared between two houses across from the park and was long gone.

Xander looked around in confusion. "So that was weird."

In the parking lot behind the Sun Cinema, Willow stood up and brushed dead vampire dust off her shirt and then shook it out of her hair. That was part of the reason she had cut it shorter to begin with.

This particular vampire had given her a rough time. Her

head hurt where she'd banged it on the side of the van. And the guy had made fun of her taste in clothes, called her "Sweet Polly Purebred."

Willow was cranky and tired. As she brushed the dust from her hair one last time, she muttered under her breath. "Yeah, well, Sweet Polly Purebred kicked your vampire butt in right-eously medieval fashion." Then she smiled to herself. "Getting the tough chick lingo down pret-ty good."

Then Buffy shouted her name.

That was right before the Slayer came flying over the hood of a car and slammed into the side of the van. Willow looked across the car and saw Pepper Roback—or Veronique, she re-minded herself—grinning at her.

"Another night, Slayer," Veronique said. "You have my promise."

Then she turned to run.

Buffy was already up, and together the girls ran after the red-headed vampire.

"Oh, I don't think so," Buffy grumbled.

She jumped up onto the hood of the car, then dove after Veronique before Willow could even begin to get around it. Buffy tackled the vampire and slammed her head through the driver's-side window of another car. Its alarm began to sound, blaring.

Willow glanced around guiltily.

"Stake!" Buffy shouted.

Without a moment's thought, Willow spun and tossed a stake through the air. Buffy snatched it in mid-flight and brought it down hard into Veronique's chest. The vampire was struggling like a hooked fish, her head inside the broken win-dow. Then Pepper Roback's body exploded, dusting the floor and the upholstery inside the car with the screaming alarm.

"Um, we should—"

"Go, yep," Buffy agreed. "We'll come back for the van in a bit, so no one sees us driving away like vandals or whatever."

They marched away quickly, even as people started to stream out of the movie theater's rear doors.

"So," Willow said hopefully a few minutes later. "Guess that takes care of her for a while, huh?"

"Who knows? " Buffy replied, preoccupied.

Then she turned to look at Willow. "Thanks for hanging with me tonight," she said earnestly, eyes wide and lost. "I really needed just to be with you."

Willow gave an embarrassed sort of shuffle and smiled. "I'm sorry I don't really know the right things to say."

Buffy nodded, managed a half smile. "That's why I needed you. There isn't a right thing to say. You're my best friend, Willow. I just didn't want to be feeling all this alone."

After a moment, Willow reached out and pulled Buffy to her. In all the time they'd known each other, even when the worst had happened with Angel, she'd never felt as if she was the strong one, as if she was the one protecting Buffy.

That's how she felt now, and part of her hated it.

"You're not alone, Buffy. Not ever," she promised.

Chapter Nine

There was a knock on Giles's door. It was quite late, but he was still awake, surrounded by reference books, a half-eaten combination plate from Sunnydale Tandoori, and a cold cup of tea laced with sugar and lots of milk.

He wore an old navy-blue Oxford sweatshirt and a pair of dark gray sweats. Perhaps that was the reason Buffy looked caught off guard when he opened the door.

"Buffy," he said. "Come in. Has something happened?"

"Yeah." She flashed him a smile. "I dusted her butt." Her smile faded. "Oh. You mean about my mother."

"No, not at all," he said quickly, but it was true. The first thought to pop into his mind was that Joyce had taken a turn for the worse.

"You've got how's-your-mom face," she accused, stepping in. She wore her dark blue hooded sweatshirt and gray sweats. Giving him a look, she grinned and said, "Aren't you glad there's an Old Navy outlet in town? For those Slayer-and-Watcher matching outfits?"

"Quite."

"Easter, I'm thinking floral patterns."

He led the way into his living room, saw her glance idly down at one of his books splayed open on his desk. It was a thick text entitled *Soul Possession and Transmigration: An Annotated Bibliography.*

You've always been one for a little light reading before bed," she commented. "Even the footnotes have footnotes."

He smiled faintly. "The sort of thing to thrill a librarian to his soul."

She chuckled in return. "You're not a librarian, Giles. You just play one on TV. You're really Indiana Jones. Your little hat and whip will be on the next plane from Adidas Arriba."

"Addis Ababa," he corrected. He gestured for her to sit down. "You said you dusted Veronique?"

"Yup." She looked mildly proud of herself as she got comfortable on the couch and picked up a throw pillow, cradling it against her chest. "Not to brag. Just like the Terminator, she'll be back."

Buffy shivered at the thought. No matter how many times she rolled it over in her mind, no matter what kind of references Giles might dig up on Veronique, the whole thing still gave her the creeps.

"It's quite probable," Giles allowed. "I'm hoping that in the interim—however long we've got—I can figure out a way to stop her." He scratched his chin. "It would help if I had more information, perhaps if more of Peter Toscano's journals had survived the fire. Or if I could find some other writings on her that were more than the usual twaddle about her immortality. It seems anyone who got close enough to her to learn anything useful died before they could pass that information on. If only we could discover what she wants. Her purpose in coming to Sunnydale."

Buffy nodded. "If the demon she's kissing up to is anything like some of the others we've dealt with, Veronique's probably playing travel agent, trying to get it a one-way ticket Earthbound."

"I'd thought of that." Giles nodded. "It seems likely, which is why I'm continuing to look into the nature of the Triumvirate. Still, if we can stop Veronique, perhaps we won't have to concern ourselves with whatever the Triumvirate might be planning.

"But you didn't really come here at this hour to discuss my research," Giles said with certainty. "What's on your mind, Buffy?"

"Nothing, really," Buffy said, then hesitated.

"Would you like some tea?" Another English person would understand that this was a gentle hint to get to the point.

Buffy, however, frowned and said, "Do you have any Diet Coke?"

"Sorry. Tea," he said firmly.

"Okay." She tapped on the pillow.

Giles headed for the kitchen. He put the kettle on and got out a cup and a spoon, filled the tea ball with some Twinings Prince of Wales. He found some biscuits in a tin and put them on a plate. Buffy remained in the living room. He glanced through the breakfast nook arch, curious about what she was doing. She wouldn't be reading, of that he was sure.

Curled up with her legs beneath her, Buffy's head was on her hand. Her eyes were closed. For a moment, he thought she had fallen asleep. Then she opened her eyes and stared off somewhere he could not follow. The look on her face was haunted, hollow.

Just how much pain is one girl supposed to endure? he thought with a flicker of anger. *She can't have the man she loves. She can't have the life she wants. And now this.*

It took a long time for the kettle to whistle, and in that time Buffy sat silently on the couch. It was unusual for her to be so open about her feelings: by saying nothing, she was speaking volumes. The Buffy he had first met—*it seems so long ago*—would have blustered on about something completely unrelated to the root cause of her distress. But this Buffy, seasoned by loss as well as years, invited conversation with her silence.

He made the tea, reminding himself that she usually took neither milk nor sugar, fetched up the plate of cookies, and returned to the living room. She barely glanced up when he put the things on the coffee table and sat a distance away from her on the couch. Quietly, he folded his hands and waited.

"She was asleep when I went back to the hospital," Buffy

murmured softly. "There was a notepad on her nightstand." With that, she glanced at him. Her large brown eyes were filled with questions he didn't know how to answer.

"Did she ask you if I can live with you until I graduate?" His lips parted. She colored and looked down at the pillow. "Because it's okay if you don't want to. It's no big."

"I just assumed your father . . ."

She took a breath. "Don't get me wrong. My dad's a good guy, and he'd be happy to have me come live with him in L.A. But I'd be able to finish school and fight the good fight around here."

Leaning forward, she picked up her teacup and cradled it in both her hands, as if she were very cold. Her blond hair draped her shoulders in a slightly unkempt manner, and she looked thin and tired. *She must have gone straight to the hospital after battle, seen something Joyce had written, and come over here immediately after.*

"I'd be most honored to be your guardian until you graduate." He inclined his head.

"Not that it's going to happen."

"Buffy, did something else happen at the hospital?" he asked gently.

Buffy took a breath. "The nurse talked to me. They did the CAT scan. They saw a mass. So they did a needle biopsy. It was . . ." She fished for a word. "They couldn't tell what it was. So they have to cut her open to get another . . . sample."

"An excisional biopsy," he said.

She nodded. "On the money. Surgery. Big time. They slice your side open and spread your ribs apart to get the sample." Privately, Giles was appalled that a nurse had taken it upon herself to explain this to the daughter of a patient. But that didn't matter right now. His Slayer mattered. His Slayer's mother mattered.

Buffy gestured toward the books. "Find me the cancer demon. Cuz I'm going to dust his butt, too."

They were quiet for a moment. Then Giles said, "I shall look for him for you tonight."

"Thank you." She took a sip of tea. "I think next time I'll have a spoonful of sugar to help the medicine go down."

"Oh." He started to get up.

She waved her hand. "No, no, just joking."

There was another stretch of silence. Then he said, "When Jenny died, I went mad for a time. I thought I should never get over it."

"I remember," Buffy said. "I wasn't sure you would, either."

He looked at her gently. "I haven't gotten over it. Buffy, everything in me wants to tell you that things are going to be fine. When I first met you, I would have been inclined to do that. But I have too much respect for you. I can tell you this. You're one of the strongest people I know."

His picked up his own teacup and held it. "You've endured much more pain than some people experience in a lifetime. Your courage inspires me. It is, in part, what kept me going, and for that I thank you."

"Oh." Buffy looked embarrassed. "Well, I, you know . . ." She shrugged. "Slayer and all."

"No. Slayers are physically stronger than other people. And most of them have had few companions. Thus, fewer risks of heartache. But your heart has been broken at least twice, and still you are brave enough to love. I take comfort in that. It gives me hope that someday I'll find someone I will love as much as I still love Jenny Calendar."

Tears welled in Buffy's eyes. She kept them fixed on her tea and then, finally, looked up at Giles.

"Me, too," she said hoarsely. She put down her teacup. "Thanks." She stood.

"Did you want to talk to me about Veronique?" he asked. "Did you discover something about her?"

Buffy shook her head. "I got what I came for." She headed for the door. "I'll see you at school tomorrow. I told everybody to meet in the library for a debriefing, see what we've got."

"Very well." He walked her to the door. "I hope you can get some rest, Buffy."

"Thanks." She turned to go. Then she turned back. "Giles, um, about the guardian thing. Thanks." She moved her shoulders.

"Let's assume it won't be necessary." He put his hand on the transom and watched her go. "But you're welcome, Buffy."

She cocked her head as if she heard him but kept going. He watched her until the night cloaked her. Then he closed the door as a wave of melancholy washed over him. *These lives we lead are so full of what might have been,* he thought.

Resolutely, he picked up Buffy's tea and took it into the kitchen. He made himself a fresh cup, poured lots of milk and sugar into it, and resumed his research.

Perhaps there were no cancer demons, but there were ancient beings purported to be healers. If one existed who could—and would—help Joyce Summers, he would find it.

The next morning, just before dawn, Willow walked nervously among the gravestones at Shady Hill Cemetery. She'd woken while it was still pitch black outside, though now a slight tinge of color burned like fire on the distant horizon, and the dark sky had become bands of ever brightening blue. The stars looked almost manufactured, even as the imminent sunlight began to erase them from the sky. Willow knew the gang would have freaked on her if they knew what she was doing. But she'd made a promise that she meant to repay, and there was no need for them all to be up this early.

Her flashlight was no longer necessary as dawn arrived, but Willow left it on. In a moment, it would be needed again. The door to the Hart family crypt hung open. From the threshold, Willow cautiously shined the flashlight over every nook and cranny, wincing at the sight of the skull and the bones. She caught her breath and whispered her ward of protection. She opened her mind and her heart. And she spoke into the darkness.

"Lucy?"

There was no answer. She hadn't really expected there to be. The restless spirits within weren't strong enough to manifest themselves the way Lucy Hanover's ghost did so willfully, and Lucy herself apparently spent most of her time on the ghost roads. It was possible she was still around Sunnydale—she had said there were a great many lost souls to be helped in the area—but it wasn't likely she'd just be hanging around the Hart crypt waiting for Willow to return.

Nervously, Willow glanced behind her, into the cemetery, and then back into the crypt. She would have felt better about it all if Lucy had been there. Not quite so alone. Which was weird, given that Lucy had been dead well over a century.

She's a ghost, Willow told herself. But then another truth came to her. *She's also a Slayer, and it's always a comfort to have a Slayer around.*

Not that Lucy could do much slaying these days.

"Lucy?" she called again.

Still, there was no answer. Willow put on her resolve face and stepped deeper into the cold tomb. She scattered rosemary across the floor and the bones.

"Spirits of the dead, I remember you," she chanted, beginning the Rite of Possession. "I am your portal."

She closed her eyes. "Through me, recall your joys, your griefs, your triumphs, and your defeats. See the world again, through me. I am the portal. I am the east, the west, the north, and the south. I am the sun and the moon. I am the five senses and the heart."

Energy began to build inside her. It was like an electric current, a tension, buzzing very deep inside her. It was as if a switch had been turned on in the very center of her body, and slowly it radiated outward. Willow was surprised at how physical it felt. She had assumed it would be more psychic, more spiritual. But this was very much a thing of the flesh.

"Spirit, join matter," she said, opening her eyes.

She dropped more rosemary on the floor, then struck a match and lit a chakra candle, which she had bought at Dragon's Cove. The warm yellow glow cast her shadow over the walls of the tomb.

Then her shadow began to separate into many shadows and to move independently of her. The tomb filled with sighs and yearning, and Willow trembled with the need of the earth-bound spirits to anchor themselves in her reality.

As the shadows glided over the moss-covered walls, Willow took deep, steadying breaths.

They caught hold of her, inhabited her. She stiffened.

"We are here," they said through her voice. "We are with you, young life. We thank you for fulfilling your promise."

"Yes," she said slowly. "I feel you."

The candle glowing on her face, she walked out of the tomb and down the hill of the cemetery, toward the town.

Cordelia lay in her room and thought about growing old. Dying was too abstract. Wrinkles and cellulite . . . now, those were fairly easy to imagine. Way too easy, in fact.

I don't want to get old, she thought unhappily. *On the other hand, I don't exactly want to die tomorrow.*

But she couldn't understand how a sagging, wrinkled old woman could be happy. How she could hold her head up high and demand better service at Neiman's or wherever. Cordelia half expected anyone who looked ugly or old to just sort of shuffle off and leave the world to prettier people.

So, age, she thought. Then she rolled over and closed her eyes. She began to doze. *How old is too old? When's it better just to throw in the towel, so to speak?*

The sun was coming up, but she pulled the covers over her head. She wasn't in any hurry to get up today.

This is too complicated anwyay, not to mention depressing.

And I need my beauty rest.

The sun rose. Willow stood under a jacaranda tree as the spirits inside her sighed with the scent. The colorful sunrise stirred them, until they were all talking at once again. Great, deep emotion surged through Willow, and she wasn't certain she would be able to withstand the onslaught.

So beautiful, so beautiful, the voices cried. *More.*

They were starved for input. Imprisoned in the tomb, their world had decayed to a powdery gray—the gray of the ghost roads, as Willow remembered, having traveled them recently—and they rejoiced now at seeing the world that their children and grandchildren thrived in. That had been the bargain. They wanted to see that world, to feel that connection to their loved ones who were still among the living, and then they could move on.

Or, rather, they'd be able to move on when Giles finally got around to calling Father Carey about reconsecrating the Hart crypt. Giles had said the priest owed him a favor and wouldn't ask any questions. Willow was happy that she was going to be able to fulfill her end of the bargain so soon.

But *soon* was a relative term. It didn't look as if Giles would get around to calling Father Carey until they took care of the whole Veronique situation.

Soon, she promised them in her mind. *Soon you can finally move on.*

There was no response. The Hart ghosts were overwhelmed with sensation and with the bittersweet knowledge that they were truly saying good-bye to the mortal world and to their offspring . . . at least, until *they* died as well. The ghosts were almost crazed with hunger for sensation. To taste, to feel, to see, hear. To speak. They made Willow talk.

"I love you, I miss you. Kevin. Marie. Dear, sweet Elizabeth."

"Miss me."

"Never forget me."

"It's too much," Willow said softly. "I can't do this much longer." She was getting dizzy and weak. The dead were taking too much out of her. They were blissful at the sight, but it also grieved them. It was time to stop, to move on at last.

"More," the dead begged.

No.

This time, the word did not come from Willow's mouth. She turned in surprise to see the form of Lucy Hanover, gossamer and faint, merely a suggestion of her face and body, shimmering in the sunlight on the hill.

You have been given a gift most souls never receive. Accept this gift graciously and move on. Soon, your resting place will be reconsecrated, and the light will beckon you at last. Leave her.

Willow felt their hesitation. But then, as one, the ghosts departed, leaving her feeling hollow and raw and, oddly, a bit hungry. She bent over weakly, taking a long breath, getting used to being alone in her body again. When she looked up, she was surprised to see that Lucy's ghost was still there, looking like little more than a trick of the light.

"Thank you," Willow said sincerely.

Not at all, Lucy replied.

For a moment, it looked as though she might have smiled, but it was so hard to focus on her, like the glint of the sun off the crest of a wave on the ocean, that Willow could not be sure.

The reconsecration? the ghost asked. *You will see to it?*

Willow nodded. "Already working on it," she reassured Lucy. "It might be a few days, though. We're kind of in crisis mode. This vampire, Veronique? She has the pesky habit of coming back after she's killed. But Buffy and Giles—he's her Watcher—are on it."

For just a moment, Willow remembered it was a ghost she was talking to. Hanging with Buffy, she'd seen a lot of weirdness. This wasn't even the first ghost she'd met. But it was still pretty amazing. Especially since Lucy seemed so nice. Willow felt she could just *talk* to her, and she had to remind herself how bizarre it all was. *Ghost.* On the other hand, she was a spellcaster. Which most people would have found pretty freaky.

Veronique? Lucy repeated darkly. *I remember the stories about her. She serves a demon, as I recall.*

"Yep." Willow nodded. "Giles said it's called the Triumvirate." Suddenly, it occurred to her that Lucy might be able to help. "Do you know anything about it? We're having kind of a hard time in the research department. We know Veronique is the high priestess, or whatever, but we have no idea what the Triumvirate is after, or even what kind of demon it is."

A strong breeze blew across the hill, and the ghost seemed to shimmer in and out of existence. For a second, Willow couldn't see her at all and thought she was gone. But then, suddenly, the ghost re-formed, appearing more tangible than she had before.

I have no answers for you, Willow, Lucy said. *But I will do what I can to find them.*

Then, before Willow could ask her to elaborate, Lucy's ghost simply disappeared.

Angel rolled over and stared at the wall of his bedroom in his mansion. The sun was up, and he was tired, but he couldn't fall asleep. He was too worried about Buffy and her mother.

He had the feeling that Buffy believed he couldn't care about people anymore. It hurt him, but he understood it. She would view it much the same as the starving Irish peasantry back in his time looked upon the wealthy, interloping English. Wealth, title, security—they had it all, and they couldn't possibly understand the plight of the less fortunate.

What Buffy didn't know about him was that Darla had sensed within him his intense longing for a bigger life than what eighteenth-century Galway had to offer. His vampiric sire had exploited his desperation. That longing had not gone away. In fact, it had intensified over the years. In many ways, vampires could not live big lives. Constrained to the darkness, unable to connect fully or for very long with humans, they were lonely and isolated, even among their own kind. Under conditions like those, immortality was almost tantamount to a death sentence.

But he was not feeling sorry for himself. He was only frustrated that he couldn't make himself understood. Mortality touched him, moved him. The pain of loss was his pain, too.

He thought of Leah Coleman, and his heart ached a little. She had been extraordinarily striking as a young woman. Dark hair, strong features, a wide mouth. Blue-red lipstick, as he recalled. Rather fast for the times.

He managed a smile. Then the smile contracted as he compared that memory to the Leah of today. Joyce was depending on that frail old lady to keep her alive. *But Leah doesn't have to carry her out of a burning building,* he thought.

Only out of the valley of the shadow.

In the protective darkness, behind the walls and shutters and drapes of his home, Angel stared at nothing and thought of death.

Buffy lay quietly in her bed, and she dreamed. She knew she was dreaming; she often did. In her dream, dawn came, and she waited until she heard her mother moving around, and then she got up.

Joyce was in the kitchen, reading a recipe book while she drank coffee standing up. A half-opened box of Cheerios, a bowl, and a quart of nonfat milk sat on the island in the center of the room.

Buffy stood in the doorway. Her mother was hunched over. She looked very young in the sunlight. The gray in her hair looked like highlights. She had on her bathrobe, but her feet were bare, and she had painted her toenails a bright pink.

"Hi." Joyce was looking quizzically at her. "What?"

"Your toes. Nice color." Buffy came into the kitchen. "What are you reading?"

"Oh, it's that old dessert book." She smiled at Buffy.

"Baked Alaska," Buffy drawled.

"We've still never made it." Joyce laughed and shrugged. "I'm thinking I'll have lots of time while I recuperate."

It was almost a joke between them. They had gone to an awards dinner back in L.A., when Buffy's old cheering squad at Hemery had won regionals. The dessert had been baked Alaska—meringue surrounding delicious ice cream and sponge cake. As it had been served, all the lights in the dining room were turned off, and the waiters poured brandy over the meringues and ignited them. The result had been a magical parade of flaming desserts. Buffy was enchanted. Joyce promised to make the dessert just for her, at home.

Almost three years later, and they had still never made it.

Joyce said, "Do you want some scrambled eggs?" She flipped through the book. "Oh, look, here's English toffee. Remember your Aunt Jamie? She used to make it for Christmas every year."

Buffy felt as though her mother had punched her in the stomach. Her mother's best friend, Jamie—not really an aunt—had died of ovarian cancer when Buffy was ten. She said, "She used too much sugar."

"You can't possibly remember that," Joyce chided. "And besides, it was perfect."

The dead can do no wrong, Buffy found herself thinking. She stirred and said, "Well, it would be fun to make for Christmas this year. You know, we could carry on the family tradition."

"Hmm?" Her mom had already turned to another page. "Oh, too bad we don't have any walnuts. This sounds really good."

Her mom was nervous. This was the kind of puttering she did when she couldn't keep her mind on anything. Buffy mentally pulled back and kind of watched over her as she struggled to find a calm place.

Then her mother turned to her and said, "Buffy, after the funeral, make baked Alaska, all right? Serve it to everyone you've ever met."

Before her eyes, her mother died. She simply ceased to be. Her face went gray, her eyes blank.

And then she started on fire, a column of fire that reached straight up to heaven.

Buffy cried out and sat up. For a few minutes, she fought to get her breath. She held herself, forcing away the threat of tears. *It was only a dream,* she insisted.

But that didn't mean it didn't hurt.

Then she heard the *fwap* of the morning paper on the porch and, more to distract herself than anything else, went down to get it.

"Three Missing, Graves Found Disturbed. Gangs Suspected," read the headlines of the *Sunnydale Gazette*.

Buffy frowned and scanned the articles as she carried the paper back into the house. Three live people were missing, and four graves had been robbed.

This is so weird, she thought, then almost laughed. In Sunnydale, when was it not?

Venice, 1872

Angela Martignetti had a secret, and it wasn't simply that she was a Slayer: she was violently in love with her Watcher.

What sane woman wouldn't be? Peter Toscano was incredibly virile, exquisitely handsome, and, to add to his irresistibility, extremely wealthy and well educated. He spoke not only Italian but English, French, and German. No matter where they traveled, he had been there before. No matter what the demon or monster, he had researched its origins and weaknesses . . . in the native tongue of the Watcher whose journals and diaries divulged the necessary information.

This great love was a dangerous and precarious situation for both of them. For Peter returned Angela's love. When the Watchers' Council learned of it—as they almost certainly would eventually—they would likely discipline Peter severely. At the least, the council would force them apart, assigning Angela a new Watcher. A band of pasty-faced Englishmen . . . what did they know of passion, of desire?

At first, they had made every effort to keep their secret to themselves. Of late, however, it had become increasingly difficult to continue that pretense. Within their household, they still tried to be circumspect, loving every night under pretext of study and discussion, with Peter retiring discreetly to his own room before the chambermaid entered in the morning to pull open the curtains and bring him a cup of coffee. But Angela knew they were doing a poor job of it, and yet she was so submerged within the affair that she found it difficult even to be concerned.

They had been tracking the notorious female vampire Veronique for almost a year. To be sure, Angela had slain many demons and vampires in that year. But it was Veronique who obsessed them both. She had not only killed Angela's cousin Lucia but now inhabited her body. Angela had sworn to put an end to this desecration of a beloved family member. That was in the early days of their war against Veronique, before they had realized what a threat she was. Not merely a vampire who was essentially unkillable but the minion of a great evil known as the Triumvirate. If she succeeded in bringing this unholy trinity into the world, there would no longer be a world in which to dwell.

Now, as they sat in their opera box and watched Verdi's *La Traviata,* Peter scanned the audience with his opera glasses, while Angela carefully took inventory of her lovely velvet reticule, the small bag in which she carried a few Slayer's weapons— holy water, wafers, and a mirror. Peter had a theory that vampires could be subdued by shining a mirror in their faces, although they had yet to test his theory on an actual fiend.

Murmurs went through the opera house as twin flutes of champagne were brought to the box, along with a sprig of orchids for Signorina. It was widely suspected that the mysterious couple were lovers. That in itself was not enough to cause gossip. But the fact that they were both so incredible to look at, well mannered, and rather mysterious caused a sensation throughout Venezia.

"There," Angela murmured, placing a hand on Peter's arm. She gestured, and he looked.

Amid the flickering candles, he caught sight of the exquisite nape of the neck of the dead Lucia, now inhabited by Veronique. What Peter would never reveal to Angela was that he had loved Lucia beyond all reason. For Lucia, he had felt incredible joy in the presence of such gentleness and innocence. Angela was not his first great love. She had not won him by her beauty and wit. She was the coda to his grand passion. The means to vengeance, if truth be admitted. Angela had flaws, including a terrible temper, an addiction to absinthe, and a tendency toward the voluptuous. She was more likely to be a man's mistress than his Madonna-like wife, at least when compared to the lost Lucia.

When he caught sight of Veronique, who had the unmitigated gall to wear the dead woman's exquisite jet-black gown, he whispered to Angela, "Tonight. It ends here."

She nodded. He could feel her tension, her excitement. He took her hand and kissed it. Perhaps, in time, he could feel the love for her that she deserved.

Outside Peter Toscano's elegant villa, a young gentleman named Gaetano DeMoliano stood within the gates. He wore a cloak and a mask, and he was terrified.

In his arms, he carried a very ancient and very sacred family heirloom: the handwritten diary of his many-times-great-grand-uncle, Jacques de Molay. Like most in his family, Gaetano believed in the innocence of his ancestor, the leader of the Knights Templar, who had been tortured into making ridiculous confessions about worshiping the Devil. Jacques had been burned long ago in Paris, and slowly, where they killed everybody, didn't they?

But now there was a new order, called in English Freemasonry, and books such as this were sacred in the extreme. The men who joined this order did so for fraternal reasons and to spread good throughout society. They did not truly believe that everything Jacques had written was true:

> And there is within the city of Paris, a fiend called Veronique. She is a vampire, and she seeks to bring to this world an unholy Trinity of Evil. . . . We seek day and night to bring her to ruin. We Templars pray constantly for her final and true death.

Many had thought Jacques's work to be a perfect example of the superstitious and florid writing of the time, but Gaetano had cause to believe it: he had loved a beautiful woman named Lucia, and she had been changed by that very fiend into a vampire.

The lover of Lucia (and such a lover was she! incredible!), he had been in her bedchamber when the monster had approached through her casement window, attacking his beloved while he watched, mute, from the curtained darkness. The monster had murmured, "They shall come for me soon."

His beloved lay still and dead after the creature escaped back out the window. Gaetano had sat beside her, weeping and in shock. And then, within three hours, his dead darling had risen, and seen him, and laughed, and told him her name: Veronique.

He had already known the name.

He knew what she was.

Through keen observation and study—and the bribing of many spies and informants—he had at last learned that Peter Toscano and his mistress, Angela Martignetti, were vampire hunters. And thus he planned to leave the journals of his ancestor with them, under cover of night. He dare not approach them openly, for he suspected that Lucia, in turn, had him watched.

And so, he snuck into the villa, aided by a confederate, one of Toscano's servants, and placed the book reverently and hopefully on the great man's writing desk.

In England, the old men gathered around a table of polished ebony. Sacred symbols and runes were carved in the surface, and the place was painted with signs and sigils to ward off the damned.

"It is confirmed," Lord Chestleborough announced. "The Slayer and the Watcher are . . . intimates."

Sir Adrian looked peeved. It was he who had stood for Peter Toscano's character when the man had asked to be assigned to the current Slayer. Now he had been made to play a fool.

Lord Covington's face was red with fury. "By God, we'll start a fire."

Across the table, Lady Anne, the only female member of the Watchers Council, rapped her knuckles on the table. "If the Slayer perishes . . . the penalties are great for the needless waste of a good Slayer."

"Watchers come twelve to the tuppence," Sir Adrian remarked. "And I suppose we're proof of that, eh, gentlemen?"

Veronique smiled to herself as the burgundy velvet curtain descended for the last time. She adjusted her long black gloves over her upper arms and flicked open her beaded fan. The opera was over.

The Slayer and her Watcher were sure to make their move.

She made a grand display of gathering her things—her spray of dark red roses, her black velvet reticule. Her black beaded shawl hung loosely and coquettishly around her waist. She knew that more than one man had stared at her with desire that night.

Of course, she had an escort—no lady would be seen in public without one—one of the vampires she had made, named Marcello. He was very stupid, and she was sorry she had bothered turning him, save for the fact that he was very handsome in his formal evening clothes.

"*Amore mio*," she murmured. "The Slayer is here. With her guard dog."

"Ah, no," he whispered back, agitated. "Do not fear, *cara*. I shall protect you."

"Yes, of course you will, my heart." She smiled adoringly at him. "When we go outside to the carriage, ensure my safety, my handsome one. Will you?"

He put his hand over his heart. "Though it cause my death."

Oh, it will, she thought, amused.

They went with the crush outside. The night was warm, redolent of exotic perfumes and nosegays. Elegant men and their astonishing mistresses sauntered toward carriages. Wives, exquisitely dressed, clung protectively to the arms of their captive husbands, who stared longingly at the courtesans belonging to other men. Young girls and their swains exchanged glances under the watchful glares of chaperones—maiden aunts, trusted married sisters, even brothers. Everyone would be off to grand suppers or midnight trysts. Veronique herself had a dozen invitations in her reticule. But tonight, she had more important business to conduct. Once she threw Marcello to the wolves, she would bring her masters into the world.

As soon as she saw the Slayer and her Watcher, she murmured to Marcello, "Where is our carriage?"

Marcello, with his mane of dark hair and his moustache, snapped his gloved fingers and shouted, "Di Rimini!" That being their absurd, invented surname.

The footman snapped to, and the carriage rolled toward them. At the same instant, Slayer and Watcher brought out their crosses.

With a snarl, Veronique pushed the hapless Marcello toward them, shielding herself, leaped into the carriage, and ordered it to be off.

Angela darted toward the vampire, but Peter held her back. "Don't make a scene," he murmured. "We're surrounded by onlookers, and he's not important."

She sighed angrily and nodded.

They went to the villa in their private carriage, loving and caressing each other the three miles to the gates. All that time, Peter thought of the lost Lucia, and his lust for revenge translated into lust of a more sensuous nature.

When they reached the villa, Peter escorted Angela inside. He poured brandies. She was clearly very frustrated. He, too.

Then he spied something on his writing desk. Crossing to it, he angled the candelabrum toward it and gasped: *Jacques de Molay: Mon Histoire sur des Vampires.*

"What is it?" Angela asked.

Peter said nothing to her. In truth, he forgot she was there. He did nothing for the rest of the night but read the story of Jacques de Molay and the vampire Veronique.

I have read such a work, he wrote later that night in his Watcher's Journal, *as would stand a man's hair on end. It concerns the vampire Veronique, who is a true Immortal.*

In the poorest section of Venice, there stood a crumbling palazzo overhanging the canal, which had once been the home of a wealthy duke. But battles had waxed and waned, his house had fallen, and the palazzo was nothing but a ruin. The duke's name was less than a memory.

In the grand boudoir of the edifice, among Corinthian columns whose gilt was peeling, and on white-and-black marble floors black with age and filth, cracked mirrors surrounded by gilt, and rotted chairs of brocade, Veronique leaned over the writhing form of her chosen vessel and urged the Three-Who-Are-One to come forth. After so many centuries attempting to bring the Triumvirate to Earth in their true form, she had finally discovered the secret. They must be separated, born into the world, and then reunited on the other side. At long last, her masters' will would be fulfilled, and they would reward her greatly. They had given her the gift of true immortality, but if she continued to displease the Triumvirate, they could easily take that gift away. Now, at last, she had found a way.

Veronique's forehead was beaded with sweat. She was exhausted and furious.

The naked male vampire, who writhed on the floor in a delirium of agony, chanted with her in the old tongue. But nothing happened. The Triumvirate did not come.

What are we doing wrong? she fumed silently, frustrated beyond speech.

Then the door to the palazzo burst open, and the Slayer stood facing Veronique and her followers, quite alone.

At that moment, the mouth of the vessel sealed shut. His back arched. His abdomen began to protrude. It was time!

Without hesitation, the Slayer slammed Veronique out of the way. A bearded vampire attacked the Slayer, but she kicked and punched him out of her way. Then another, and another.

She skidded to a halt within the sacred rune pentacle and staked the vessel in the heart.

The Three-Who-Are-One shrieked in mid-birth, as the vampire exploded.

"No!" Veronique screamed. Signaling her minions, she raced after the Slayer.

Angela had hired a gondolier, a man she and Peter had used many times as their agent. Thus, when the Slayer had prevented Veronique from completing the horror she was perpetrating, she ran and leaped over the balcony of the grand boudoir and landed in the gondola, and the gondolier had them moving instantly. They slipped rapidly into the blackness of the night, barely a ripple in the canal.

Veronique gave chase, but by the time she reached the water's edge, she knew it was too late. She balled her fists. Nothing would keep her from murdering this Slayer.

Angela reached Peter Toscano's villa an hour later, and it was engulfed in flames. The huge blasts of flame soared into the warm, starlit night, blazing with the force of the Devil's breath. Animals and servants screamed; dark forms darted in silhouette across the brilliant colors.

Without hesitation, she forced her way inside, racing to Peter's room. He was surrounded by fire, and when he saw her, he shook his head.

"Don't," he ordered. Then he reached for the heavy book, which was ablaze, and his smaller diary and hefted them at her. "Save my work. Stop her."

"Peter." Tears streamed down her face. "Peter, no."

"I beg of you." He hesitated. "I loved her, Angela. I loved Lucia. Veronique destroyed her, destroyed it all. It is a vendetta now."

Her heart broke, in many places, in many ways, as the blaze forced her away.

The villa burned all night. By its ghoulish glow, Angela read the charred journal of Jacques de Molay and that of her unfaithful lover, Peter Toscano. She learned the secret of Veronique's immortality.

And she formulated a plan.

In a fury, Veronique paced in the crumbling palazzo, her skirts trailing through the ashes of the one who was to have been the vessel for the Three-Who-Are-One. The stars were perfect, the rituals performed. That damned Slayer had ruined everything.

She traveled the city on horseback to challenge her at Villa Toscano. As the flames played over her face, she prayed to the ancient gods that the Slayer was still here.

I will be the death of you, she promised Angela Martignetti. *You will suffer as no Slayer has suffered before.*

She had been so close. Her demon lords had pushed against the membrane of the reality of this world. Soon they would have punctured it and come forth in all their glory, giving to her dominion over the mortal creatures, the expendable races. She would have been the queen of death, and the Triumvirate would have reveled in a feast of souls.

I would have drunk the blood of the last living man on Earth, she thought in a fury.

And then she turned and saw the Slayer, standing in traveling clothes on top of a carriage. She beckoned to Veronique; then she cupped her hands and bellowed over the consternation: "Follow me if you dare." Then the Slayer hopped into the driver's seat and snapped the reins of a four-in-hand.

This is far too easy, Veronique thought as she gave chase. *The head of a Slayer will adorn the Traitor's Gates of Hell tonight. My name will be a refrain in the chants of the demon heroes of the ages.*

But the victory will be so quickly won.

Veronique smoothed the ruches of lace on her ebony dress and pulled up her gloves. Then she whipped the horse and cantered after the Slayer's carriage.

Chapter Ten

In the basement of the condemned police station, Konstantin scanned the stockpiled dead for the most rotten among them and did not inhale. While vampires did not breathe, precisely, there was an instinctive in-and-out exchange of gases that allowed for speaking, the sense of smell, and smoking, if one was so inclined. Thankfully, it was a simple matter to cease that function completely.

The dead stank. And the one they wanted was the one that was the most repugnant.

"What about this?" Catherine asked.

Konstantin turned to look. She stood not far from the line of corpses they had brought back the night before. But beyond them were an older pair, one of which was relatively far gone into putrefaction. It wasn't as ripe as some of the dead they had fed to the demon hatchlings in the first couple of days, but it would have to do.

"Good," he agreed.

Together, they stepped over the fresher corpses and went to the ruined body Catherine had chosen. As Catherine bent to grab its hands, Konstantin studied her. Certainly, she was beautiful. And she seemed amiable enough. But as Veronique had begun to trust Konstantin less, it was clear that she had begun to favor Catherine more. To take Catherine into her most intimate confidence.

It did not bother Konstantin, really, that Veronique did not trust him. Though he certainly did not plan any kind of rebellion, even philosophically, he could not say for certain that he had faith in their actions.

In his heart, Konstantin was troubled by that lack of faith.

"They're always hungry now, aren't they?" Catherine said, as Konstantin lifted the corpse by its legs and they started for the stairs. "It makes me nervous to be near them, when what we feed them isn't enough."

Konstantin nodded thoughtfully.

"The Harbinger gave us explicit instructions, however," he reminded her. "We must be careful how much we feed the hatchlings. If they grow too much, too fast, it might be impossible to reunite the Three-Who-Are-One."

They started up the stairs. Konstantin had thought the conversation at an end, until Catherine paused on a step and looked at him meaningfully.

"Would that be a terrible thing?" she asked.

Konstantin stared at her. "Veronique would go mad. She has spent hundreds of lifetimes working for this."

Catherine glanced away. "Please say nothing to her," she asked. "It's only that I wonder . . . I fear what might be in store for us when the Triumvirate walks the Earth, whole once again. What need will it have of us?"

With one eyebrow raised, Konstantin urged her to continue up the stairs. They carried the corpse between them.

"You must have faith," he said, aware of his hypocrisy. "I will say nothing of our conversation, however."

"Thank you," Catherine said earnestly.

But he suspected she was not in earnest at all. It did not make sense to him. And it did, in a disturbing way. Close as Catherine was to Veronique, who clearly did not trust Konstantin himself, the girl might well have been commanded by the Harbinger to tempt him, to draw him out.

Wisely, he had kept his own counsel. He was not a heretic, a betrayer. But he could not be certain that would always be the case.

In silence, they made their way up to the first floor. Konstantin left the door to hang wide behind him as they emerged. Some light from the early-morning sun spilled in through cracks in the boarded-up windows and sent spikes of invisible fire across the floor. Even with their horrible burden, they were very careful to step around the shafts of sun as they made their way along the corridor toward the front of the building, where the hatchlings nested in an office that had become almost too small for them.

In another room, not far off, the newly made vampires lay, still dead, awaiting their resurrection. One of them would be Veronique, of course. A very special target, chosen by the mistress herself, for a very special purpose.

Konstantin smiled to think of it. Cruelty, cleverness, war, those were the things that aroused his interest. In certain ways, serving a demon like the Triumvirate, which would lay waste to everything in its path in what he thought might be a failed attempt to destroy human society, was a huge waste of time.

But for the moment, he could not think of any alternative.

As they approached the nest, he could hear the clacking of human bones, stripped clean, as the hatchlings lumbered about like voracious manatees in the remains of their many meals of these past days. Unlike manatees, however, the hatchling demons had arms and legs and tails. They were sheathed in golden scales and had molted their outer skin several times while growing. It had occurred to Konstantin to collect those skins, and he had secreted them away in his own space within the old building. One day, if he lived long enough, he might fashion some kind of armor from the scales of the demons. He imagined it would be quite effective.

"I don't like to be near them," Catherine whispered.

"They are your masters," Konstantin reminded her, still playing the dutiful worshiper. And, in a sense, he was not playing at it. The Triumvirate had the most raw power he had ever been in the presence of, and it was exhilarating.

But Catherine was correct. It was also frightening.

The Three-Who-Are-One, or would be again, heard them

coming, or scented the corpse they carried, for the clacking of bone against bone grew louder and more frantic, and as they approached the office, Konstantin could see their tails flashing in the air above the nest. A pair of arms came over the edge of the nest, and one of them hauled itself up to look over the edge.

Its eyes nearly froze him there. He was a demon himself, really. But the evil and the power of this thing, its golden eyes, overwhelmed him. Konstantin smiled at it and moved forward.

"Not too close," Catherine told him in a hushed voice.

Together, they went to the outer door of the office and, with a mighty heave, tossed the corpse inside, where it flopped with a wet thud next to the nest. A pair of golden-scaled tails whipped over the edge of the nest, wrapped around the dead, rotting human form, and hauled it up and into their filthy lair.

The sounds of the hatchlings eating were enough to chill even the vampires. Konstantin moved a little closer to Catherine as they heard the gnawing and sucking and tearing and snapping of bones from within. They saw heads bob into the air, lightning quick, and tails waving with ecstatic pleasure.

A tiny sound escaped Catherine's throat.

"Don't be afraid," Konstantin told her in a whisper.

"I'm not," she said. "The evil, the savage purity of it . . . it's beautiful."

"Do they still remind you of dragons?" he asked.

"Not really," she replied thoughtfully. "Though I wonder if it wasn't the father of dragons."

Konstantin considered that. "Or," he added softly, "the dark dreams that inspired the legends."

A kind of numb quiet had fallen over the library. Willow sat at the computer terminal, clack-clacking away at the keyboard. Oz and Cordelia sat at the long study table leafing through volume after volume of Giles's books—the ones in English, at least (though Willow could decipher some of the Latin and Greek now). Xander had gone out to get pizza.

They had spent the day popping into the library as often as

they could and convened there after the last bell. Now the tension level had risen to terrible proportions, as another evening approached and they were no closer to solving the mystery behind Veronique's machinations.

Buffy sat in a far corner thoughtfully whittling the ends of crossbow bolts to a fine point.

Giles moved silently, sternly, from the stacks to his office and back, trying to figure out the best place to begin looking for more information about Veronique or this Triumvirate she served. He had called the council, hoping for some information he did not have, but to no avail.

He paused at the center of the room and cleared his throat. They all looked up immediately, save for Buffy. It took a moment, it seemed to Giles, for things to sift through the fog of emotion that surrounded her now.

"We are at an impasse, it seems," he began. "I'm not certain how to stop Veronique without knowing what her plans are. Clearly, there are two facets to her scheme. First, the breeding, which we seemed to have an impact on last night, though according to this morning's papers, not quite enough. Secondly, there are the grave robbings. Until we discover what use she is putting these stolen corpses to, I fear we won't know what she's up to."

The Watcher looked thoughtful. "While I'm fascinated by these meetings with the Hanover ghost and her apparent willingness to aid us in our search for information, we certainly cannot expect any news from that quarter. We have no way of knowing what, if anything, she will find or even if she will remember us. Ghosts are not generally very reliable."

"She won't forget," Willow told him confidently.

"Yes, well." Giles nodded in acceptance. "Be that as it may, we've got to rely on ourselves for the moment. If we knew exactly what the Triumvirate was, we could perhaps infer what Veronique's plans are."

"Well, I've got a big, fat zero," Willow admitted. She took her hands off the computer keyboard like a concert pianist wrapping up a great session of Liszt's greatest hits. "I mean, graves, vampires. Vampires usually come out of graves. But vampires digging up graves? I don't think so."

"The vampires are digging up the graves because the corpses are people they wanted to vampirize, and it was a nice thing, like giving a really ugly girl a makeover," Cordelia ventured. Then, at the looks from the others, she said, "Or not."

"We could follow them," Oz suggested.

"My thought precisely," Giles replied. "If we can track them to their lair, perhaps we'll be able to determine precisely what Veronique is up to. Unfortunately, it means effectively losing another night or two of ground with these disappearances and corpse thefts, but once we've found their headquarters, we can bring the fight to them, and—"

"No."

Giles blinked and looked over at Buffy. She stood up and walked toward him, then turned to face the others.

"All we've been doing is reacting. We're flailing around blindly, waiting for more people to die," she said, and paused, glancing away before turning to face Giles again. "We need to take the fight to them *now*. It might not get any better results, but at least we'll be making some kind of progress."

For a moment, Giles thought about arguing with her. But then he realized that she was right. Beyond that, he knew that it was far better for her mental health right now to feel as though she were accomplishing something.

It occurred to him, for the very first time, that Veronique must seem to Buffy very like her mother's cancer. She was a phantom enemy, something truly evil, and yet something the Slayer was incapable of destroying.

"What did you have in mind?" he asked.

"Willow, make up a list of likely places to search. Empty warehouses, closed-down businesses, abandoned houses, that sort of thing; places in town that are big enough to hold a bunch of vampires during the day, not to mention their little private stock of dead guys, and remote enough that they might not be noticed. Then you and Oz, Cordelia, and I will start looking," Buffy said.

Xander pushed in through the library's double doors with a smile on his face. "Hey, pizza! Don't forget the tip!" Then he looked around the room, and his smile faltered. "I see we're still living in Fun City."

"Go ahead and eat," Buffy told him. "Then I want you to get over to Angel's."

Xander rolled his eyes. "Why again?"

"You like playing the tough guy at Willy's, right?" she asked. "I want you and Angel to hit the Alibi Room, maybe some of Angel's contacts, see if we can't figure out where Veronique and her crew are crashing during the day."

"You said that's after pepperoni, though, right?" he asked hopefully.

"You're still a growing boy," Buffy agreed.

"Agreed, then," Giles said. "Once we've eaten, we'll all set out on our appointed rounds."

Though it was many, many centuries earlier, Veronique could still remember when she had first awakened to the life of the vampire. It had been a bit frightening at first. That was part of the mystery of vampirism to begin with. The demon soul rooted in the human mind took on all the memories and knowledge of the dead host body. Veronique had always been her name, and the human taint in her had felt the fear as well.

For waking to the world as a creature of the night, a blood predator stalking humanity, was new for both of them.

From body to body, the original human mind of Veronique traveled along with the demon soul. With each new host, she gained knowledge and memories, but her persona remained that of the girl from the foothills of the Pyrenees who had first given her life's blood up to a handsome man on the roadside, shrieking all the while.

Each resurrection was different. Sometimes they were incredibly swift, and other times they might take a night or two after a new vampire had been made for her to rise in that form. But in the many times she had inhabited a new host, Veronique had never awakened with such a vital sense of immediate purpose.

With the failing light of dusk just beyond the walls that kept her safe from it, Veronique's eyes snapped open.

"The Slayer," she snarled, and rose quickly to her feet.

Veronique strode impatiently into the corridor. Catherine was coming down the hall toward her. The Harbinger was about to speak when Catherine brushed past her.

"Stand aside, newborn," Catherine growled. "Or I'll teach you to respect your elders."

With a snarl, Veronique's face changed, yellow eyes blazing, and she grabbed Catherine by the hair and drove her hard into the wall. Catherine spun, face also contorted into the countenance of a vampire, and prepared to attack.

"You forget yourself, girl," Veronique snapped. "Don't make me kill you."

For a moment, Catherine only looked confused. She stared at the new body that her mistress wore, and then their eyes met. And Catherine *knew.* She fell to her knees and prostrated herself before Veronique in abject terror.

"Mistress, I did not know," she pleaded. "I did not know which of those taken last night would . . . would be you. How could I have recognized—"

Veronique crouched by her and reached out. Catherine's words stopped abruptly, and she winced, expecting an attack. Instead, Veronique caressed her hair.

"You know, I think I like you like this," Veronique told her, fingers trailing down to Catherine's face and lifting her chin. She stared into the other vampire's eyes.

"Yes, Veronique. Thank you," Catherine replied.

"You would be wise not to dismiss the newborns so," Veronique said. "Sometimes the youngest of vampires are very strong, and certainly they are impetuous. If you insult me again, you will die."

"Yes, mistress," Catherine whispered. "Your new body is very beautiful," she added.

Veronique agreed. It was beautiful, and it would serve her very well indeed. She knew that she had probably overreacted to Catherine's slight. But she was still enraged over the actions of the Slayer the night before. It was becoming tiresome for her to have to lose time again and again because the Slayer destroyed her hosts.

This time, however, they had planned ahead.

Veronique reached out to stroke Catherine's cheek, to run her fingers through the girl's hair. She pulled Catherine toward her and kissed her lightly. "Come to me later, Catherine," she whispered. "For now, though, gather the others. I want to know exactly where we stand."

"Yes, Harbinger," Catherine replied hoarsely.

Shortly thereafter, they were all arrayed before Veronique. All.

"Six," she growled. "We began the night last night with six. How is it that we begin this night also with six?"

Konstantin looked away, then glanced back up at her. "The Slayer and her comrades are—"

"I am not pleased," Veronique snapped, cutting him off. Then she smiled cruelly. "Fortunately, I have a plan."

Willy's Alibi Room was nowhere near as much of a dive as the Fish Tank. It wasn't that kind of place. It was filthy and dark and stank of stale beer and cheap whiskey and cigarettes, but Willy catered to a much different kind of clientele from the Fish Tank. Unlike the bikers and dock workers and the criminal element that frequented the Fish Tank, the regulars at Willy's were a relatively peaceful group. Of course, from time to time there'd be a random bar fight, which usually only happened when there was someone new in town.

A lot of Willy's customers were from out of town.

A lot of Willy's customers weren't human.

It was the kind of place where one could hide from an angry spouse or lover or the cops or a process server. If Willy answered the phone, and one of the regulars had a call, he'd always raise an eyebrow in that customer's general direction to see if they were officially there or not.

On the other hand, that generally only referred to the human customers. The others—the vampires and minor demons and other creatures that didn't quite fit the definition—for the most part were just there because they had nowhere else to go at the moment. Or they were meeting someone, gathering information, or planning something horrible.

Willy honestly didn't mind. This was the only place in town they could come and let their hair down, so to speak. They weren't about to kill him. And the money that came from the pockets of the undead or evil Hellspawn spent just as well as anybody else's.

There was also the fringe benefit that Willy was a born listener. If you ran a bar, you sort of had to be. Willy listened. And he heard. And some of the stuff that he heard, he might share with someone who was asking. For a price. There had been a few times when that cute little girl who was the Slayer had roughed him up a little for some info he didn't feel comfortable sharing. He could have gotten in trouble for that stuff.

So far, he was okay.

In fact, he was so okay that he'd wised up. Instead of waiting for her to rough him up, he held out his hand and waited for his palm to be crossed with silver. Then he gave with the goods. It was a nice arrangement.

As long as Buffy, or that Angel guy, or the punk Xander who always had a little swagger in him that Willy knew covered up for his fear (something Willy knew because he'd once had a swagger like that—before he'd given up bothering with trying to hide his fear) came in relatively early, when the place wasn't busy, he was pretty safe.

It was going on eight o'clock, and business was already pretty good. Three vampires and a chaos demon, all of whom were regulars—guys who never got in trouble with the Slayer because they kept their heads down and did their business out of town or not at all—were in the midst of their weekly poker game at a round table in the back.

Tergazzi, a minor demon who made a small fortune twice a

year stealing and then reselling arcane artifacts on the black market—and then lost it all in Vegas—was at the bar, along with half a dozen other regulars.

"I'm tellin' ya, Terry," Willy said to the demon, "ya gotta love this town. I mean, with all its faults, it's still a beautiful place to live."

"That's why I always come back," Tergazzi replied. "I mean, let's face it, it ain't for the company!"

They both laughed.

"Plus," Terry went on, "I don't worry so much about hiding my face here. Sure, I cover up and all, but not like in other places. People 'round these parts are so used to looking the other way, or just not seeing what's in front of 'em . . . well, as long as you behave and steer clear of the Slayer . . ."

The diminutive demon shrugged and scratched the green, wrinkled flesh at the top of his head, right between the twin ridges of horns that ran down the back of his scalp.

"An' I don't say this above a whisper much," Willy told him confidentially, "but I think that Slayer does a world of good, keeping out the riffraff, y'know? I like paying customers, demons who ain't too big for their britches, y'know?"

"Absolutely," Terry agreed, and raised his beer mug in a toast.

"Yeah," Willy said absently, gazing around his place. *His* place. "Life is good. Life is—"

He raised both eyebrows and stared as Angel and Xander walked through the door together. Then Willy shook his head and sighed and picked up a rag to wipe down the bar.

The new arrivals said nothing but scanned the place for trouble before they walked over to the bar. Willy shot them a glance that let them know he was a little pissed off that they'd come in late enough that the place was busy. They both glared back, and Willy had the idea it was important, and maybe he should keep his mouth shut for once.

He nodded to the right slightly, then wiped the bar in that direction, moving down and away from the regulars sitting at the bar. The vampire and the punk kid sat down just a few seats away from Tergazzi. Willy saw the demon's pointed ears move slightly, like a dog's, and he knew Terry would hear the conversation, but there was nothing to be done for it. And, anyway, Terry pretty much looked out for himself.

"What can I do for you boys tonight?" he asked, in the same friendly voice he used on everyone who came in.

"I'll have a beer," Angel said, playing along.

"And a Shirley Temple for your sidekick," Willy replied, grinning.

Xander frowned, stared hard at Willy. "Don't make me have to hurt you, Willy," he said in a low, dangerous voice.

Willy figured he'd been practicing. Kind of like De Niro in the mirror in *Taxi Driver.*

"Sure, kid," Willy agreed. "No doubt. Coke?"

"Yeah." Xander nodded agreeably.

Willy drew Angel's beer from the tap—Guinness, as usual—and set it down on the counter as he grabbed a glass for the kid's Coke.

"New game in town," Xander said quietly. "Veronique. Connected to some kind of demon called the Triumvirate."

"She's out to breed, and quickly," Angel added, glancing around. "And she's the one who's been digging bodies up lately."

"We need to find where she and her buddies are crashing," Xander said. "And we need to find out now."

Willy screwed his mouth up, thinking. He slid Xander's Coke across the bar and then scratched his chin. After a long minute, he looked around the room, trying to figure out if any of the mooks who were in there would have any leads for these boys.

"What's in it for me?" he asked, pretending to wipe the bar down again.

"An even hundred," Angel told him.

Willy nodded thoughtfully. "Tell you what," he said. "I got nothing. Not a damn thing. But you leave me fifty, and I'll see what I can find out. I get you a location, you cough up another hundred, and we're square."

Angel thought about it, but it was the kid who answered.

"Twenty now," Xander said, sliding the bill across the bar. "Another Benny when you've got answers."

Willy smiled. "Deal. And the Coke's on the house. But you still have to pay for the beer."

Angel reached into his pocket and dropped a five on the bar, even though he'd only had a few sips of the beer. The two of them were getting up, about to leave, when Tergazzi moved a couple of seats closer to them.

Willy glared at him. *What're you up to, Terry?* he thought. Willy knew he had a good thing going with Angel and the Slayer and all, but he also knew that Buffy might beat him within an inch of his life if the need arose.

"Pardon me, gentlemen," Tergazzi said politely. "I couldn't help overhearin' your conversation, and I think I can help."

Angel glared at him.

"You know where we can find Veronique?" Xander asked under his breath.

"No," Terry replied, shrugging. "But I get around, y'know? Pick things up here and there. Valuable things. Sometimes magick things. Books, too. And I think I may have a book in my collection that would interest anyone who planned to go up against Veronique."

Xander rubbed his hands together. "Maybe we can do business after all, then."

But Angel wasn't as trusting. As Willy watched, the vampire's hand snapped out, and his fingers closed around Terry's throat. Angel leaned in close, and Tergazzi's back was to the room. To the others in the bar, it would look like nothing more than a bit of private conversation.

"Don't screw around, demon," Angel snarled. "We don't have time for it."

"Wouldn't dream of it," Terry rasped.

"Then let's go," the vampire replied.

The three of them left the bar together.

* * *

Oz drove the van, and Giles rode shotgun, with Buffy, Willow, and Cordelia in the back. The pall that had hung over them earlier remained, and they spoke surprisingly little. There was a gravity about their work that night that was unusual. When Buffy rose out of the dark blue funk she was in long enough to recognize it, she took the blame upon herself.

It isn't just Veronique, and it isn't all this mysterious body-snatching and breeding stuff. It's me. And Mom. And the fact that they all know what's going on, and nobody had any clue what to say or do about it.

It would have been so much easier for her if they'd found what they were looking for.

But they didn't.

Still, they made the rounds, hoping against hope that their search would lead them to the hidden lair of the little family of vampires that Veronique was putting together. Logically, they began by checking places that had housed similar gatherings in the past. The ruins of the factory, where Spike and Drusilla had held court for so long, were silent save for the rats and the echoes of the evil that had been perpetrated there. Beneath the surface of Sunnydale, in the warren of maintenance tunnels—and others whose purpose had never been quite clear—the hovel that had been headquarters to the Master showed no signs of recent occupation.

When they stood in the broken church that had crumbled into a hole in the earth during a quake many years before, and looked around at the cold stone and shattered walls, Buffy had shivered. She had died there, right in that room. Only for a few seconds, but death . . . there was so much about it she was beginning to believe nobody really understood. Yet that was not the sole reason for the chill that ran through her. That place was also where the barrier between Earth and Hell was the thinnest.

They didn't stay longer than necessary.

After that, they were a bit more random about their choices, though never without logic. A place big enough to hold a large group of vampires and yet isolated enough that they could come and go in relative obscurity. They drove by the old Sunnydale Twin Drive-In, long since closed down, and checked out the big cement bunker that had once doubled as concession stand and projection booth.

Nothing.

They actually broke into the old Bairstow place, a mansion not far from Angel's, which had been vacant for half a year.

Nothing.

They checked the rusted-out cannery down by the docks off Shore Road and an empty warehouse that stood right next to it.

Nothing.

Though it was getting late, they drove through the old downtown section of Sunnydale, where there were a number of condemned government buildings, ready to be torn down, but they all seemed locked up tight. At the old courthouse, which stood at the end of the block, they'd seen something moving inside and had completely overreacted, going in hard and fast with stakes raised and crossbows drawn. But all they found were several frightened squatters, a couple of junkies, and a homeless family whose child shrieked with fear when Buffy kicked in the door.

Giles gave them fifty dollars and suggested they hide it from the junkies.

As they drove along the street again, it became clear that they were likely to find similar situations in each of the buildings, at least until the city council finally demolished the half block.

It was after ten o'clock when they finally agreed to call it a night and head back to the library. At least until they could come up with a secondary list of locations to search. As Oz pulled into the driveway, it was, as usual, Cordelia who put voice to the despair they were all feeling.

"Well, that was useless," she grumbled. "I could have used my time better just about anywhere. Maybe Veronique left town? I mean, if she's as classy as she sounds, she'll have figured out by now how tacky this whole place is to begin with."

"Now, *there's* something we can hope for," Buffy said, scowling at Cordelia. "I didn't see you coming up with any ideas."

Cordelia looked appalled. "Yeah. I'm just so well-versed in the dives and crackhouses of Sunnydale, Buffy. I'm going to be offering a walking tour starting next week. Here's an idea. Wait till she shows her face again, and then torch her. I mean, obviously, a stake isn't getting the job done. Maybe some fire would—"

"Do nothing," Giles said bluntly. "From what I've read, it's been tried."

"You're the expert," Cordelia said emphatically. "I'm the girl who gets cranky without beauty sleep."

"That explains a lot," Buffy sniped.

"Don't start with me," Cordelia replied angrily, then she fluttered her hands. "No, I don't even have time for that. I'm going home and going to bed. Have fun storming the castle, or whatever it is you people do in the library when the research runs dry."

With that, she turned and went to her car, slipped behind the wheel, and drove away. The four of them stood in the parking lot for a few seconds, watching the embers of her taillights burn low and then wink out in the dark. Willow was the first to speak.

"So . . . research?" she asked.

"That's on the Giles agenda," Buffy admitted, then turned to look at Willow and Oz. "But in some ways, Cordelia's right. I don't know how much more any of us can get done tonight."

Oz raised one eyebrow slightly. "But you're staying. Doing more research."

"That's the job," Buffy admitted.

"Yes, and we'd best get on with it." Giles sighed. "Perhaps I shall make yet another angry call to London."

"I can't believe the council hasn't come up with any more than we have," Buffy grumbled.

"Well, that's not precisely true," Giles admitted. "They have provided records of a great many of Veronique's escapades in the past, but nothing that reveals the nature of the Triumvirate or their intentions."

For a second, it appeared as though he might say something more, but then Giles turned and headed for the library. "Damn it," he muttered angrily.

Buffy knew he was frustrated; they all were. But only now did she begin to realize how angry Giles was becoming. She understood. The knowledge was his specialty, and he wasn't coming through. It wasn't his fault, but she knew it would be useless to tell him that. Instead, she watched him go, then turned back to Willow and Oz.

The two of them exchanged a look, and Willow nodded. "We'll stay," she said. "That way, Oz can drive you home after."

Buffy thought about protesting, but she just didn't have the energy. And she wouldn't mind the ride, either. Not tonight. She was tired, and frustrated, and afraid.

"Just another hour," she said. "After that, I think my head will explode."

"Whatever you need us to do." Willow reached for Oz's hand and twined her fingers with his. "I was thinking as we were driving around that we haven't cross-referenced all notations about tripartite demons to see if any of them might be additional names for the Triumvirate. That's a place to start, at least."

"Giles will be happy," Buffy said.

Willow looked troubled. "I just wish I'd thought of it sooner."

"We've had our hands full," Oz reassured her.

"Still do," Buffy said.

Together, the three of them walked into the school and down the corridor to the library. Giles was at the end of the hall, and they saw him push through the double doors of the library. Buffy saw him tense and pause with the doors held open.

Somebody's here, she thought, and quickened her pace. The others kept up right behind her.

"What's the meaning of this?" Giles demanded as they came into the library behind him.

Buffy reached around to the rear waist of her belt for the stake she had stashed there, just in case. But then she saw who the intruder was and left it there. With a quizzical look on her face, Buffy studied the girl. Behind her, Willow gave her the name to go with the familiar face.

"Damara?" Willow said, her voice soft, almost conspiratorial.

The girl—a Sunnydale student whose older sister had once roomed with Pepper Roback—could not possibly have looked more alone and lost and afraid, sitting there in a chair at the study table, hugging herself and looking up at them with wide eyes. Terrified eyes.

"Oh, thank God you're here," Damara whispered. "I was so scared."

"Of what?" Willow asked immediately. "Damara, are you in danger?"

Buffy narrowed her eyes and tilted her head slightly to one side. "I have better questions. Like, what the hell are you doing here?"

The girl blinked, shocked, and seemed to inch back farther into her chair, as if that were possible.

"Buffy, I really don't think—" Giles began.

But Buffy wasn't done. She walked over toward Damara and stared at her closely.

"All right, then," the Slayer said, "answer Willow's question. What are you afraid of?"

Damara glanced at the floor. "Vampires," she whispered. "They're after me. First it was Pepper, my sister's old roommate. Now it's some other woman I've never seen before. But I know she's a vampire. I saw what her face looks like. I mean, really looks like. I never believed the things they said about you, Buffy. Never gave you much thought, really. But now—"

Buffy sighed. *Never gave you much thought.* That sounded like Damara, all right. "What things?" she asked.

Damara shrugged. "Stuff. You know what stuff. Monsters, all of that. Around school, y'know? And it's no secret that you guys hang out here. I figured it must be kinda safe, and if I hid here tonight, maybe you'd show up in the morning. I only got here myself a little while ago. And I've been doing some thinking. I want to leave Sunnydale. Go live with Tanisa in L.A. I'm gonna call her as soon as . . ."

The girl's voice trailed off, and she looked around the room. "Is there a phone in here I can use?" she asked, her tone desperate and tense.

Giles raised his eyebrows and looked at Buffy. She didn't know what to think now. She shrugged.

"Right over there," Giles told her, pointing into his office.

Damara thanked them all profusely and went into Giles's office. She picked up the phone and dialed. The first thing Buffy noticed was that she only dialed seven numbers. If memory served, Tanisa Johnson had moved to L.A., which would have been eleven digits.

Buffy frowned and moved toward the office door.

Damara turned to look at her, phone clutched to her ear. Slowly, the scared rabbit look drained from her face and was replaced by a smile.

"It's me," Damara said, her voice strong and clear as she spoke to whoever was on the other end of that phone line. "They're not all here, but feel free to begin any time you like."

Buffy sensed Giles, Oz, and Willow moving into a kind of odd waiting formation behind her. They had all realized something was not right. Not at all.

Then Damara tore the phone out of the wall, and they knew it for certain.

"Veronique," Buffy said flatly, her voice betraying none of the anger she felt, none of the frustration that made her want Veronique dead perhaps more than any other creature she had ever faced.

Damara snarled, and her fangs seemed to thrust from her open mouth, her face contorting into the ugly countenance of the vampire.

"Oh, no, I've been discovered," Damara said dramatically. And then she laughed, and Buffy knew she was absolutely right.

The Slayer held out a hand, and Oz slapped a stake into it. Behind her and to her left, she heard a familiar click as Giles nocked a bolt into the crossbow and prepared to fire.

"Something's funny?" Buffy asked.

Veronique's smile disappeared. "Not really," she said. "You've been quite a nuisance to me, Slayer. Taking this girl, your peer, was my way to find out more about you, figure out where I might track you down. But I have suffered enough aggravation that I don't find it very amusing at all.

"What I do find amusing is the look of fury and sadness and defeat that will be on your face tomorrow morning."

Buffy frowned, gestured with the stake into the office. "Maybe you're not paying attention," she suggested. "You realize you're trapped? I've dusted you twice myself, but there are four of us out here, and the only way you get anywhere is past us."

"I don't need to get past you," Veronique said.

Then, without any further explanation of her words, she lunged at Buffy. But instead of attacking, as Buffy expected her to do, Veronique grabbed her by the front of her sweatshirt and hauled her forward into Giles's office and threw Buffy across the room and into Giles's desk. Before the Watcher and the others could follow, the vampire slammed the door and easily tipped a glass-faced bookcase over to block them from entering. At least for a precious few seconds.

Buffy was already up. Already moving toward her.

Veronique faced her, and for the first time, Buffy thought there seemed to be more than raw fury in the vampire's stance. The Slayer moved in fast, launched a kick at Veronique's face. The vampire spun and brought her forearm up to block the kick, to grab Buffy's ankle in midair and spin her out of the way.

"Be careful, Slayer," Veronique said triumphantly. "I've been watching you. I know your moves."

Buffy punched her in the face, and when Veronique went to defend against another, similar attack, Buffy tried to bring the stake down to her chest. Veronique slapped her hand away, then cracked Buffy a savage backhand across the face, rattling her teeth and sending her crashing into the downed bookcase, forcing the door closed again after Giles had wedged it open a few inches.

Veronique lifted up Giles's desk chair. Scowling, she brought it crashing down onto the bookcase . . . but not on Buffy. The Slayer had rolled clear at the last second. She vaulted to her feet and moved in quickly, ducking Veronique's blow to drive an open palm into the vampire's chest. But Veronique backpedaled, turned Buffy's strike aside, and dodged in to punch the Slayer in the face.

Buffy was staggered.

"I told you, I know all your moves," Veronique sneered.

"All the ones you've seen," Buffy countered.

In the blink of an eye, she dropped to the floor onto her palms, as though she were an Olympic gymnast, and swept her legs around with blinding speed to knock Veronique off her feet. The vampire tried to roll free, to get back up, but Buffy didn't give her time. The Slayer slammed her down on her back, grabbed her hair, and drove her face into the hard floor of the office.

Buffy had nothing against staking a vampire in the back—against the undead, there was no honor in battle—but she wanted Veronique to see her face as she died. She turned her over, and still the vampire struggled. She lifted the stake above Veronique's chest.

"What was that phone call?" Buffy demanded.

"The end of things between us," Veronique replied hatefully.

"No," Buffy told her, realizing Veronique would never tell her what she wanted to know. "*This* is the end."

"Oh, I'll be back," Veronique said. "You mean less than nothing to me, Slayer, because I always come back. But you won't see me next time until it's too late."

Buffy brought the stake down hard, and it splintered the bones of her chest as it crashed through to pierce the heart. What remained of Damara Johnson erupted into a cloud of dust.

A moment later, brushing dust off her sweats, Buffy shoved the bookcase out of the way and hauled open the office door.

"What was that phone call about?" Willow asked right away.

"Wish I knew," Buffy replied.

Giles looked troubled. After a moment, he let out a long breath. "If I had to hazard a guess," he said, "I would think that aside from taunting you about our inability to stop her, it would seem that she wanted to be certain we were occupied here while her followers were involved in something elsewhere."

"Makes sense," Buffy agreed. "Any ideas what that might be?"

"Something mighty nasty," Oz suggested.

Giles removed his glasses and glanced distractedly away. "I suppose we'll find out."

Seventeen Missing in Horror Film Mystery

Sunnydale—In one of the strangest events in the recent history of Southern California, at least seventeen people are known to be missing after not returning from the final showing of a horror film at the Sun Cinema here two nights ago.

When workers arrived at the Sun yesterday morning, they found the theater open, including the box office and the projection booth. On the seats inside the theater, police found pocketbooks, several jackets, sweaters, and other items of clothing, some torn and stained with blood.

Blood was also found spattered inside the box office, behind the concession stand, in the aisles, and, perhaps most notably, inside the projection booth itself, including on the lens of the still-running projector, so that the screen in the empty theater was showing nothing but a splash of blood when authorities first arrived.

Despite the overwhelming evidence of foul play, however, local authorities were not yet ruling out the possibility that the entire gruesome scene was little more than an elaborate prank or hoax, but they expected to have more information in the coming week. Thus far, however, police have admitted that none of the missing patrons has been located, and many of their cars, as yet unclaimed by relatives, remain in the lot at the . . .

Chapter Eleven

"Are we almost there?" Xander groused. "Or is this Bataan Death March, the Sequel?"

Xander had no idea what time it was, but he, Tergazzi the demon, and Angel had walked east across town, leaving beautiful Sunnydale in their wake, then down into a ravine left muddy by the rain that allegedly never happened in Southern California. Now they were tromping across open land. The moon and a flashlight were their only source of illumination; when Xander stepped on something that gave way squishily beneath his shoe, he winced and didn't try to see what it was.

"Don't you know the saying?" the demon asked, turning back to look at Xander. He wore a hat low over his forehead, and he looked fairly ridiculous, even for a minor demon. "All things come to him who waits."

"Pithy," Xander said. "Also, generally untrue." He was beginning to smell a rat. Or else Tergazzi was wearing Eau de Road-kill. *Or else I stepped on a dead skunk.*

Angel said, "Definitely untrue. We're done. C'mon, Xander." The vampire hung a U and started back across the field.

Xander wasn't sure if Angel was bluffing, but he caught up with him and said, "I'm missing the *New Match Game* for this."

"Next time, miss the dead squirrel, too," Angel bit off. Dead Boy was clearly pissed off.

"Wait, you guys," Tergazzi called, catching up with them. "I'm not conning you. I really have the book."

Angel glared at him. "Have you ever heard of taxis?"

The demon was clearly distraught. "I didn't think you guys would get in a car with me." He slogged along beside Angel, trying to keep up as the vampire strode along, his duster flapping like bat wings. The demon's hat blew off, and he grabbed it, holding it against his chest. "Enclosed space, you know, like that."

"Yeah, like you could take us," Xander shot at him, glancing for affirmation at Angel. But DB only rolled his eyes.

"Look, I'm, um, kinda short," Tergazzi said, waving his hands in front of Angel's face. "Vegas. It's like a drug with me. It makes me crazy."

Angel swept by him. Xander was trying to keep pace, but one of the things vampires had on humans was endurance.

And, man, do I not want to go anywhere near there, Xander thought, as an image of Buffy popped into his mind.

"Veronique," Tergazzi pleaded. "This book's got the whole prophecy. I swear it."

Angel stopped. "How convenient."

The demon bobbed his spiny green head. "My thinking also. It's, like, karma." He mimicked tossing a pair of dice. "The minute you two walked into Willy's, I thought, 'Hey, tonight my luck is gonna change.' " He smiled hopefully. "Same for you, looks like."

Angel glowered at the little guy. "How much farther?"

"Half a mile, tops."

Angel kept glowering.

"Three-quarters. I swear." He held up his hand.

Angel glanced at Xander, who had finally managed to catch his breath, then glared at the demon again. "If that book's not in my hands in twenty minutes, your luck's going to run out."

"Sure. Sure," Tergazzi said, bobbing his head. "No problem, Angel. Not a problem at all."

"I didn't say you could call me Angel," the vampire said stonily.

"Not a problem." Tergazzi raised his hands. "What would you like me to call you?"

Angel pointed in the direction they had originally headed. "Just get the book."

"You got it. It's as good as in your hands."

As promised, they walked for about another fifteen minutes. Then the demon veered off the level fields and urged them toward a stand of trees. Angel frowned and murmured to Xander, "I don't like this."

"Should we split?"

Angel looked at Xander thoughtfully. "Maybe *you* should."

"Hey." Xander raised his chin. "I've held up my end of lots of fights."

Tergazzi whistled three times. Xander and Angel both tensed.

Then a light blinked on and off three times.

"Okay." Tergazzi smiled at them. "Coast is clear."

He whistled three times again.

The light blinked on and off three times again.

"Is there a point?" Xander said.

"Sorry. Precautions. You know how it is." The demon gestured them forward. An owl hooted, and Xander nearly jumped out of his skin; luckily, he caught himself before he did anything obvious and, hence, embarrassing.

Why do I care so much about what Angel thinks, anyway? he thought angrily. *Just because Buffy thinks the sun rises and sets on him—ha ha—doesn't mean I have to compete with him.*

Oh, yes, it does.

"Jeez, you stink," Angel muttered to Xander. "Next time, watch where you're going."

"Oh, excuse me, Mr. Fee Fi Fo Fum. Since I'm not a freakin' demon, I can't see so well in the dark."

Angel grunted in response, which took Xander aback. Maybe he had just scored a direct hit. He could always hope.

"Someone's coming," Angel said.

"Wow. I'll say."

She was tall and tan and—what was the word Xander was searching for?—*developed*? With shiny black hair that tumbled over her shoulders and brushed the tops of her . . . developments, which were encased in silvery spandex atop a pair of shiny black leggings, she was most definitely a babe.

"Hey, Queenie," Tergazzi said happily. "Ya miss me, baby?"

"We got customers?" she asked, batting her eyes at Angel.

"Believe it." The short demon came up to her and put his arm around her waist. He pulled her close and gave her a proprietary squeeze. "For the book."

"That's great, Terry." She bent over and gave him a kiss on his spiny head. "I knew something good was going to happen tonight." She giggled. "I mean, something *else*."

The demon preened. "Some babe, huh? We met in Vegas."

"Really," Angel said, deadpan.

"Yeah." The woman—Queenie?—chomped down hard on a wad of gum and nodded. "I never was with a demon before. It's very exciting." She leered at Angel. "You know what I mean, honey?"

"Yeah, he does," Tergazzi said curtly. "He's a vampire."

Her eyes widened. "Really? *Wow*."

"Hey." Tergazzi gave her a light smack on the hip. "Go get the book."

"Sure, baby." She gave him a little-girl pout. "I didn't mean anything. You know I'm your girl."

As she turned, she gave Angel a little wink. Xander caught it. Angel did, too. But the demon was oblivious. His gaze was glued to her as she walked back into the stand of trees and disappeared.

"Ain't she something? Chick like that, she could have all kinda men. But she knows where the smart money lives."

"Just get the book," Angel said.

"She is, she is." Tergazzi gestured. "She'll be right back."

Sure enough, Queenie hurried back, carrying an enormous dark shape in the dark night. Xander strained forward, very curious. He wasn't sure he had ever seen such a thick book.

Queenie set the shape down on the ground. It was some kind of box, Xander realized. With a flourish, Tergazzi opened the lid. Then he aimed the flashlight beam down.

Angel swore. Xander did, too.

The box was filled with half-charred fragments of ancient pieces of what appeared to be sheepskin, if Xander remembered his ancient writings on the black arts.

"What is this?" Angel rushed the demon and grabbed his coat by the collar. The demon's legs flailed for purchase as Angel hoisted him off the ground.

"It's all there, I swear it." Tergazzi tried to loosen Angel's grip, but no way was he getting anywhere. "It was like that when I got it."

Angel released him. He dropped to the ground on his butt. Queenie bent over him and made sad comforting noises.

"It's true, Mister Vampire," she said in a come-hither voice. "It's the real deal." She leaned forward so Angel could get an eyeful.

Angel sighed heavily. Xander said, "Hey, man, it's better than nothing."

"I'm not so sure of that." Angel narrowed his eyes at Tergazzi. "If you wasted my time . . ."

"Our time," Xander corrected. "Hey, man, you've got a lot more of it than I do."

"Tell you what," Tergazzi said anxiously. "You boys just take it. Look it over. It's useful, you look me up at Willy's and pay me what you think it's worth." At Angel's dubious expression, he picked up the box and shoved it toward him. "Go ahead. I trust you."

"You have no reason to," Angel retorted.

"No. Seriously, you have a good rep in the underground. You're tough but fair."

Xander snorted. Angel took the box and snarled at Tergazzi, "Get the lid. We'll talk later."

"Sure. Sure." Tergazzi stumbled over his own feet as he bent down to grab up the lid. Queenie helped him put it on the box.

He gave it a pat and smiled nervously at Angel. "We'll be in touch."

Angel gave him another look. Without another word, he walked away.

"Good-bye, Mister Vampire!" Queenie called sadly.

Angel said nothing. Having, apparently, nothing to say.

After a while, Xander paused for a breather, lungs aching.

"Tired?" Angel asked.

"No," Xander rasped in reply. "I'm good. Let's get this thing to Giles."

Three nights later, Buffy stood before another open grave in Restfield and kicked large dirt clouds into the pit. She was still furious over the way she'd been set up that night—the night of the attack on the Sun Cinema. Veronique had kept Buffy distracted long enough for her hench-vamps to take out three dozen people, and now they'd all gone to ground. There'd been no sign of them for days, except for the grave robbing. And they were getting smarter about that. Buffy had yet even to catch sight of one of them in the act of stealing the dead, much less stop them.

It was getting bad. News of the desecrations was beginning to show up in the local press. Apparently, some poor little old lady had come to visit the grave of her three-weeks-dead husband, only to find the coffin hacked to bits. Also, one of his shoes had come off.

When she returned to Giles's place later that night, meeting up with the Watcher and Willow and Oz, who had patrolled Shady Hill that night, she was quite preoccupied with their predicament and kind of embarrassed that the vampires had been able to rob graves pretty much right under her nose.

"And did you know the bottoms of the coffins are made of cardboard?" she said to Giles as she paced in his living room. "Oh, they say they're moisture-proof and air-tight, and maybe they are in the great big elsewhere, but the best you get in Sunnydale is like, like, particle board. Did you know that?"

There had been another grave robbery at Shady Hill, even though Willow and Oz had been on patrol at the time. They'd found the grave while on a final sweep of the cemetery before reporting back to Giles's place.

"Actually, yes," Giles said absently. The box of charred pages was on his desk. Numerous faxes and books were open on the floor, and he was peering over the tops of his glasses as he tried to fit two pieces together.

"I think you need a new prescription," Buffy said, glancing at him. "Maybe we all need glasses. I don't know."

Oz gently cleared his throat. "Not to cause additional tension, but Willow is due home."

Buffy exhaled. Oz was her ride. And there was no point staying here, anyway. Giles was busy, and she was probably annoying him at the least and distracting him at the worst.

"I'll get my jacket," she grumbled.

"I'm sorry I have to go, Buffy," Willow said. "It's . . . nice hanging out, isn't it?"

"Oh, yeah." With a wry sigh, Buffy slipped on her jacket. Cordelia had bowed out of patrol the day before, pleading her busy social schedule. Xander was home sick with a cold. Angel was moving among the shadows, trying to locate the vampires. Oz and Willow were trying to help, but they'd come up with nothing. And they couldn't help tomorrow because Willow had to go to a bar mitzvah, and Oz was playing a frat gig at Crestwood College. To put it bluntly, the Scooby Gang were going about their regular lives, on hold until Buffy needed them.

But this is my regular life, Buffy thought, a little down. The Watcher researching, the Slayer pacing and frothing over some evildoer. *We now return the Slayer to her regularly scheduled programming.*

Giles looked up from the fragments and said, "You may be right about the glasses." He rose and walked them to the door, ever the polite British guy. "Good night, Buffy. Willow, Oz."

"Roger that," Buffy said with a half-hearted wave. "I'll check in first thing at the library."

"Perhaps I'll have some good news."

"Yeah. That'd be . . . good." She managed a smile.

Willow and Oz took Buffy to the hospital. She tiptoed into her mother's room, remembering the many times Joyce, having waited up for her, would lift her head off the back of the couch and slur, "That you, Buffy?"

But her mother was still in the hospital. The normal pattern of their lives had been completely disrupted. The doctors were waiting for Joyce to get over her bronchitis or whatever it was, so she would be strong enough to endure the surgery to take out the thing in her lung. On doctor's orders, Joyce got a sleeping pill every night. But Buffy often heard her stirring when she came into Room 401, no matter the hour. It bothered her to think that her mom couldn't sleep until she knew her daughter was safe. It made her want to come in early, even when she had patrolling to do.

She's here, Joyce thought gratefully, dozing against the thin hospital pillow. *She's safe.*

Quickly, she closed her eyes. Buffy would be upset if she knew Joyce waited up for her every night, fighting the medication. She was on strict orders to get as much sleep as possible so she could have her operation.

Surgery. Her heart thudded in her chest. Her mouth was dry.

Dr. Coleman had come by and gently suggested they try another regimen of antibiotics and steroids to make Joyce better. The implication was that the specialist was getting worried about her patient.

"Mom?"

Buffy's silhouette was framed by the light in the hall. Joyce said softly, "Hi, honey."

"I know I didn't wake you," Buffy said accusingly. Then she hesitated. "Did I?"

"Guilty as charged, sweetheart." She waved a hand and smiled weakly at her beautiful child. "Any luck?"

Buffy shrugged. "We'll see."

With a pang, Joyce hid her worry as well as she could. Giles had made it quite clear that there was something very big and very dangerous loose in Sunnydale and that he and Buffy were having a hell of a time tracking it down.

"But we'll nab it," he'd assured her, in all his British stiff-upper-lipness. "It's only a matter of time."

But Joyce had nearly run out of time. She was very sick. She knew it. She felt it.

"Mom?" Buffy's face wrinkled with concern as she drew closer. "Mom, aren't you feeling well?" Her voice was shaky and shrill with fear.

"Yes. I mean, I feel . . ." She took a deep breath. "I'm still sick," she confessed.

"Well, nothing's happening Slayerwise, so I can devote all my time to being with you." Buffy swallowed hard. "Do you need anything? Some, um, juice or medicine?"

"It's fine," Joyce assured her. "Everything's been taken care of."

Buffy nodded. Joyce's heart went out to her. So much rested on Buffy's shoulders, and yet she wasn't really all grown up yet. Joyce saw before her the little girl Buffy had once been, prancing around the room in a ballerina tutu and a pair of Joyce's high heels. The dreams of childhood. Joyce felt bitter regret that she had not been able to spare Buffy from the nightmare her life seemed to have become.

"Honey, we have to be positive," she said carefully. "If you need anything, your father is standing by. He was going to come out, but I told him to stay in Los Angeles until we . . . know." Her voice was wistful, and she couldn't help it. "You know he's awfully busy."

"Yeah." Buffy crossed her arms over her chest. "Busy."

"He wanted to come. He'll be here as soon as I have my surgery." Joyce cocked her head. "Come here, sweetheart."

Buffy walked to her bedside. Joyce moved her hair away from her face, then pulled her hand away slightly. "Does it bother you, my touching you? Are you afraid I'll make you sick, too?"

"Mom," Buffy said, shocked. "How can you think such a thing?"

"I've been thinking a lot." She stroked Buffy's cheek. "I spoke to Mr. Giles, and he's agreed—"

"I know. Guardian." Buffy looked down. "You're going to be fine."

"Yes. I am."

They looked at each other. Buffy leaned forward and kissed her mother's cheek.

"I love you," she whispered.

Joyce put her arms around her little girl and rocked her against her chest. "I love you, too. With all my heart."

Buffy stayed with her mother until Joyce fell asleep. It didn't take long.

Then, numbly, she made her way home, her face an expressionless mask. When she finally let herself into her house, the tears came hard and silent. She did not sleep for the rest of the night.

Angel watched from the shadows, his heart breaking for her. He was an unwilling witness to her pain, and yet he was glad he was there, if she could find comfort in his presence. The problem was, he wasn't certain of that.

"Buffy," he said softly, at the open window. "I'm here."

She nodded. "I know. I knew when I came into my room. I just couldn't . . ." She trailed off.

Then he was slipping into the room, surrounding her as she lay on her stomach, his body cupping hers, holding her. She turned over, and he slid his hands underneath her back; he rocked her as her mother had, and murmured, "Shhh, Buffy, my love. Don't cry."

But she was lost in pain, awash in it. She was terrified, and helpless, and he ached for her. This was what death brought. This was the iron mask it smothered your smile with. If he had not been cursed with remorse, then grief surely would have ensured his torment until the end of his existence.

"You don't know what it's like," she insisted. "You have no idea—"

"I do." He kissed her very gently. "Believe me, I do."

"No." She shook her head. "You can't keep feeling this kind of hurt and stay sane."

"She's got a fantastic doctor. One of the most compassionate people in the world," Angel insisted.

Buffy peered at him. "And you believe this because?"

"I knew Leah Coleman. It's been half a century, and yet I remember her."

Buffy sat up, crossing her legs Indian-style. Angel leaned back against the headboard of her bed. He looked back through time and saw himself in that alley again, a wreck of a creature, when Leah came out again one night, smoking her cigarette.

Manhattan, 1944

"Okay, come out," she'd called impatiently. "I know someone lives back here."

Damn, he'd thought, and slid deeper into the shadows.

"Come on, I won't bite," she insisted.

Angel had almost laughed at that.

Then she surprised him. She darted forward exactly where he was sitting—behind a pile of orange crates—and grabbed his wrist.

"Got you!" she cried with satisfaction.

He made sure his face was human and allowed her to drag him into the light.

"Oh," she said, startled.

For a moment, he thought he was wearing his true face—the demonic grin of the vampire—but a quick, furtive touch reassured him otherwise. His evil nature was concealed from this dark-haired vision.

She puffed on her cigarette and tamped it out with the toe of her clunky black shoe. Then she started leading him back toward the open door.

"What are you doing?" he asked.

She appraised him. "What's wrong with you? Why do you live like Frankenstein out here?"

"Frankenstein was the doctor," Angel said, a smile playing around his lips.

"What was the name of the monster?" she asked, obviously puzzled.

"The monster," he replied simply.

"Hmm. I didn't know that." She gave his wrist a shake. "You have no idea what I've been imagining about you." She laughed. "You were deaf. A blind mute. Crippled. But you're a man. An able-bodied fellow with deepset eyes and in sore need of a little sun."

"You've got that right," he drawled.

"So I ask you, why on earth are you living like a beggar?"

He hesitated. "It's a very long story."

"I'm making doughnuts," she informed him. "It takes forever. I'll be awake for hours."

At the door, he stopped. She hadn't really invited him in, and he couldn't enter unless she did.

"Are you sure you trust me?" he ventured.

"No. I'm sure I don't." She grinned at him. "But what's life for, if not to take a little risk now and then? Come on in. I'll make you some soup."

"And she did," Angel said to Buffy. "Back then, I'd lived off rats for so long I didn't know if I could keep anything else down. I was afraid I'd get sick. Maybe die."

"From soup?" Buffy asked incredulously.

"From soup."

She rubbed her forehead. "My mom's going in for the surgery tomorrow. With your old girlfriend as her doctor."

"She was never my girlfriend."

She regarded him askance. "Angel, more women lust after you than Captain Kirk on classic *Trek*. I can't figure out if you're just clueless or you're trying not to flaunt your major sex appeal around me."

He chuckled. "Maybe a little of both."

"Accent on clueless," she chided. Then she slumped, suddenly exhausted. She was completely drained. She felt as though she could sleep for a week.

Make that two.

Angel picked up her right leg, drew off her black leather boot, and put it carefully on the floor. Then he drew off her other boot and placed it beside its mate. He eased her up on the bed, lifting the coverlet. She took off her jacket, and he laid it over a chair.

Then he tucked the covers up around her chin.

"Just go to sleep now," he murmured, kissing her forehead. "I'll do the worrying for you."

"I always said you were a gentleman."

He turned off the light. She was terribly afraid he would go. But he sat on a chair in the darkness, the moon and the stars glowing on his chiseled profile. Then he silently said the Serenity Prayer for Buffy. It had hung over the doorway to Leah Coleman's Shelter for the Destitute, and he had memorized the words:

> *God grant me the serenity to accept the things I cannot*
> *   change;*
> *the courage to change the things I can;*
> *and the wisdom to know the difference.*

"Amen," he whispered.

Buffy was asleep.

Giles was exhausted.

He had stayed up all night working on the charred pages. Faxes and phone calls to researchers the world over had provided him with vital clues: this was not one but two books. The first was a portion of Peter Toscano's journal. The second appeared to be another journal, but thus far he had no idea whose, or what it might contain. It was medieval French, and he needed some help in translating what was there.

For the moment, Toscano's words were enough to concern him, however. His journal contained in its entirety the prophecy about the Three-Who-Are-One, otherwise known as the Triumvirate.

He'd been able to decipher approximately one-quarter of it last night, and now, armed with more knowledge about the Italian dialect in which Toscano wrote, he was nearly a third of the way through the manuscript.

What he had learned horrified him.

They shall come when the stars cry their tears across Orion's Belt . . . the Maid of the Sky shall weep . . . the heavens shall tremble.

The Three-Who-Are-One shall be born into this world as Children of Hell, feeding upon the carrion and rot of the grave. Their handmaiden will serve them, and tend them like a loving mother. And when they become the One, they will bestow upon her greater blessings and gifts than ever vampire had known: true immortality. They shall enslave the race of man, make cattle of humanity entire, until, in the end, the handmaiden will drink the blood of the last man on Earth.

But that is not the worst that awaits mankind beneath the shadow of the Three-Who-Are-One. Not by far.

It is a thing of damnation, a Hell beast like no other. Where its shadow falls over the faces of human beings, so those creatures become damned, never to see the light of heaven.

The Triumvirate will not bring Hell to Earth, but rather bring us all, saints and sinners, to Hell, one by one.

Chapter Twelve

Bloodlust.

It was painful.

Days had passed since he had tasted a single drop of blood. Konstantin didn't know if the others were affected in exactly the same way, but he knew what it felt like to him. The demon inside, the beast within, raged just beneath the surface at all times now, and his features seemed to change to their more feral aspect with little or no prompting.

His gut and his veins felt as though they were made of the thinnest glass, and with every moment they cracked, splintered, and began to shatter.

Konstantin wanted blood.

Veronique had forbidden it, of course. They weren't to leave the dusty, crumbling structure. In their bid for power, their play to free the most evil of creatures from Hell, they had made their stronghold into their prison. And all to avoid a conflict with the Slayer.

The Harbinger's plan had seemed brilliant to him at first. While she went to face the Slayer, distracting her from any possibility of interfering, even to the point of sacrificing herself—with the knowledge, of course, that she would return to life again that very night—Konstantin and Catherine and the others attacked the Sun Cinema. They'd killed seven humans during the initial attack, and all of the bodies were brought back and stored for later to feed the hatchlings—which had grown so large now they could hardly be called hatchlings any longer.

Ten others they had taken alive, but not without brutality. The first night, Konstantin and Catherine and the others had each drained one of the survivors and shared blood with them, so they would rise again as vampires. The handful that remained were saved to feed the newborns when they arose.

And that had been that.

They'd all eaten well that night, but not a drop of blood had stained his teeth since. Some of the others didn't seem to be as disturbed by the hunger. Perhaps they had a greater tolerance for it, or the hunger was not upon them so quickly as it had begun to haunt him.

But Konstantin was nearly shivering with his need. His head ached with it, and with the grating sound of the hatchlings stomping and sliding around on the piles of human bones within the nest. There were so many now that the hatchlings seemed to be existing within the pile, and bones slid over the edges of the nest from time to time as the demons shifted within.

He watched them now, in the darkness amid the bones and the refuse that made up their little home. Each had grown to at least four feet long, not including their considerable tails. Konstantin had expected them to speak, once they had grown so large. But they were incomplete creatures, separated like this, and little more than ravenous beasts without their union.

Still, there were times when they looked at him in such a way that he felt their intelligence, felt the flames of Hell licking at the back of his neck. During those times, he wondered what his reward would be, what the Triumvirate would do to repay his loyalty. And though he would never share such doubts, not even with Catherine, whom he was coming to admire greatly, Konstantin was not at all certain he wanted to know.

"They are terribly beautiful, aren't they?"

Konstantin turned quickly, snarling as his fangs protruded, his face taking on the monstrous appearance of the vampire. But it was only Catherine, her soft beauty taking him off guard, as his features slid back toward human. Her eyes had widened when he rounded on her, but now she narrowed her gaze and studied him.

"You're in pain, aren't you?"

Konstantin nodded. "I'm sorry," he growled low. "You startled me. The hunger is growing to be too much."

"I understand," she said, voice filled with regret and powerful desire.

He blinked. "Truly? I thought I was the only one who was feeling it so strongly. I know there are those who can go much longer, but I am obviously not one of them. It's making me crazy, making me . . . lose control."

Catherine nodded slowly and licked her lips slightly. For the first time, Konstantin really saw the hunger in her. She was as edgy in her way as he was.

"Her plan was to take enough from the theater to last until the ritual," she said. "But there were too few people in that place. And now we starve because of it. I don't know how much longer we can survive in here, with the world locked out, without blood."

Konstantin was about to reply, but he froze as he saw Veronique appear just down the hall. Catherine turned to see what had caused this reaction in him, and they both stiffened slightly.

"Hello, Harbinger," Catherine said.

Veronique moved toward them swiftly, almost irritably. Her new form was that of a tall woman, a warrior's height, in her early thirties. When Veronique had confronted the Slayer in order to draw attention away from the attack on the movie theater, she had sacrificed the form of Damara Johnson.

And woke in the body of a man.

"It would suffice if I had no choice," she had told them. "But I do have a choice."

Veronique had sent Catherine out to find her a suitable form for what she believed would be her final shell, her host, her body for eternity. In life, the former owner of that body had been a martial arts instructor named Anita Barach. She had short-cropped black hair and a ring in her left nostril, as well as an intricate tattoo of a howling wolf beneath a full moon on her shoulder blade. But Anita Barach was no more.

That body now belonged to Veronique.

When she smiled, Konstantin could see the Harbinger in this new face. Her cruelty and her faith were there at the edges of the new mouth, in the glint of the new eyes.

"Have the stars shown you the way?" Catherine asked her. "Do we know when the alignment will occur?"

"Indeed they have," she replied, the words rolling off her lips with an odd kind of accent, as if the mouth speaking them were not used to such work.

Konstantin wondered if the dead woman whose form Veronique now inhabited had spoken a language other than English.

"How many meals do we have left for them?" Veronique asked, nodding toward the hatchlings.

"Enough to last until tomorrow afternoon," Konstantin replied, twitching slightly with his hunger. "But no longer. We will have to go out shortly to find more dead. If the ritual isn't soon—"

"Tomorrow night," Veronique interrupted. "The stars have shown the way, they have aligned just as the prophecy foretold, and this time, I have prepared the way properly. Nothing will prevent the Three-Who-Are-One from joining. Their shadow will fall, and their rule will be eternal."

Konstantin frowned as he looked at Veronique and realized that her eyes weren't even focused on him. She was lost somewhere, off with her prophecies. Her lips parted almost sensually, and he realized something else. She was also hungry.

"Mistress, while we are out, you must allow us to feed," he

said. "We are starving. I am nearly unable to control myself, and I don't think Catherine is far behind."

Catherine hung her head. "Konstantin speaks truth, Harbinger. I hunger, and the need is almost overwhelming. Could we not try, just for tonight, to bring sustenance back with us as well?"

Veronique snarled, face transforming, silver nostril hoop swaying a bit and reflecting the candlelight that dimly illuminated the room.

"You will obey me," she growled. "Or you will die."

"Of course, mistress," Konstantin replied, though he imagined himself offering a very different response.

"The Slayer still searches," Veronique said. "She knows that something is coming but is unaware precisely what horror awaits her. If I lose any of you now, there may not be time to replace you before the ritual. We cannot afford that, not for anything. Certainly not because of your hunger pangs."

This last she said quite bitterly, and Konstantin winced at her tone. Fortunately, Catherine was there to soothe them both. She reached out to Veronique and ran a hand through the short hair at the nape of the Harbinger's neck.

"Mistress," Catherine said, her voice a supplication in itself, "if we do not feed soon, I fear we will be unable to control ourselves. That will not serve the ritual, either. The others may not be as bold as Konstantin in speaking their minds—perhaps it is fear, or perhaps they are not yet as hungry as we are, though they soon will be—but that does not mean they are not affected as we are. If something is not done—"

"Enough!" Veronique snarled, and slapped Catherine's hand away. "Do you think I do not hunger as well?"

She shook her head and took several paces away from them, toward the small pile of bones that had spilled from the demon nest. For several moments, the three of them stood in relative silence, listening to the sound of the bones jostling beneath the demons. When Veronique finally turned to face them again, it was with a new composure.

"Tomorrow night, not long after dark and well in advance of the time of the ritual, we will feed. I know of a way we might do so without immediately attracting the Slayer's attention. By the time she realizes what has happened, the ritual will be completed. In addition, we will need several living humans to be fed to the Triumvirate after its facets have been reunited. We will get those tomorrow night as well.

"But tonight, no one feeds. No one moves without my command. We will strike at the San Rafael Cemetery, retrieve three of the dead, and return here without incident. Is that understood?"

Konstantin and Catherine exchanged a glance. He saw her lick her lips again, and he knew that she was filled with the rush of anticipation, of knowing that the following night they would taste blood once more.

Now, it was only a matter of keeping his wits about him until then.

"Yes, mistress," they said together, their voices hushed.

"Excellent."

As swiftly and silently as they were able, Buffy and Angel moved through the overgrown field and toward the line of trees on the opposite side, keeping low. They slipped into the forested area, and the darkness enveloped them. Strangers would have been lost to each other then, but the Slayer and her companion were hardly strangers. They had done this sort of thing together time and time again. Like wraiths, they moved through the trees, sometimes in sight of each other, sometimes not, but never losing track.

It was several minutes of this before Buffy came upon Angel crouched beside a thick tree, peering into the starlit clearing just beyond. She moved down next to him, even more silent than Angel himself. An eerie thought crept through her mind. *I make less noise than the dead; I'm hardly more than a ghost myself.*

Buffy shivered. And yet, creepy as the thought was, the truth of it was always helpful to her. Her duty was to kill and destroy creatures of darkness, things of evil. It wouldn't serve her purposes to have them hear her coming.

Like now, for instance.

Angel studied her features, and Buffy locked her gaze with his. She nodded toward the clearing. Unspoken, but Angel understood the question. *You're certain this is the place?* He nodded.

Buffy held up a hand, lifted one finger. Then a second. On the third, the two of them launched themselves into the clearing, running for the other side. Perhaps it would have been wiser to work their way in silence around the edges, but Buffy didn't have much time to think about anything right now.

Her mother finally had begun to feel a little better. Which ought to have been good news. But what it really meant was that she was now well enough to have her surgery. Joyce's operation was in the morning. Before that happened, she wanted to put an end to Veronique and the whole mystery surrounding her intentions. Whatever the eternal vampire was up to, Buffy intended to stop it tonight, so that the next day, she could be with her mother with a clear conscience, without worrying what Veronique might be preparing to unleash upon Sunnydale and the world.

The only problem was, Veronique and her brood were in hiding. Whatever they were planning, they didn't want Buffy to know what it was. They'd gone to the extent of nearly disappearing from Sunnydale altogether. It had been several days since she had encountered a vampire. But they hadn't *really* disappeared. They were still around, somewhere. Buffy and her friends had searched the more obvious places, but a door-to-door search of every possible hiding place in town, and even beyond the city limits, would take forever.

Maybe Angel had forever, maybe Veronique did, but the Slayer certainly did not. And her mother might have even less time than Buffy did. The thought haunted her every breath.

So they sprinted across the clearing toward the place that

Angel had told her about. Even as they approached, Buffy saw movement in the trees on the other side of the clearing. The quick flash of green skin under the starlight . . . and possibly some flesh that wasn't quite green.

The demon Tergazzi burst from the trees and stood before them for a moment as if trying to decide which way to run but unable to do so.

"What do you . . . ?" he started to ask.

But then he must have gotten a good look at the expressions on their faces and thought better of it. Because the demon turned and ran. He made it less than a dozen feet across the high grass of the clearing before Buffy tackled him, driving his face into the ground. Tergazzi actually screamed, whimpering like a child.

"I don't mean to hurt you," Buffy snapped quickly. "But I will if I need to. Believe that."

"Oh," he said breathlessly as she rolled him over. "I do. Really I do. And I'll cooperate. Just ask your buddy Angel, there. I'm really very much the cooperative type."

"Cooperate by shutting the hell up," Buffy said, hauling Tergazzi to his feet.

Buffy turned to see Angel standing just beyond the tree line. He was looking into the trees, through them, and Buffy frowned, trying to see what he saw. Then she remembered the other skin that had flashed among the trees. Pale skin. Human skin.

"What were you doing in there?" Buffy asked Tergazzi suddenly, yanking on the spines on his head.

The demon cried out in pain. "None of your business!" he said, trying to sound brave.

Buffy yanked again, and the demon started to cry.

"Oh, boy, you're pitiful," Buffy sighed. "I don't have time for pity. What were you—"

"Come out, Queenie," Angel said quietly, though his tone carried.

Buffy turned to see a very breathless, very ruffled-looking

human woman emerging from the trees, clothed only in a long man's shirt that was haphazardly buttoned up the front. Her eyes widened, and she looked back at Tergazzi, who raised his eyebrows with a sly grin.

"Queenie?" Buffy repeated in disbelief.

The woman in question—all five ten and surgical enhancements of her—turned to look at Buffy and smiled with embarrassment. "Hi," said Queenie. "You must be that Slayer girl that Terry told me about. Pleased to meetcha."

"Terry?" Buffy asked, baffled.

Angel nodded toward Tergazzi. Buffy looked at the demon again, and suddenly a lot of the anger drained out of her.

"Look," she said to him, exhausted, "I don't want to have to hurt you. I mean that. But I have to find Veronique, and I mean tonight. I don't have time to be nice about it."

Tergazzi looked confused. "I wish I could help you," he said. "But I really don't know where she is."

Buffy shook her head sadly. Then she grabbed Tergazzi around the throat and ran him backward into a thick tree. The demon gasped for air and tried to rasp something. The Slayer let up on her grip a little.

"You don't need to do this. I'd be happy to tell you if I could."

"Hey!" Queenie cried shrilly. "You can't do that to him, got it? He's a powerful demon. You're lucky he doesn't just tear your freakin' head off. Tell her, Terry. She can't do that to you!"

The half-naked woman rounded on Angel. "I liked you, mister. I thought you were nice, and kinda cute in that broody way. But cute or not, you can't just waltz into our home and—"

"This is the forest," Angel countered.

"It's where we live!" Queenie screamed. "It's all we've got right now, and Terry is working hard to change that. Most girls woulda left, sure, but I love the little freak, okay? And now you guys think you're gonna rough him up just 'cause you don't know where to find some vampire chick? After he gave you those papers and stuff, not even askin' for money. You got a lot of nerve." She rounded on Buffy. "And I'll tell you something, missy, you lay one more hand on my little demon, and I'm gonna kick your ass from here back to Vegas."

Buffy blinked, staring at her in horror and a little bit of sympathy. Angel's face went from human to vampire in an eyeblink, and he leaned in toward Queenie, leering.

"Maybe you should shut up," Angel suggested in a savage rasp.

Queenie looked at him and nearly swooned, a small smile playing across her features.

"Oh, yes, sir," Queenie gasped, moving closer to him. "Whatever you say. Just don't *hurt* me."

Buffy scowled in disgust. Then she remembered Tergazzi and glanced at him again, frowning. He seemed harmless enough, but he was a demon. She shook her head.

"What are you?" she asked Terry.

"Um . . . a collector and seller of antiquities?"

"Besides that," she growled.

"Say 'demon,' " Angel suggested.

"Demon?"

"Very good," Buffy told him. "And what am I?"

"Slayer?"

"What does the Slayer do to demons, in your experience?" she demanded.

Terry shrugged. "Um, I don't have any firsthand knowledge, really. Though I've heard some stories about other demons who've run into Slayers."

"So tell me," she insisted. "What have you heard?"

"Slayers kill demons," Tergazzi said with a gulp.

"See." She nodded. "That's where we're going with this. I should perforate you just on principle, just 'cause that's the job. Neither one of us really wants that. You're not really getting in anybody's way, out here committing God knows what kind of crimes against nature with your girlfriend there."

Suddenly, it was as though storm clouds had moved through her eyes, lightning flashing there, and thunder rumbling deep within her. She didn't touch Tergazzi again, didn't hit him or even lean toward him imposingly. Instead, she merely let him see the truth in her eyes.

"I want Veronique," she said. "Tonight. I'll meet you in front of the Bronze at one A.M. If you don't do what I'm telling you to do, I will hunt you down and break every bone in your body, one at a time. If you're not where I'm telling you to be, I'll know that you didn't look for Veronique hard enough, and I'll hunt you down and break every bone in your body."

Tergazzi was cowering. Buffy felt like a jerk. But the mere thought of how weak her mother had looked the night before and early that morning was enough to alleviate her guilt.

"We clear?" Buffy demanded.

"How do I find her?" he asked weakly.

"You're even more of a weasel than Willy," Angel snarled. "And you don't have a business here, or a life here, really. You find out what's happening, you give up the location to us, and then you leave town. No repercussions. Once we've taken Veronique out of the picture, you're welcome to come back as long as you don't cause any trouble."

Tergazzi grumbled. "Oh, and then I'm Slayer's pet snitch for the rest of my life."

"Not necessarily," Buffy said reasonably. "Just for the rest of *my* life. Which, in demon years, probably won't be long."

"What a shame," Terry said miserably.

Then he shrugged. "Look, if somebody has the knowledge, I'll get it. But even if I don't have it, I'll be at the Bronze. If I'm not there, it means I put my nose where it didn't belong."

Queenie preened. "Honey, that's one of your strong points," she said, giggling.

Buffy shot Angel a look. "Let's go before I retch," she said bluntly.

Angel nodded but reached inside his jacket to withdraw a wad of cash that he handed over to Tergazzi. The demon's eyes widened, and he grinned broadly, showing long rows of silvery needle fangs.

"There's gotta be a grand here," he said excitedly.

"That's for the box with the pages," Angel told him. "From my pocket. You behave, maybe you'll have a profitable life in Sunnydale. You don't . . ." Angel grabbed Terry by the back of the neck and drew their foreheads together, glaring at him, demon to demon. "You have any doubt the Slayer will rip your heart out of your chest?"

"Not a one," Tergazzi replied, and swallowed hard.

"Good boy," Angel grunted.

They rode back from the edge of town in Giles's car, which Angel had borrowed earlier that night. It was quiet in the car, and Buffy knew that they were both thinking of her mother. She still didn't really believe that Angel could understand what she was going through—the distant memory of grief and dread was not the same as the current understanding of it—but she knew that he felt for her. That he was there for her, as much as he was able.

But that was the kicker. Just as her mother was alone with her fear at the surgery she had to have the next day, Buffy was alone with the terror she felt at the thought of losing her mother.

As they pulled into the parking lot at Sunnydale High, Angel glanced over at her from behind the wheel.

"How are you holding up?" he asked.

"Not, really," she confessed. "I just . . . I can't imagine life without her."

She bit her lip, and though she tried to fight them, tears began to roll down her cheeks again. Only for a few seconds, though, and then she got herself under control.

"I'm sorry," she rasped. "I never thought of myself as the weepy type."

"There's no shame in being afraid, or being sad," Angel told her as he shut off the engine. He reached over and drew her into an embrace. "I'd be more worried about you if you were trying to hold all this stuff in."

Buffy nodded. "Yeah, that'd be good. The first Slayer to die because her brain exploded and blood poured out her ears."

Angel grunted.

"What?" Buffy frowned and looked at him oddly.

"Actually, you wouldn't be the first."

She made a face. "Eeeew."

Angel smiled. "Bad joke, huh? My weak attempt to distract you."

"Thanks for trying, anyway," she said gently. "Still, eeew."

They got out of the car, locked the doors, and headed for the front entrance of the school. The place seemed quiet, and Buffy figured that meant Giles was alone. Willow was at a bar mitzvah, and Oz was playing with the Dingoes out of town. Xander and Cordelia, Buffy reasoned, must still be out on the hunt for vampire grave robbers.

In the meantime, Giles was research central, working overtime to try to get to the bottom of all the madness.

"We'll go back out as soon as we've checked in," Buffy told Angel. "See if we can't hook up with Xander and Cordelia."

"That'll make my night," Angel told her, with unusual sarcasm.

At the double doors to the library, he stopped her with a gentle hand on the shoulder. He didn't ask this time, but Buffy knew that he was inquiring once more about her emotional state.

She didn't smile. Instead, she gnawed her lip a little and nodded slightly. "I'll be better after we meet back up with Tergazzi. If he can't find out where Veronique is, I don't know what we'll do."

"You really gonna break every bone in his body?" Angel asked.

Buffy shrugged. "I don't know," she said honestly, and then pushed through the double doors into the library.

Giles looked up immediately from the burnt pages Xander and Angel had brought him several days earlier.

"Oh, Buffy. I'd hoped you would check in before continuing your patrol."

"Why don't I like your tone?" she said instantly.

"I've translated most of the prophecy, or at least what wasn't charred," he explained, rising to his feet and moving toward them several paces. Giles looked down at Buffy, his expression troubled. "I've finally gotten the first bit of information about the nature of the Triumvirate."

"And?"

"I'm not sure what it means, exactly. According to Toscano's writings, any human to fall beneath the shadow of the demon will be instantly damned to Hell. I don't know if that's literal, either the shadow reference or the bit about Hell."

"But you think it is," Angel said.

Giles nodded. "I need to learn more. If we're to combat this thing, I've got to find out exactly what its powers are, figure out how to stop it before it can spread its evil."

Buffy was staring at him.

"What is it?" Giles asked.

"You're giving up," she said, her tone accusatory. "You're just assuming we're not going to be able to stop Veronique, so you're moving on to Plan B. Not that Plan B is bad, but have a little faith, Giles."

He looked directly at her. "I have all the faith in the world in you, Buffy. But I must also go about this logically. We must be prepared for every eventuality, and given the dearth of information we've managed to acquire thus far . . ."

His words trailed off. Then, at length, he inclined his head, glanced away from her. "There's something else."

Buffy only looked at him, heart filling with dread.

"In addition to the Toscano papers, I've also managed to translate some of the other document. It's the journal of Jacques de Molay."

"Which is significant. For some reason." Buffy raised her eyebrows.

"He was the master of the Knights Templar in France. It seems he ran afoul of Veronique, and his order was destroyed as a result. However, his journal included a great many helpful bits of information, including the formula for determining the night when all of Veronique's preparations will go toward performing a specific ritual. A ritual that will bring a true demon, the tripartite thing I told you about, the Triumvirate, to Earth."

"Here in Sunnydale, of course," Buffy sighed.

"Well, as we're on the Hellmouth—"

Angel interrupted. "The barrier between Earth and Hell is weaker here. Yeah, we know. You found a formula to figure out when the stars are aligned so that the ritual can be performed. So what's our deadline? When's the big night?"

Giles glanced away, then looked back, meeting Buffy's anxious gaze.

"Tomorrow."

For the first few seconds after he'd said the word, she could only stare at him. No words would come, nor could she even draw a breath. Then, finally, a quick intake of air, and she began to shake her head, denying the truth he had just given her.

"I'm sorry, Buffy, but we must be prepared," he said, and she heard in his voice how his heart ached for her.

But it wasn't enough.

"No," she said at last, managing to eke the words out, though she still felt as though she had been somehow disconnected from herself. "No way, Giles. I'm going to be with my mother."

She stared him down, daring him to contradict. For a moment, it seemed he might do exactly that. Then he looked away.

"Yes," he whispered. "Of course. That's where you should be. We'll prepare without you. When your mother comes out of her surgery, once she's settled in and we all know that she's well . . ."

He let his words trail off. Buffy wanted to argue, to tell him to stop pushing. But she knew that he wasn't pushing at all. He was being realistic. Her first priority had to be her mother, and Giles knew that. But he also knew that when it all hit the fan the next night, when this prophecy about Veronique and the Triumvirate came to pass and they started doing the chicken dance or whatever for this ritual, the Slayer would be needed.

The thing that pained her the most was that she knew her

mother would understand as well. *She shouldn't have to*, Buffy thought. But there was nothing she could do.

As the Slayer, she might be able to save the world, but she sure as hell couldn't change it.

Angel came up beside her and softly slid his arm around her waist. She wanted to rage at him as well, to tell him that she didn't need support, that she was all right. She wasn't some fragile creature who would fall apart when faced with such dreadful considerations.

But Buffy knew she couldn't say that. Because she'd be lying.

Slayer she might be, and in the face of the hordes of darkness she would stand without fear and do what her duty to herself and her family and her friends and her world demanded. But she was also just a girl. Not even really an adult yet. She'd begun to think she was, and the irony of that was not lost on her. Buffy had started to think she was all grown up. After all, with the things she'd seen, the horrors she'd been up against . . . if that hadn't made her an adult, she hadn't known what would.

Now she knew she'd been fooling herself.

In a part of her she did not want to examine at all, she knew that what would truly make her an adult was the moment when her mother was no longer there to watch over her, to care, to worry, even when Buffy herself didn't want her to.

When she really started to understand death, she wouldn't be a child anymore. Not merely the knowledge of death; she had acquired *that* long ago, when she herself had died, though only for a few moments before Xander revived her. This was different. People died all the time, she'd seen it too often. But now death threatened to tear violently away from her a huge part of her world. Her mother's strength had been invaluable to Buffy time and time again. The bond they shared as mother and daughter, the memories they had lived together, would be sharp, painful things if they were splintered by death.

If, Buffy thought. *But it isn't if, it's when.*

"How can I fight this?" she whispered to herself.

Angel pulled her more tightly to him, and she let him, comforted by his presence.

She didn't cry again, though. And she wouldn't. She promised herself in that moment that she would not cry over her mother's illness again, not unless the unthinkable happened.

As soon as she made herself that vow, though, Buffy feared that she would break it.

If she dies, Buffy thought, holding Angel tight as she allowed herself to really consider it for the first time. *If she dies, the world might as well end. It just won't matter anymore.*

Giles had been silently watching her, mute witness to her pain. But now he moved toward them and reached out to her, and Buffy let go of Angel, and she and Giles embraced each other tightly. It was unlike them, and very awkward in its way. But she needed him so desperately, in a manner very different from the way she needed Angel or Willow. They stood by her, and always would. Buffy knew that. But Giles . . . Giles watched over her. Looked out for her as best he could.

Buffy needed that now.

"There's nothing more to be done tonight," Giles told her. "Go home. Get some rest. Tomorrow you be with Joyce. We'll all try to come by as we're able."

Buffy withdrew from him. Looked into the Watcher's eyes. "And I'll be back here by dark."

Giles nodded.

Together, she and Angel walked toward the double doors. As she pushed through, Buffy turned and looked back at Giles, who was once again examining the charred pages of the journal of Peter Toscano.

"Hey," she said, and Giles looked up. "You get some sleep, too, okay?"

"Thank you, Buffy," he replied. "Just another twenty minutes or so, and I'll be off."

Buffy smiled thinly and gave a small nod. But as she and Angel left, she knew that Giles was lying, both to her and to himself. He had deciphered most of the prophecy and much of de Molay's journal, but if there were some other clue in those charred pages to how they might destroy the Triumvirate, he was determined to find it.

He would fall asleep over the study table, or at his desk, as he did too frequently.

The light of dawn would wake him.

And then he would begin again.

"I can't believe we're out here by ourselves," Cordelia sniffed.

"Yeah," Xander agreed. "Sort of spooky, huh? Guess you feel like cuddling up so I can protect you now, right?"

She scowled at him. "In your dreams."

Xander nodded reasonably. "Your point would be?"

"My point would be I'd rather plead with the dentist for rusty tools and no novocaine." Cordelia sneered.

She always was good at sneering, Xander thought.

They stood in the middle of Crestwood Cemetery, a quarter of a mile from the college of the same name. It was also the name of the entire neighborhood, and Xander figured whoever this Crestwood guy had been, he'd had major identity issues if he'd had to go and paste his name all over everything.

"I don't know what you're worried about," he told Cordelia. "I mean, we're not actually supposed to slay anything, right? We look, we find, we use the cell phone to call Giles, he brings the cavalry. We go home and share a nice, long Jell-O bath."

Cordelia answered that one with a glare.

"Besides," he went on, "it's not like we're actually going to run into any vampires. They've been pretty much steering clear of us lately, right? They're trying their best not to be seen, never mind dusted. And of the dozen cemeteries in this town, what are the chances we'll be in the same one they are, even for a couple of minutes?"

She rounded on him, nailing him with a withering look. "Did we or did we not come here because of all the cemeteries in town, this was the only one they hadn't hit more than once?"

"Well—"

"And we figured that gave us better odds of finding some vampires?"

"Well—"

Cordelia lifted her chin, rolling her eyes in disgust. "Or do you honestly think that even if I were this fretting damsel in distress you seem determined to make me out to be, you could ever possibly be the knight in shining armor?"

Xander cocked his head angrily. Now he was miffed. "Hi-ho, there, Trigger," he snapped. "First off, if you're not fretting, I don't know what else to call it without cuss words. And second, I have been your knight in silly armor plenty of times, or don't you remember my saving your precious bacon in the past?"

"Please," Cordelia drawled. "In an Archie Comics world, Xander, you'll always be Jughead."

Then she walked off, leaving him desperately trying to come up with an Archie-related comeback and failing miserably. In the end, he could only set off after her, muttering under his breath. Moments later, as he caught up to her, an odd sound caught his attention.

The sound of shovels in soil. And it was coming from straight ahead.

"Hold it," he whispered, grabbing Cordelia's arm.

"What?" she said, a bit too loud.

The shoveling stopped. Xander grabbed her arm and pulled her down behind a large marble grave marker. In place of the shoveling, he now heard voices, though they were a bit too low and far away for him to make out exactly what was being said.

He pointed to her bag, making wide-eyed expressions with his face. She looked at him as if he was insane as he tried to mime putting a phone to his ear. Cordelia only responded with similar crazy gestures and threw up her hands. Exasperated, he grabbed her bag and reached in, digging around until he had the phone.

Xander punched the memory button, and then dialed *12. On the other end of the line, in the library of Sunnydale High

School, the phone began to ring. Xander looked at Cordelia and gave the thumbs-up sign.

Just as the first vampire snarled at them, lunging over the top of the marble marker.

Xander cried out and rolled out of the path of its attack. But he dropped the phone to the soft cemetery earth as he did so. Cordelia shrieked, more because of her phone than the vampire.

But then there were more of them.

Almost before they knew what was happening, Xander and Cordelia were surrounded.

They didn't stand a chance.

In the library, Giles's eyelids fluttered up, and he went groggily to the phone.

"Hello?"

At first, he couldn't make out the odd sounds on the other end. There were grunts and the sound of flesh on flesh, and he wondered if it were some sort of obscene prank.

Then he heard a girl begin to scream, and he knew it was Cordelia. He knew that she and Xander were searching for some sign of Veronique and her clan, but he had no way to know exactly where she was calling from.

There was quite a bit of screaming.

Chapter Thirteen

It had still been dark when Buffy reached Sunnydale Hospital. Roused from sleep and informed by the hospital social worker that her mother's surgery had been rescheduled at the last minute for reasons Buffy couldn't begin to understand, she had thought at first that she was dreaming. She dressed and left the house bleary from lack of sleep but jittery from the adrenaline rushing through her bloodstream. She was trembling and terribly alert.

As she walked through the hospital's entrance doors, she noted a scattering of cars in the lot. The parking structure looked nearly empty. *Not a lot of operations today,* she thought. *Or else they get to show up later than me.*

Her interior tension level was reaching the boiling point. *Get it together,* she chided herself. Not for anything did she want to make her mother comfort *her* or calm *her* down. Joyce had more than enough on her own plate to deal with.

The lobby was eerily quiet. But there were the ever-present little old ladies behind the information console. A man was staring at the Weather Channel, and a little girl beside him was playing with a teddy bear. A young woman with a chestnut ponytail walked beside a man in scrubs who was pushing a wheelchair. Her face was grim and set. An old man sprawled in the wheelchair, his head bobbing, his eyes half closed. His mouth lolled open. He looked as if he were a thousand years old. He looked as if he were already dead.

Buffy flashed, *Why bother keeping him going?* and felt horribly ashamed of herself. She cleared her throat as she realized that she was staring.

Buffy crossed to the elevators and pressed the button. After about half a minute, the doors opened. A woman in a business suit carrying a briefcase smiled and swept out. Her beeper trilled, and she sighed and unhooked it from the waistband of her skirt. She squinted at the number and sighed again.

The ride was extremely short. The doors opened, and Buffy took a huge gulp of air. Her throat was killing her, and she was bone-weary. She wished she'd had some advance warning that the surgery was going to be moved up like this.

And then what? The Slayer could have gone to bed early?

She stepped out into a corridor much busier than the downstairs lobby. People in scrubs pushed carts of machinery. A young man in a long white coat frowned as his beeper trilled. Two men in suits strolled past, each carrying a briefcase.

The nurses' area was dead center in the middle of all the activity. Two of them were seated behind computer monitors, one busily entering data from a set of charts at her right elbow.

"Good morning," said the other nurse, a young blonde, smiling helpfully at Buffy.

"Hi," Buffy rasped. "I'm Buffy Summers. My mom's in for a . . . a thoracotomy."

"Her name?" the nurse said, typing Buffy's last name in. "Oh. Here it is. Joyce Summers. Oh. Dr. Coleman's on the case." She looked impressed.

The other nurse, this one significantly older, looked up from the pile of charts and glanced at the younger nurse's screen. "Equivocal mass," she said. "So you want to code in C1. Cancer."

Buffy's stomach clenched. "They don't know what it is. That's why they're doing the surgery."

"It's just procedure." The older nurse leaned slightly in front of the younger one. "We have to put something down."

"It's okay," the younger nurse said. "It's just the way we have to do it."

"No." Buffy shook her head. "It is *not* okay. She has not been diagnosed with cancer."

"Now, honey," the blond nurse began. "It's okay."

Buffy placed her hand on the desk. "Think about it. A single mom, with a preexisting condition of cancer? What if her business folds and we need to get different insurance?"

"Oh." The younger nurse looked confused. The older one glared at Buffy, which shocked Buffy. *I'm here because my mom is sick, and she's treating me like a criminal.* Buffy glared back.

"If you were qualified to determine that my mother has cancer," Buffy said to her in a low, seething voice, "you'd be performing her surgery."

The woman narrowed her eyes at Buffy. "I'm an R.N., and I've been with this health-care system for fifteen years, and—"

"Well, this is a hospital, not a health-care system, and you aren't an M.D.," Buffy shot back. "Do we need to get your supervisor?"

The nurse narrowed her eyes. "I *am* the supervisor. And I suggest you talk to Dr. Martinez and Dr. Coleman about the diagnosis, if you're having so much trouble accepting it."

The blond nurse murmured, "We can update the chart once we have more information, Miss Summers. And I'll be sure to take care of it," she added, her cheeks reddening as the other nurse aimed her venomous glare her way. "Your mother's in prep. It's just down the hall." She pointed. "Would you like someone to show you how to get there?"

"No. I'll figure it out," Buffy said frostily. Then she reminded herself that this woman had been nice to her and was probably going to get in trouble for it. So she made herself smile briefly and said, "Thanks."

"I know it's scary," the nurse began. Then the older one cleared her throat, and the younger one fell silent. Still, she smiled sadly at Buffy.

Buffy made her way in the direction the nurse had indicated. She heard someone crying. Footsteps squeaked on the shiny linoleum floor.

It was still dark out.

Very dark.

It was nearly dawn when Oz and Willow dashed into the library. Giles looked pasty-faced, even for him. It would have been improper for him to call Willow so late at night, but he had been able to reach Oz by phone. Giles had asked him to e-mail Willow and then get to the library. He had also suggested they hurry.

"Thank you both for coming," he said.

"Not a problem," Oz said.

"What's wrong?" Willow asked.

"I received a call from Cordelia. All I heard was a quite a bit of screaming on the other end. When I press star six nine, a message tells me the phone is out of service."

Willow blinked at Oz, and vice versa. Willow chewed her lower lip and said, "And you don't have any idea where they were?"

"None whatsoever. They were doing a bit of reconnaissance, hoping to find a lead on Veronique's whereabouts, or even to find some of our grave robbers and follow them back to their lair. I've been hoping she'd manage to call again. But . . ." He shrugged.

"We'll start looking," Willow promised him.

As she turned on her heel, Oz caught up her hand and said, "Where?"

"Where? Why, there are lots of wheres." Willow drew herself up. "And the sooner we start searching all the wheres, we'll have a better idea of where not."

"On the other hand," Giles cut in, "Buffy is off-duty, and if we can ascertain where Xander and Cordelia are, we can help them as a team. If we separate, we may prove less effective."

"The hospital," Willow said softly. "Oh, poor Buffy."

There was a momentary silence. Then Oz said, "Perhaps not

showing my sensitive side, but the Slayer can't be off-duty. Not for this."

Giles sighed. His shoulders sagged with fatigue as he nodded. "My thinking likewise. Though I hadn't wanted to put it into words. It's most unfortunate that this is all happening at the same time, but Buffy is the Slayer. She has a clear duty."

"She's also a daughter." Willow's voice was whisper-thin. "And I really like Mrs. Summers."

The three regarded one another.

"Hospital," Giles said.

They left campus.

After answering a hundred questions about her health, her previous surgical history, if she had complied with fasting the night before—*what do they think, I slipped out the window and went for pizza?*—and a million other things (including if she wanted to be an organ donor), Joyce was given a hospital gown to change into. Also, a paper bouffant shower cap and a pair of paper booties.

She sat on her hospital bed and regarded her uniform. To Buffy, she said, "I feel so . . . disposable."

"Just your outfit, which I've longed to tell you many times before," Buffy said. Her voice was shaking. "Some of the stuff you wear . . ."

She turned away.

"Stay with me, honey," Joyce asked quietly. "I know you're scared. I'm scared, too."

"I'm sorry." Buffy was horribly ashamed. "I'm okay, Mom. Really." She wiped her tears away to prove it.

"Mrs. Summers? We'll be walking you down in about five minutes," said a nurse in salmon-colored scrubs and a matching shower cap.

"No dignity," Buffy huffed after the nurse left. "I thought they'd wheel you down in a hospital bed with violin music in the background."

"Only in the soaps, I guess."

Joyce didn't want Buffy to know how unsettling it had been to discover that she would actually be escorted to the operating room. She would walk into the room with all the equipment and the beep-beep-boops and climb up on the table. Apparently, the reason for this was that the anesthesiologist was running behind, and another doctor would begin the process of knocking Joyce out.

They had been waiting more than an hour past Joyce's scheduled surgery in a sort of clearinghouse area, with one bed, a shower, and a restroom in it. Buffy had already been at the hospital for five hours.

She was weaving, nearly asleep on her feet, except for her heightened anxiety. That kept her going. She had had nothing to eat, nothing to drink, but she was certain that if she tried to eat or drink something, she would throw it back up.

"All right, Joyce, here we are," the nurse said again. It had only been about two minutes since the last time she had popped her head in.

I'm not ready, Buffy thought frantically. *Please, I am so not ready.*

"All right." Joyce took a deep breath. "May my daughter accompany me?"

The nurse looked apologetic. "Only as far as the O.R. doors."

"Better than nothing," Buffy murmured.

Joyce stood, looking tall and thin in her gown. Her paper booties were ridiculous. The shower cap was silly.

Buffy thought her mother had never looked more beautiful in her life.

They walked out of the room and into the hall. Joyce took Buffy's hand and squeezed hard. To Buffy's surprise, the nurse took her mother's other hand, and Joyce squeezed her hand, too.

"My mother had a very bad prognosis," the nurse confided. "Twelve years ago. She just went on a cruise to Puerto Vallarta with a brand-new husband."

"Her own?" Joyce asked. The two older women chuckled. All Buffy did was stare straight ahead. Her heart was thundering.

This cannot be happening. This is not happening.

The nurse's voice dropped. "If you can believe it, she met him on a blind date. At a nudist colony."

"Get out!" Joyce shrieked, scandalized. She giggled. "I guess you can't call it a blind date, then."

The women snickered and cackled. Buffy thought she was going to scream.

Then her mother turned to her suddenly and put her arms around her. "Hey, you," she whispered into Buffy's ear. "We're going to be fine."

"I know." Buffy's voice was small and timid and lonely.

She was bereft when her mother let go and waited for the nurse to buzz the light gray operating-room doors. They clicked and opened. Beyond, there were people dressed in scrubs milling up and down a corridor lined with other doors. Joyce walked through them, arm-in-arm with the nurse, leaving Buffy behind.

The operating room was exactly the way Joyce had seen them on TV. In the center of the room, a flat, padded-looking table with an enormous light overhead, all kinds of equipment on roll-around carts, and people bustling everywhere.

"Just climb up on here, Joyce," the nurse said, helping her onto the table.

"Oh, it's warm," Joyce said, surprised.

"We heat it. And we're going to encase your arms and legs in special warmers. They look like they're made out of aluminum foil. But you'll probably be asleep before that."

Joyce lay down on the table. Someone came over with a mask and cap on. She saw two piercing, rich brown eyes.

"Joyce? I'm Dr. Charaka, a staff anesthesiologist," the masked figure told her. "Dr. Jones is still in surgery, so I'm going to take care of you. All right?"

"Yes," Joyce murmured, wondering what would happen if he said it wasn't all right. *And why does it matter so much about Dr. Jones? Is he better than Dr. Charaka?*

"Now, I'm going to give you a mild sedative. Then I'll give you your morning margarita." His eyes crinkled, and she guessed he was smiling. "It's quite a cocktail."

"Will I feel sick afterward?"

"No way," he said firmly. He gave her a pat. Then he looked up and said, " 'Morning, Dr. Coleman."

Joyce was confused. "I thought Dr. Martinez was going to be here?"

"He asked Dr. Coleman to head the team," Dr. Charaka explained. "He'll look in on you later."

"Oh, but . . ." She felt a sharp jab in the back of her hand, and she began to feel dizzy. She heard something whining *beep beep beep.*

A short time later, she was aware of someone saying, "Joyce? Please breathe into the mask. Good. Very good."

Then a disembodied voice said, "Joyce, I'm Dr. Coleman. We've met. Can you hear me?"

"Help," Joyce whispered.

"Don't you worry, Joyce," said the voice. "Just go to sleep."

Joyce Summers dreamed.

She was young again, and with her husband, Hank. Buffy was somehow still the same age as she was now . . . whenever now was.

They were walking through a forest. Everyone was dressed in white. Joyce and Buffy wore coronets of wildflowers in their hair, and as Joyce smiled at her daughter, she thought, *She's my child. I brought her into this world.*

The forest dripped exquisite petals—roses, violets, lavender—and Buffy held out the hem of her dress to catch them.

From a stand of weeping willows, a shape parted the drooping branches. It was a snow-white unicorn, a magnificent creature, stately yet delicate. Its golden horn glistened in the magical forest light. It stamped a silver hoof once, chuffing, and bobbed its head in Buffy's direction.

"Oh, it's beautiful," Joyce's daughter whispered.

She reached out a hand to pat the creature's forelocks. It dipped its head lower.

It charged.

It slammed its horn through Buffy's side.

Buffy screamed.

And then she became a shower of petals which fell to the moist, rich earth.

Buffy was pacing in the waiting room. She could make no sense of what was on the TV—she, who used to skip school on such a regular basis back in L.A. that she had memorized the entire daytime programming lineup, including all the major cable channels—and she hadn't been able to read any of the out-of-date *Time* magazines heaped on a number of coffee tables around the room.

"Buffy."

She looked up and walked straight into Willow's arms. They held each other for a moment. Willow whispered, "Any news?"

"The surgeon was delayed," Buffy said in agony. "This is taking forever."

Oz came in next, followed by Giles. The Watcher's expression was grim at best. Buffy gazed levelly at him and said, "What?"

"Xander and Cordelia are missing."

Buffy closed her eyes. "As in, they didn't show up at school, or as in, you don't have any idea where they are?"

"The latter." When she stared at him, he said helpfully, "Door number two."

She remained silent.

"I heard Cordelia screaming on her cell phone."

She took that in.

Giles said, "How's your mother?"

"Funny thing. I'd like to know that, too." She ran both hands through her hair. "They're in there cutting her open. Spreading her ribcage apart with, like, these huge nutcrackers. Don't ask me to leave her, Giles. Because I can't."

"She's in good hands," Giles ventured.

"No." Willow took a step in front of Buffy, inserting herself between Slayer and Watcher. "It's not right to ask Buffy to leave."

"Next he'll say there's nothing I can do here," Buffy muttered, staring at Giles with a tormented expression on her face. "Which is true. And a lot I can do if Xander and Cordy are in trouble."

"She's your mother, Buffy," Willow insisted.

"Of course, you're both right," Giles said. "I shouldn't have presumed—"

"And why not?" Buffy burst out. "Just because I happen to be the Slayer with the sick mom? You're supposed to tiptoe around me because I have split loyalties or something? Is that in the Slayer's Handbook, or is it just more proof that I'm all wrong for the job? Because I love my mother?"

"Buffy, please, calm yourself," Giles begged, as interested faces glanced their way.

A little boy tugged the pants leg of a man who was getting a cup of coffee from a vending machine and said, "What's a Slayer? What's wrong with her mommy?"

"Oh, God." Buffy wiped her face and marched into the corridor. Giles accompanied her. "All right. What do you want me to do?"

Giles shook his head. "I was wrong to come here. We can search for them. And we're quite a formidable team."

"Oh, yeah." She was not being sarcastic in the least. "You guys can kick evil bootie from one end of the Hellmouth to the other."

"We're going. We'll be back to check on you," Giles assured her. "Cordelia and Xander in tow, bickering as always."

"A sight for sore ears," she replied.

"Right, then."

He ducked his head into the waiting room and gestured for Willow and Oz to follow him. With one last tight hug, Willow brushed past Buffy, wrapping her arm around Oz's.

Then, as abruptly as they had arrived, they left.

"Are you sick?" the little boy asked Buffy.

Buffy only stared at him.

The day had seemed endless. Now, at last, the dusk was upon them. In the condemned police station, Veronique imperiously clapped her hands. The sun had barely set when she spoke.

"We will depart. It is time to feed."

The vampires, though sluggish with hunger, responded eagerly to her announcement. Konstantin took Catherine's hand in his—a gesture not overlooked by their mistress—and they smiled at each other, oblivious of the consequences.

Konstantin was so hungry he had been tempted to taste the humans held in reserve for the hatchlings, including the newcomers, the dark-haired boy and girl. The two were young, and filled with vitality. Their blood smelled clean and fresh and rich, and whenever he stood near their cage, he swayed with his need.

Now his lot was about to become even worse. Veronique had determined that he and Catherine were the only two among her brood that she trusted to obey her, despite their hunger. Thus, the two of them were to be left to watch the prisoners—the first meal for the Three-Who-Are-One after their reunification—while the Harbinger led the others on the blood quest.

Konstantin wished that he could be certain Veronique's trust in him was warranted. But he was not. He did know, however, what the consequences of slaking his thirst would be. If he and Catherine fed, their lives would surely be forfeit when Veronique returned and saw what they had done.

Over the racket of the clacking, active hatchlings, Konstantin and Catherine stood back and listened to the Harbinger address the others. The brood was very attentive.

"The blood bank is on the third floor," Veronique reminded them. "The same floor as the surgical recovery unit, which is excellent. Most of those patients will be so groggy they won't notice us."

"Why don't we drink of the patients?" the Brit, Niles, asked.

Veronique narrowed her eyes in distaste. "Anesthetized human blood? Diseased cattle? I'll not allow it. No taking of lives. No attacking humans. We'll steal the blood bank's plastic dinners and drink when we are safe and away. You will not risk yourselves, you will not draw undue attention or waste time."

"Cold, dead blood." Catherine shivered.

"Be grateful for it when we bring it to you," Veronique snapped. "Or die of starvation. I don't care."

She stomped away. Catherine was stunned. Konstantin patted her hand and said, "Don't worry. She won't harm you. She needs all of us for the Ritual."

"But what about after?" Catherine asked nervously.

"We must not speak like this," Konstantin replied, his guard up. He still didn't fully trust her when she talked like this. Now was not the time to be branded a traitor, no matter what assurances he might give the beautiful vampire. After all, there were live humans in the police station. Any one of them could be transformed if another vampire were needed.

Konstantin watched as they all filed out after the Harbinger. When they were gone, he allowed himself to change. It had been all he could do to control himself in those minutes. The hunger was wracking his whole body. His face kept morphing from vampire to human and back again. It had been stupid, cruel, and arrogant of Veronique to bring them to this state. He was not sure he would ever forgive her. But one thing was certain: his trust in her leadership was permanently destroyed.

She is immortal, he reminded himself. *I can't kill her.*

It became a mantra as he tried to control himself, bloodlust clouding all other thoughts.

She is immortal.

"Miss Summers."

Someone was shaking Buffy's shoulder. She sucked in air and half jumped from her chair, to see the wrinkled face of Dr. Leah Coleman inches from her own.

"Mom," Buffy blurted.

Dr. Coleman smiled gently. "Your mother is recovering nicely. We took out the mass and did a frozen section. It was not malignant."

"But . . . was it . . . is she . . . ?"

The doctor's thin white hands cupped Buffy's own. Buffy saw now that the doctor wore turquoise scrubs. She had a bonnet stuffed in her breast pocket, along with a stethoscope, and a white mask was draped around her neck, dangling from two sets of ties in back. Her hair was cropped short and very white. She looked positively ancient.

"It appears your mother had Valley Fever," the doctor said. "She's going to be pretty weak for a time to come. But most people make a full recovery."

Buffy stared at her. "Most."

"Oh, I think she'll be fine," the doctor said. "The mass was caused by a fungal infection, which we found in the tissue when we examined it. But there's no evidence of it having spread. Now that we've taken it out, she should be right as rain."

Dr. Coleman cricked her neck and stifled a yawn. "Excuse me, dear. I've been on my feet a long time. I'm sorry your mother had to wait. Delays are routine nowadays." Her face softened. "So much has changed since I started practicing medicine."

Buffy looked at her closely. It was so hard for her to picture what Dr. Coleman might have looked like when she was young, when Angel had known her, and she had given him just a little bit of hope. She found herself feeling sad for Angel, and for Dr. Coleman, too. She could afford to feel bad for someone else, now that she had hope that her mother would be all right.

"We still want to keep an eye on her, of course. Make absolutely certain we've gotten rid of it all. But I think we're in the clear. Would you like to see her?" Dr. Coleman asked.

"Oh. I can?" Buffy said quickly. She jumped to her feet. "Yes. Of course I do." She swallowed. "I've been having trouble swallowing. Dizziness . . ."

"Classic anxiety symptoms." Dr. Coleman patted her. "They'll go away eventually."

Buffy was uncomfortable with that. She didn't know why, exactly. But she nodded and followed the doctor out into the corridor.

"Go down the hall and then to the left. She's in 311." Dr. Coleman gave her another smile. "I'm going to go to my hotel and make a pitcher of margaritas."

Buffy was a little surprised; this staid old grandmother didn't seem the margarita type. But she nodded and began to leave. Then she whirled around and called, "Dr. Coleman!" to the retreating figure.

"Thank you," Buffy said feelingly. "Thank you so much."

"You'll be fine. Both of you." The doctor gave her a salute and slowly walked away.

Buffy started running, then slackened her pace when a nurse behind a large console glared at her. She wheeled around the corner and headed for 311. She passed by a room where a man was moaning, "Hallo? Hallo?" with a foreign accent. There was weeping in another room.

The door to 311 was open, and Buffy sailed in.

Joyce opened her eyes and smiled at her. There was an IV needle in the back of her hand, and she was pasty against the white pillow. But she was her mom.

And she didn't have cancer.

"Did they tell you, Mom?" Buffy asked, bursting into tears.

Joyce held out her right arm. "Buffy, honey, come here."

Buffy knelt beside the bed and cried. Her heavy sobs wracked her body; her throat became even tighter, so tight she could barely breathe.

She didn't know if she cried for five minutes or five hours, but after a while, she couldn't do it anymore, even though everything in her wanted to. She realized that through it all, her mother had been stroking the crown of her bowed head.

Buffy looked up. Her mother was wincing with pain.

"Mom?" Buffy asked, alarmed.

"I'm just sore. They're going to bring me a morphine drip."

She touched Buffy's hair. "I was afraid I was going to leave you behind."

"I was afraid . . ." Buffy began, then sagged. "I was just afraid."

"My poor little girl. You've been through so much." Joyce's face was radiant. "I'm still here for you, honey."

"They told me you're still sick. You have something called Valley Fever."

"Sounds hokey, huh?" Joyce grinned. Then her smile started to sleep. Her lids fluttered. "Honey, I'm so tired. Go help Mr. Giles."

"No," Buffy protested.

"I'm okay. I'm very tired." Joyce patted her. "Ask the nurse to bring me some painkillers, okay?"

"I'm not going."

"Honey, I need to sleep. I need this." She tilted her head and studied Buffy's face. "When I look at you, I still feel the same sense of awe as when I gave birth to you. They laid you in my arms." Her eyes closed, opened. "About five minutes ago."

"And now I'm all grown up. Almost." Buffy was terribly wistful for the earlier, simpler days.

Joyce chuckled. Then she drifted.

Buffy reluctantly left the room. She found some nurses gossiping about a new doctor and asked them to give her mom something for the pain.

"We'll take care of her, honey," one of the nurses told her.

"Right," Buffy murmured.

She left, trying to focus on the problems at hand—Xander and Cordelia in trouble, an immortal vampire, the Tri-whatever, yadda yadda. But all she could think about was, *My mom isn't going to die.*

She left the hospital, oblivious to the shadows pooling around the back entrance.

Oblivious to the fact that they brought death with them.

Chapter Fourteen

The Sea of Crete, 1862

They navigated by the stars, the wind filling their sails, the rigging pulled taut. But Veronique paid no attention to the stars or the wind or the fullness of the sails. She stood on the bow of the ship and stared out at the choppy sea, imagining that she could see her quarry ahead of her. She could almost taste the blood of the Slayer mingling with the salt in the air.

Cresting the swells, the ship came in sight of a tiny island off the port bow. Veronique turned slightly to catch the captain's eye and pointed at the island. The wind whipped the man's long hair across his face, but he gave her a meaningful stare and nodded ruefully.

Veronique smiled. This, then, was their destination.

For weeks, she had pursued the Slayer along the eastern edge of the Adriatic. She had killed at her leisure and taken clothing and currency wherever she found it. Once, near Tirana, she had nearly overtaken the girl. But Veronique must take cover by day, and the girl had no such restrictions. Save sleep. That was the only reason she had not escaped Veronique completely——she needed sleep.

In retrospect, though, Veronique thought that perhaps there was one other reason. The Slayer was a beautiful young girl, traveling alone, who had encountered more than a few bands of ruffians who would challenge her virtue. Veronique scowled in amusement at the thought of the little harlot in fear for whatever virtue she had remaining to her. Angela's confrontations with those men had left a trail behind clearer than Veronique might have hoped.

Upon arrival at Athens, it had been a simple enough task to discover that the girl had gone ahead by boat, hoping still to escape her wrath. But Veronique had made a vow to herself and to her masters. She would not rest until the Slayer was dead.

For centuries, Veronique had tried time and again to bring the Triumvirate to Earth, where they would transform the land into an inferno. To her disappointment, she had relied for far too long upon the daunting magicks they had taught her, rituals they vowed would bring them forth. Only when she realized that it was not working did it occur to her to think for herself, to find a solution.

Truly, she would be eternally blessed.

For she *had* found a solution. The Three-Who-Are-One could not pass into the plane of man in their whole, united form. They must be broken down into their component parts, born unto death, and reunited under the aligned stars.

Veronique had rejoiced with this discovery, and the Triumvirate had been very pleased with her. At long last, their lusts would be fulfilled.

And would have been, if not for Angela Martignetti.

The translucent flesh, the hatchlings writhing beneath, pressing to be free . . . and then the Slayer bursting in, thrusting the stake into the heart of the vampire shell, their vessel . . . turning it to dust . . . closing the way.

In all the weeks she had pursued the girl, Veronique's fury had not abated even a fraction. If anything, it had grown. This girl knew too much about her, as had her Watcher, Toscano.

Who had burned. Veronique smiled at that thought, the wind whipping her face as the ship closed in on the island. The ship she had hired in Athens to pursue the girl to Crete, where all reports indicated she had gone. And in Crete, there were whispers that she had set out to sea, running, hiding from some horrid pursuer.

"But I am her mother," Veronique had said, wearing the stolen garments of a noblewoman. "I have come to fetch her home. The danger has passed."

And with gold likewise stolen, she had paid the captain to continue on, to take her out to the island to which the Slayer had fled. This little whitewashed bit of stone in the midst of the Sea of Crete.

Kefi.

In a small dip in the land, away from the wind, the people of Kefi were burning their dead. It was just after dawn, the third day after the *bucolac* had come. Upon her arrival, the first thing she had done was to make other vampires.

Just as Angela had expected.

Veronique was not a fool. She knew how far from any other land the island was, how far from other vampires. Should she die here, on this island, it might be some time before another vampire was created nearby, allowing her to live again. But the Slayer knew it as well. Which was why, when she had first arrived on the island nearly a week earlier, she had tried to convince the people of Kefi that they must leave.

To do so, she had broken a cardinal rule of the Council of Watchers; she had told the truth. But the truth was the only way she could see to get these people not merely to leave their homes but never to return.

They had mocked her.

They had stayed.

And upon Veronique's arrival, they had begun to die.

Angela absolved herself of blame. She had done all she could to prepare these people, to send them away. Veronique had now made at least three new vampires. And killed dozens of other islanders, those now in flames atop the enormous funeral pyre.

As the bodies burned, and Angela watched with a numbness

inside where her tears ought to have come from, one of the older men from the island approached her carefully. Though his face was weathered and wrinkled, his eyes were young and blue as the Aegean.

"We were fools not to listen," he told her in Greek, a language she only half understood.

It had been difficult for her to express her concerns to them in the first place. But she had made them understand, if not believe. Now, though . . . now they believed.

For she had killed Veronique twice in as many nights. Here on this island. Both times, with islanders bearing witness. And yet, because she had made other vampires of their loved ones, the islanders were not rid of Veronique's evil. She would continue to plague them for as long as there were humans living there, humans who could be made into vampires.

"We will go," the old man said.

He was weeping.

All through that morning, homes were abandoned, belongings were gathered, ships set out to sea. Angela watched the exodus for a time, but when the sun was highest in the sky, she knew that her work must begin. The island was small, yet it took her many hours before she finally found the abandoned whitewashed hut where Veronique's offspring lay resting, away from the rays of the sun. Their mistress was not there, but this was the primary job in any case.

Angela tore the shutters from the small home and heard the shrieking within as the sunlight splashed onto the dusty floor inside. When she entered, they were cowering in the corner, three of them, though there was a small puff of dust that might have been a fourth before the sun had burst through.

They attacked as best they could, but Angela used the sun against them, dancing in and out of its rays, leading them in to be burned. Within minutes, two of them were dead, leaving only the last.

"Do you want to live? To sleep the day away and emerge in the shadows, to set out to sea and find some other hunting

ground? Shall I spare you, demon?" she asked, sneering, her
heart beating and sweat dripping from her brow.

The vampire nodded.

"Where sleeps your mistress?" Angela narrowed her eyes.

The creature hesitated only a moment. "In the church," it said.

A tremor of disgust and hatred like none she had ever felt
rippled through Angela. She remembered Peter, burning to
death. Remembered Lucia. Her emotions were in turmoil, but
within that chaos, one thing was clear: none of her heartache
would exist save for the evil of Veronique.

Now it would end.

Angela moved on the remaining vampire quickly. It tried to
attack but was hesitant because of the light. She brought her
stake down, but it was knocked from her grasp. The vampire
grabbed her around the throat, but Angela only smiled grimly
at it as she broke the grip. She struck out, crushing its nose,
splitting its lip over fangs. Then she grabbed it by the hair and
hauled it across the dusty floor, shrieking, into the sunlight.

It exploded in a shower of burning dust.

The Slayer brushed what remained of the vampire from her
clothes as she went out and started to climb up the long hill toward the church and the trio of bells that sat, one upon the others, on the overlook above the sea.

They were alone on the island, then. The Slayer and
Veronique.

The immortal vampire had nowhere to run.

Curled in a small alcove near the back of the church,
Veronique lay with her eyes tightly closed, only barely asleep.
Though they might come here in worship, they would not see
her unless they were looking. And none of the superstitious
fools would ever guess that she was hiding from the sun within
the walls of their sacred church.

She slept with the security of that knowledge.

Shattered, as the door slammed open with a crash and crack
of wood.

Veronique's eyes opened, and she vaulted to her feet. This was no mere worshiper, come to pray for deliverance from evil. The sheep came quietly to the shepherd. No, she knew there was no hiding from this intruder. She knew that it must be the Slayer.

"Come out, vampire!" the girl cried.

There was another crash, perhaps a bench tipping over. Veronique smiled to herself, thinking how foolish the girl was. She stepped out from the shadows of her hiding place and noticed immediately the dim sun stretching its fingers in through the open door. Dim, because out over the ocean, the orb burned the water as it sank on the horizon.

Dusk.

"Hello, Slayer," Veronique said, speaking the girl's native Italian. "Have you come to kill me yet again? I am so frightened." The vampire stretched sleepily, bored. "Or it may be that this time, I will kill you? Ah, but you won't come back, will you?"

Veronique was a bit taken aback by the Slayer's smile.

"You are so very wrong, Veronique," Angela said happily.

Her clothes were torn, and there was blood on her collarbone and her upper right thigh. Veronique wondered how she would taste. A Slayer's blood, she knew, held great power.

"Truly? Educate me, then, girl, before I kill you."

"You believe you are immortal," Angela said. "Perhaps that is so. But I am also immortal."

A flicker of doubt went through Veronique's mind, and then she smiled cruelly. It was not possible, of course.

"You don't believe me, I see," Angela went on. "If I kill you, you will be reborn. But if you take my life, my blood, so will I be returned to life. For the very moment I breathe my last, somewhere in the world another girl will find herself gifted with the strength and the duties of the Slayer. Strike me down, I will rise again in her."

Veronique nodded in understanding. There was truth to what the girl said. But it mattered not. For before a new Slayer could find her, she would go to ground, to plan for the next time the stars aligned, that she might bring the Triumvirate to Earth at last.

"An eternal war," she told the girl. "Or so you think."

"No," the Slayer replied, and her smiled returned. Then she stepped aside and gestured toward the door, beyond which the sun had finally slipped beneath the waves. "It is a long way to Crete, Veronique."

The vampire frowned, confused. Then she pushed that confusion aside and stepped toward the girl. "Come then, Slayer. Let us engage in this struggle once more." Her features changed, fangs protruding, and her eyes blazed yellow in the dark.

The Slayer nodded, reached into the folds of her ragged garments, and withdrew a stake. "Oh, yes, let's," she whispered. "Just you and me, Veronique."

The vampire lunged for her, and the Slayer dodged to one side and brought an elbow down on Veronique's skull, driving her to the floor. The vampire rolled, leaped to her feet, and turned to face the Slayer again.

"Just you and me," Angela repeated. "The battle comes down to the two of us, demon, because we are the last. We are alone here, on the island. No human, no vampire remains, save for we two."

Veronique paused to stare at her, understanding beginning to sink in. Crete *was* ever so far away. Too far. If she were killed here, it would mean she must wait for the island to be settled once more, long enough that a vampire might come, and take one of them. Unless her masters aided her. But she had already failed them so very often; she had no faith that they would.

"Come, then, vampire," the Slayer snarled. "Perhaps we'll die together."

Then the girl lunged for her prey. Veronique barely moved aside in time. Her eyes darted around the church, to windows and broken door, out to the ocean beyond, longing to be anywhere but there in that room with Angela Martignetti. The Slayer.

For the first time in many centuries, the creature called Veronique was afraid.

* * *

Angel stood among the cars in the parking lot at Sunnydale Hospital, blending with the shadows as best he could. He knew that Buffy was inside, thanks to the message she had left him, but he had decided it would be best for him to wait out here. When she emerged, he would go to her, and stay with her as long as she needed him.

The minutes ticked by unnoticed. What did they mean to him, after all? Long hours filled with nothing were not uncommon for his life. But keeping this vigil for Joyce, and for Buffy, was enough to occupy his mind and heart.

Until he saw Leah coming out of the hospital. A small smile spread over Angel's features, and he stepped even more deeply into the shadows, crouching a bit, as she came toward him. She stopped only a row away, and he watched her. With a striking suddenness, he was overwhelmed by the memory of the first time he'd seen her, when she'd come into the alley and he had watched her, skulking in the darkness. This was so similar, it was painful for him to remember.

For a moment, he dropped his gaze.

Then he heard Leah Coleman scream.

Before his mind had begun to register what was truly happening, Angel was vaulting onto the hood of the car in front of him. Several vampires had come from the darkness deeper into the lot to attack Leah, and he saw many others moving as shadows toward the hospital.

"You should have kept your mouth shut," one of the vampires snarled at her. "If you hadn't seen us, you would not have to die. But we cannot afford to have you sound an alarm, old woman."

Angel ran across the hoods of cars, his heavy boots denting the metal, and then he dove at the nearest of the vamps, tackling it to the ground. The vampire tried to rise, but Angel was up first. He kicked the vampire in the head, and then the chest, and turned on the others.

"Dear God, what is this?" Leah cried. "What are they?"

The other two vampires advanced on Angel, and he prepared to fight them, trying not to be distracted by Leah's fearful questions. Then he heard a scraping behind him, knew that the other had gotten up, and started to turn. They were all on him at once. Angel lashed out, shattered the cheek of one of them, and the others began to pummel him.

He went down. Leah screamed at the vampires, trying to drive them away, and he heard a blow, and a cry. He felt the roar building in his chest, and though he did not want her to see him that way, he gave in to the vampire, let his face change to feral. Angel screamed at them, a guttural bellow, and threw them off. He grabbed one and drove it face first into a car window, which shattered.

Then he ran to Leah's side. She was on her knees, trying to use the front of a car to drag herself to her feet. Her face was bleeding, and she clutched her chest in pain.

Angel willed his face to change again, praying she hadn't seen him.

"What is it? Are you badly hurt?" he asked.

"She'll be dead in a second," one of the vampires snarled.

Angel started to turn to face them.

"No," said another, a stout bald male with tattoos on his arms. "We cannot afford the time, or any defeat. You know what Veronique said. Leave them. Before they can do anything, it will be too late."

Then they were running across the lot toward the hospital. Angel wanted to give chase, but Leah groaned beside him.

"Leah, hold on," he said, fearing for her. "I'll get you into the hospital. Just hold on."

He lifted her in his arms, dismayed by how frail she seemed.

"You . . . know my name," she rasped. "Have we met?"

Angel looked in her eyes and saw that she truly did not know him. Even now, in this frightful moment, she had no idea who he was. Once, he had felt that he loved her. She gave him the tiniest bit of hope when he needed it so desperately. And she didn't even remember his face, though he had not changed at all since they had last met.

"No," he said. "You don't know me."

Then he went toward the hospital entrance with her, moving as swiftly as he dared, given her pain.

The Sea of Crete, 1862

Angela Martignetti lived by herself on Kefi for nearly four months before the Council of Watchers finally tracked her down. When her new Watcher arrived in the back of a fishing boat to retrieve her, he greeted her without any civility whatsoever. Even his stance was hostile.

"I am Jason Cromwell," he said. "Where is the de Molay volume you retrieved from the fire?"

"In a stable in Tirana," she replied icily. "It was a choice between the book and my life."

Cromwell looked down his nose at her. "Given the way you have disgraced your station, it's possible you chose poorly."

Not a word was spoken on the boat as it sailed back to Athens.

Though their attitude toward her changed greatly over time—out of necessity—Angela Martignetti never lifted a finger to aid the Council of Watchers again. She had planned to die on Kefi.

For many years thereafter, she wished that she had.

Between bites of her meatball sandwich, Willow glanced around the library guiltily and sighed. "I feel like we're betraying everyone," she said. "Buffy and her mom are still at the hospital. Xander and Cordy are still missing. Who knows what that Veronique thing is up to tonight?"

"Really, Willow, I understand your misgivings," Giles replied. "But we spent half the day searching for Xander and Cordelia. There is nothing we can do to aid Buffy at the moment other than what we have been doing. And the very reason we came back here to the library was so that I could confer with my notes once more to attempt to determine the location of tonight's ceremony."

"Then there's the eating," Oz added. "It isn't guilt-free."

"See!" Willow said, exasperated.

"We must eat if we plan to go on. For the moment, I'm afraid our search for Xander and Cordelia must take a lower priority than locating Veronique and preventing her from performing the ritual that will bring the Triumvirate to Earth. That creature must not escape its Hellish domain and break into our own.

"In fact, as soon as we are done here, we must go to the hospital and retrieve Buffy. Until now, it has been possible for us to function without her. But to stop this ritual, the Slayer must be with us. Otherwise, there is really no point to saving her mother. By tomorrow morning, all of Sunnydale will be nothing but scorched earth, and the people along with it."

"You always know just the right spin to put on things," Willow told him. "If, y'know, you're trying to *terrify* me."

They ate. Giles continued to read.

Willow tortured herself wondering if Xander and Cordelia were still alive, and wracked her brain trying to figure out where Veronique might have jailed them, if for some reason she was keeping them alive.

Suddenly, she had it.

Jailed them!

"Oh . . ." She started to speak, and then paused to swallow her food. "They're in Old Town. That's got to be it. It's one of the only places we didn't search that well, 'cause we thought it was too close to civilization, that they'd be noticed. But I'll bet they're holed up in one of the buildings down there, maybe the old police station."

"I'm afraid I don't know Sunnydale as well as you two," Giles said slowly.

But Oz just nodded. He dropped his foot to the wrappers on the study table and stood up.

"Let's go."

Cordelia glared expectantly at Xander.

"What?" he asked, not for the first time.

"Why are we still alive?" she demanded.

"You have a problem with this?" he asked. " 'Cause, I've gotta tell ya, I'm kinda yay life right now. And despite the fact that the last hours or minutes of that pitiful life may be spent having to listen to the Queen of the Shallow Parts of the Nile whine about how being incarcerated in a crumbling building with demons and vampires just plays havoc with her hair . . . I'm still feeling pretty warm and fuzzy about life."

Cordelia rolled her eyes. "Are you through?"

Xander shrugged. "Pretty much."

"Why are we still alive?" she asked again.

Xander slapped himself in the forehead and stared imploringly at the gray ceiling, mutely praying for some kind of help. He received no answer.

"We're not the only ones, either," she said.

"What was your first clue?" he asked. "The screaming?"

Indeed, there was screaming. They were in a jail cell in what was obviously the closed-down police station in Old Town. There were vampires here. Lots of them. But so far, they hadn't taken a bite out of Xander or Cordelia, or, as far as they knew, from any of the other handful of people also in captivity down here.

Xander was thinking that was a good sign.

Which was about the time he heard the scraping of the metal door at the end of the hall and then footsteps coming down toward them.

"Get back from the door," he whispered to Cordelia. "If they come in, maybe we can rush them."

Just as he glanced back out through the bars, there came a snarl, and a vampire lunged at him, thrust its hands between the bars, and grabbed his shirt, hauling him up hard against the metal.

"Oh, yeah," the vampire whispered. "That's gonna work."

"Or not," Xander said reasonably. "If you have a better plan, feel free to speak up."

It took a moment, what with the snarling in his face and the fangs and such, but Xander realized he recognized the vamp in front of him.

"Wait, I know you," he said.

"Oh, great, you're just buds now?" Cordelia sighed. "Always the schmooze-hound. Gotta know someone everywhere we go."

"You're Konstantin, right?" Xander asked, badly faking an amiable smile. "I'm Xander."

"I'm hunggrreeeee!" Konstantin screamed into Xander's face, yanking him hard against the bars again and again.

Then Konstantin let him go, and Xander stumbled back, grabbing onto Cordelia. "Please to meet you, hungry," he said meekly.

Konstantin stepped back a bit, into the shadows of the darkened corridor.

"And if Veronique does not return with blood soon," he growled ferociously. "Then I will have yours, no matter what punishment may come."

Buffy walked across the parking lot toward the grass beyond. It wasn't a really long walk from the hospital back to school—which is where she figured she'd meet up with Giles, Willow, and Oz—but it certainly felt far away.

Valley Fever. What the hell is that? Sounds like something only soap opera characters could get.

Her mother was still sick. Buffy wanted to stay. But she also knew that at midnight, she had somewhere to be.

"Yeah, great," she muttered to herself. "Got a date with a demon."

A sudden scream slashed through the night. Buffy stopped, stood completely still, and listened to the sounds coming to her on the wind, trying to pinpoint the direction of the scream. She couldn't, but she started slowly back toward the hospital, her every muscle tensed.

There were things she had to do, but she couldn't just walk away from a scream.

Moments later, she heard the sounds of a struggle, and she started to run along a row of cars. She heard talking, saw several figures dodging among cars, moving toward the hospital. Then she spotted Angel carrying Dr. Coleman in his arms. She called out to him, but he seemed not to hear her.

Buffy ran to him.

"Angel," she said, coming up beside him. "What's going on?"

"Vampires. Veronique's, I think. They're infiltrating the hospital. Leah saw them, and they attacked her to silence her. I think she's having a heart attack."

Buffy heard the strain in his voice, his fear for Dr. Coleman, and she sympathized. But there were so many other priorities at the moment.

"Get her inside," she said. "I've got to figure out what they . . . wait! You don't think they're after my mother?"

"For what purpose?" he asked as they hustled toward the entrance. "No, the ritual is tonight. They've been hiding from you, and they're not here for trouble now."

"Then why are they here?"

Angel glanced at her. "Maybe for blood? They weren't expecting trouble, so maybe they were going to go after the stored supply. That's third floor."

"How do you—" Buffy cut herself off. "All right," she said with a nod. "Meet me up there. My mother's room is on the third floor. And if they already know they've got trouble, that things aren't going to go as smoothly as they think, maybe they're going to try to grab some fresh stuff after all."

The moment they went inside the doors, with Angel calling out for a gurney and a doctor, they separated. Buffy ignored the elevators, just as she expected the vampires would have done, and headed for the stairs. Just inside the door on the ground floor, there was a guard.

Not a human one, of course. That would have been too convenient.

The vampire lunged at her, but Buffy brought her foot around in an arc and kicked him hard in the side of the head.

He went tumbling down the stairs toward the basement, and she didn't even bother going after him. Instead, she pulled out a stake and started up the stairs two at a time.

As she emerged onto the third floor, she heard shouting and the shatter of glass. She slammed the door open and stood in the corridor, looking in both directions.

In the midst of the chaos was a female vampire Buffy knew must be Veronique. She was very tall and muscular, with short black hair and tattoos. She looked dangerous, nothing like the other bodies the immortal vampire had taken. This one seemed more suited to Veronique's arrogance. Still, that wasn't the give-away. There was just something in the way she carried herself that Buffy recognized now, no matter what body she was in. And, of course, she was screaming orders at her followers.

"Damn you fools!" she roared. "Quick and quiet. Those were my commands. You have jeopardized the Ritual, and for that some of you will surely pay. But not tonight!"

"You know, it didn't hit me till just now," Buffy told her, "but you kinda remind me of my second-grade teacher."

Veronique snapped her head around to glare at Buffy. "Slayer," she growled, her voice low. "Why must you always interfere? It was true, what you said long ago. It is an eternal war."

"I don't remember that," Buffy told her. "Must've been my evil twin. Oh, wait, that's Willow with the evil twin."

Veronique bristled and attacked. "You mock me, girl? Even after all this, you don't fear me? I will teach you fear."

Buffy held the stake out to one side and readied herself. When Veronique lunged, she dodged to one side and grabbed the vampire by her hair. She yanked back Veronique's head and raised her stake.

"See, there's that resemblance to Mrs. MacWhirter again."

She brought the stake down.

"Buffy?"

It was her mother's voice. Buffy turned, slightly, wavering, to see Joyce standing in the doorway to her room, looking pale and weak and impossibly vulnerable.

"Get back in your—"

Veronique roared and snapped her head forward, slamming her skull into Buffy's. The Slayer staggered backward, and then shook it off, facing Veronique again.

"Mistress?" called a vampire who was coming up the hall behind her.

"Go!" Veronique snapped, without turning. "Take the others, take the blood, and get back to the nest. I will deal with this."

"But Harbinger—"

"Go!" Veronique screamed, and launched herself at Buffy.

The vampire obeyed. They all did, running for the stairs at the other end of the corridor.

Buffy tried to dodge again, bringing the stake up at the ready. Veronique feinted and then punched Buffy, hard, in the side of the face. Rattled, Buffy staggered, and Veronique knocked the stake from her hand.

"You're too arrogant for your own good, Slayer," Veronique hissed, smiling. "Perhaps there will be another after you, but after tonight, it won't matter. Not at all. The stars have told the tale. By dawn, this place will be only the first foothold of my masters on Earth."

"Not if I have anything to say about it," Buffy snapped, and leaped up into a roundhouse kick.

At the precise moment that Veronique ducked past her. Buffy started to come down, thrown because her target was no longer in front of her. Veronique grabbed her around the neck and flipped her into a glass partition. It shattered, and Buffy crashed down on the broken shards of glass. She staggered to her feet, bleeding from a dozen tiny cuts.

"That's the point you're missing, Slayer," Veronique said. "You don't have anything to say about it at all."

She moved on Buffy. The Slayer brought her left arm up to block. Veronique was expecting it, grabbed Buffy's arm, and spun around behind her, striking her a hard blow across the back of the neck. Buffy went down on her knees.

Veronique bent over her. "I've fought you enough, girl.

You've killed me too many times. I've studied you; I've paid attention. I know your style now. Every time you make a move, I'll already have guessed what it's going to be."

Buffy's instinct was to thrust her legs out behind her, to sweep Veronique off her feet. It was the smartest move, as it would give her a chance to rise, to regain her balance. But she couldn't do that. It was what Veronique would have expected.

She drove her head back as hard as she could, slamming the back of her skull against Veronique's nose, shattering it. She felt the vampire's blood on her scalp as she rose and rammed her elbow behind her.

But Veronique was ready for it. She grabbed Buffy by the elbow and twined the fingers of her other hand in Buffy's hair. Then Veronique drove her down the corridor and slammed her headfirst into a wall. Buffy tasted blood, and this time, she knew it was her own.

"Get away from her, you bitch!"

Buffy blinked into full consciousness to see her mother, haggard, in a hospital gown, facing off against Veronique with only a small crucifix that she had packed with her things for her surgery.

Veronique hissed.

Then she laughed. "It doesn't matter," she said. "Soon, it will all be done. Another few hours, Slayer. Enjoy them."

With that, the immortal vampire turned and ran down the corridor, following the path her blood children had taken. Almost the instant that she disappeared beyond that door, the elevator pinged and the doors slid wide, and Angel stepped in with security guards and orderlies behind him.

"Buffy!" he cried in alarm.

Angel and her mother were both crouched by her. Buffy tasted her own blood again, and it enraged her. She used the sleeve of her shirt to wipe the blood from her face. A security guard tried to ask her what had happened, and Joyce shooed the man away.

"Buffy, just wait for a doctor," her mother was saying. "You'll be all right."

"I don't *need* a doctor," Buffy insisted.

She dragged herself to her feet, despite the protests of her mother and the man she loved.

"Buffy, maybe—" Angel began.

"Maybe nothing," she snapped. Then she spun to face the security guards. "Hey. You. This woman over here is my mother. Those freaks who were just in here, they have a grudge against her for something. They might be back. You keep someone on her room until dawn. After that, they'll have left town."

The guard frowned and looked at her. "Miss, I don't know who you are, but I can't just take all this on your say-so," he began.

Angel started toward him, but Buffy grabbed his shoulder and forced him to be still. She moved forward and stared up into the eyes of the much taller guard. She didn't stand on tiptoe. She didn't have to. It was more like he shrank.

"What's your name?" she snarled.

"Al Scott."

"Al," she said, trying to sound patient through gritted teeth. "I'll say this again. That's my mother. I will be back here to see her at dawn. If any harm should come to her, then I. Will. Come. To. You."

Without waiting for a response, Buffy spun and headed for the stairs. Angel followed instantly. Buffy was expecting her mother to call out, to try to talk her out of going. Instead, she heard one of the other security guards—not Al Scott, for sure—ordering her not to leave.

Then Joyce did speak. "I wouldn't do that, if I were you," the Slayer's mother said dangerously. "I'd just move out of her way."

I love you, Mom, Buffy thought. *I'll be back.*

Chapter Fifteen

Cordelia was terrified. For hours upon hours, she had kept up the façade of bravery, expecting Buffy and Giles and the others to show up and rescue her and Xander. But Buffy hadn't shown up.

And the vampires were hungry.

Konstantin and his bizarro girlfriend had moved them out of their cell and into a room with the most disgusting things Cordelia had ever seen. She didn't know why they'd been relocated, but neither one of them thought it was a good sign. Considering their life goals amounted to escaping or being rescued in the nick of time, it was definitely a move in the wrong direction.

Wherever in the condemned police station the rest of the human captives were, they were still screaming. Which was good, because that meant they were alive.

But so were the revolting monsters in the big bone pile, chomping and slithering and staring hard with their unnerving red eyes at Cordelia and Xander. They were disgusting things, scaly and taloned, with bits of pink stuff—*don't let it be pieces of people*—stuck to to their faces and legs.

Almost worse than the sight and sound of the creatures was their overpowering stench. The entire room reeked, the stink of death so thick that when Cordelia inhaled, it coated the inside of her mouth and throat and it was all she could do to keep herself from throwing up.

Meanwhile, the two vampires left to guard them had been semi-arguing, semi-commiserating together about their hunger for more than an hour. The problem for Cordelia was that she, the veteran of many, many, many diets, empathized with their plight—until she reminded herself that she was the object of their temptation.

"Hey, Cor," Xander whispered, trying his best to comfort her. "We'll be all right. Really."

She stared at him, frowning. "Please. Even you're not stupid enough to believe that. Don't insult me, all right? Cavalry? Not coming. We've got to figure something out before those two decide cocktail hour is more important than Veronique ripping their heads off."

Xander looked crestfallen. "You think they're gonna lose it, huh?"

"I don't know," she confessed, glancing down. "They're starving. But it's like when Harmony and I used to diet together. If they both stay strong, we'll be okay. But if one gives in, the other will. Even though Veronique would be pretty peeved."

"That's a comfort," Xander murmured.

She looked at him and nodded. "It is, Xander. They're terrified of her. If they weren't, we would already be dead."

He gave her a look. "Which brings us back to the notion of yay life."

"Okay, all right. " She ran her hands through her hair and dropped them in her lap. Her back to the vampires, she was sitting Indian-style, and her legs were starting to go to sleep. "You win. Whatever. I don't care. I just want to live to a ripe old age." *And so much for my thoughts on dying young and beautiful,* she thought.

"Ripe old age of what?" Xander jibed. "Twenty-four?"

"Oh, you think you're so smart," she said, but the truth was, she was a little wigged because he had practically read her thoughts.

"Actually, I don't," he admitted. He looked scared, but he smiled at her crookedly. "You've reminded me so often that I'm a cretin that, well, frankly, Cor, I think I might have started to believe it. Thus, I have rejected all my escape plans, and I'm sitting here like a dead duck."

She was taken aback. "Oh."

He sighed. "Also, facing death, I just don't have it in me to engage in cheap, meaningless banter any longer."

Cordelia was alarmed. "Xander, don't freak out on me." He said nothing. "Xander!" She smacked his arm.

He smiled. "Ow?"

"Don't give up," she said angrily. "We'll get out of this. We always do."

But even as she said it, Cordelia knew how hollow it sounded. They'd been lucky up until now. But eventually, their luck was bound to run out.

Xander's face drained of color. He murmured, "Uh-oh."

"Uh-oh?" she echoed shrilly, then dropped her voice as she looked over her shoulder. "Why?"

The two vampires were staring straight at them, and they were morphing. As the two vamps attacked, Xander grabbed Cordelia's hands and yanked her to her feet. The female caught Cordelia by the hair and threw her halfway across the room onto her back. Pain rattled through her like a cold, harsh wind.

As Cordelia tried to crawl away, the male caught Xander in a headlock and forced him to his knees.

"I can't stand it," Konstantin bellowed. "I am starving. The Triumvirate will have an entire world of souls to feast upon when it rises. These two won't be missed."

"Don't," Cordelia blurted at Catherine as the vampire kicked her. "Veronique will rip you guys to shreds."

With a wicked, scary growl, the female lowered her fangs toward Cordelia's neck. Cordelia's ribs ached as she gasped in terror. Her entire body was bruised and swollen.

"Shut up," Konstantin said in a hoarse rasp. "Just shut up. You are only food."

"The blue plate special," Xander moaned. His head was bent forward as if Konstantin were going to shoot him in the back of the head. "What'd I tell you, Cor?"

"Oh, my God!" Cordelia cried. "Xander, we're going to die!"

"The good news is," Xander grunted, "we can finally stop worrying about it." Then, as Konstantin yanked his head back, he cried out, "Ow! Hey, *ow!*"

Oh, my God. Cordelia shut her eyes. Catherine's fangs pricked her skin. *This is it. This is finally it.*

Then it was as if the entire room exploded. There was a horrible banging and footfalls and screams. Catherine was torn away from Cordelia, taking with her a good chunk of skin.

Cordelia sat up and shouted, "Buffy!"

But it wasn't Buffy. It was Veronique, in her latest incarnation, all slick black hair, leather, and funky tattoos. *But it doesn't make her look like a biker chick,* Cordelia thought. *It makes her look like a killer.*

"Idiots!" Veronique snarled at Konstantin and Catherine, who cowered, backing away. "I have spent centuries preparing for this night. Much of that time was wasted because I did not have the correct rituals, did not understand how to bring my master to Earth. When, finally, I corrected that error and found the way, one of those damned Slayers destroyed the vessel before the hatchlings could be born.

"Now, finally, the time has come! Despite the presence of this modern Slayer, the girl, Buffy, I have done it. Thirteen vampires from my bloodline, ready to perform the ritual. Ephialtes sacrificed himself to bring the hatchlings to this world, and they have been fed and have grown. The stars are in alignment, the portents are right! The Triumvirate will be reunited and will consume the souls of mankind, consigning them to a Hell even the biblical scholars never imagined."

Veronique strode across the room and peered into the nest of bones and garbage. The creatures within quieted as they looked out at her, almost adoringly. She lowered her gaze and shook her head.

"The hatchlings have been weaned on rotten human flesh, yes. But when they are rejoined and the Triumvirate walks the Earth, it will be incapable of taking such food. Its only sustenance will be the powerful, thriving souls of living human beings."

She rounded on Catherine and Konstantin, eyes blazing yellow, fangs protruding. Her hands were curled into claws, ready to attack.

"And you want to destroy the very humans that are to be the first offering?" she roared.

The two starving vampires could do nothing but cower and whimper. Veronique crouched down beside Konstantin, who would not meet her gaze.

"I'm sorry, mistress," he whispered.

"The gift of true immortality they have given me is ephemeral," Veronique told him in clipped tones. "They can take it away at any time, trapping me in one flimsy shell of flesh and cold blood. I would be like the rest of you, then. But if I succeed . . . the shadow of the Three-Who-Are-One will fall across the land, leaving humans without mind or motivation, wandering, helpless, ready for us to feast.

"Would you take that dark and beautiful destiny away from your brothers and sisters? Away from *me?*" she demanded.

Then, disgusted, she spun and walked over to lift Cordelia roughly from the ground. "Are you still human?" Veronique snarled, examining her neck.

"Yes," Cordelia stammered. "I—I think so." She tried to touch her neck. "Did I get vampirized? Am I a vampire now?"

Veronique smiled evilly. "I think that would be a good idea. As two of my followers are about to die." She turned her head and glared at Konstantin and the female, now surrounded by the rest of Veronique's followers, who had entered while their mistress raged on. Konstantin's head was lowered, as if in shame, but Catherine glared at Veronique.

"You can't kill us. You don't have time. Even if you did, you don't know what you'll get," the female said defiantly. "The new ones could be sentient, or they could be like that ravening maniac these humans staked in the tomb."

"Yeah," Xander chimed in. "You go, girl."

The female looked in Xander's direction and hissed. He made a face and hissed back, and a few of the other vampires chuckled.

"*He* has spirit," Veronique commented. She put Cordy in the care of a couple of vamp henchmen and sauntered over to Xander. She cupped his chin. "Would you like to live forever, boy?"

"I'd be happy to make it through today," Xander suggested hopefully, his eyes wide and frightened. "A trip to Acapulco would also be just peachy."

"Or perhaps you shall be my consort, after this is over," she mulled, trailing her nails down the side of his neck.

"What is it with you and monster chicks?" Cordelia demanded, as she struggled in the vampires' clutches. "I so do not get it."

"Veronique," Catherine interrupted angrily. Then her tone became more respectful. "Harbinger. We were starving beyond reason. It was cruel of you to leave us here with warm, living blood, when we two were the ones who warned you of the danger."

For a long moment, Veronique stared at the female. Then she whispered, "Catherine." There was no missing the finality in her tone: Catherine was dead meat.

So to speak.

Catherine's eyes widened. She swallowed, hard, looking for all the world as if her bluff had been called. "I'm young among our kind," she said. Her voice quavered. "You have had centuries of life to prepare you for trials such as this. Mistress, please. Haven't I pleased you before?"

Veronique smiled cruelly. "I brought you to my chambers, girl. Don't presume that means very much. Ask Konstantin, before you start to believe that intimacy with me gives you some privilege. It does not.

"I can no longer trust you. At least Konstantin shows remorse. You can only argue with your mistress."

She advanced on Catherine. Cordelia's pulse pounded in her forehead. *If Veronique kills Catherine, she's going to need another vampire. I don't know why, but I don't want to know why. And I don't want it to be me.*

Cordelia cleared her throat. "I really hate to interrupt," she said, "but, gee, if I were you . . ." She trailed off as Veronique morphed into vamp face and narrowed her golden eyes at her. The vampire's fangs glistened. "Which I am not," she finished nervously. "Sorry."

Veronique surveyed the group of vampires. Catherine had begun to tremble. The two vampires holding Cordelia's arms watched Veronique's every move.

The rest of the room was silent, except for the clacking and a strange whining and growling from the three monsters in the pile of bones.

The noise evidently meant something to Veronique, for she said, "We're almost out of time." She glared at Catherine. "Against my better judgment, I spare you. But make no assumptions."

"No, I won't. Thank you, Harbinger," Catherine said in a rush. As Veronique moved away, Catherine's knees buckled, and she held on to one of the guards to steady herself. "I won't disappoint you again, I swear."

Then Cordelia allowed her gaze to wander over to the bone pile. The grotesque creatures were watching everything with their reptilian, glowing eyes, and their snouts were covered with gore and a lot of weird, squiggling white things. *Maggots.*

And the monsters have gotten bigger, Cordelia realized as her stomach did a flip. *They've grown since the last time I looked at them.*

Veronique must have read Cordelia's expression. She grunted and looked over her shoulder. Her face became radiant.

"Gather up everything we need," Veronique ordered. "We shall leave for the unification site in half an hour. The ritual must be conducted by midnight."

Manhattan, 1944

The alley would never be clean. There was always more garbage, more discarded junk. But at least it was clear, and sometimes even orderly. Angel tried to keep it that way for Leah.

He didn't see her every night, and he hid away in the basement of a nearby tenement during the day. But when he did see her . . . it was just the tiniest bit of pleasure and hope.

She had invited him back into the shelter time and again. Sometimes he would go and share in the soup that was offered. Other times, when there were a lot of people inside, he preferred the few minutes he could speak to her in the alley.

Leah had stopped asking personal questions after the first week. She knew he wouldn't answer. But Angel never tired of hearing about her life, her past, even her love for Roger Giradot, her fiancé, who was abroad fighting the war in the Pacific.

He cared for her, as much as he was able. But that part of him had been crippled so long he thought it dead.

Still, he cared enough that when the door to the alley burst open that night and Leah emerged, sobbing uncontrollably, unable to catch her breath for the tears that streamed down her face, he went to her in alarm.

"Leah?"

She turned, then, the beautiful girl he had admired from afar and for whom he had dared to thaw the ice in his heart, to hope for something other than the life he led.

"Oh, Angel," she sobbed, and she threw her arms around his neck and fell into his embrace, crying horribly. "I just . . . they sent a telegram. He's dead, Angel. My Roger is dead."

He held her awkwardly. It had been so very long, and longer still since he had held a woman without hurting her. Drinking of her.

But he cared for Leah.

And now he hurt for her.

Her pain was clear and terrible to behold. She sobbed into

the filthy fabric of his jacket, and Angel stiffened. *This is wrong,* he thought. *This . . . this isn't meant for me. These feelings . . .*

He wanted to tear himself away. Wanted to spurn her, to leave the alley and never see her again. He wasn't human, and this . . . this humanity was beyond him now, forever. He knew himself to be the worst of monsters, the cruelest of evils. He did not deserve even a single moment free of the guilt that haunted him.

Holding Leah tightly, Angel closed his eyes, wracked with self-loathing, horror, and guilt. *You don't even have the courage to destroy yourself,* he thought. *But at least you can do this. Leave this girl alone. Don't interfere with her life. You'll only end up . . .*

His eyes snapped open. Leah's crying had begun to subside. She was thanking him, apologizing in embarrassment, and at the same time mourning again for her lost love.

Angel barely heard her. He was staring at the soft white length of her neck, and the veins that pulsed there, just under the surface. It had been nothing but rats for so long.

He could almost taste her.

Holding her, he felt his face change. His fangs elongated, and his eyes became yellow and fierce. She felt him tense and tried to pull back to look at him. Angel held her close.

"Angel?" Leah asked, sounding a little frightened.

It took all the power of his will to rein in the vampire within him. But even then, he didn't let her go. He didn't ever want to look into Leah Coleman's eyes again.

"I'm so sorry," he whispered. "For everything."

Then he released her and turned, and walked from the alley, a prisoner of the death he had wrought and the death that still lurked inside him, waiting to strike.

Buffy looked at Angel, concerned by the expression of dismay on his face. "Hey," she said, "what's on your mind?"

Angel blinked, as though he'd been drifting. "I'm okay," he said. "Just a little frustrated with all this. We've got to find Tergazzi."

Buffy seriously doubted that was what Angel had been think-ing about, but she didn't want to pry. With all that was hap-pening, they had both had a lot to think about lately.

"Okay, my thinking on Tergazzi?" she said. "Either he's hid-ing in the forest with Queenie, or he's at Willy's scrambling for the knowledge."

"Or he's blown town," Angel added darkly, "with a grand in his pocket."

"That would be your fault."

He shrugged.

"Plus you talk too much, Angel. It just totally drives me crazy." Shrugged again.

She gave him a small smile. "Well, at least the Summers fam-ily had a little bit of good news before the grand finale. If there's going to be one. Which I doubt." Her smile faded. "But I guess there's always a first time. Or a last. And don't mind me. I al-ways chatter after a good battle. Or the attendant double latte. Or to fill an awkward silence."

"I know."

Buffy sighed at Angel's lack of responsiveness. When he was on a mission, he was on a mission.

They walked on until they came to Willy's. Inside, they scanned the room as assorted creatures of the night scuttled out of range.

Willy looked up from washing beer glasses, saw the two of them, and ticked his head to the right. At the far end of the grimy bar, someone sat hunkered over a shot glass full of amber liquid, wearing a trench coat and a fedora.

Angel closed his eyes and shook his head while Buffy snick-ered. Then they walked over and flanked Fedora Man. Buffy took off the hat.

"Good evening, Terry," Buffy said to the top of the demon's spiny green head. "Whatcha got?"

"Hi, guys," he murmured. "Please. Go away. I think I'm being watched."

"What do you have for us?" Buffy said, sternly.

He shook his head. "I ain't saying nothing, even if you tear my head off. They threatened Queenie."

Buffy took that in, but Angel didn't even flinch.

"If you don't help the Slayer, your girlfriend's as good as dead, anyway," he said.

"Are *you* threatening her, too?" Tergazzi asked shrilly.

Angel said nothing. The demon looked at Buffy. "This isn't fair. She's my weak spot." He made a little face. "Well, that and, you know, playing the odds."

"Let me tell you something," Buffy said, taking the bar stool beside his. "You-know-who is about to do a ritual. This ritual will bring a very evil creature into this world. So evil that eventually, there won't be any Las Vegas."

"No," he breathed.

"Or Atlantic City," Angel added.

"And everywhere else. And Queenie will die. And it won't be pretty."

Tergazzi said, "That's not what Veronique's guys told me."

Buffy blinked in disbelief. "When you go to Vegas, do you ever win anything?"

"I do okay." He drew himself up. "I am a hundred and twenty-seven years old, you know. I made it this far following my hunches."

"Which is why you're living in the forest," Buffy said.

Angel leaned over the demon. "Where are they holed up?"

The demon stared at his drink. "I spent a lot of money on this glass of hooch. It's good stuff."

"Are you hitting us up for money?" Buffy asked, stupefied. "After what I just told you?"

He shrugged. "Us demons, we usually don't go along with the package, know what I mean? Most of your end-of-the-world scenarios, they mean end of the human world."

"Queenie," Angel said. "Vegas."

"Plus, I'm calling your bluff," Buffy said. "We've got the Slayer card. And let's face it. Veronique is not playing with a full deck."

Tergazzi sighed and threw back his liquor in one huge gulp.

He coughed and sputtered, almost choking until Buffy whapped him one on the back. Then he shrieked in pain.

"All right, all right. I heard something about the station. They were all going back to the station."

Buffy waited. Then she prompted, "The bus station? The train station?"

"Didn't sound like that kind of place. They were all moved in, like."

"The radio station," Buffy said.

He was quiet a moment. "I could use another drink."

Angel nodded at Willy, who picked up a fifth of something and poured it into the shot glass. As Tergazzi wrapped his scaly mitt around it, his hand—or whatever—shook. He threw it back.

"They kept talking about the old part of town," he said.

Angel knitted his brows. "Old Town?" He looked at Buffy. "The old police station."

"Yeah." Tergazzi moved his head up and down. "Something about the cells. I was thinking cell phones, you know, but . . ."

Buffy turned to go. Then she grabbed Tergazzi and hauled him off his bar stool. "You're coming with," she said.

He cowered away from her. "Oh, no. They see me with you, Queenie's dead."

Buffy exhaled and looked past Tergazzi to Angel. "Shall I hit rewind, or do you want to?"

"You're the Slayer," Angel deadpanned.

Tergazzi raised his hands. "Okay, okay, but make it look like I'm very reluctant. Like maybe you've got a knife at my back."

"I'm the Slayer. I don't need a knife."

"Point made," he said miserably.

When Angel, Buffy, and the still-whining little demon arrived at the police station, the stench was shocking, overpowering. Angel feared the worst: that the ritual had been completed, and the Triumvirate had been formed.

Hell had smelled like this.

Buffy was caught up short by it as they neared the dilapidated building. Then she gamely covered her mouth and took the lead. Tergazzi groaned and moaned until Angel glared at him. Then he shut up. Angel wasn't sure why Buffy had insisted that he come along. Maybe it was out of pity—and to save his life.

Pretty much everything looked boarded up, but when Buffy grabbed the handle of the back door, ready to tear it open, they were both surprised to see that it was unlocked. With a glance over her shoulder at Angel, Buffy crept inside.

Angel made Tergazzi go next. He wasn't going to be running off as long as they kept him between them. In silence, they followed Buffy down a long corridor with offices on either side and ended up in what Angel figured had once been the booking area.

Up ahead, the bright beam of a flashlight swept the wall to Buffy's right. She froze. Tergazzi took an awkward step forward, trying to halt his movement, and his foot landed on something that made a crackling noise. Angel winced and thought hard about knocking him out.

Then Buffy murmured, "Willow's here."

Angel didn't know how she knew, but he believed her.

"Will? It's Buffy," she called out.

Tergazzi sucked in his breath, eyes wide. "We're all gonna die," he blurted.

"Buffy?"

"Yeah. It's okay."

Flashlights panned the room. Then Giles, Oz, and Willow strode in. As Giles silently greeted her and Oz inclined his head, Willow said simply, "They're gone."

"Damn." Buffy glared at Tergazzi.

"Hey, hey, not my fault," he said, raising his hands.

"But there's good news, kind of," Willow continued. She looked at Giles.

"Yes." He pushed up his glasses, and Angel felt a rush of impatience.

He's going to go on and on, he thought, *and we don't have time.*

"Who is this?" Giles asked, indicating Tergazzi.

"He's the guy who sold us the fragments," Buffy said.

"I'm an antiques dealer," Tergazzi said.

"Also a demon," Buffy explained. "And a card-carrying member of Gamblers Anonymous. Or he should be."

Willow cleared her throat very softly. "I used a picture of Xander and Cordy and did a locator spell, and some of the text in the fragments makes a little more sense," she murmured. " 'Earth, air, wind, fire . . .' We're thinking the ritual's going to be performed in the woods."

"There's a lot of woods," Buffy said, not feeling very hopeful.

"Indeed," Giles said. "But the Toscano journal talks about the alignment of the stars, as I told you before. In order to see them in the proper alignment, this evening, one would have to be somewhat to the northeast and preferably at the highest elevation available."

"Miller's Woods," Buffy said instantly. "I wouldn't call it a mountain, but there's a pretty decent hill there."

"If only we could be certain," Giles said anxiously.

Angel didn't want to say it, but it didn't look as if anyone else was going to. "What else do we have to go on?"

"So we go," Oz said.

"We find them, and I dust Veronique again, and in the morning, when we don't have to worry about the Triumvirate anymore, we'll figure out how to get rid of her for good," Buffy said.

"Which works in theory," Oz noted. "But what if we don't get there before she lets the demon loose? It would help to know what we're fighting. Or how to fight it."

"We'll just have to do our best," Angel said grimly.

Willow cleared her throat. They all looked at her. She smiled shyly. "I have an idea."

Chapter Sixteen

They sat in a circle on the floor of the old police station, trying to concentrate in spite of the horrid stench of death within that place. Save for the demon, of course. Tergazzi stood in a corner, looking nervous and impatient. He hadn't offered to join the circle, and Giles hadn't asked. Summoning a frightened human spirit might be difficult if one of those doing the summoning were a demon.

Angel was another matter. He still had a human soul.

Giles glanced around at the others. Angel, Buffy, Oz, and Willow—so brave, all of them. Once more, lives depended on their actions. Xander's and Cordelia's in particular. But he allowed himself just a moment to be grateful that Buffy's mother would be all right. She was a good and decent woman, and observing what a strong and caring mother she was to Buffy, Giles had come to care for her. He would have grieved for her.

Even in their darkest moments, there were signs of hope. He clung to them.

"Join hands," he said, and they obeyed. "Clear your minds and reach out in sadness and charity to those who were horribly murdered in this building by Veronique and her followers. It is likely at least some of them are lost souls, and remain here, helpless, directionless. Reach out to them."

They were all silent. For his part, Giles focused on his sorrow for all those who had died there. But Willow's suggestion was an excellent one. It was logical to think that at least one of the people murdered here would have remained behind, one of the lost. A ghost.

It was a handicap that they had no candles. Instead, their flashlights were on, pointed at the center of the circle, providing some kind of focus for any spirit that might need guidance. Something for it to concentrate on.

"Willow?" Giles said.

"I am the portal," she said. "Speak through me. See through me. My voice is yours."

Giles feared for her, but he approved. She was proving to be quite an adept spellcaster and had the potential for great power. She had allowed herself to be the receptacle or medium for spirits twice recently, however, and he worried that she might become susceptible to ethereal attack, to possession without her consent, if she allowed it too often. He would have to warn her of that possibility later.

For now, however, they had little choice.

Suddenly, Willow's eyes went wide.

"*Oh, thank God,*" she breathed.

But it was not Willow speaking.

"*Can you help me?*" asked the ghost within her. "*I . . . I think I'm lost.*"

Giles mourned for the deluded spirit. He glanced at the others quickly. Buffy and Oz were staring at Willow, but Angel's eyes were tightly closed, focused. In the far corner of the room, Tergazzi swore under his breath.

"You know you are more than lost," Giles told the ghost.

Willow began to cry. "*I know,*" it said through her, voice choked with sobs. "*I just hoped it . . . oh God. Why am I still here, in this horrible place?*"

"It's up to you," Buffy spoke up suddenly. "You didn't want to believe, and it kept you trapped. You have to let go to find your way."

The expression on Willow's face changed from horror and despair to fear. "*I don't know if I can.*"

"If you do not, you will remain in this place forever," Giles said plainly. "But there's someone who might be able to help you. And help us, as well. Someone you can speak to, can find for us."

Willow stared at Giles with a ghost's eyes, and he shivered.

"*Tell me,*" she said.

It was Angel who spoke up. "Can you hear voices?"

Willow nodded.

"Call out to them," Giles said. "Pass the word along. We need to speak with Lucy Hanover. She's there, with you, wandering the paths of that world."

Willow's eyelids fluttered, and her head dropped, as though she had fallen asleep sitting up.

Buffy stared at Willow. It had been several minutes. She didn't think she could take it anymore. Time was passing, and now they might have put Willow in jeopardy as well.

"This is a waste of time," Tergazzi moaned. "I just want to keep Queenie alive. Could we just—"

Buffy glared at him, and Tergazzi shut up instantly. She glanced at Giles. "How long—"

Willow looked up suddenly, and Buffy knew just from her eyes that it was really Willow again. She looked terribly disappointed.

"Hey," Oz said, moving toward her. "You all right?"

"I think so," she said weakly, and nodded.

"What happened?" Buffy asked, glancing from Willow to Giles, who shook his head.

"He went away," Willow said reluctantly. "The ghost, I mean. I don't think it worked. I don't know what—"

He has moved on.

They all turned around. Buffy leaped to her feet, and for the first time found herself face-to-face with the ghost of Lucy Hanover. The girl's spirit hovered slightly above the ground, her body little more than mist from the waist down.

Buffy could see a boarded-up window beyond her—through her.

For a moment, Buffy couldn't breathe. This wasn't just a ghost to her. Buffy saw, floating there only a few feet away from her, absolute confirmation of her fate. Lucy Hanover was a Slayer. She looked as though she might have been twenty when she died.

And if what Willow had told them was true, Lucy was still doing her part to fight the darkness.

"Hi," Buffy whispered.

The ghost smiled. *I am honored to meet you, Slayer.*

"The feeling's mutual. Call me Buffy."

Lucy inclined her head. *You sought me out to see if I have discovered anything of the Triumvirate,* she said, her voice low and keening, like a mournful whistle.

"Yes, that's exactly right," Giles said, clearing his throat as he approached.

But he didn't get too close, Buffy noticed. She herself hadn't moved any closer to Lucy, and she thought she understood why, at least a little. The ghost seemed so surreal, so not really there, that she was afraid if she got too close, Lucy might disappear.

She was also severely uncurious about what it might feel like to touch a ghost.

Ah, Lucy said, noticing Giles for the first time. She inclined her head in what might have been a ghostly bow or curtsy. *You must be the Watcher. My respects to you, sir. I am at your service.*

"Wow," Buffy heard Willow whisper to Oz behind her. "I guess Slayers really have changed."

"You ain't kiddin'," Tergazzi told her. "But no matter the century, they're usually babes. Check out the ghost girl. She's smokin'."

Buffy didn't even bother to glare at him this time. Instead, she just ignored him.

"Were you able to find out anything at all about the Triumvirate?" Giles asked the ghost.

A great deal, Lucy replied, and she began to float toward them.

Buffy and Giles both took a step back, and she instantly regretted it. The ghost noticed their reaction, and a look of sadness swept over her gossamer features. It passed quickly, but Buffy never forgot it.

Their surroundings were awful, the place only escaping the title of slaughterhouse because the walls were not splashed with blood. Their friends, their town, possibly the human race itself, all were in great peril. And this woman, this girl, was a ghost, her shimmering, translucent form unnerving to look at, the fact of her death a harsh reminder.

But she was still a human soul. She still felt, though she no longer had a flesh-and-blood heart. She could be hurt.

"I'm sorry," Buffy said quietly.

Lucy smiled gently. Then her face changed, her expression grim.

I'm afraid the news is not good, she told them in a voice Buffy now realized sounded like wind chimes. *I have learned precisely what the Triumvirate is, and what it plans.*

The infernal realms are vast, as you must realize. Most of the creatures that find their way to Earth are not true demons but hybrids of some sort. The Triumvirate is pure demon, but even so, it is not like others. If any of them could be said to be like the others.

The Triumvirate was once three relatively powerless demons. When joined, however, they became an evil unto themselves. A Hell unto themselves.

The ghost paused then, and Buffy thought she actually shuddered. Lucy was dead. The Triumvirate could do nothing to her, but even so, she was afraid.

"I don't think I like where this is going," Buffy said softly.

"The prophecies say that the shadow of the creature will damn those upon whom it falls," Giles said. "How can that be?"

It is worse than that, Lucy replied.

Angel came up beside Buffy, and she stole a quick glance at

him, saw the anxiety on his face. She looked over at Oz and Willow, whose expressions were filled with dread.

A dread Buffy shared.

The Triumvirate is a soul-drinker, Lucy whispered, shuddering again. *If its shadow falls upon a living human being, or it can get a human in its clutches, it absorbs the spirit of that person. It is more than a demon, you see. For within its body, somehow, by some terrible form of unnatural physics, lies an infernal landscape of torment and horror.*

If the Triumvirate takes your soul, you are damned to spend an eternity in the Hell that exists within the creature's own body.

"Oh, my God," Giles muttered.

"Xander?" Willow said weakly. "And Cordelia. We've got to save them."

"Don't forget my Queenie!" Tergazzi interjected, speaking for the first time since Lucy had appeared. "You gotta get her back."

"We will," Buffy said.

"What I don't get," Oz spoke up, "is where Veronique fits into all of this. The demon needs her, fine. But what does she get out of it?"

"Besides an endless supply of bodies, you mean?" Tergazzi said. "What else does she need?"

Giles looked troubled. Buffy watched him closely, and the others all seemed to be drawn to him as well. He was the Watcher. He was supposed to have the explanations. Even the ghost looked to Giles. After all, Lucy was a Slayer, too.

"Sheep," Giles said bluntly.

He looked up, and his features looked drawn and sickly in the weird light thrown by the flashlights on the ground.

"People without souls wouldn't die?" Willow asked.

"Some would. Most would just wander around aimlessly," the Watcher replied. "Sheep."

At Buffy's side, Angel tensed. "And Veronique would be the shepherd," he said. "We better get moving. If we can't stop her, maybe we can at least take care of this demon before dawn."

Buffy was about to ask what was so important about dawn, but then she understood. "When the sun comes up—"

"There'll be shadows," Willow finished.

"Then good. So let's go," Tergazzi said. "Or my Queenie will be doing all her talking via the remote here." He stuck a webbed thumb out at Willow, who glared back.

Angel and Tergazzi went out the front door, with Oz and Willow behind them. Giles hung back with Buffy, who thanked the ghost sincerely. "We owe you, Lucy," Buffy said. "Will we see you again?"

I would like that very much, Lucy said. *I'll look in on you whenever I can, and if you need me . . .*

"We'll use the Willow-phone," Buffy said. "Thanks again."

As Giles said his good-byes, Buffy turned to leave, trying to figure out how they were going to fight the Triumvirate. Even without shadows, it could steal the soul from any living humans just by touching them. When she thought of Lucy's description of the Hell inside the creature, she shuddered.

Then she stopped and turned.

"What is it?" Giles asked.

Buffy stared at the beautiful, ghostly girl and smiled. "Lucy," she said. "I have an idea I think you may be able to help us with."

As I said, I am at your service.

In a clearing at the top of Nob Hill, in the middle of Miller's Woods, Veronique stood triumphantly atop a smoking pyre of downed trees, flames flickering around her. Draped in black robes, she lifted her face to the brilliant, ice-blue starlight. The moon shimmered a deep azure like the Sea of Crete.

She lifted her arms and chanted the words that would let her manipulate the shadows. Then she drew them down from the night sky. Power sizzled around her, causing a stir among her vampire followers as they prepared for the ritual. The pine forest outside Sunnydale echoed with the shrieks of the human captives as they were bound in a circle around the pyre and marked with fire and blood.

There were five of them now, chained to the ground, including the lover of that loathsome demon, Tergazzi, who had handed the Slayer the writings of de Molay and Toscano the Watcher. Veronique seethed at the thought of the demon's arrogance—that he could even imagine that she would not learn of his heinous act.

There, too, were the young man and woman who had been favorites of the Slayer. They had been branded with the rest, signs and sigils on their arms and feet, and three cuts made into their chests, to signify the three-headed Triumvirate, which would soon drink their souls, damning them to eternal torment in its own belly. The girl had stopped whimpering and now stared dully around herself. The young man, Xander, continued to struggle, and Veronique promised herself that if the Three-Who-Are-One had sufficient souls to sustain it without consuming his, she would favor Xander with a place at her side.

For souls were necessary to the completion of the ritual. If the Triumvirate did not feast upon human souls when the hatchlings were first rejoined, when the demon itself first trod upon the soil of this world, then the ritual would not succeed. Her master might even die. Veronique could not allow that, for it would mean the end to her power, trapping her forever in this single shell.

The hatchlings had been secured in a box made of iron, and Veronique's offspring, all vampires of her bloodline as required, now carried it with due reverence to the top of the pyre. As they moved aside, she unlatched the box. Konstantin lifted the heavy lid, and the three heads of Veronique's lord and master shot upward, raging, snapping at the air.

They had not the cruel intelligence of their true self in this form, but, once rejoined, they would be unstoppable. Their eyes glowed with evil, and they stared with anticipation at Veronique, who rejoiced to see in the irises the power of her master. She clasped her hands across her chest and sank to her knees in obeisance.

Soon, I shall be truly immortal. Staking will do nothing to this body. I will own it forever, and longer than forever.

Veronique clapped her hands over her head. She gestured to Catherine, Konstantin, and a newborn whose name she could not even remember.

"Bring the dead ones," she cried, "and prepare the pyre."

She watched with satisfaction as the three departed to a place behind a stand of trees. Each pulled a sort of travois, upon which was placed one or more decomposing human bodies. The smell was like that of a charnel house . . . or the streets of Constantinople, where it had all begun, so long ago. She had endured much; she would savor this night of triumph for centuries, as she had nursed the frustration over her failures.

The bodies were brought to three large stone vessels, baptismal fonts she had defiled, each with multitudes of blood sacrifices. Their pitted interiors were stained with layers of dried blood. Catherine, Konstantin, and the newborn vampire each loaded the remains into the fonts, as Veronique began to chant, in a tongue older than the whispers of demons:

> *"I curse the air, the earth, the fire, the water.*
> *I curse the breath of man, I curse his soul.*
> *I curse all living beings that are not of Hell.*
> *I shall drink the blood of the last man on Earth.*
> *His garden shall be my place of pestilence.*
> *His cities, my burial grounds.*
> *His children, my forks, my drinking cups.*
> *His race . . . a distant, feeble jest."*

The vampires took up the chant as three of their number picked up jeweled blades. Beside each armed vampire, another knelt, with a bronze bowl positioned beneath the outstretched arms. The vampires with knives sliced open their wrists, and the blood drained into the bowls. Some howled with pain. That was permitted, even encouraged, for according to the ancient writings Veronique had gathered, "They shall howl with rage and agony when the Triumvirate cometh forward. And their souls will be damned to suffer eternity in its bowels."

The vampires traded places; those who were still bleeding profusely staggered to their knees, while those who had held the bowls now cut themselves. One faltered, hesitating; Veronique narrowed her eyes. When the ritual was complete, that one would die.

Meanwhile, two vampires crushed the human remains in the fonts with large stone pestles, making a vile stew of the rotten viscera and bones. The human sacrifices began fresh screaming at the smell, their panic level rising.

"Anoint the hatchlings," Veronique commanded.

The vampires who had blended the rotten flesh and organs into a vile paste, now scooped up the mix with more bronze bowls. They carried it up the pyre, which was growing warmer, and smeared the thick matter onto the hatchlings, darting back nervously as the hungry creatures snapped and clacked their teeth and talons at them.

Once they were covered, Veronique chanted again. Her followers, well trained, joined in.

Veronique gave the signal. Konstantin ascended the pyre with a torch in his left hand.

He ignited the hatchlings' heads, each in turn. They burned like flimsy paper, and the hatchlings began to shriek in agony.

"As from the fires of Hell, it is born!" Veronique shouted.

The flames rose; Veronique leaped off the pyre. The humans, still chained, screamed in terror as the searing fire licked at their bodies. One of them, an older woman, wailed in agony as her clothes caught ablaze. The boy and girl who were beloved of the Slayer struggled against their bonds.

Veronique laughed.

The pyre ignited in an immense conflagration. A huge fountain of blue fire shot straight into the dark sky. Stars burst; comets soared. The moon dripped with blood.

The trees lining the clearing burst into flame.

From the box, the hatchlings screamed as they burned.

"Behold the inferno, the purifying fire!" Veronique shouted.

The vampires crossed their hands over their chests and knelt in submission. Thirteen, as the ritual demanded, in their appropriate places around the pyre, creating with their own bodies a circle of evil magick and dark possibility. Surrounded by a firestorm, they were quaking with fear. But none of them dared to move.

Let them burn, or not? Veronique thought gleefully. She gazed with delirious joy as the hatchlings were reduced to a thick heap of ash and gore.

I'll let my master decide.

From the ash, the Triumvirate began to rise.

The forest went up as if it had been touched with an enormous torch.

Queenie, the beloved of Tergazzi, was hidden from Veronique's sight by a wall of living fire. She could barely see the boy, Xander, and the girl beyond him, but she watched closely. It would not do for the fire to destroy them before the Triumvirate could descend upon them.

If they died first, it would not be able to drink their souls.

Halfway up the side of Nob Hill, Buffy and the others froze as every tree, bush, root, fern, and dry, dead leaf around them began to burn.

Chapter Seventeen

The firestorm raged through the forest.

"Aw, jeez, we're all gonna die!" Tergazzi cried. "We'll never save Queenie and your friends now!"

"Hey, Glum," Buffy said, choking on smoke. "Panicking will not help."

Tergazzi stared at her a moment, completely freaked. He turned to the others, who were trying to make some kind of forward progress on the fiery path through the burning trees on the hillside.

"Do I look panicked to you?" the weasely demon shrieked, then began to run wildly back and forth on the path, searching for an escape route.

Buffy thought about tackling him, but she needed to concentrate on how to save not only his skin but everyone else's. It was blazing hot; sweat rolled down her face, and the skin on her arms was beginning to blister. Oz stood with his arms around Willow, jerking her to one side when a towering pine spit sparks and branches that rained down in a shower of intense heat.

Willow's eyes were closed, and she was chanting. Of late, Willow's inventory of spells had been growing at a healthy rate, but she was still only a spellcaster. Fortunately, what she seemed best at were spells of protection—which they needed pretty badly right then. Buffy had no idea what Willow could do about their current situation, but just about anything aside from gasoline would improve it. She figured, therefore, that her own best bet was to make sure that Willow didn't roast to death.

She joined Oz in shielding Willow. Giles, his face scarlet, nodded at her and did the same. Willow stood in a protective huddle, and after a few moments, Giles took up her chant.

Tergazzi was about to run past them, still freaking, when Angel stepped up and grabbed him by the throat.

"Calm. Down."

"I'm calm," Tergazzi said obediently.

Angel came up behind Buffy and shielded her from the fire with his own body. She heard him gasping with pain and winced at her apparent lack of ability to do anything more than what she was doing. Slayers were built for action, not passivity, and it galled her that this might be the way she finally went out.

"You know," Giles said, looking meaningfully at Buffy, "there are a lot of dangers inherent in your plan. But I think it would be a shame if we didn't get to test it."

He started coughing violently, his eyes watering from the smoke and heat.

Around them, trees began to collapse and tumble. The earth shook. Buffy looked up the hill past Angel. Past Tergazzi, who followed them meekly, trying not to get burned. Where the trees had fallen, a path of sorts was being cleared through the blaze. She looked back at Willow and wondered if her friend was the cause of what clearly was their only escape route.

But that didn't matter. Reeling from the heat and the smoke, she broke apart the huddle and, coughing from the smoke, gestured for the others to follow her through the narrow firebreak.

She could only trust that they were behind her as she bounded through the firestorm. She couldn't risk a single look back, in case she lost her footing; she found herself thinking, *If Mom were back there, I would look.*

So she looked. And they were all there, even Tergazzi.

*   *   *

"Oh, God, Xander, do something!" Cordelia shrieked.

I am doing something, he thought. *I'm dying.* It wasn't technically accurate, but it might as well be. They had been through so much, and he'd always faced it with humor, not matter how frightened he'd been.

Yet somehow Xander couldn't think of anything funny to say. Not a single thing.

Damn, he thought. *I'm going to die really badly. Screaming and begging for my life. No dignity, and lots of pain.*

The begging part hadn't happened yet, but the pain was already there. The fire was close, but Veronique seemed to be keeping it back somehow. Just far enough so that it didn't burn them. But the heat . . . Xander's skin felt tight and much too hot, as if he'd touched a frying pan with his whole body. He thought his hair was getting singed and worried that it would start to burn.

"Cordy," he grunted.

Then he heard the hunger cries of the Triumvirate above him. The three-headed demon at the top of the burning pyre looked out over the sacrifices laid before it, and it roared, its voice the sound of eagles screaming.

Xander stared at it in horror. He heard Cordelia shrieking, and his own voice joined hers. He could barely feel the pain anymore. The fear was too great. He screamed and screamed, and he didn't care, not at all. Dignity was very, very low on his list of things to worry about.

Then, suddenly, he had the strong, clear sense that someone was moving underneath him, hands pulling him down below the ground.

You are going to die, said a voice in his mind. *Let me in. Give your body over to me.*

Xander gasped. *I don't think so!*

What choice do you have?

"Xander!" Cordelia shrieked. "The ropes are burning!"

What do I do? he thought.

Let me in, let yourself slip away. It will be like dying, the voice told him.

But I won't die? Xander asked.

If you would save her, act now, it told him.

Cordelia's screams were unbearable. Xander's mind, awash in pain, flashed past words to surrender.

Yes, he thought. *Anything.*

For just a second, he felt it, filling him up, a presence there with him, a mind . . . and then he was gone. No more pain, no more monsters, no more fire. Only nothing. Cold and gray.

Oblivion.

Cordelia shrieked as her bonds began to burn. Through a haze of pain, her skin blistering, she tried to turn her head, tried to get a look at Xander. She let out a harsh sob of frustration as she realized she had to be hallucinating. He had been tied up, right there beside her, but as she looked, Xander easily snapped his bonds and sat up. Head jerking around, face cold and expressionless, he saw her.

In an instant, he crawled to her and used his bare hands to tear at the thick ropes that were tied around her ankles and wrists, just as the ropes really began to burn. Xander picked her up in his arms and staggered away from the fire.

"Xander," she groaned, looking up at him. Her eyes widened. His face was slack, his eyes dull. He didn't even register her presence, though he had just saved her life. If she had to guess what was wrong with him, she would say he was dead. There was no spark of life anywhere on his face.

A deafening howl buffeted her ears. She cried out, but Xander didn't even blink. She raised her head to look at the tower of fire and screamed.

From a pile of smoking ashes, a single creature of gleaming scales topped by three brutish, serpentine heads rose from the smoke and towered above the pyre. It stood at least twenty-five feet high, almost above the Hellish inferno of the woods. It threw back its heads, opened its mouths, and blue flame gouted from its jaws into the sky.

As Cordelia watched, dumbstruck, pieces of the sky actually disappeared. In their place, red, gaping wounds formed, and a gory ichor rushed down in streams like waterfalls. Where it hit the fires, enormous gaseous clouds formed, roiled, and expanded. Then they popped, disgorging hideous monsters— skeletal beings dragging pieces of dark purple and black matter that at one time might have been portions of their bodies; strings of eyeballs trailed behind them on the ground as they capered and slid down the pyre, eagerly grabbing at the one of the humans still chained to the ground.

They were people, Cordelia realized. *These were human beings once.*

The heads and body were covered with talons and spikes, the faces evil and reptilian. Eyes glared at her with a cunning and ferocity so powerful it vibrated through her and deep into the marrow of her soul.

They opened their mouths and spoke one word: *Apocalypse.*

And then, almost more incredibly, the three heads of the Triumvirate seemed to yawn, and all of it, the Hellish creatures— demons, suffering mortal souls, whatever they might be—the blood and the dark and the blot on the sky, were drawn back inside the creature.

"Oh, my God," Cordelia whispered. "Oh, my God."

Standing unharmed atop the pyre, Veronique spread wide her arms. "At last!" she shouted.

Willow opened her eyes and blinked hard. The blazing forest was being sucked upward, and everything with it—rocks, undergrowth, even squirrels and the half-rotten carcass of a coyote. She felt the vacuum tug at her and cried out. "I forbid it! By Hecate and all that is divine to Maia, I forbid it!"

As the hellfires blazed around them, Willow stood her ground and shouted her incantation. Buffy grabbed a burning tree root and held tight, grunting with the pain.

Then gravity reasserted itself. When Willow turned around to face her friends, she was startled to find the ghost of Lucy Hanover hovering beside her.

It is working, Lucy told her. Then the ghost turned to look at

Buffy and Giles. *But you must hurry. Any moment now, the Triumvirate will have its first souls, and then it will be too late for your friends, and for the rest of the mortal world as well.*

"Can't the lost souls help?" Angel asked, approaching the ghost.

Lucy looked at him carefully. Willow wondered if this was the first time she had realized that he was a vampire.

Haven't they already helped? the ghost asked. *I cried out to all of them, all the spirits of the angry dead, the lost souls who died horribly in these woods and were unwilling or unable to move on. I pleaded for their aid, and they have given it. Not only have they led you to this place, but they are willing to lend themselves to you, to fight the Triumvirate in your stead, as your proxies.*

"Can we trust them?" Oz asked suddenly.

Willow looked at him. "Oz?"

"Hell, I wouldn't trust them," Tergazzi interrupted.

Willow stared at him. She'd almost forgotten the demon was there, he'd been so quiet, cowering among them.

"Seriously," he went on. "Think about it. Okay, the Triumvirate can only drink the souls of living humans. So sure, let the spirits of the dead into your body, hoping maybe they can shield your own soul and use your body to fight the thing at the same time.

"Pretty far-fetched to begin with. But I'll tell ya what's really crazy: believing those angry ghosts are gonna give up those bodies after they're done. Hell, they're pissed off that they're dead. You think they hung around out here 'cause they liked the scenery?"

A burning tree cracked and collapsed across their path, flames jumping from tree to tree. Willow had spoken every ward, charm, and spell of protection she could think of, but the fire was just too strong.

"This is not the time!" she cried.

It was Giles who asked the question again. He looked at the ghostly girl and lowered his gaze as if in apology. But he asked it. "Can we trust them?"

Lucy looked sad. *If you fail here, most of them have loved ones they have left behind. I have explained what the fate of those mortals will be if the Triumvirate drinks their souls. You may trust the lost ones, because it is not you they fight for.*

Buffy led the way through the inferno.

The three faces of the Triumvirate glared down at Veronique. *I hunger.*

"Yes," she said triumphantly. "I have brought you mortal souls."

Xander had broken his bonds and had carried Cordelia in his arms, but he had not gotten far. Several of her vampire brood had risen to block their exit, and the fire blazed high around them. They could not escape.

And there were still the other three, the woman, Queenie, and the two who remained from their attack on the theater. Veronique gestured to the figures on the ground.

Cordelia stood beside Xander now, leaning on him, skin burnt an angry red. She looked up, coughing from the smoke. Her gaze locked with Veronique's, and the hatred there was . . . exciting.

I should find a way to spare them. The boy is so intelligent and bold. Veronique stared at him. There was something odd about him, about the way that he stood, the slack expression on his face.

From atop the pyre, where she stood in her rightful place beside her master, Veronique began to descend. Even as she did so, she stretched her consciousness out, using magick taught to her by Empress Theodora so long ago. She reached out with that magick and touched him, and found . . . nothing.

He is dead.

She was shocked.

Dead, and yet he walks, but he is not a vampire.

Nothing in her magick had prepared her for this.

The Triumvirate dipped its heads, flames curling from its nostrils, toward Xander.

"No!" Veronique screamed.

This undead-yet-living thing held no mortal soul. If her master tried to drink that soul, Veronique feared that all would be lost.

But the Triumvirate did not know that. All it heard was her scream . . . her command.

Veronique dropped her gaze, knowing that it would be useless to try to explain. The hunger for souls was upon it, the thirst for mortal spirits to torment in the eternal suffering of its gullet. Their suffering would give it even greater power.

She awaited punishment.

A burning tree stood in the middle of their path, and there wasn't enough room on either side to go around it. Buffy stopped and turned to speak to Willow, who was standing behind her.

Willow's face was a blank slate; her eyes were unfocused. She was murmuring in a language Buffy didn't understand; she gestured to Giles and Angel, who came forward, clearly straining to hear over the cacophony of windstorm and earthstorm.

"Protective wards," Giles shouted. "But she can't keep it up much longer."

"I'll guide her," Oz said, snaking past Angel and Giles. He laced his fingers through Willow's. She made no response, completely focused as she was on the spell she was casting.

"Let's go," Oz told Buffy.

The Three-Who-Are-One rushed down toward Xander as Veronique shouted again.

"No!"

The enormous demon knocked him down, hard, and lunged for Cordelia. She screamed and dove aside, falling to the ground, shrieking as her hand flattened over a white-hot rock. Her palm sizzled, and she tried to pull her hand away, but she was in such pain she couldn't remember how to work her body. It lunged for her again.

"Oh, my God!" Cordelia screamed. She fell forward, slamming her chest and face against more superheated rocks. The pain was unbelievable. Every nerve ending in her body was seared, rushing along the synapses to fire the neurons in a confused riot of misinformation; her heart beat too fast, then skipped a beat.

Oh, God, just let me die, she thought wildly.

Another hallucination, she thought, but she couldn't quite convince herself of that, as Angel raced forward, leaped into the air, and kicked at one of the demon heads.

The creature reared back, then snapped at Angel with its razor-sharp teeth. He punched it in the mouth, shouting in pain and bringing his knuckles back, shredded and bleeding.

"Thanks," Cordelia muttered, and tried to crawl out of the way. She had never felt so weak and stupidly helpless, which was something she had hated, and hated even more now.

Open your mind, said a papery, whispery voice below her. *You must give yourself over.*

"Wh—wha—" she stammered.

I have been trying to touch you, but in your pain you could not hear me. Now, open yourself to me, and you will live. For if the demon touches you now, your soul will be damned.

Confused, terrified, Cordelia tried to make sense of it all. She was about to protest, to argue that the demon had touched Xander and Angel, but the voice came again.

Yes. But the vampire is not mortal. And Xander has given his body up to the dead. We protect him, as you must let us protect you. Let me in.

Xander shuffled forward. Cordelia's mouth dropped open.

"Oh, my God," she whispered. "Xander?"

Xander stared at her. There was no emotion on his face. He shook his head.

"*Let her in,*" his mouth said. "*To live, you must die.*" But the voice that spoke did not belong to Xander.

"No!" she screamed.

But then Angel was in front of her.

"Do it!" he snapped. "It's the only way!"

Cordelia closed her eyes and wept, and she let the ghost in.

Buffy had dusted three vampires before they even knew she was there. Oz and Willow and Giles and Tergazzi were all moving around the circle as well. The vampires did not expect them at all.

We have the element of surprise, she thought. *But then, they have the element of forest fire, and that whole evil thing.*

Still, they were doing what they could. They had thought about getting closer, trying to help Angel against the demon. But the fire was so intense and so widespread that the Triumvirate threw shadows in all directions.

In the middle of the clearing, at the base of the huge burning pyre, Angel beat at the heads of the Three-Who-Are-One with a thick burning tree limb. Xander held a large stone, and he threw it at the demon. Of course, it wasn't really Xander, only his body. Their attacks weren't doing much more than buying time.

But time was what they needed.

Even as Buffy watched, Cordelia—who was also no longer herself—tore away the ropes that bound Tergazzi's girlfriend Queenie and another woman not far from the base of the pyre. Veronique stood behind the demon on the other side and thus far hadn't seen her.

You go, Cor, Buffy thought. Then she remembered again that it wasn't really Cordelia, and that preyed on a fear that she dared not voice. The fear that Tergazzi had been right, and the dead would not give up the bodies of her friends when this was done.

"Worry about it after you win, Summers," she muttered to herself, and then lunged at a fourth vampire.

It saw her coming. That didn't help it any. A heartbeat later, it was just another cloud of ashes sucked into the inferno.

When she turned again, Lucy Hanover was there.

Well done, the ghost said. *You are far more skilled in battle than I ever was.*

"It's time?" Buffy asked.

Lucy nodded.

Buffy ran into the clearing, dangerously close to where the shadows of the Triumvirate might fall. Cordelia had gotten extremely lucky, but Buffy wasn't going to leave it to luck. She stayed just out of range. In a moment, the demon would come after her. For a moment, she doubted the whole plan once more. It was her fight, she was the Slayer. She could not bring herself to give up control.

But what choice did she have?

Angel was there. He ran toward her. On the other side of the clearing, silhouetted against the fire, she saw Giles and Tergazzi. Off to her left, Willow and Oz staked the last of Veronique's vampires and then hustled toward Buffy as well.

In the center of the clearing, above it all, hung the shimmering form of the ghost of Lucy Hanover.

Now! the ghost screamed.

Let me in, a lost soul whispered into Buffy's mind.

All right, she sighed.

Angel saw Buffy fall to the ground. A moment later, she climbed to her feet once more, powerful but unsteady, and he knew that she had become like Xander and Cordelia, host to a spirit, one of the ghosts that haunted these woods. They were all possessed now, their minds and spirits submerged deep inside their subconscious, their bodies occupied by the angry dead.

He was afraid of what might come of it. Lucy Hanover had been a Slayer in life, but she was a spirit now. She had recruited these ghosts to help defeat the Triumvirate, supposedly to protect their own still-living loved ones. But there were no guarantees.

Angel might have argued the plan, but it had been Buffy's idea.

"I hope you're right," he muttered as he watched the now possessed Oz, Willow, and Giles climb to their feet as well.

"Well, that's a creepy sight if I've ever seen one."

Angel spun, ready to attack, but it was only Tergazzi. He didn't have a mortal soul, and Angel was dead, so neither of them was in any but the usual physical danger from the Triumvirate.

The three-headed demon shrieked and dodged its heads at them, and Angel and Tergazzi dove aside.

Maybe I was too quick to discount the physical danger, Angel thought.

Buffy was chilled to the bone, weighed down, and smothered in unending gray oblivion.

Not finished. I wasn't finished.

I was unfinished.

There were no brilliant white lights; there were no loved ones with outstretched hands waiting for her. The void was without form; there was no one else there; nothing but endless, vacant emptiness. Nothing had any shape or texture, except her immense regret.

I am dead, inside and out, she thought. *I've . . . stopped.*

Veronique watched in horror as the dead Slayer and the others, all somehow animated though without living souls, attacked the Triumvirate. Their attack should have been beneath its notice. Its shadow fell over them all, its heads darted down, fangs flashing, its talons slashed.

They couldn't hurt it, not really. But they protected themselves. And Veronique knew they would not have to do that for very long.

Her scream of fury and failure rent the darkness, a hard wind fed the fire and then snuffed it out in many places. Scorched trees fell in the forest.

The Triumvirate searched for souls to drink, but there was none to be had. It fought, but it was growing weaker, even disoriented. Confused. Six golden eyes glared at Veronique where she stood, raging helplessly.

Souls! it demanded in utter fury.

Its mouths opened, and it vomited huge streams of black
 or, which doused the blazing pyre.
 Elsewhere, the fire stopped spreading. Began to burn low.
 The Triumvirate howled, and more of the horrid liquid
 ewed from its maws. It collapsed in a heap, covered in the
 rk liquid. Then, beneath that thick tar, things began to move.
 d they emerged.
 The hatchlings.
 Veronique shrieked again. She had failed. But this was not
 e her previous failures, for they were here now, on this world,
 d Veronique did not know how to send them back.

Good-bye.

 Buffy's eyes fluttered open. The ghost had been as good as its
 ord. She leaped to her feet, feeling somehow more energized
 an she had been. With a quick glance down at her hands,
 ffy saw that somehow her burns did not seem so severe now.
 e didn't understand it, but she wasn't going to argue.
 "Buffy!"
 She looked over and saw Willow coming toward her, waving.
 was behind her.
 "Behind you!" Oz roared.
 Buffy spun and saw one of the hatchlings lumbering toward
 r, disgusting demon drool slipping from its mouth. It leaped
 her, fanged mouth snapping. She spun into a high kick and
 ught it in the jaw with the heel of her boot. It was turned
 ay, and before it could come at her again, Buffy was on top
 it. The demon hatchling was covered in black, sticky slime,
 d she nearly slid off. Instead, she clamped on tighter,
 apped her arms around its throat from above, and then
 oke its neck with a loud crack.
 The demon crumbled to the ground beneath her.
 "Way to go, Buff!" Willow cried, coming up behind her.
 Oz gave her a hand up, and Buffy turned to see that one of
 e remaining hatchlings lay dead, with Xander and Giles still
 bbing at it with long, partially burned tree limbs.

The third was on Angel.

"Hey!" Buffy screamed.

She ran for the thing. But she needn't have worried. From beyond the hatchling, nearly in the fire itself, Tergazzi appeared, roaring a battle cry unlike anything Buffy had ever heard. He grabbed the hatchling from behind and drove his taloned hand through the creature's back. His hand exploded out the other side, the hatchling's black, twisted demon head clutched in his grasp.

"Hello? Eeew!" Cordelia was moaning as Buffy approached. "Who invited him?"

Buffy saw Queenie coming up behind Tergazzi, now that the danger was over. The weasely little demon looked at her.

"I can fight," he said. "When there's somethin' worth fighting for."

"Guys!" Buffy said sharply. "Aren't we missing something? Where's Veronique?"

Giles looked aghast. "I thought you'd killed her," he said.

That snapped them all back into battle mode. Buffy and Angel moved to stand side-by-side, staring around the clearing where the fire was burning down on the blackened trees.

"Maybe she just took off," Xander suggested. "If I'd had such a wicked ass-whuppin', I'd beat feet, too."

"And often do," Cordelia sniped.

"No," Willow said, coughing a little from the smoke she'd inhaled. "Look over there."

They did. Veronique was bent over the corpse of the hatchling Buffy had killed, holding it in her embrace.

And it moved.

"It's not dead," Angel snapped.

Buffy was already moving. She ran toward Veronique, and the vampire turned to look at her and screamed.

Veronique had lost her mind, and some small part of her knew it. It was over. Though one of the hatchlings yet lived, it was fast dying. Once again, a Slayer had stolen her destiny. First

Angela Martignetti, and now this creature Buffy Summers. But this was worse.

There would be no coming back from this. Veronique had felt it the moment the first hatchling died. Something was different: she was no longer truly immortal. She was trapped now, in this shell, and when she died, as she knew she would, at the hands of the Slayer, she would be dust. Once she had been more than immortal; she had been *eternal*.

Now she was nothing more astonishing than a vampire.

Shrieking in fury, she ran at the Slayer.

Veronique had lost it. Buffy knew that the moment the vampire lunged at her. She was out of her mind with rage. They had fought enough times that Veronique knew what to expect from her. That focus had made her a formidable opponent.

No longer.

In her fury, she was barely paying attention.

The once-immortal vampire attacked her savagely, fingers curled into talons, and Buffy kicked her in the face. Veronique rose again and leaped into the air. Buffy ducked in with a hard elbow to the gut that drove her back to the dirt.

"Buffy!" Angel said from behind her.

The Slayer turned, for only a second, and Angel slapped a stake into her hand.

Buffy turned on Veronique, stake at the ready.

And Veronique ran, screaming, back to the dying hatchling.

"No!" she cried. "You cannot leave me to this!"

The vampire began to beat the demon thing's slimy hide. The hatchling glared balefully at its former handmaiden with a half-lidded eye. Then it growled, low and dangerous.

"Oh, master, no," Veronique whispered, backing up.

Buffy backed up, too. The hatchling was not dead yet. It still held some power, particularly over Veronique, to whom it had given so much of that power over the centuries.

"Please," Veronique begged.

The vampire turned to face Buffy and reached out her hands,

though whether she was seeking help or casting blame, Buffy would never know.

As Buffy and the others looked on, Veronique was suddenly bathed in an eerie matte nothingness that was more a lack of substance than of anything else. In a strange slow-motion progression, Veronique was stripped of everything—hair and eyebrows, then layers of skin, disappearing into the matte, until she looked like some strange creature composed of bloody muscles. Her eyes and the cartilage in her nose were stripped away. Her veins and arteries and then her unbeating heart. All her organs.

And then her bones.

For a moment, there was a strange imprint of black on black, and then Veronique was gone.

She had never even screamed.

"Ashes to ashes," Buffy whispered, wiping her grimy hands on her grimy pants.

The fires were out. The forest around them for a quarter mile was a charred wasteland of ash and smoke that flurried across the clearing.

Angel came up beside her.

"It's over," he drawled.

Thunder rumbled overhead, and it began to rain.

Epilogue

The morning after the fire, Buffy slept in. She didn't sleep very well, however. Despite her evil, Veronique had died a pitiful creature, and it had been disturbing to see. But that didn't keep her awake. The burns did that.

It wasn't much, all things considered. Giles had explained that the doubling of the life force in each of their bodies while they were possessed had likely speeded the healing process—though as the Slayer, Buffy naturally healed faster than everyone else. But all of them had still suffered burns. Willow had cast a healing spell for them and whipped up a salve. It was working for Buffy. *But then again, Slayer.*

She hoped everyone else was doing all right.

When she finally gave up and decided that despite her exhaustion, she had to face the world, she dragged herself out of bed and into the shower. She hoped her mother would be discharged that day and wanted to get to the hospital.

An hour later, when the elevator doors opened at her mother's floor, her heart began to beat faster, and a broad smile spread across her face.

Buffy hurried into the room, to find her mother sitting up in bed and eating a turkey sandwich. When Joyce looked up and smiled weakly, Buffy grinned happily.

"You're too late for breakfast, lazybones," her mother said. "But you can share my lunch if you want."

"You stay right there, lady," Buffy chided her. "I can get my own lunch." She walked over and kissed Joyce on the head. "How do you feel?"

Her mother looked up, and her smile started to fade a bit. "I was going to say great."

"But?" Buffy asked with concern.

Joyce glanced away. "It was pretty scary, honey."

Buffy put a hand on her shoulder. "You can say that again. You had me terrified. Let's not do that again anytime soon, okay?"

"Deal," her mother said, and then she looked at Buffy closely for the first time, studying the skin of her arms. "Hey, what happened to you?"

"I'll be okay," Buffy said lightly.

"Do I dare even ask about last night?"

"Probably better if you don't," Buffy said reluctantly.

"Oh, Buffy," Joyce sighed, shaking her head. "You're going to be the death of me."

That night, when Angel walked from Dr. Coleman's room, Buffy was waiting outside the door. When she saw him, she smiled, too brightly, and they walked down the corridor.

"How's your mother?"

"Much better." She laughed uncomfortably. "She's embarrassed to have such a hokey-sounding disease. She says it'll sound very stupid on the annual Summers Christmas card."

"She could skip it."

"Mom's a stickler for the details," Buffy replied. "You know that."

"Yes." He paused. "No sign of Tergazzi?"

"Figure he skipped town. Maybe went back to Vegas with Queenie. He's gotta think his luck is changing."

Angel smiled wanly. "What about the ghost? That Slayer?"

"Lucy? I have a feeling we'll see her again."

She glanced at him. "Is Dr. Coleman going to be okay?"

"She had a mild heart attack when Veronique's bunch jumped her the other night. Unfortunately, she had another, much more severe, last night. I'm pretty sure she's going to die soon. So is she."

Buffy stared at the squares of linoleum, wheat-colored and very bland, very boring.

"We all are, compared to you." Her voice was harsh. "We're like the small towns of life expectancy. Blink, and poof! You've just driven past our entire downtown."

"A lifetime is a lifetime, no matter how long it is," he ventured.

"Please. Politically correct vampires I can do without."

He stopped and touched her shoulders. "Buffy, if you did die, I would die."

She raised her chin. "No. You wouldn't." When he opened his mouth, she raised a hand to stop him from speaking. "You would grieve. I'll give you that." She sighed and gazed at him levelly. "Maybe you'd even put roses on my grave for the first, oh, fifty years or so."

Angel looked down.

Say something, she thought desperately. *Come on. Deny it.*

Instead, Angel took her hand in his.

Together, they walked down the hospital corridor.

Alone.

Christopher Golden is the award-winning, *L.A. Times* best-selling author of such novels as *Strangewood* and the three-volume *Shadow Saga*; *Hellboy: The Lost Army*; and the *Body of Evidence* series of teen thrillers (including *Soul Survivor* and *Meets the Eye*), which is currently being developed for television by Viacom. He has also written or co-written a great many books, both novels and non-fiction, based on the popular TV series *Buffy the Vampire Slayer*. As a comic book writer, Golden has worked with such characters as Batman, Wolverine, Spider-Man, the Punisher, the Crow, and Buffy the Vampire Slayer, and he is the regular co-writer of the *Angel* comic book series. His non-fiction work includes *Buffy the Vampire Slayer: The Monster Book* and *The Stephen King Universe*. Golden was born and raised in Massachusetts, where he still lives with his family. He graduated from Tufts University. He is currently at work on his next novel, *Straight On 'til Morning*. Please visit him at www.christophergolden.com.

Bestselling author Nancy Holder has sold 42 novels and 200 short stories. She has received four Bram Stoker Awards for fiction from the Horror Writers Association. Writing with her frequent collaborator, Christopher Golden, as well as working alone, she has sold fifteen *Buffy the Vampire Slayer* and *Angel* projects. Her most recent Buffy project, *The Watcher's Guide, Vol. 2*, written with the assistance of Jeff Mariotte and Maryelizabeth Hart, will be out next fall. A graduate of the University of California at San Diego, she lives in San Diego with her daughter, Belle, and their two Border collies, Mr. Ron and Dot.

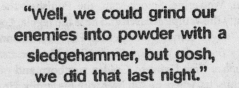